better than your reality

XO-

CAMBRIA HEBERT

Mr. FANTASY

Cambria Hebert

B... your reading!

MR. FANTASY Copyright © 2019 CAMBRIA HEBERT

Published by: Cambria Hebert
http://www.cambriahebert.com

Interior design and typesetting by Sharon Kay of Amber
Leaf Publishing
Cover design by Cover Me Darling
Photograph by Regina Wamba
Cover model: Shen Kai
Edited by Cassie McCown
Copyright 2019 by Cambria Hebert

This is a work of fiction. Names, characters, places, and
incidents either are the product of the author's imagination
or are used fictitiously, and any resemblance to actual
persons, living or dead, business establishments, events, or
locales is entirely coincidental.

ISBN: 978-1-946836-26-7

better than your reality

CAMBRIA HEBERT

FANTASY

The Fantasy

One

Nora

"I can't believe the week is almost over." Val groaned, then consoled herself with a large gulp of the fruity cocktail sitting in front of her.

I sighed sadly, silently agreeing with her. Spring break needed to be a lot longer than a week. Pretty soon, it would be back to work, back to classes... back to reality.

Reality sucked.

Especially when I gazed around this tropical resort and realized some people lived like this all the time.

"One week in paradise just isn't enough," I said out loud, playing with the pink umbrella perched in the coconut drink I held. Rotating the barstool, I spun to face the turquoise water of the ocean and pure-white sand beneath it.

Grass umbrellas dotted the beach, and under them, people lounged and played. Beyond the beach, people also played in the water, running around in skimpy bikinis and golden tans.

The breeze off the ocean blew through the tangled strands of my blond hair, and sand clung between my toes. Focusing past the shoreline, I gazed across the water, past the floating cabanas, and out to a small island filled with palm trees.

"I'd like to see the guy who owns that island just once while we're here." My voice was wistful as I plucked the cherry out of my drink and popped it into my mouth.

Sweet juice from the fruit burst over my tongue as I stared.

Val made a sound and slapped me on the shoulder. "Don't even tell me that's the reason you haven't had a fling yet!" she practically yelled.

Swiftly, I swung in her direction. "Shh! God, Valerie, don't announce our sex life to the entire resort."

"At least I have a sex life," she muttered, fitting her straw into her mouth. "That's what spring break is for. Letting loose, having fun… no regrets."

"Hey, I've done that, too."

She made a rude sound. "You've turned down three guys since we got here."

I shrugged and looked back at the ocean. "I'm picky."

"You have to let him go, Nor," Valerie said gently. Leaning in, she rested her cheek on my shoulder. "I know you loved him, but Alan wasn't good enough. And he hurt you."

Yeah. Yeah, he did.

I sucked on the straw until it made that annoying slurping sound because my alcohol had officially run out.

"Having a fling is the best way to get him out of your system. Let someone rock your world for a night, and forget about him completely."

I smirked. "You think a one-night stand will erase a guy I dated for nearly a year?"

Val sat up and wagged her eyebrows at me. "The right guy will."

I laughed, and she snagged the empty coconut out of my hand and held it over her head. "Bartender, another!"

"Now, about that." My best friend pointed out toward the distant island. "Please tell me you haven't been holding out to see if Mr. Island shows up to rock your world."

I scoffed at her assumption.

"I knew it!" she yelled.

People around us turned to look at her.

I smiled at them, "Sorry. She's a bit extra."

"You're still hung up on your cheating, scumbag ex, and now you're hung up on some faceless guy who might not even exist?" Val dropped her forehead into her hand. "I've failed as a best friend."

I slipped an arm around her shoulders. "You have not."

A tap on my shoulder made me turn, my eyes colliding with a set of piercing green ones. "Oh," I said, a little breathless.

"Your drink is ready," the bartender said, leaning over the bar, holding out my refill.

"Oh!" I glanced down at the drink. "Thanks."

"Anytime, gorgeous," he quipped and winked.

I nearly spilled the drink in my lap right there. He wasn't wearing a shirt, and he had the bronze tan of a local with an accent to match.

"You need anything else, just wave."

I nodded, unable to reply.

"See!" Val said, putting her arm around me, bringing me back around. "This is exactly what I'm talking about. You're gorgeous. You could have any guy here you wanted. Even the bartender. Yet you're busy mooning over some guy who's probably old enough to be your grandpa."

"I am not mooning!" I insisted. Then I grimaced. "And ew… grandpa."

"You really expect some young, hot single to own that island over there?"

I shook my head. "Not just the island… this entire resort."

Valerie moaned. "That's just a sexy rumor the staff here likes to tell women like us. It makes us even more excited about this place."

"It could be true," I murmured, staring out to sea. "He really could be some young, rich computer genius who sold off an app and bought this place."

"Uh-huh. And he has a hot body and the stamina to make you forget all about Awful Alan."

"Hey," I accused, salty. "I didn't judge you when your fantasy was to sleep with a yoga instructor to see if they really were more flexible than other guys."

Valerie giggled. "They are. They totally are."

I rolled my eyes. "You're incorrigible."

"Hey, I'm young, single, and being safe. What's wrong with a little fun?"

I drank some of my cocktail.

"Besides, at least my fantasy was attainable. Yours is practically from the pages of some cheesy romance novel."

"Whatever." I sighed. This conversation was bringing down my buzz. "Finish your drink so we can go lay on the beach."

"Your time is running out." She reminded me. "We're going home tomorrow night. If you don't have a fling soon, you're never going to get over Alan."

I'd had enough of this conversation, and if she said my ex-boyfriend's name one more time, I was going to scream. I jumped down off the barstool and tripped on my flip-flop, stumbling.

"Whoa," I stammered as I fumbled forward. Seconds later, I collided into the back of a chair, falling over the shoulder of whoever was sitting there and dumping my drink down their chest.

The shoulder under my waist stiffened, and I scrambled to leap back.

"Oh my gosh, I am so sorry!" I exclaimed. Dumbly, I looked down at the drink in my hand. It was empty.

Horrified, I skittered around the chair as the person sitting in it stood, pushing it out from beneath him.

Our bodies collided and I tumbled back, but he caught my arm to keep me from falling. Another apology formed on my lips, but the second I looked up, it dissipated.

He was tall. So tall I had to crane my neck back to look up at him. His shoulders were wide, and his jaw was chiseled. His skin had the same deep bronzed look as all the locals, and his hair was the color of midnight.

I didn't know if his mouth was just sexy as hell or if the way he pursed his lips as he regarded me made them look pouty, but the effect was still the same.

Everything inside me tightened and then went liquid, as though he'd melted me with just one glance.

My mouth moved, but no sounds came out. I was exceptionally aware of his large hand wrapped around my upper arm. Even though we were sitting in the shade, his hand felt warm like he'd been in the sun. Goose bumps erupted along my bare arms and legs, and my scalp prickled with awareness.

Glancing down to where he held me, I couldn't help but notice how his hand was so big it wrapped around my arm completely. Involuntarily, I shivered as I thought about what else his hands would completely cover.

Embarrassed, I jerked away from his touch. His hand dropped beside him, and then I realized the entire front of his shirt was completely soaked with my drink.

Gasping, I tossed aside the empty coconut and let my hands hover near him. "This is all my fault," I exclaimed. "Can I get some napkins over here?" I yelled. "Valerie!"

My best friend, who was standing there just as speechless as I was, burst into action and turned toward the bar.

"I'm so clumsy," I told the guy. "I'm so sorry. I'll buy you a new shirt," I offered. "And whatever you're drinking today."

"No need," he said. His voice was quiet but so commanding it didn't need to be loud. "It's just a shirt."

Glancing down at the ruined garment, I groaned again. It was blue silk. Probably cost more than I made in an entire week. And because of the material and the fact that it was soaked, it was plastered to his chest as if he'd been caught in the rain.

He was thin… but imposing. Everything about him was.

Val shoved a towel in front of my face, and I snatched it quickly. Rushing forward, I didn't even think twice about reaching out to try and dry the shirt.

The thin material was saturated, and it seemed no matter how much I patted and wiped, nothing helped.

Above me, a throat cleared. "Are you done?"

I froze, towel still pressed against his shirt, and looked up. His chin tilted down, and our eyes met, pure desire sliding through me.

I jolted back, flushing. "Sorry, I was trying to…" What was I trying to do?

He smiled, reached up, and unbuttoned the shirt to peel it off his body and drop it in the sand. "I'm pretty sure it's not savable."

My mouth ran dry. I couldn't look up from his tan, smooth chest.

A second later, he snapped in front of my face, making me lift my eyes. "You might want to lay off the alcohol the rest of the day. I think you've had enough."

Dumbly, I nodded and held out the towel for him to take.

He glanced between me and the offered towel, then smiled. "I'm good," he replied, then turned around and walked away.

I stared after him long after he was gone, still holding out the towel like a moron.

Val jumped in front of me, eyes wide. "Oh my God!" she whispered. "That guy was hot!"

The towel fell out of my hands, landing beside his forgotten shirt.

"Hey!" Val yelled toward the bar. "Who was that guy?"

"Never seen him before," one of the bartenders called back.

"Sucks," she muttered, then grabbed my hand. "C'mon, let's go get some vitamin sea."

"Wait!" I exclaimed, pulling back before she could drag me away. Bending down, I picked up the wet, sandy shirt he'd just discarded from his body.

Val tsked and dragged me toward the beach. "First the island guy, and now this." She sighed. "You're completely hopeless, Nora. Hopeless."

As I stared down at the shirt clutched in my hand, I couldn't help thinking she might be right.

Two

Carter

I sat there listening to quite an amusing conversation going on behind me.

One bad girl and one good... The bad trying to corrupt the good. I guess I could understand the appeal. The good ones were always the best at being bad.

I never got involved in guest affairs, even though all these scantily clad women were ripe for the picking. It was too easy. Too boring.

I liked a challenge.

Like being able to erase a man from the mind of a woman who couldn't let go.

I wondered if the good girl behind me was as open to that kind of fling as she pretended to be or if she clung to the rumors about a man on an island because she knew he probably didn't even exist.

Sometimes holding on was easier than letting go because at least the pain of holding on was familiar.

The second her drink spilled over my shoulder and across my chest, I wondered if it was my karma for listening to their conversation or if there was something else here at work.

The sparks between us were practically visible, and the way she shivered beneath my touch excited me. Still, I pulled away, because sometimes being a mystery was better than being real.

I felt her eyes against my back the entire time I walked away. I pondered if I would ever see her again, if I would be able to rise to her challenge.

The way my life had turned out so far was all because of fate. So I decided to leave this up to fate, too.

Three

Nora

"I can't believe I let you talk me into this!" I groaned for the hundredth time.

"You'll thank me later," Val assured and tossed something black in my direction. "Put that on."

"What is it?" I asked, holding it up. "A shirt?"

"It's your dress for tonight."

Glancing at the slinky fabric, I grimaced. "I'm pretty sure this borders on indecent."

"It stretches. Put it on."

The straps were so thin there was no way I could wear a bra. In fact, as I shimmied into it, I wondered if there would be room for panties.

As if she could hear my thoughts, Val tossed a black thong into the bathroom on her way past. "Here!"

"I'm not wearing your panties!" I gasped.

"They're brand new!" she countered.

Sure enough, there was a tag on them still. I pulled it off and slid them up my thighs under the black dress.

Standing in the mirror, I gazed at my reflection. It seemed I had bathing suits bigger than this dress, but the way it hugged my body was pretty impressive.

"You bitch," Val said, stepping into the bathroom behind me. "I knew you would look killer in that!"

I reached behind me to tug the string out of my ass. "I'm pretty sure this thong is going to kill me."

"Red lip, for sure," Val instructed, then hurried out.

Reaching for the red lipstick, I sighed. "I have no idea why I'm doing this."

"Because you're on vacation! Because you need to let loose a little!" Valerie called.

I stepped out of the bathroom, and she bounced over in front of me. "Zip me up."

Dutifully, I zipped up the strapless, sparkly dress she'd put on.

Turning, she put her hands on my shoulders. "You know I love you, right?"

I nodded.

We'd been besties since third grade. We'd been through everything together.

"If you can't do this for yourself, then do it for me. Okay? I'm worried about you."

"I think you're the only person in this world who thinks a one-night stand will cure everything."

"Not everything," she rebuked. "But it's definitely the Alan hangover cure."

I winced. *Alan hangover*. Was that what I had?

"Besides, I saw you checking out that bartender. You totally think he's hot."

I smiled. "He's not unfortunate-looking."

Val laughed. "Yeah, and neither is his friend. *His friend with a boat.*"

"Yeah, yeah." I agreed.

She'd been going on about the bartender's friend all afternoon. Right after the guy I spilled my drink on vanished, we'd been invited for some sailing and fun by the green-eyed bartender and his friend.

"I can't think of any better way to spend our last night here in paradise than on a boat with two hot locals."

A knock sounded on the cabana door, and Valerie's eyes lit up. "They're here!"

"I'll be right there," I called after her as she raced out of the room.

I heard her chattering a mile a minute to the guys as I stepped back into the bathroom and picked up my favorite perfume. After spraying a bit behind my ears, I went to the window where white gauze curtains billowed with the ocean breeze.

The sky was turning a twilight color. Everything lit on fire with the lowering of the tropical sun. Warm air caressed my bare shoulders, and the scent of salt wafted over me. I glanced in the direction of the island, wondering again about the man who supposedly lived there. Was he as good-looking as they said? What was a young, rich man doing living alone on his own private island?

"Nora!" Valerie called from the other room.

Tearing my eyes away from the view and putting my thoughts away for later, I hurried out into the main room where green eyes and his friend were waiting.

* * *

The bar was stocked, the boat beautiful. It was the kind with large sails, and string lights lit the deck. Valerie and her conquest were at the large wheel, him reaching around her as she tried to steer the boat.

I was standing near the edge, champagne glass in one hand and holding back my blowing hair with the other.

Xander, the bartender with the green eyes, came up beside me. "You cold?" he asked in a sultry, accented voice right beside my ear.

I glanced over my shoulder and shook my head. "I'm good."

Smiling, he took the flute out of my grip and took a sip of my champagne, then handed it back, making sure our hands brushed when he did.

My cheeks heated with the contact, but otherwise, I felt nothing at all. Maybe Valerie was right. Maybe I was still too hung up on Alan. I wondered if all his betrayals had broken me and I'd never be able to feel anything for another man again.

The boat suddenly lurched, and I pitched forward. Strong arms came around me from behind, firmly pulling me back against a taut body. Even after I was steady, he didn't let me go. Instead, the other arm came around, and I was encircled from behind.

Timid, I glanced around to that pair of unfamiliar green eyes with seduction practically dripping from the corners.

Fingers tightening on the bubbly, I turned back and took a fortifying gulp.

A rich chuckle filled my ear and slid down me just like the alcohol in my throat. "I've had my eye on you all week," he said, his lips brushing against my ear. "I see lots of beautiful girls, but you are by far the prettiest."

Really? That was the best he could do?

I wondered vaguely if any girl every really believed that. *They probably don't care enough either way.*

Val would have giggled and let herself be charmed. I just wanted a refill on my drink.

The second his lips grazed the top of my ear, I pulled away and turned. Holding the glass between us, I smiled up at him. "How about a refill?"

"That I can do." He agreed, taking the glass and going off for more.

Turning back to the night sky, I marveled at the way the millions of stars glittered like fine diamonds. A few moments later, a full flute of bubbly appeared before me, and the second I took it, his arms were back around me.

I sipped at the drink, settling a little more firmly against his body. Behind us, Valerie's laugh carried on the wind, and the boat bounced over the waves gently.

Xander's lips found my ear, his teeth nibbling at the sensitive skin. I closed my eyes and succumbed to the sensations, waiting for desire and want to crash over me.

A short while later, the boat slowed, and footsteps behind us brought my head around.

"Man the boat," Xander's friend said and picked Valerie up off her feet. "We're going below."

The second they were gone, Xander pulled me around, clamping his arms around me, his lips crashing down over mine. He tasted like alcohol and eagerness, the combination dampening most of my desire.

Squeezing my eyes closed, I stepped a little closer, telling myself I needed this.

The boat lurched again, and my champagne sloshed over the rim and onto Xander's shirt. I pulled back and wiped at the spot, but he grabbed my hand and tried to pull me back into him.

"What about the boat?" I asked, feeling it bounce again.

"Just leave it," he murmured, clamping his lips at my throat.

An uncomfortable feeling slithered around inside me and made me squirm. Xander mistook that for an invitation, thrusting his hips into me.

Another wave rocked the boat, and I shoved away from my date. "I think you should check," I said, shaky.

His green eyes were glittering, his lips swollen from kissing. Swiping a hand over his lower lip, he nodded once. "All right. Come on," he said, taking my hand and towing me along behind him.

My bare feet slapped against the deck as we went to the steering wheel and Xander checked all the controls. After a moment, he righted our course, and the boat continued on smoothly.

Barely a second after the course smoothed out, he was on me again. This time he sat down in the captain's chair and pulled me into his lap. His hands were rough when he pulled the thin strap of my dress down and uncovered my breast. The sea breeze brushed over it unforgivingly, making my nipple harden in an instant.

His thumb and forefinger clamped around it and pinched, making me squeak.

He chuckled. "You like that, huh?"

Actually, I didn't.

I moved away, hoping he would get a hint. Instead, he grabbed my hips and pulled me back over him, this time grabbing the fabric of the dress and pushing it up toward my waist.

"Hey!" I said, trying to push it down as he pushed up.

"I know you want me. I saw it this afternoon at the bar. I heard your friend saying you needed to get laid."

Oh, ew. Gross.

"I guess manhandling me is your idea of getting laid?"

"You'll like it. Just relax." He bent forward and tried to take my exposed breast into his mouth.

I shoved his head away and stumbled out of his lap.

The problem with a boat is there isn't much place to run.

So I ran out on the deck, noting how there was nothing but water surrounding us for miles.

Xander caught me. Of course he did. He laughed like we were playing some cat-and-mouse game, like my resistance was foreplay.

He spun me around, planting his mouth over mine. His tongue pushed against my lips, demanding entrance, and I wanted to gag.

I pushed him off me, chest heaving. "Stop! I don't want this."

Confusion rolled over his handsome features. "You were just kissing me five minutes ago."

Yeah, and I could barely fake that.

"I know. I'm sorry. Look, I didn't mean to lead you on. I just… I changed my mind."

He laughed and rubbed a hand through his hair. "Are you serious right now?"

I nodded.

He grabbed his crotch and jerked it. "And what do you suppose I do about this?"

"I'm sure if we go back to the bar, you could have a replacement for me in two minutes flat."

Anger lit up his eyes. "No one ever turns me down."

"I know. I'm sorry," I said again, then pressed a hand to my stomach. "I think I-I'm seasick... This is my first time on a boat. I think I might throw up." To prove the words, I ran toward the railing and leaned over, making retching sounds.

I wasn't actually seasick, but, hey, it seemed like my best option right now.

Valerie was never going to let me live this down, but I didn't care. Xander was not the guy with the ability to cure my Alan hangover.

As I fake retched, Xander cursed and stomped back toward the steering wheel. I breathed a sigh of relief, thankful he was at least a nice enough guy to take me back to shore.

The sound of the motor speeding up and the boat propelling forward gave me a great sense of relief. I dared a glance over my shoulder at Xander and nearly squealed when I saw him glaring daggers in my direction.

I leaned back over the railing, once again pretending to puke. I was pretty sure he wouldn't actually come close enough to know if I was truly sick or not because this guy wanted sex tonight, not to hold back my hair.

The boat cut through the water more quickly than before. Unease trickled down my spine when I looked up and realized Xander hadn't turned the boat back to shore.

Clutching the rail, still leaning slightly over, I looked back to where he was. The second our eyes connected, he smiled.

Gave me the finger.

Then cut the wheel sharply to the left.

My scream got lost out at sea as my body pitched over the rail like a feather in a strong gust of wind. I hit the black waves with a splash, the cold temperature a shock against my bare skin.

My eyes sprang open as my body sank under the surface, and panic gripped me like never before when all I saw was black. It felt as though I sank forever, like my body was no match for the endless inky black of the night sea. It had the arms of an octopus, skillfully dragging me under, turning me around until I wasn't sure which way was up.

I struggled and fought, screaming against the current. Eventually, my head broke free, and sweet oxygen filled my burning lungs. Just a few gasps in, a wave crashed over my head, and I was tumbling upside down all over again.

Coughing and sputtering bitter salt water, I found the surface again. Nearly gagging, water dripping in my eyes, I tread water, looking for the boat.

"Help!" I screamed. "Help me!"

In the distance, I caught the twinkling of the string lights on the sailboat.

"Valerie!" I yelled. "Valerie!" I screamed so loud my throat ached.

Panicked but unwilling to give up, I started swimming toward the boat. My arms and legs moved furiously through the heavy water, dragging me backward with every stroke I took.

When my arms were quaking with exhaustion and my legs felt like rubber, I finally slowed. I was no closer to the boat than before... If anything, I was farther away.

"Help!" I cried out again, my voice much weaker than before.

I didn't bother calling out again because I knew they wouldn't be coming back.

Four

Carter

Through the high-powered telescope, I watched the good girl and the bad girl step onto a sailboat.

Even beneath the twilight sky, even only after seeing her once, I recognized her. It had nothing to do with my photographic memory and everything to do with the way she made me feel.

Even with the distance between us, she still affected me, still intrigued me.

Good girls are just girls who haven't met the right man yet.

True, I said I was going to leave what might be between us up to fate.

But sometimes fate needed a little help.

Five

Nora

Overboard. I'd just fallen overboard from a boat that left me in the middle of the ocean.

Correction.

I hadn't just fallen; I'd been purposely tossed.

I'd be really freaking pissed right now if I wasn't so terrified.

What did a person do when they were cast overboard? How long could I tread water until my arms and legs gave out and I sank like a rock to the bottom of the sea?

It was cold out here. And dark. There were no signs pointing in the direction I needed to go. When I looked around, all I saw was vast darkness and nothing… absolutely nothing.

I wanted to cry, but crying would only expel energy I so desperately needed. The only way out of this was to swim to shore. After settling on the way I thought land might be, I started out, trying not to let my teeth chatter, trying not to think about all the things swimming around beneath me.

Sharks!

The thought made me whimper and stop pushing through the waves. My body floated, carried by the moving water as I stared anxiously down, trying to see below me.

I could be eaten at any moment. A giant shark could be circling.

Would being eaten by a shark be better than drowning? Both seemed like cruel fate, but unbelievably, I was leaning toward getting eaten alive vs drowning.

Floating silently in the endless black sea seemed imminently more depressing and lonelier than being chewed up by Jaws.

"You're losing your mind, Nora," I muttered, then spun around, looking to see if my voice had brought out any predators.

The loud, disruptive sound of a blaring horn cut through the night, and I screamed. Water splashed everywhere in the force of the way I jumped, and I sputtered and coughed when a mouthful of salty sea filled my throat.

The horn blasted again, and I spun, spotting a hulking craft moving into sight.

"Help!" I screamed. "Help me!" I waved my arms over my head, slipping a little beneath the surface as I did.

The second I burst upward, I yelled again, squinting against a suddenly bright light. Flinching away, I threw my arm over my face to shield my eyes.

Wait. There was a light!

Smacking the surface of the water, I blinked at the blinding beam focused right on me. I couldn't see anything or anyone beyond it, but really, I didn't care who it was. It could be pirates from hell, but at this point, I'd take my chances with Blackbeard over Jaws.

"Please help me!" I cried, my voice watery and hoarse.

Something hit the water close by, and more splashed into my eyes. Eyes stinging from salt, I saw a life preserver and dove at it. The second my arms clamped around it, I was towed out of the bright light, through the waves, toward a giant white boat.

This was a different kind of boat than the one I'd just been on. This one was bigger, whiter… and I didn't really care. It could have been a raft with a hole in it and I'd have been grateful.

"Hang on," someone yelled down.

"Like I have any other choice," I yelled back.

Muffled laughter reached me, but I scarcely paid attention because as I watched, a figure climbed over the side and started down a ladder attached to the boat.

It seemed to take forever for them to get to me. Anxious, I swam over and grabbed the bottom of the ladder and started to pull myself up. My arms were weak and my fingers stiff from the cold. I couldn't grip the metal rungs solidly enough to help myself.

I tried again and fell back into the water, a wave of hopelessness washing over me.

"Don't give up," a low voice said, and a hand appeared before me.

The second my hand grabbed his, my lack of strength no longer mattered. Instead, I was hoisted up onto the back of someone with enough muscle for both of us. Standing on the ladder, he pulled my arms around his neck and reached around to lift me higher.

"I need you to hold on," he said.

I nodded against him, my cheek pressed firmly against his back. He was warm. Like the sun. Like a sun that didn't disappear even when the moon came out.

I don't know how he did it, but he climbed up the ladder with me on his back. The feel of his muscles working under me imparted a serious sense of security.

The second we were at the top, hands grabbed us both, pulling us over the side and onto the deck. I collapsed there, trying to grip the floor, wishing it wasn't so solid so I could take a handful and never let go.

I coughed and heaved as salt water expelled from my lips and dripped off my limbs. The black dress I'd been wearing was saturated and clinging to me. My fingers and toes were numb.

When I felt my body being lifted off the floor, I struggled because nothing was more reassuring than a firm surface beneath my quivering limbs.

"Shh…" The voice drifted over me, and I was cradled against a wide chest.

Automatically, my arms wound around his neck and my cheek pillowed against his shoulder. I let my eyes drift closed, knowing I might have left one danger and dropped into another, but I couldn't find the energy to care.

I felt safe right now.

Safer than I had been in a very long time.

I could let myself have that, right? Even if it was only fleeting.

The sounds of his heavy footfalls were like music to my ears, and the gentle swaying of the boat was so much kinder than the buoyancy of the sailboat I'd been cast off.

The sound of rain met my ears, and my fingers clutched against the shirt of the man holding me. "You saved me just before the rain," I whispered.

A second later, warm spray cascaded over me, and my eyes sprang open.

"You need to get warm," a low voice assured, carrying me a little farther beneath the spray.

Looking up, I saw the giant silver showerhead and sheets of marble all around. The warm, gentle spray of the water seeping into me felt like heaven, and my cheek fell back against his chest.

"Thank you," I whispered. "Thank you."

And then I promptly passed out.

Six

Carter

Fate often provides opportunity. We just have to be paying attention to see it. Fate saw me watching, so she delivered.

A faint knock on the other side of the door made me look up in time to see Aaron step inside, carrying a wooden tray with two large black mugs. He didn't glance at the bed or even at me sitting in a chair beside it. Instead, he focused on sliding the tray onto the bedside table, lifting one mug, and handing it over to me.

"I know this is the tropics, but you should warm up with something hot."

"Thanks," I said, taking the offered drink.

"Should I call for the doctor?" he asked, still averting his eyes from the girl in my bed.

"No. Steer the boat back to the island."

He didn't offer any reaction or opinion on my decision, just nodded and left the room.

Setting the mug back on the tray, I adjusted my position from the chair to the side of the mattress. She was sleeping, as if she had no clue what trouble she could be in.

I didn't get the impression earlier today that she was a stupid girl, but after tonight's events, I might have to revise my previous appraisal.

"You need to wake up," I told her, reaching out to jostle her shoulder.

She didn't do anything other than sigh. Just that contented sound tightened my groin, and my hand fisted in my lap.

"Hey." I tried again.

Clearly, she had no intention of listening, which just wouldn't do. Planting a hand on either side of her, I leaned close, intently staring at her smooth, pale skin.

"Good girl." I beckoned. "You need to open your eyes now."

Slowly, her eyelids fluttered, and unfocused blue eyes came into view. A few seconds passed before she seemed to realize I was there.

Alarm flared, and her mouth opened to scream.

Quickly, I pressed my palm over her lips. "The staff will think I'm torturing you if you scream."

Her heavy breathing puffed against my hand, and against my palm, I felt her tongue dart out to wet her lips.

Carefully, the girl nodded, silently telling me she wouldn't scream.

Removing my hand, I sat back in the chair I'd parked beside the bed and watched her. She was beautiful. Even half drowned, drowsy, and confused, she was beautiful.

I saw beautiful women on a daily basis. Hell, they flocked to the resort in droves. This good girl sitting in front of me wasn't any more beautiful than the rest of them, so I wasn't quite sure why I was so intrigued.

Perhaps because I'd heard her talking about me. Because it seemed she'd been passing on other men because the idea of me was in her head.

A girl who passed up reality because the fantasy in her head was that much more appealing made me think there was a lot of passion simmering beneath her skin.

Her body slid up beneath the heavy comforter as she pushed into a sitting position. Immediately, she glanced down and gasped. Graceful-looking fingers pressed against the white silk draped over her as she fumbled with the buttons down the front.

"Where are my clothes?"

"Your dress was soaked. After your shower, I put this shirt on you so you'd be dry."

Swallowing, she glanced down at it again. "Is it your shirt?"

"I thought you might like the feel of silk against your skin."

Her head shot up, and her eyes roamed my face. Recognition came into her gaze, and her mouth fell open. "You're the guy from the bar. I spilled my drink on you."

I half smiled. "That's two of my shirts you've managed to procure in one day."

Gazing around quickly, her hand pressed to her neck. "Where am I?"

"On my boat. You fell overboard the one you were on, and the bartender left you there to drown."

Her body pressed against the pillows, blue eyes wide with alarm.

Clearing my throat, I tried to gentle my voice, realizing I'd been a little harsh in the way I spoke before. "Are you okay? Do you need a doctor?"

Her hand fell from her throat to clutch the blankets in her lap. Her hair was damp, and strands of it clung to her cheek.

"How did you know about the bartender? How did you know I was in the ocean?"

"I was watching you," I said, matter-of-fact. Lifting the mug Aaron had brought for her, I held it out. "Here, drink this. It will warm you up."

She gazed between me and the offered mug. Her lips were colorless, and her cheeks were pale. "What is it?"

Tilting the mug toward me, I gazed inside. I couldn't tell, so I leaned down and smelled it. "Hot tea," I replied. "The butler made it."

"The butler…" she echoed.

"Are you worried it's drugged?" I asked, lifting an eyebrow. I took a drink of the liquid and let her see me swallow. "It has honey it in," I added. "Do you like honey?"

She nodded.

"Here, then." I offered it. When she still didn't take it, I sighed and lifted her hand to place it around the mug.

"It's warm," she said, her fingers curling around the ceramic. Soon after, her other hand came up to wrap around the other side.

"You were watching me?" she repeated.

I nodded.

"You know that sounds like the start of a horror movie, right? You have some kind of room on this boat where you grind up helpless women into fish food?"

"I think the horror movie you're thinking of is the one where a girl almost gets raped on spring break, but instead, the angry bartender just tries to kill her."

She collapsed back against the pillows, clutching the mug against her chest. "So that really happened, huh?"

"It really happened."

"I guess I should be glad you were stalking me, then." She glanced into the mug, then peeked up at me. "Thank you for rescuing me. I probably would have drowned."

I didn't try to hide my smile. "Probably."

Offended I'd agreed, she sat up. "Hey! I might have survived! I was swimming back to shore when you showed up!"

"You were going in the wrong direction. You would have ended up farther out to sea."

She pursed her lips and said nothing. After a tentative drink of the hot tea, she asked, "Why were you watching me?"

"I was intrigued after our meeting."

"You could have just asked for my number," she grumped.

"I like to let fate do her thing."

Grabbing the blankets, she tossed them back. "I should go. Val is probably out of her mind with worry."

The second she tried to stand, she pitched sideways, her legs giving out.

Catching her around the waist, her body fell into mine, making my heart race. The silk of my shirt beneath my hand was all that separated my palm from the skin of her back.

"You need to lie back down," I said, setting aside the mug and picking her up completely.

Hearing her breath catch, I looked down. Our eyes locked and time froze for unspecified moments as sparks ignited between us.

"Can I borrow your phone?" she finally asked, breaking the spell we were both under.

I tucked her back in the bed and went across the room to my cell.

"I'll have her meet me at the dock. That's where you're taking me, right?"

"I'm taking you to my island."

She forgot about the cell in her palm. "Y-your island?"

"Weren't you curious about the man who lived there?"

Her mouth dropped open again. She seemed to do that a lot. It made me want to kiss her. "You heard our conversation?"

"I'm pretty sure everyone within earshot heard it. Your friend is not quiet."

"She was drunk," she refuted, surly.

"What's your name?"

"Don't you already know?" she rebuked.

"I want you to tell me."

Her eyes narrowed. "Why?"

"Because then I'll have permission to use it."

Her eyes dipped to the bed, but she replied, "Nora."

"I'm Carter, Nora."

"Carter," she repeated. "So are you trying to tell me, Carter, that you are the guy who lives on the island and owns the resort?"

"I actually own several resorts, not just this one."

She blinked. Had she thought I'd been joking?

"There is one thing you got wrong, though."

32

"What?"

"I didn't get rich from selling an app. I got rich off selling a video game. But I'm working on some apps now."

She started to cough, and I pushed the mug back under her. "Here, drink this."

Obediently, she took the mug and drank.

"I must have hit my head," she murmured after swallowing. I watched her search her head for bumps and cuts.

There weren't any. I'd already looked.

A second later, she gasped again. She was very dramatic. "How did I get in this shirt? And in the shower?"

"I dressed you."

"You saw me naked?"

"Yes."

Her fingers clutched at the neckline of the silk shirt.

"Should I have left you drenched and in that tiny dress?"

"You didn't see anything, right?"

Staring at her intently, I replied, "I saw everything."

"You could have at least pretended to be a gentleman!"

"I'm no gentleman. And I think you already know that."

Red spots formed on her cheeks, and it pleased me because it was better than seeing her pale.

"Drink more of that. Do you want something to eat?"

"No," she refuted, but the loud grumble of her stomach betrayed her.

"Call your friend," I said, going over to the phone attached to the wall. "Word about a missing woman at my resort will not be good for business."

I hit a button on the phone and held it to my ear. Aaron picked up on the first ring. "Yes, sir?"

"Bring a sandwich and some bisque."

"Right away." He agreed, and I hung up the line.

"I'm fine, Valerie. I promise." Nora was assuring her friend on the other end of the call. After a moment of listening, she made a sound. "Tell them to call off the search. I'm fine."

"He said what?" Nora exclaimed after another minute. "That liar. Liar! He purposely tossed me off the boat! He's a scumbag! When I see him next, I'm going to kick him so hard in the balls he's going to have to get them medically pulled back out!"

Feisty.

Amused, I crossed my arms over my chest and watched her.

"Wait, what?" she said after a minute. "Seriously? How…?" After a few beats, she looked up at me while speaking to her friend. "A witness?"

Uncrossing my arms, I strode across the room to snatch the phone out of her hand. Putting it up to my ear, I said, "Nora won't be home tonight. She'll be back tomorrow. Don't worry about her. She'll be fine."

"Who are you?" her friend yelled into my ear.

"I'm the guy who lives on the island. Surprise, I'm not old enough to be her grandpa." The second I said the words, I disconnected the call.

A second later, it started ringing in my hand. "Ah, sometimes the call back feature really is annoying." Instead of answering, I powered down the phone completely.

Nora was staring at me when I looked up. Raising an eyebrow, I asked, "Is there something you want to know?"

"Valerie said the bartender was already fired and taken to the police station on charges of assault."

"Did you think I would let him get away with what he did?"

"You can do that?"

"Protect you? Protect my resort and everyone in it? Of course."

"You seriously own this place?" Her eyes began looking around the large bedroom, then back at me.

"I don't lie," I deadpanned.

"This is all just a little… unbelievable."

"Most fantasies are."

Realization dawned over her face. "I'm dreaming," she whispered. "I must have blacked out in the ocean, and I'm still dreaming."

Aaron rapped on the door and entered, carrying a large tray with a plate and bowl in the center. Nora's eyes widened, and she lifted the covers as if she could hide behind them. Aaron pretended not to notice but set the tray over her lap and then left the room without a word.

"Eat," I commanded.

"This is some dream," she mused, looking over the food.

Stalking close, I leaned over the tray, making her sink back into the pillows once more. Taking her chin in my hand, I lifted it so I could stare into her good-girl face.

"This might be a fantasy, but it's no dream. Before this night is over, you'll learn to tell the difference."

Before she could reply, I lowered my head, fusing my lips to hers. I felt her shock, but I didn't pull away. Instead, I moved, caressing my lips over hers and drinking in the faint taste of salt still on her skin.

A few seconds ticked by, and I felt her relent. I knew without looking that her eyes drifted closed because the mouth beneath mine began to move.

Desire so swift cut into me like a deadly sword. Aggressively, I went at her mouth, trying to quench the thirst, trying to satiate the need she so desperately made me feel.

One kiss wasn't going to do that, so I yanked back and put some distance between us.

Nora stared at me with giant eyes and pink, swollen lips. Slowly, she fingered her mouth, and the urge to kiss her again was swift.

Holding back, I cleared my throat. "Eat," I demanded again, pointing to the food. "You're gonna need all the energy you can get."

Seven

Nora

Was I insane?

Someone just dumped me in the ocean and left without looking back. Then another guy came along and hauled me out, saw me naked, put me in his bed, admitted to being a stalker, *then* kissed the crap out of me.

What was I doing about these events?

Sitting in his lavish bed, wearing his silk shirt, and eating lobster bisque like nothing was wrong.

I had to be insane, right?

Or maybe I really was dreaming. Maybe I was dead, and this was the afterlife I was given. If that was the case… death wasn't so bad.

The spoon dropped into the bowl, splashing a little of the soup.

"Careful," my savior said without even looking up. He was lounging in the chair beside the bed, his feet propped up on the side of the mattress. A tablet was in his lap, and his fingers were flying over the screen.

"I should wake up," I murmured, then slapped myself on the cheek. "Wake up, Nor. Wake up!"

I went to slap myself again, but a large, warm hand wrapped around my wrist, preventing me. My eyes met his very dark, very intent ones. The grip around my wrist was gentle, but it was imposing.

"Now why would you want to wake up? We haven't gotten to the good part yet."

I swallowed, my arm going slack in his palm.

"I'm going to let go now," he intoned.

Why was the sound of his voice so damn delicious? Why did he look like so dangerous yet make me feel so safe?

"Don't try and hit yourself again, or I'm going to get angry."

I pulled my arm back, but he wouldn't let go. His eyes implored me, and I found myself nodding, silently promising I wouldn't hit myself again.

Satisfied, he let go, lounged back into the chair, and resumed whatever he was doing. "Finish eating, and I'll show you the island."

"Really?" I asked, excited.

His lips turned up even though he didn't break focus on what he was doing. *What is he doing?*

"Yes, really."

I went back to eating. I guess almost dying made a girl hungry.

"Aish!" he spat, sitting up.

The sudden outburst startled me, and the spoon slipped out of my mouth. "What happened?"

He glanced at me, then turned the tablet around for me to see the screen. "I died."

He was playing a game. Some colorful, simple game on the screen with the word DEAD flashing in red in the center.

"I'll beat it next time." He encouraged himself. "Next time."

I couldn't pull my eyes away as he tossed the tablet at the end of the bed and dragged a hand through his sleek, dark hair. The second he let it go, it fell over his forehead and brushed over the tops of his eyebrows.

Desire curled my toes, and even though it was overwhelming, I didn't look away.

When his eyes met mine, he laughed beneath his breath. "You're not too good at feeding yourself."

"Huh?"

Leaving the chair, he dropped on the side of the mattress again. I forgot to breathe when he leaned near, his eyes straying to my mouth. The rapid pounding of my heart thundered in my ears as I anticipated his closeness.

I thought he was going to kiss me again, so I slammed my eyes closed and waited. His chuckle brushed over my body, and then something brushed against my lips.

"You have soup on your face," he said softly.

My eyes snapped open. Carter was still as close as before, but his thumb was brushing away the mess I'd apparently made of my mouth.

When he was done, he sat back just a little and pushed the pad of his thumb between his lips to clean it off.

The bottom dropped out of my stomach, and my limbs tingled.

Carter glanced at the tray between us. "You finished?"

I nodded.

When it was gone, he reached for my hand and pulled me out of bed. My legs were bare beneath the white shirt, the silk fabric brushing over my thighs like a caress.

I started to tug it down, though it was longer than the dress I'd had on earlier.

He noticed my fidgeting and reached for my other hand to pull it away. "No one else is here to see." He assured me. "And I've already seen it all."

Ducking my head, I tucked some damp hair behind my ear.

"You steady on your feet now?" he asked.

I nodded.

Truth was I was starting to wonder if I'd ever be steady again. Good Lord, he had some power. He tilted everything inside me so much I seriously wondered if it would ever right itself.

When he didn't walk forward, I glanced up. He was gazing at me with dark, unreadable eyes.

"I don't think you are," he said as if it were a sincere observation.

"I really am," I argued, wanting to see the island. "I feel much better after the food."

His lips pursed and doubt was written plainly on his features. Releasing my hand, he turned and crouched.

I stared down at him, dumbfounded. "What are you doing?"

He patted his shoulder. "Come on. I'll carry you."

Before I could, he reached around, tugging my hand, and I fell against him. Carter rose, tucking his hands beneath my legs and lifting me farther onto his back. My arms looped around his shoulders and clasped in front of his collarbone.

The balmy night slipped against my exposed skin and my cheek when he stepped onto the deck. Without thinking twice, I buried my face in his neck, seeking warmth.

"Look," he beckoned, so I did.

We stood on the deck, a perfect view of his private island laid out before us. Drawing in a breath, I gazed at it all incredulously, resting my chin on his shoulder. "I seriously haven't seen anything this amazing."

He didn't say anything, but I could feel my words pleased him.

The island was filled with swaying palm trees. Even in the dark, the sand glowed bright white. Nestled farther up between the palms was a lit-up house with giant windows and a deck wrapping around the entire back.

The yacht was pulled up to a giant private dock, which looked as if it stretched for miles before we actually got to the beach. On the way, we passed jet skis and smaller boats, which all bobbed in the water quietly, waiting to be used.

"You're cold," he said, glancing over his shoulder. "I'll show you the beach tomorrow, in the sun."

"Tomorrow?"

His footsteps halted in the sand, and with agility I didn't really think he had, Carter pulled me off his back and around his body so my legs were wrapped around his waist and we were face to face.

"I'm not letting you go tonight. Tonight, you're mine."

I lifted my chin. "Will you toss me back out to sea if I tell you no?"

He smiled. "Are you going to tell me no?"

My stare dropped to his lips.

"I didn't think so," he retorted and started walking again.

He carried me down a sandy path through some tall grass and flowers. The air was fragrant here with whatever bloomed nearby and the unmistakably salty air. When we got closer to the house, lit torches lined the path, creating a warm glow against the stark-white sand.

"You live here all alone?" I was amazed.

"I like my privacy."

I pulled back to look into his face. "But you brought me here."

He stopped walking again, pinning me with those endless dark eyes. "I must like you, too."

I kissed him this time, wrapping my arms tightly around his neck and arching into his body. His hands tightened where he held me, his tongue stroking into my mouth and making me moan.

Without breaking the scorching kiss, he carried me up some steps, across the deck, and into the house. We broke apart for a second. Carter tilted his mouth in another direction, and then he was kissing me again.

Sensation after sensation rolled over me, muddling my thoughts and stealing my breath.

The soft hum of an overhead fan buzzed in my ears, and suddenly, he was draping me across a bed with blankets so soft I sank into them.

He rose beside me on his knees, towering over me with dangerous intensity. I watched by the light of the moon shining in through the windows as Carter peeled the shirt off his body and tossed it away.

His body was long and lean. There wasn't much softness to him. The wide set of his shoulders drew my eyes again and again. When he leaned down, I clutched his biceps, offering up my lips and letting him consume them. My legs were trembling when his pouty, full lips dragged down my neck and across my collarbone.

With a deep growl that made my stomach flip, he sat up again, staring down with glittering eyes. With deliberate slowness, Carter unbuttoned the shirt around me one button at a time.

With every new button released, he would start at the top, dragging his finger down the center of my chest, caressing the bare skin, until he reached the next button that needed undoing.

By the time he pulled the shirt apart, I felt flushed and overheated. My chest heaved upward when he peeled it the rest of the way off and threw it to the floor.

Lying beside me, our bare skin brushed together. Nuzzling my ear and neck, that large hand of his covered my breast and squeezed.

A low sound built in my throat, and I turned my face toward his so we could lock lips again. He kissed me until I couldn't think, until I thought perhaps his tongue was mine. My lips were swollen, my limbs completely slack.

I don't know how, but this man owned me so quickly that if I'd been able to think, I might have been scared.

At last, he moved between my legs, holding his weight on his arms.

"What's my name?" he asked, his voice low and rough.

"Carter," I answered, reaching up to cup his jaw.

Lips closed around my nipple, and his palm went to the apex of my thighs. I was ready and drenched, literally quivering for relief.

My hands shook as they trailed over his body, marveling at the dips and curves, getting drunk on the restrained power he exuded.

When his mouth left and he rose above me again, I tried to grab him back. His low chuckle made my teeth sink into my lower lip as I watched him quickly cover himself with protection.

Those large hands covered my thighs, pushing them apart, opening me wide. Between us, he palmed the erection standing proud and stroked it only once.

The second I felt his sleek, hard head brush over my core, I moaned. One arm slid between me and the mattress, pulling me firmly against his naked chest. He whispered my name at the same moment he thrust into my body.

Pleasure unlike anything I'd ever known before erupted over my entire being, blocking out absolutely everything else. Everything was suddenly condensed down to the way he felt moving inside me, how incredibly hard and throbbing he was.

Bracing himself above me, Carter started to move more urgently, spearing me again and again until I could barely breathe. As I gasped, he lowered to capture my mouth, twisting his tongue against mine.

Pushing deep, I felt my body begin to splinter. Wrapping my arms around his neck, I pulled him closer, holding on like I was afraid I'd somehow fly away.

Cupping the back of my neck, he pulled me in and thrust again, rocking gently deep inside me.

Light burst behind my eyes, and my body bucked up against his. He used his body to hold me down while sensation after sensation ripped me apart in the best way. I moaned, and his lips caught the sound.

Eventually, my body went completely boneless, and I collapsed against the bed. Carter rose over me again and began to move.

Even though I'd already been ripped apart with immeasurable pleasure, incredibly, it rose within me again. The second a growl built up in his throat, I knew he was about to spill over. Seeing the corded muscles in his neck and the way his eyes glittered made me bold.

Reaching around, I grabbed his butt and pushed him so deep we both cried out.

We fell at the same time, bodies convulsing together and the room filled only with the sound of gasps.

When he was able, he rolled off to the side, arms flinging across the wide mattress. Scooting closer, I pillowed my cheek on his chest. Almost like he was surprised, he glanced down. Gazing up, I asked without words if it was okay.

He answered without words as well, putting a hand against the back of my head and pulling me closer.

Eight

Carter

I wrapped my hand around her ankle and dragged her toward the edge of the bed. She made a sleepy sound and reached for me, but I avoided her touch. Slipping my arms beneath her, I lifted Nora and the sheet tangled around her into my arms.

"Where are we going?" she asked, pressing a kiss against my bare shoulder.

I didn't answer. Instead, I just went across the room and stepped out the large sliders onto the private deck. Sitting down with her in my lap in the single chair outside, I tucked the sheet around our naked bodies and hitched a chin toward the view.

"Look."

Nora lifted her head. "Wow," she mused. "It's so beautiful."

The sky was just awakening as the sun rose behind the endless ocean. Pink and peach clashed on the horizon, painting the water line in glowing shades. Clouds spread up toward the heavens and the blossoming sun's rays sparkled on the ever-moving water, making it glitter.

Palm trees filled the island and grew right around the house, their waving fronds sort of like a frame for the sunrise filling the horizon.

"You get to see this every day," Nora said, staring.

"Usually, I'm still asleep."

"Mm, sleep."

I made a sound. "You can sleep on the plane tonight."

Tearing her eyes off the sunrise, she glanced behind her at me. "You really listened to everything we said."

"You're noisy."

She turned back to the view, and I put an arm around her from behind, pulling her into my body.

"How often do you do this sort of thing?" she asked a little while later.

"Does it matter?"

She didn't reply, and we sat there until the sun looked like a giant ball of fire resting right on the ocean.

The light wind blew, pushing the blond strands of her hair off her bare shoulder. Her skin was so creamy, I couldn't resist leaning forward and sucking it into my mouth.

Her head tilted to the side, allowing me greater access, so I reached around her body to wrap my hand gently around the front of her neck.

I kissed and nipped at the skin, making her shiver. When I started to pull away, she reached around and pulled my head back, holding it there until my lips latched on again.

I sucked on her skin until she was satisfied and her arm slid away. Lifting my head, I saw the already deepening mark my mouth had left behind.

Something about leaving that mark on her skin made me satisfied in a bone-deep sort of way. Nora turned in my lap, grabbing my face and kissing me thoroughly. As we kissed, I peeled the sheet off her body, exposing her naked flesh.

Wind from the ocean blew around us, and the rustling sound of palms overhead seemed to be the music to the desire pounding in my veins. I didn't know how I could still want her. I'd already claimed her three times.

I don't know how my body kept responding, but this good girl had awakened something primal inside me, and as long as she was in my hands, I would want to claim her over and over.

Abruptly, I stood, picking her up with me. The sheet fell at my feet, and my lips locked around her breast. Nora arched into me with a purr as I sucked and licked at the hard pebble.

Impatient and demanding, I swung her down to her feet. Swiftly, I spun her so she was facing the view and her back was to me.

"Don't move," I ordered as I turned and went to retrieve a condom from the nightstand.

Gripping her hips, I walked until I could place her hands on the railing, then covered them with mine.

My already throbbing cock nudged her ass, causing a swift intake of her breath.

"Someone might see."

"This is my island," I rasped, nudging her again. "No one else is here."

Reaching around, I slid my fingers into her center, finding the secret spot. Her knees buckled, and I wrapped an arm around her waist.

"Spread them," I whispered in her ear.

Nora planted her feet farther apart and lifted her round ass in the air.

Gripping her hips, I pushed inside her, and we both hissed.

I fucked her hard and fast on the balcony, leaving finger marks on her hips. She cried my name like it was a chant, and I grinded against her bare ass like a hungry wolf.

Her shout of pleasure was carried by the wind out to sea, and when she collapsed toward the ground, I held her up until I emptied every last ounce of satisfaction I had left inside me.

We sat completely naked in the chair, the sheet long forgotten, until I trusted my legs to hold us up. Only then did I carry her into the shower, where we played beneath the spray.

Both of us dressed in robes, we exited to find a tray filled with fruit and pastries, along with a pot of coffee and fresh cream.

I watched her fill a plate and bring it over to me, still intrigued by everything she did. I grabbed her hand when she turned away.

"Am I not allowed to eat?" she asked, playful.

"I'll share." I pulled her down on the bed, and we fed each other fruit until the plate was empty.

We took our coffee out onto the beach, me dressed in a pair of shorts and her in nothing but my white silk shirt.

The sand was warm beneath our toes, and her bold hair looked like golden fire underneath the morning sun.

We didn't talk much on the boat ride back to the resort, even though it was only her and me. At the dock, I tied the boat and lifted her out of the craft so she was standing right in front of me.

"Thank you for pulling me out of the water last night. I'm pretty sure you saved my life."

Slipping my arms around her, I indulged us both with one last kiss. It was long and thorough, reaching all the way down to bone.

When I pulled back, she caught my lip and sucked it into her mouth, lifting up on tiptoes to kiss me long and hard.

Nora was smiling when she pulled back, her blue eyes dancing with mischief. "Thanks for the shirt," she said and started to walk away.

"Hey," I called out, and she tilted her head in reply. "You figure it out yet? The difference between a dream and a fantasy?"

Lifting the collar of my shirt, she ducked her chin inside. After a moment, a smile lit her eyes, and the shirt fell back into place.

"You!" she called out.

Chuckling, I crooked my finger, and she came running. I caught her in midair, her legs wrapping around my waist. "You forget about that ex yet?" I asked against her lips.

"Who?" she asked blankly.

I watched her walk away, the silk of my shirt molding against her curves.

Just when I thought she wouldn't turn back, she did, and it made me smile.

"Thanks for the fling!" she yelled, and people nearby stopped to stare.

I laughed and got back into my boat.

She might be a good girl, but she sure as hell knew how to misbehave.

Nine

Nora

It rained last night. The streets were still damp and puddles dotted the sidewalks. It wasn't a refreshing kind of rain, though. It was the kind that left the air humid and sticky. Honestly, there weren't many refreshing rainstorms here in the South, but even if there were, I probably wouldn't have noticed.

There was only one type of rain for me now.

Water splashed the backs of my calves as I jogged over the sidewalk, pulling open the café door. The strong scent of coffee and the sound of grinding beans welcomed me as I casually wiped the bottom of my sneakers on the large rug by the door.

Valerie waved at me from the line and pointed to a table someone was vacating. Nodding, I went to grab it, tossing my bag in one of the empty chairs and sitting beside it.

A few minutes later, Val dropped into the chair across from me, holding a cup in each hand. "Seriously, Nor?" She complained. "Again?"

I glanced up. "Huh?"

My best friend offered a coffee across the table while giving me a sour look. Following her expression, I glanced down at myself and held back a grimace.

"What?" I asked innocently. "It's comfortable."

"*Yeah*, you're wearing that because it's comfortable."

I cleared my throat and lifted the cup to my lips. The movement caused the silk material to graze against my arm like a teasing caress. Tingles of memory shot along my spine, making my stomach dip. I took another sip of the coffee, using it as a shield while I held on to the feeling for a second longer.

"It rained last night." Valerie's voice was all-knowing.

Making a sound, I put the cup down. "I never should have told you that."

"Please," she said, arrogantly. "Even if you hadn't told me all the details from that night, I would have known because you wear the shirts you stole from him all the time."

"I didn't steal them," I muttered, fingering a button on the front.

One dark eyebrow arched dramatically over Val's eye.

Okay, fine. Maybe I stole one of them. The one I spilled the drink all over. But the stain came out, so what was I supposed to do? Throw away a genuine silk shirt?

What a waste.

And the one I was wearing now—the white one I'd worn when I was with him—well, he'd given it to me.

Besides, it looked really good partially unbuttoned with a lace bodysuit underneath and tied at the waist over a pair of cut-off denim shorts.

Val leaned across the table toward me. "Did you dream about him last night?"

Of course I did. Every single time it rained, I dreamed of Carter. Of that night. I was beginning to think that for the rest of my life, the rain would only ever serve as a vivid reminder of him.

When I didn't answer, she sighed. "Like I even need to ask. You're sitting over there half dazed and wearing his clothes."

I wondered how ballistic Valerie would go if I told her I dreamed about Carter even when it wasn't raining.

"You're terrible at one-night stands, Nora," she announced. The girls at the table nearby snickered.

"Oh my God!" I whispered, sitting forward. "You have the loudest mouth of anyone ever."

Valerie shrugged, not the least bit offended. "It's nothing to be ashamed of."

I groaned.

"Ashamed? Who's ashamed?" someone asked, pulling out the seat beside me.

My back stiffened, and Valerie practically snarled. "Get lost."

"Nice to see you, as always, Valerie," Alan said, picking up the bag I'd put on the chair and dropping it on the floor so he could sit down.

"Hey!" I sat forward so I could lean down and pick my stuff up off the floor.

"Leave it," he said, brushing my arm away. "I have news."

"Shouldn't you go share that news with people who care?" Val quipped.

Alan turned his blue eyes to me. "Nora cares, don't you, Nora?"

"No," I answered, not having to think about it. "I think I've made it clear that I don't."

Alan draped an arm across the back of my chair and leaned in. I used to like when he did that. It made me feel secure, like he cared about me. I knew now it was just his way of claiming ownership over me. Of using the way I felt to control me.

"How long are you going to punish me, sweetheart?" he asked as if he were in pain. "I said I was sorry."

"You think saying sorry makes up for you being a giant, cheating dick?" Valerie declared.

Again, the girls at the nearby table snickered.

"You're so crude." Alan sneered at my friend.

Pushing his arm off the back of my chair, I scooted away. "I'm not your sweetheart. And we aren't together anymore."

Seriously, though, when was he going to get the hint?

I took another sip of my coffee, deliberately looking away from my ex, wondering for probably the thousandth time if I hadn't had that one night in paradise, would I be this resolute about Alan?

Would I have already taken him back? Would we be back in the same pattern of him being a giant jerk face and me making excuses for him?

I cringed just thinking about it. I cringed thinking about *him*.

The girls at the nearby table were still covertly paying attention to the drama, so I sweetly gave them an encouraging smile, letting them know I was glad someone found my life so entertaining.

"Don't you want to hear my news?" Alan said, leaning his elbows on the table and flashing his dimple in my direction.

I used to love that dimple. Now I thought it was annoying. And childish. In fact, the blond-haired, blue-eyed, boy-next-door good looks that I used to swoon so hard over just seemed tired and immature.

I wanted something darker, something more commanding.

"Nora," Alan snapped, the charm he tried so hard to maintain slipping away as irritation took hold.

"What?" I snapped back.

"Face it, bro. You just can't keep her attention anymore." Val taunted him.

Alan's face flushed with anger and his hand fisted on the tabletop. An uncomfortable feeling slipped down my back, chasing away some of the lingering dream I'd been holding on to since I woke up this morning. Closing my eyes, I clutched tightly at the dream and the feelings it left me with, not quite ready to let them go.

But it was too late.

Awful Alan and his stinky presence was too much reality for my fantasy.

"I'm coming to Boston with you this summer."

Eyes springing open, my head nearly rocked on its shoulders when I swung around to face my ex.

"What?" Val and I both exclaimed at the same moment.

He smiled a Cheshire cat smile. "I sent Net Tech my resume to see if they had an opening, and they called right away." He leaned forward, bringing our faces just inches apart. "I'm in."

I sat back, flabbergasted.

Val and I shared a look. I could practically hear the storm brewing in her head, and I knew in just a matter of moments, she would open her mouth and unleash it all.

I was tempted to sit back and watch.

But then I glanced over at smug-faced Alan and down at the silk shirt draping my body. Valerie's lips parted, and I cut her a look, shaking my head just slightly.

Her eyes narrowed, and I shook my head more firmly. Sighing, she sat back and indicated for me to do whatever.

"You got a summer internship at Net Tech," I repeated to Alan.

Valerie made a sound, clearly not happy with my opening line.

"It's not an internship. I'm getting paid. I'm too skilled to work for free."

I crossed my arms over my chest and regarded him. "But you don't mind having your father call in a favor to get you a job."

He shrugged one shoulder. "That's business. It's all about who you know."

"I thought you were going to New York City," I rebuked.

Reaching out, he tucked a strand of hair behind my ear. "Why would I go there when you're going to Boston?"

Valerie made an angry sound and practically leapt over the table. Without looking, I held up my hand, stopping her.

"I don't get you, Alan." I began. "When I first started talking about going to Boston for a summer internship months and months ago, you were dead set against it. You wanted nothing to do with Net Tech at all. When I landed a spot, you practically laughed in my face and told me how stupid I was for wasting my time there,"

"I don't think I was that harsh," he said, tugging on his earlobe.

Tugging on his earlobe = he knew exactly how much of an ass he'd been about Boston. So much so that I'd nearly called and given up my spot.

"You were worse," Val and I intoned at the same time.

"And now…" I forged on, pinning him with a hard look. "You stroll in here this morning, announcing that you're coming to Boston for the summer like it's some grand gesture that will make me fall all over you."

He reached forward to touch my hair again, and I recoiled. Dropping his hand, he leaned close. "Just think about it. Me. You. Summer nights in Boston and the weekends in The Hamptons."

My mouth dropped open.

"I rented us an apartment near the office. It has a view of—"

"Are you insane?" I burst out.

Alan glanced up sharply, and the girls nearby giggled.

"We broke up, Alan. Months ago. Remember that day I walked in on you in bed with another girl?"

"Shh," he implored, rubbing the back of his neck.

"What? You don't want everyone here to know what a shitty boyfriend you are? Maybe you should have worried about that more before I dumped you."

"You did not dump me," he hissed, anger flashing in his eyes.

"Yes, Alan, I did. Is that what bothers you so much? Is that why you've been trying so hard to get back with me? Because *I* dumped *you*? Because I'm no longer interested and it kills you? You pay more attention to me now than you did when we were actually in a relationship."

"Mm-hmm." Val agreed from across the table.

Alan's shoulders rose and fell with his deep breath. Swiping a thumb across his lower lip and regarding me with serious eyes, he smirked. "This is getting really old, Nora. I said I was sorry for what happened that *one* time."

For the record, it was not one time. Alan was a chronic cheater.

"I've been trying to make it up to you ever since, including giving up an incredible opportunity in New York so I could be with you this summer."

"I didn't ask you to do that," I spat. "I don't want you there. I don't want to see you at all."

"You're surprised. I surprised you. You never were very good with surprises," he allowed and pushed out of his seat. Pushing his hand down into the front pocket of his jeans, Alan pulled out a business card and slid it in front of me. One hand rested on the back of my chair and the other on the edge of the table beside me. He leaned down, bringing with him the scent of his cologne.

Memories and feelings welled up inside me with the familiar scent, and tears rushed to the backs of my eyes. His voice was low beside my ear, smooth like honey and cajoling like a lullaby.

"That's the building manager for our new place. The place I got for *us*. You can call him anytime, and he'll send you pics of everything. All you have to do is ask. I put your name on the lease. Yours and mine. This is what you always wanted, Nor. I know I messed up, and I'm trying to make it up to you. You just have to let me."

When I didn't respond, he leaned around me farther, trying to get a glimpse of my face.

Turning my head away and keeping my posture rigid, I said, "Just leave."

He sighed as though I'd hurt him, but I felt him nod. "Fine, I'll go. But I'm not giving up." Finally pulling away, he tapped on the card still lying on the table. "Give him a call. You're going to love our new place."

"You have two seconds before you're wearing this coffee," Val threatened.

"Pleasure as always, Val," Alan quipped, turning away.

Just when I thought he was gone, he appeared on my other side, stepping right into my line of sight. I turned away, but as I did, he caught my chin with his hand. "I'll call you later." He spoke softly, then leaned down to kiss the top of my head.

I sat rigid even after he walked away, afraid to move or react until I knew for certain he wouldn't reappear. My stomach felt knotted and my fingers ached from the tight fist I was making beneath the table. Why couldn't he just leave me alone? He didn't even want me. He just didn't want to lose.

"He's gone," Valerie said, setting aside her coffee like it suddenly tasted bad.

I let out a breath I hadn't realized I was holding. Slumping forward, my elbows hit the table, and I groaned. "Can you believe him?"

"Usually, I'm not surprised by anything that moron does, but Boston?" Val shook her head. "I didn't see that one coming."

"He hated the idea of going there. You know that." Glancing down at the business card in front of me, I shook my head. "What is he thinking?"

"He's desperate," Val said, licking the lip of her lid. "He can't stand the fact that you want nothing to do with him."

I laughed without humor. "Maybe if I cared a little less when we were dating, he would have cared a little more."

Val slapped her hand down on the table in front of me. "Fuck that. Head games don't belong in relationships. You deserve better than that."

"I know." I agreed. And I did. Sometimes, though, I would momentarily slip back into the past and feel all the pain he'd inflicted.

"I take it back," Valerie announced.

"Take what back?"

"What I said earlier, before Awful Alan showed up. You know, the hard time I was giving you about Mr. Fantasy." As she mentioned Carter, her finger pointed to the shirt I was draped in.

Glancing down, I sat back in my chair and put one hand over the other arm, lightly stroking the fabric with my fingers.

"If it wasn't for that guy, Alan probably would have his nasty hooks back in you."

My head whipped up. "He would not!"

Valerie gave me a look, calling me a liar. "You were totally wavering before spring break. During spring break. But when you stepped off that guy's boat the morning we came home, Alan was nothing but a bad memory. You totally swapped hangovers."

"I didn't!" I objected.

"It's okay, Nor. Being hung over from one epic night of sex is a lot better than being hung over on an ex who treated you like shit."

Looking down at the business card on the table, I frowned. "I really wanted this internship. It will look really good on my resume when I start applying for jobs next year."

"Call up there. Tell them you can't work in the same place as your stalker ex."

"And given the choice between some no-name unpaid intern and the guy with an already incredible resume and a father with a big name in the tech industry, who do you think they would choose?"

Valerie put her chin in her hand. "What are you going to do?"

I shook my head. "I'm supposed to move up there next month. It's too late to try and get another internship. Everything worth having is going to be full."

"I should have dumped my coffee on his head."

"I have to go," I said, standing. A moment of alarm burst through me when I looked down for my bag and it wasn't there. Then I remembered Alan tossing it on the floor.

Jerk.

Leaning over the chair, I fished around for the strap. As I leaned, the chair under me slid backward and banged into one behind it.

The man sitting in it jolted, and I leapt up. "Oh, I'm sorry!"

"No problem," the man said, not even bothering to turn around. His attention was fixed on the screen of the laptop in front of him, and there was a black hat pulled down over his head.

Pushing the chair all the way under our table, I reached for my stuff.

"Throw that away for me?" I gestured toward the card Alan left.

"With pleasure." Val agreed.

Outside, the thick, humid air smacked me in the face and stole my breath. It wasn't anything at all like the balmy tropical breeze from the island. We'd been home a little over a month, and I still thought about our trip every day.

Dreamed about Carter almost every night.

Maybe Valerie was right. Maybe I had traded one man-hangover for another.

Ten

Carter

The screen on my phone lit up with a notification, giving me an excuse to avoid work. Pushing off my desk, the chair I sat in rolled backward as I snatched the phone and stood. Turning around to the window, which offered a hella nice view, I pulled up the message.

The photograph filling the screen made my fingers tighten around the device. It was just an ordinary photo, taken from a distance.

It didn't matter.

It was enough.

Enough to transport me out of this office, out of reality, and back to that night.

Skin on skin. Lips on lips. The look in her eyes when I was inside her... Shaking my head, I tried to clear the memories rolling over me. Laying a palm flat against the window, I stared down at the photo again, bracing most of my weight on my arm.

Even set in reality, my good girl looked like a fantasy.

The cut-off shorts she wore were too short, exposing long, slim legs that sometimes I still felt wrapped around me. The sneakers on her feet splashed through the puddles on the streets, kicking up droplets of water that were frozen midair in the photo, making it appear as though raindrops danced around her.

The sudden image of her in my arms beneath the spray of the shower flashed in my head, and my throat constricted.

She was wearing my shirt. Seeing it knotted at her hip imparted a deep sense of satisfaction. It might have been just one night, but she hadn't forgotten.

The pad of my thumb swiped over the image, bringing up a second, then a third.

One was of her sitting at a table with some man beside her. Jealousy was quick to kick up in my stomach, churning like a bad burrito and leaving a sudden foul taste in my mouth.

Closing out of the images, I pulled up the accompanying report. The second I finished reading the words, I hit the screen on my phone and brought it to my ear.

"Come in here," I ordered, then disconnected.

Seconds later, Aaron let himself into my office and perched on the corner of my desk.

I didn't beat around the bush. I wasn't that type of guy. "There's something I need you to do."

Eleven

Nora

I was right. Every internship worth having this summer (and even some that weren't) were all full. Ever since Awful Alan decided we should play house in Boston, I'd been scouring the internet for something—*anything*—that wasn't in Boston.

"Why?" I cried, shoving my laptop away so I could lay my head on the table and moan.

"I take it the search isn't going well?" Val asked, coming into the kitchen to grab a soda from the fridge.

I made a grabby hand at her drink, so she handed it over, then reached in to get another. The sound of the tab popping open was satisfying. After a long drink and the prickly sensation of all the carbonation going down my throat, I shook my head miserably.

"You have to apply so early for this stuff. If I don't go to Boston, I'm screwed."

"Which is exactly what Alan wanted," Val said, carrying her drink over to the table to drop into the seat across from me. "He knew you wouldn't be able to find anything else. He's totally taking advantage."

"Why couldn't I see what a colossal jerk he was when we were dating?" I grumped.

"He's good. I'll give him that," Val allowed.

Pursing my lips, I said, "You never liked him."

"I'm a bitter bitch. I don't like anyone."

"You like me," I sang.

Without missing a beat, she replied, "You pay half the rent."

Snatching the pen off the table, I threw it at her.

Val laughed and let the pen skid across the floor without batting an eye. "So are you going?"

I didn't want to. However, if I didn't, it would basically put me a year behind. True, I could still apply for jobs next year after I graduated, but I would be at a serious disadvantage to everyone else who had internships and letters of recommendation and actual experience.

Taking another sip of soda, I stared off into space while debating.

My phone started ringing, and I glanced at it, then away.

"Aren't you going to get that?" Val asked.

"It's an unknown call."

"Ooh! My favorite!" Val exclaimed, snatching up the cell and answering. "City morgue. You kill it; we chill it!"

I snickered into my soda.

Instantly, Val straightened and her eyes went wide. "Uh, yes, hold on, please." Lowering the line, she put her hand over the front of the phone. "They're asking for Ms. Williams."

I rolled my eyes. "Telemarketer."

"He says he's from Ansoft…" Valerie added, her voice trailing away.

My mouth dropped open. "Ansoft? Like *that* Ansoft?"

"Is there any other Ansoft?" Val asked.

I shook my head slowly. There was only one Ansoft... and it was huge in the technology world.

Holding out the phone, Valerie urged me to take it. I did but hesitated before putting it up to my ear.

"Hurry up!" Val whispered, motioning at me.

Swallowing, I answered, "This is Ms. Williams."

"Ms. Nora Williams of the Digital Art and Design College of Savannah."

"Yes," I replied cautiously.

"I'm calling on behalf of Ansoft Corporation. Are you familiar with Ansoft?"

"Yes, of course."

"Good. We recently decided to open a few spots for interns in our company, so we reached out to your university for a list of potential candidates that might fit who we are looking for. Your information was sent over, and we like what we see."

Glancing at Val, I sat up straight. "You've seen my work?"

"Some of it,"

"Ah..." I didn't know what to say. I mean, what did one say when a huge gaming company called to tell you they liked your design work?

"We'd like to offer you an internship at our company headquarters in Florida. You would report here at the end of May and finish up work mid-August."

My mouth dropped open again.

Val knocked on the table, drawing my attention. "What?" she mouthed. "What?"

Shaking my head at her, I focused on the conversation. "I, ah, already have an internship at Net Tech for the summer."

"Net Tech is a solid company. A safe choice. But based on what I see in your work, you would be more suited to the type of creative freedom a company like Ansoft allows."

My head was spinning. Never in a million years would I have expected a phone call like this today. Glancing at my laptop, I noted the long list of technology and design companies I'd just been searching to try and find a replacement for Net Tech. Ansoft wasn't even on my list. As far as I knew, they didn't even take interns.

"Is this for real?" I blurted out.

There was a pause on the other end of the line. The man cleared his throat. "I can assure you that this is a genuine offer. If you agree, I can send over some paperwork and a formal written offer today."

Val was hopping around in her seat.

Lowering the phone, I leaned toward her. "They're offering me an internship."

"Take it!" She gasped. "Good-bye, Awful Alan!"

"Miss Williams?" the man on the line called.

Quickly pulling the phone close, I cleared my throat. "I'm here. I'm sorry, this is just unexpected. I didn't even know my department sent my information."

"As part of the internship, we are offering lodging located here in Miami, not far from our offices. In addition, we can offer a daily wage, though it's not anything substantial."

Housing, pay, *and* a chance to get away from Alan?

"I'll take it!" I announced.

Across the table, Valerie clapped silently.

"Wonderful. If you could confirm your email, I will send all the information, as well as some HR forms we will need you to complete and send back as soon as possible."

I confirmed my email, and he promised to send everything right away.

"If you have any questions or concerns, just call the number on the form."

"Right." I agreed. Then, because this was all happening so fast, I asked, "Is that everything?"

"That's everything," the man replied. "Welcome to Ansoft, Ms. Williams. We'll see you next month."

I stared at the screen on my phone long after it went black and didn't look up until Valerie banged on the tabletop.

"I got another internship," I said dumbly.

"I can't wait to see Alan's face when you tell him."

Pulling my laptop close, my fingers flew over the keyboard as I pulled up my email, half expecting the papers confirming my new job not to be there.

They were.

Right there at the very top was the email from Ansoft Headquarters with everything they promised enclosed.

Butterflies fluttered in my stomach, and a smile bloomed across my lips. It almost seemed too good to be true, but it was.

Twelve

Carter

"Good you're still here," Bryan declared, walking right into my office without so much as a knock.

"Not for much longer," I quipped and pointed up toward the ceiling. "The chopper is on its way."

"You're the only person I know who actually takes a helicopter to work."

"Perks of being the boss." Standing from behind the desk, I grabbed the navy-blue suit jacket off the back of my chair and pulled it on over the polo I was wearing.

The monitor on my desk was still on, still displaying the brand-new artwork just sent over for approval. It looked wicked cool.

"Hey, check out the new specs the art department sent over for *Zero*." Still adjusting my jacket with one hand, I reached out with the other to spin the monitor around for Bryan to see. "The graphics upgrades are better than I expected."

Bryan came closer, eyes roaming over the design of the main character of what was going to be the biggest game launch in Ansoft history. He whistled beneath his breath, tucking his arms over his chest as he looked it over. After a moment, he swiped a finger over the screen, bringing up an additional angle of the character design.

"Well?" I asked, waiting for his feedback.

His eyes swung up to me, then back to the monitor. After momentarily pursing his lips, a smile curved them. His fist appeared over the desk. "Bro."

Laughing, I bumped my fist against his. Then we transitioned flawlessly into the handshake that was exclusively ours.

"Anyone else see this yet?" Bryan asked, pulling back.

I shook my head. "It came straight up from the art department."

He blew out a breath. "That's good."

Swinging the monitor back around toward me, I began the process of shutting down the computer. "What's going on?"

"Some info about *Zero* leaked."

"Has the marketing department been notified so they can stay on top of it?"

"It wasn't leaked to the media."

Glancing up from my desk, I asked, "Then where?"

"Regal Tech."

Straightening, both hands went to my hips, and I laughed under my breath. "Seriously? They just won't get off my ass, will they?"

"They're already threatening a lawsuit."

Anger sparked inside me, and I ran my tongue over my teeth. "They want to waste their money on a lawsuit they won't ever win, that's not my problem."

"You're sure they won't win?"

The anger in me flatlined, creating a quiet buzz in my skull. "You actually asking me that?"

Bryan swore. "I'm the president, Anders. I have to ask that."

"*Because* you're the president, you should know better."

"Stop looking at me like that. It's scary." Bryan dropped into one of the club chairs across the room. "It's business."

"Exactly." I agreed, going around the desk, leaning against the edge to regard my friend and business partner. "Regal Tech knows they're about to lose a shit-ton of money."

"How can you be so cool about this?" Bryan asked.

I shrugged. "They've been watching us from almost the beginning. It doesn't surprise me they managed to get an informant inside this company, which is exactly why the team working on this project is small and all progress is sent directly to me."

"You know he's not going to let this go." Bryan advised.

"He doesn't have a choice."

He rubbed the back of his neck and sighed.

"Why don't you come to my place this weekend. You look like you need to de-stress," I offered.

"Sold!" Bryan agreed. "Some drinks and a girl in a bikini are exactly what I need."

"I'll have a room at the resort blocked off for you," I remarked, making a mental note out loud.

"Or you could babe hunt with me, and we could take the festivities back to your place."

"You know I don't bring random sand dollars back to my island."

Sand dollars = random women we hooked up with at the resort I owned.

"Bro, if I were you, I'd be using that island as a mecca for the ladies."

"That's why you aren't me." A mental image of a blue-eyed good girl smiling over her shoulder flashed in my mind.

"Oh," I said, stopping midway on the way to the door. "I hired a summer intern. She starts next month."

Bryan's face screwed up in surprise. "You did what?"

"Her paperwork should be in HR by now. Put her with the design team."

"What in the hell possessed you to hire an intern?"

Stopping in the open door of my office, I didn't turn around. "She's special," I said, not offering anything more.

"So's my mom, but I didn't hire her," Bryan quipped.

I turned back, smirking. "Your mom doesn't know how to work a computer."

Bryan laughed.

"I'll send the chopper back for you later."

"I need details!" he yelled after me as I went down the hall.

I waved and kept walking.

Thirteen

Nora

The sound of someone beating on our apartment door was not a pleasant alarm.

Okay, there was no pleasant-sounding morning alarm, but this one was especially annoying.

Still drunk on sleep, I half fell out of bed, tripping on the blankets as I went. Bleary-eyed and stumbling through the living room, I grunted at the continued banging as it took me two tries to unlatch the locks before I was able to pull it open.

"Is there some kind of emergency?" I grumped, a burst of air brushing against my bare legs when the door swung inward.

"What the hell is this?" Alan demanded, slapping a hand in the center of the door and forcefully shoving it wider.

Unprepared for the sudden force, I stumbled backward, nearly falling onto my butt.

"Alan?" I said stupidly. Hey, my brain was still trying to wake up, okay?

"I want an explanation!" he demanded.

The anger he was projecting chased away the drowsiness clinging to me, and adrenaline started to pump through my limbs. Alan stalked close, putting his hands on his hips while staring at me with flared nostrils.

He kinda looked like an angry bull.

I decided not to say that out loud.

"What are you talking about?" I asked instead.

His upper lip curling, my ex reached into the inside pocket of his jacket to pull out his cell. Holding up the screen, he showed me the text I'd sent him the night before.

Oh. Right.

Glancing between him and the phone screen, I pointed at the text. "I think my text was clear. What exactly do you want me to explain?"

The fingers gripping the phone turned white, and his eyes flared. Alan hated to be challenged. He liked to be the one in control. He liked to feel superior.

It made me feel really stupid that I never noticed just how bad he was until after I broke up with him. How had I stayed with him so long? What did that say about me as a woman?

Swallowing, Alan turned the phone toward him and read the message I'd sent. "Alan, I'm not going to Boston after all. Sorry for the inconvenience."

After reading it, he gazed back at me, accusatory. "I need an explanation for this."

"What's to explain?" I asked. "I'm not going to Boston."

His phone vaulted across the room and hit the couch with a thud. Quickly, he launched forward, grabbing my upper arm and yanking me toward him. My feet skittered over the floor, my bare toe stubbing the hard ground. I made a sound, rubbing my toe against my bare calf for some kind of relief.

My heart was pounding, and I didn't like the look in his eye.

"Let go," I intoned, trying not to show I was any kind of intimidated.

When his fingers tightened around my arm, I lifted my chin and practically dared him to continue. With a huff, he released me.

Moving around him, I shut the front door because it was still wide open from him barging in.

Turning back around, I noted some movement in the hallway where Valerie hovered, peeking around the corner. Giving a slight shake of my head, I told her to stay where she was. Seeing her would probably just piss off Alan more. Hell, he'd probably blame her for me not going to Boston. It wasn't her fault. This was my choice. It was time I faced Alan and put a stop to all his nosy, controlling ways.

When I looked back at him, he was glaring at me, waiting.

Crossing my arms over my chest, I regarded him coolly. "I got offered another internship. A better one. I took it."

His laugh sounded like a bark. "Another internship? When?"

"Just the other day."

"Where?"

"It doesn't matter where. I'm not going to Boston."

Alan's blue eyes narrowed, and his square jaw hardened. "Do you have any idea what I gave up to come to that second-rate company with you?"

"I never asked you to do that."

Tossing his hands in the air, he roared, "Are you kidding? You didn't shut up about Boston for months!"

"That was last fall. When we were still together. We aren't together anymore."

Putting both hands on his hips, he heaved a sigh and stared at the floor, acting like he really had to rein in his temper just to deal with me. Maybe before, I'd would have seen that as passion, as how much he really cared.

Now it was exhausting. I wanted him to leave.

I *really* wanted to put on pants.

"How much longer are you going to punish me? I know I hurt you, but this is ridiculous. Get over it already."

I bristled. Back in the hallway, Val stepped into view, brandishing a giant hairbrush as if she were about to come out and brain him.

Averting my gaze from my BFF, I looked directly at Alan and took a step forward. "I am over it. I got over it the minute we broke up." Okay, that was a lie, but he didn't need to know that. "It's you who can't seem to let it go. I dumped you. I don't want anything to do with you. Stop acting like I'm just throwing a fit for attention, because I'm not. If you're that hard up for a girlfriend to look good on your arm, go find another one."

His mouth dropped open, and a small sound forced its way out. Closing his lips, Alan scratched his temple and chuckled. "You want me to find another girlfriend?"

"Please. Take her to Boston if you want to go that bad."

"Be careful what you ask for, Nora," Alan said quietly.

Walking over to the sofa and picking up his cellphone, I held it out over the coffee table between us. "Please leave."

He reached for the phone, but instead of taking it, he latched onto my wrist instead. Pulling me forward, I fell onto the coffee table. Scrambling up onto my knees, my heart pounding, I twisted my arm, trying to get it out of his hold.

"Get out!" I yelled.

"You're going to regret this," he said, dragging me farther over the table. The books we had piled there all tumbled onto the floor.

"I'm calling the cops!" Val said, bursting into the living room with her phone out.

Alan ignored her, continuing to drill holes into me with his blue-fire stare. "This is the only chance a girl like you is ever going to get at a better life. No one else is going to be willing to put up with you. Think hard. Think real hard, because when I walk out that door, everything I could offer you goes with me."

Using all the force I had, I pulled my wrist free of his grasp. His phone clattered onto the floor near his feet. Tucking my burning, sore arm against my chest, still on my knees on the table, I rose to my full height and met his gaze.

"Don't ever show your face to me again."

Shock flickered in his eyes, and then his tongue ran over his teeth. He laughed. The dimple everyone thought was so charming appeared vile to me. Bending down to scoop up his phone, he went to the door. Before pulling it open, he glanced over his shoulder. "You're a stupid girl, Nora."

"You're right," I replied. "I am. Stupid for wasting an entire year of my life with *you*."

Leaving the door, he rushed forward again.

Valerie leapt between us, holding up her phone. "Out."

Alan divided his stare between us, then slammed out of the apartment.

I wilted on the tabletop while Valerie ran forward and threw the locks. Turning around, her back against the door, she pressed a hand to her chest. "Nora," she said after a moment of us just breathing.

I avoided her eyes.

"Nora," she said again.

"I'm going to take a shower," I said, climbing off the table to stand on wobbly legs.

"Did he ever hit you?"

I stopped but didn't turn around.

"Did that son of a bitch ever manhandle you like that before?"

"It doesn't matter anymore, Val. It's over," I replied, soft, then hurried out of sight.

Sure, maybe it seemed a little too good to be true that I got offered a last-minute internship at Ansoft. But I didn't care. That internship felt like a savior and an escape all in one. I couldn't wait to get the hell out of here for a few months and go to a city where none of this could follow.

Fourteen

Carter

The helicopter landed on the roof. My office was on the top floor of our building, but I took the elevator all the way down to the ground floor.

Ansoft's lobby was shiny and clean, with a wall of glass doors for employees to enter through and a wide, white tile floor to walk across on their way to security.

Large posters of all the games and apps we produced hung everywhere, providing all the color the space needed. There was a single "lounge" type area near the doors with modern-style couches and oversized green plants.

Strolling through the lobby, I went to the couch and took a seat. My security team cleared their throats and gazed around, then at me, in confusion.

Amused at their flustered faces, I waved a hand toward them. "Have a seat."

They didn't. Instead, they planted themselves in front of me, barricading anyone else from attempting to sit down alongside me.

I rolled my eyes at their backs.

Aaron glanced over his shoulder with a sour expression. "I saw that."

"Stop acting like the secret service. I make video games."

"Sir?" another of my security asked, not sure what to do.

"Ignore him," Aaron ordered.

"Who's the boss here?" I wondered out loud, taking out my phone to gaze down at the screen.

"A boss belongs in his office."

I'd get there eventually. I had something else to do first.

About ten minutes went by, and I continued to sit there. People stared when they realized it was me, and my security stood around, shuffling from foot to foot occasionally because they had no clue what the hell I was doing.

This was kinda fun.

Why had I never thought to mess around with them before?

The sound of heels clipping over the tile made me glance up. She was dressed in a light-pink dress that hugged her body but flared out at her hips. Long, tan legs stretched down to the nude-colored heels elevating her feet.

A small bag on a gold chain hung from one shoulder, and her blond hair was pulled back into a ponytail at the nape of her neck.

I watched her walk for a few moments, smothering a smile when she teetered a bit on the heels before righting herself to go through security.

An air of nervousness wafted around her as she nervously dug into her bag to find her ID and show to the guard. Bypassing the checkpoint, I went around, then leaned a shoulder against a wall, watching as she shoved her ID away and walked toward the elevators.

After pushing the button, she waited quietly until the doors opened with a chime.

Nora stepped into the elevator, and I strode forward, catching the door just before it slid closed. Our stares collided briefly, and satisfaction filled my chest when her eyes flared with recognition.

Turning around, I motioned for my team to back off and take the next elevator.

Two of the guys seemed worried, and when another employee tried to board the same car as us, Aaron put his arm out. "Take the next one, please."

I grinned in thanks, and he merely rolled his eyes.

The elevator doors slid shut, leaving the two of us alone.

"What floor?" I asked, glancing around at her.

Her mouth fell open, and I realized it still made me want to kiss her.

She didn't answer, and the elevator continued to stand still, waiting for a command.

"Not sure?" I asked and turned back to the panel of buttons. I hit the one for my floor because it was at the very top of the building and it would take the longest time to get there.

Nora's blue eyes followed me as I moved beside her, kicking out one foot and resting a shoulder against the wall.

"Hey there."

Her stare roamed my face, but still she said nothing. Half smiling, I reached out and pushed her chin up with one finger.

Eyes traveling down her body, then back up, I said, "Nice dress. But I prefer you in my shirt."

"What are you doing here?" Her blond brows twisted in puzzlement.

I couldn't look away from her. Everything inside me was utterly captivated by her presence. "Me?" I said, casual. "I own the place."

Her mouth dropped open again, then snapped closed. "You own what place?"

"This place." I smiled. "Ansoft."

Straightening, Nora turned to face me completely. A low laugh bubbled out of her. "You're actually trying to tell me you own Ansoft Corporation right now?"

Adjusting the open jacket I was wearing, gesturing to myself, I asked, "I don't look like a CEO?"

Her eyes dropped, running over my body and giving me a little satisfaction. Clearing her throat, she forced her stare back up. "You own a resort and an island... not Ansoft."

"I can't own both?"

Adamantly, her head shook. "No. No. Ansoft is owned by a young, twenty-something video game genius who..." Her voice trailed away, and her eyes turned round.

Pressing my lips together, I waited for her to finish.

She burst around me and hit the giant red button on the panel. The smooth-riding elevator ground to a sudden halt.

"Did you miss me that much?" I teased.

"You can't possibly," she said, gazing at me suspiciously.

An earsplitting alarm rang out overhead, cut off abruptly by a loud buzzing.

Startled, Nora's hand shot out and grabbed a handful of my jacket, pulling herself so close she was almost against my chest. "What was that?"

"Mr. Anders." Aaron's voice cut through the intercom. "Are you all right?"

I stepped toward the panel on the wall, but Nora grabbed me back, refusing to let go of my jacket. With a sigh, I wrapped an arm around her, keeping her close. Lifting her off her feet, I took her with me to the panel. Once there, I let her go and hit a small button. "Everything's fine. We, ah, accidentally hit the stop button."

"And what would you have me tell security?" Aaron asked, his voice bland.

I grinned up at the ceiling.

"Nothing. I'll be in my office in a minute." Releasing the button, I glanced down at the woman still clutching the front of my jacket. "You're the one who stopped the elevator. Why are you scared?"

Her cheeks flushed a rosy color, the same color they'd been the night I had her in my bed. Clearing her throat, Nora released my jacket and stepped back.

"Anders," she said to herself. Then, "Carter Anders." Gasping, she spun to face me.

I stuck out my hand. "Carter Anders, CEO of Ansoft, owner of a few tropical resorts, and resident of an island you spent the night on."

Nora looked between me and my hand. Instead of putting hers in mine like I wanted, she crossed her arms beneath her breasts and scowled. "Have you been stalking me again?"

Was she scolding me right now?

Shit, she was cute.

"I've been keeping an eye on you."

"Stalking!" she accused.

I shrugged. She could call it what she wanted.

She gasped, her mouth falling open.

I reached out and pushed her chin up, then, not wanting to pull away, let my thumb trail the underside of her lower lip. "You better stop doing that."

Her eyes went out of focus, and I dropped my hand. Blinking, she came back to her senses. "This internship! That was you!"

"I thought our night together erased your ex from your brain."

She pursed her lips and regarded me. "Maybe you should sleep with him, too. Maybe then he would forget about me."

I threw my head back and laughed. Our eyes collided and held, my laughter faded, and we were left standing in the enclosed space, alone, with electricity suddenly crackling the air.

"He's not nearly as pretty as you," I whispered, still holding her gaze.

Nora broke free from the tether between us first, leaning around me and hitting the button to make the elevator move once more. "I can't accept this internship."

"You already did."

"Well, I changed my mind."

"Why?"

"Because I didn't earn it!" she burst out.

Without looking, I reached behind me and hit the stop button again. The elevator lurched, and she stumbled into my chest.

Her hands wrapped around my biceps, her head falling back to look up at me. "What are you doing?" She gasped.

What, so she could stop the elevator, but when I did, it was shocking?

Hmph.

Overhead, the alarm went off again. Nora's fingers flexed around my arms. Memories of the way she clutched at me that night as I was above her came roaring back.

"Mr. Anders." Aaron began again.

My entire hand slammed on the intercom button. "If you buzz me one more time, Aaron, you're fired!" I snapped.

He didn't reply.

I turned my attention back to Nora. "Do you know how many interns we hire at Ansoft?"

She pushed away from me, retreating to the other side of the small space. A strand of hair came loose from her ponytail and brushed against the side of her cheek.

An indelicate sound ripped from her throat. "None. I knew this was too good to be true." She glanced down at her feet. "Hired by a stalker," she muttered.

Stifling a laugh, I kept my voice authoritative. "That's right, none. But I liked your portfolio. I think you'll make a good fit here. And after I made some inquiries, I found you needed an internship—"

"What were you doing making *inquiries* about me?" she reprimanded, giving me a squinty-eyed look.

"I wanted to see you."

"Oh," she said. The suspicion in her face was replaced with softness.

Ah, there she was. There was my good girl.

I've missed you.

"You could have just asked for my number," she shot out. I recalled she'd said the same thing back on the island.

I half smiled. "Fantasies usually don't have phones."

A few moments of silence stretched between us.

"Did you really look at my portfolio?" She wondered, looking everywhere but at me.

I nodded once. "You ever thought about doing graphics for video games?"

"Not until Ansoft called…"

"And now?"

"And now I really want to be here, but I can't because you're stupid!"

I blinked. "Are you whining and pouting right now?"

She lifted her chin. "No."

"You're really not going to stay?"

"What will people say?" she said, horrified.

I bent so we were eye level. "Why?" I mock gasped. "Do you plan on trapping me in the elevator like this every day?"

Horror dawned over her features, and she rushed to hit the button again. She kept her back turned, straightening her dress and smoothing a hand down the length of her ponytail.

Once she was composed, she glanced around. "Don't talk to me at work. People will think I slept with the boss to get my job."

Unable to help myself, I stepped up behind her and put my lips against her ear. "Didn't you?"

Gasping, Nora spun. I couldn't help but notice the gooseflesh along her arms.

"I did not sleep with you to get this job! I didn't even know you were… *you*!" she insisted. "I didn't even know you would be here when I accepted!"

Behind her, the doors slid open, revealing the top floor. Across the way was a huge desk with two assistants wearing headsets stationed behind it.

My security team stood close to the open doors, but they all kept their gazes averted.

With a huff, Nora started out. Snaking an arm around her middle, I dragged her back into the car. She shrieked a little, and I shushed against her ear.

"What are you doing?" she whisper-yelled.

"This is my floor, not yours."

"Oh." Her body went slack against mine, and awareness flowed through me.

Mindful of watchful eyes, I forced myself to let her go. Stepping around her, I hit the floor she needed on the panel before glancing her way once more. "Be sure to get a badge from HR so you don't have to dig for your ID every morning."

"Right." She agreed.

I didn't say anything else, and I didn't step out of the car either. Instead, I stood there staring.

"What?" she hissed. "Don't talk to me!"

Smirking, I stepped farther into the elevator, and the doors started to close behind me. "Aaron," I called, and his arm came in to keep the doors open.

Nora's eyes ripped away from Aaron to gaze up at me as I moved closer. She backed up until her back hit the wall. "What are you doing?" she whispered.

Without a word, I reached up, grasped the band holding her hair back, and slid it out in one fluid motion.

"Hey!" She gasped, affronted. Her hand shot out to snatch the hairband from my grasp, but I tucked it into my front pocket before she could steal it back.

Using both hands, I spread her hair over her shoulders, trailing my fingers through the strands. "I prefer it down."

The second I stepped out of the elevator, Aaron pulled his arm back, and the doors began to close. "Have a good first day," I called, watching her through the shrinking doorway.

"Don't talk to me!" she hissed.

I was still laughing when the doors closed completely. This was going to be fun.

Fifteen

Nora

"He's here," I said the second Val answered the call.

My best friend didn't miss a beat. "Nor, this is going too far. I think you seriously need to consider a restraining order."

Stumbling over the pavement, I gripped the phone tighter as though it would somehow make it easier to walk. "He's not dangerous," I mumbled, righting myself. I was a little offended she would say something like that about him.

Beyond flustered would be an apt explanation of my feelings. I'd hardly slept at all last night, which was totally disappointing, considering the amazing bed in my new place. I could barely enjoy the first day at my new job because, literally, everything was overshadowed by Carter stepping into the elevator.

Learning the guy from my fantasy one-night stand was now my boss.

"Are you serious right now?" Val exclaimed. "He manhandled you the last time he was in our apartment. If I hadn't threatened to call the cops, he would have hurt you."

She's talking about Alan. Not Carter. Realizing that made me feel a little less affronted on his behalf.

Just the mention of Alan made my stomach clench. I was glad to be away from him.

"Not Alan." Tucking the phone closer to my lips, I whispered. *"Him."*

Valerie paused. I could practically hear her brain catching up. Her gasp was like a lightbulb illuminating above her head. "No!"

Up ahead, a door opened onto the sidewalk, and a woman stepped out, carrying a big cup of iced coffee. My stomach grumbled, reminding me I hadn't eaten breakfast.

Or dinner last night.

Veering right, I caught the door as it was closing and stepped into the small coffee shop, taking a place in line.

"You mean to tell me that Mr. Fantasy is in Miami right now? You saw him?" Val pressed.

"He isn't just here," I said. "He's my boss."

Valerie shrieked so loud I pulled the phone away from my head and made a face. The man in front of me turned around to stare, and I gave him an apologetic grin.

"She's very dramatic," I whispered, motioning to the phone.

Flashing a bright-white smile, the man laughed and turned back around.

"Nora!" Val hollered in my ear. "Focus!" Pulling the phone in close again, I listened. "What do you mean he's your boss? He's a graphic designer? *At Ansoft?* I thought the dude owned an island and some resorts."

I made a sound and moved ahead with the line. "Apparently, he owns a lot more than we realized…"

She gasped again. "No way!"

A sound of agreement erupted from my throat. "I'm kinda freaking out."

I could hear Valerie's fingers flying over the keyboard that must be in front of her. Then seconds later, she yelled again.

The guy in front of me glanced around.

"I'm so sorry," I mouthed.

"Are you telling me that Mr. Island is Carter Anders... *the* Carter Anders, CEO of Ansoft?"

"Guess he comes up on Google," I murmured.

"Holy shit, Nora! You sure can pick them."

"I didn't pick him..."

Valerie sucked in a breath. "There's no way this is a coincidence."

"I didn't say that either," I replied, dubious. I was very aware of the people in this café with me. I couldn't exactly go around blurting out my personal business with Carter freaking Anders just a block down the street from the building he owned.

"He gave you that internship on purpose?" Valerie concluded. "How did he know...?"

"Excuse me, miss? What would you like?" The guy in front of me turned from his place in front of the cashier and gestured for me to order.

"What?" I asked, still completely flustered.

"It's on me this morning."

His words made me look at him, really look. He was good-looking. Dressed in a suit and clearly on his way to an office. His brown hair was back off his forehead, and it was cut close around his ears.

"Oh," I said, realizing both he and the cashier were waiting for me to order. "You don't have to do that. I can get mine after you."

"You're holding up the line." He gestured behind me.

Glancing around, I saw the several people waiting.

"I'll have an iced coffee. Leave room for me to add some cream."

The cashier hit the screen in front of her and spit out a total.

"Hold on, Val," I said, cutting off my friend midsentence. Putting the phone down on the counter, I fumbled in my bag to pull out some cash.

"I said it's on me." The guy beside me reminded me, reaching out to lay a hand on my arm.

I jolted, my hand flying out of my bag, along with half its contents. A sound of distress burst from me as I quickly scooped up the lip-gloss, cash, and credit card that scattered all over the counter.

"I'm such a mess this morning." I apologized.

"Got it all?" the man beside me asked, humor in his tone.

I nodded, and he wrapped a hand above my elbow and tugged me off to the side. "Coffee will be down here."

He let go of my arm, and I finished fastening my bag, making sure everything was stuffed inside.

"I'm so embarrassed." I groaned. "I'll never be able to come in here again."

The guy chuckled. "Half the people in this place are still zombies because they haven't had their coffee yet. No one even noticed."

"You think?" I asked hopefully.

His eyes settled on mine, and he smiled again. "Coffee's up." Reaching toward the counter, he picked up my iced coffee and held it out to me.

"Thank you," I said sincerely.

Taking the cup over to a nearby bar, I set it down, popped off the lid, and added a few splashes of cream to the brew. After stirring it all in with my straw and putting the lid on, I turned to leave, nearly colliding with him.

"Oh," I gasped out. "You're still here."

"Hope that's okay."

"Of course," I said, sipping some coffee.

"Good?" he asked, watching me.

I nodded.

His hand settled near the base of my spine, guiding me through the growing line and back outside on the sidewalk.

"Nora!" Valerie yelled from a distance, and I remembered we'd been on the phone. Quickly pulling it up again, I spoke into it. "I'm sorry, Val. I was ordering a coffee."

"I need details!" she insisted.

The man who bought my coffee fell into step beside me, making me glance out of the corner of my eye.

Clearing my throat, I spoke to Val. "I'll call you tonight after work."

"You can't make me wait all day—" Valerie began to protest, but I cut off the call and stuffed the cell into my bag.

"Busy morning?" the guy asked.

First Alan, then Carter… and now this guy. Were all men this nosy? Good Lord.

I nodded. "Yes. I just started a summer internship, and—"

"You're new in town?"

"Only been here a couple days." I confirmed.

Nodding, he said, "That explains why I haven't seen you before."

Releasing the straw from between my teeth (I chew straws; it's a bad habit), I asked, "You work around here, too?"

"Just up the street."

"Well, thank you so much for the coffee. I'll be sure to drink the whole thing so your money doesn't go to waste."

He laughed.

I didn't know why that was funny. I was trying to be sincere. Smiling, I started to move off down the sidewalk, wishing I had on sneakers so I could get away faster.

His legs were longer than mine, and he wasn't wearing stilettos, so catching up was a piece of cake. "Next time, you can buy,"

Glancing over at him, I asked, "Next time?"

"I stop there every morning on the way to the office. Maybe we'll see each other again."

"Maybe," I answered, noncommittal. The large building that was Ansoft towered ahead, and relief made me take a breath. "Well, that's me, so—"

He made a sound. "You work at Ansoft?"

"I'm the new summer intern."

"No way," he mused, chuckling.

"You work there, too?"

He nodded. "In the coding department. I'm on the third floor."

Bobbing my head, I pretended to know where all the departments were located. The truth, after seeing Carter yesterday, I was lucky I retained where the design department was located.

As we approached the large glass doors, the man jogged ahead, pulling one open and holding it.

I smiled, ducking my head a little when I went through ahead of him. "Thank you," I said when he fell into step beside me once more.

"I'm Seth, by the way."

"Nora," I replied absentmindedly. My eyes were already roaming the lobby, scanning the security line, and checking every face in search of one in particular.

He's the freaking CEO. He won't be in the lobby! I yelled at myself.

He was down here yesterday.

A light touch on my elbow made me jump and teeter on my heels.

"Whoa," Seth mused, reaching out to steady me.

"I'm okay," I said, tugging back from his touch. "You just startled me."

"You were saying what department you worked in."

I was pretty sure I wasn't telling him that. In fact, I'd all but forgotten he was there because I was too busy hoping I'd see Carter.

The last thing you need is to see Carter! You shouldn't even be here!

"Badges," the security guard called as we drew to the front of the line.

Inwardly, I groaned. *I forgot to get my ID badge from HR yesterday.*

Because everyone else in this building was a good employee and not completely and totally distracted by some guy, they all had badges hanging around their necks and passed through security in seconds.

Then there was me.

Lifting his eyebrows, the guard gave me a stare when he noted I was not wearing a badge, nor was I holding one out.

"I'm new," I explained. "I don't have my badge yet."

"ID," he instructed.

Nodding, I stuck a hand into my bag, searching around for my ID. When I didn't find it immediately, I grew anxious and embarrassed.

Giving a sweet smile to the guard, I held out my coffee. "Can you hold this?"

He blinked, then reached for the coffee.

With both hands free, I went back to digging in my bag. It wasn't even that big, yet it was suddenly like the Grand Canyon! A nervous laugh bubbled out of me, and I shifted on my feet. "It's here somewhere…"

Oh my God, where is it? Why is this happening to me right now? I look like a complete and utter idiot on my second day of work.

"Ah!" I said, relief pouring through me when my fingers closed around a card. Ripping it out triumphantly, I held it out toward the guard.

He cleared his throat.

I looked down.

It was my bank card. Not my ID.

The scene in the coffee shop where all my things spilled out of my purse flashed through my mind, making me gasp. "I must have left it there!"

"Ma'am, if you don't have ID—"

"I do!" I insisted. "I dropped it back there." I pointed toward the doors behind me.

"I'm going to need to ask you to exit the building."

"Whoa, wait a minute, Paul," Seth said, materializing behind the guard. He'd already made it through security and stood on the other side. "She's telling the truth. She—"

"No ID, no admittance," Paul said, matter-of-fact.

My cheeks were flaming. "I'll just go see if I can find my—"

"Let her through," a new voice commanded.

A blanket of thick silence fell over everyone for the span of a few heartbeats. My body rotated around, automatically moving toward the voice.

My heart fluttered wildly, seeing Carter striding toward us, hands tucked into a pair of well-fitting white jeans and black leather sneakers, not making a sound across the shiny floor.

The black jacket he wore over a grey silk shirt fit him like a glove, accentuating the width of his shoulders and the narrowness of his waist.

Shiny, dark hair fell over his forehead and almost into his dark eyes, which locked on me like a missile acquiring a target.

"Mr. Anders," the security guard greeted. "This woman here doesn't have an ID."

Carter's eyes didn't leave me. They glittered like black diamonds, making my throat constrict.

"I-I think I dropped it at the café down the street," I explained, breathless.

I was well aware of the stares around us, prickling the back of my neck and burning my shoulder blades.

"Let her through," Carter said again, authority clear in his tone.

The guard stepped aside immediately, sweeping his arm out in a gesture for me to pass.

I hesitated, feeling as if I were breaking the rules, like I was getting special treatment because Carter was standing here.

Carter didn't care. When I didn't move, he did, striding forward, wrapping his hand around my wrist, and tugging me onward.

My heels slapped against the floor as I scurried to his side, my bag bouncing against my hip as we went.

"Miss, your coffee!" Paul called out behind us.

Carter stopped walking, and so did I.

"I'll take it," Seth offered. Yes, he was still there.

I could almost taste the waves of displeasure emanating from Carter as Seth strode forward and held out the coffee for me to take.

"Didn't you just tell me you were going to drink this entire thing?" Seth teased, holding it out.

I reached for it, but Carter was faster, taking the cup and holding it down at his side. "You two know each other?"

"We met at the coffee shop," I explained.

"I can't leave you alone for three seconds, can I?" Carter asked.

My eyes went wide. "What?"

Seth turned curious eyes to me. "You know our CEO?"

"She calls me Carter."

Gasping, I was quick to try and refute him. "No! I—"

"C'mon, you're going to be late." Carter didn't let me finish what I was trying to say and tugged me alongside him.

I tripped and stumbled. Carter released my wrist to put an arm around my waist.

"Let go of me!" I hissed. "People are watching."

"If you don't want me to help you walk, then you should wear more sensible shoes."

The elevator dinged open the second he approached, as though it too obeyed his every command. Without stopping, he stepped inside, pulling me right along with him.

"I'll see you tomorrow!" Seth called, and Carter's security stepped in front of the doors as they began to close so he couldn't try and get in the elevator with us.

The second they were shut, Carter let go of me and turned. His eyes were dark and bottomless as they intently stared down at me. "You will not see him tomorrow."

"I need to go back to the coffee shop. I dropped my ID."

"I'll have someone go get it."

"I'll go," I insisted.

One dark brow arched, disappearing behind the curtain of hair on his head. "Are you defying a direct order from your CEO?"

Smiling sweetly, I pushed up onto my tiptoes. "But just downstairs, you said I called you Carter."

The elevator jolted, making me pitch to the side. Teetering on my toes, I would have fallen, but he was there. Both arms shot out, catching me around the middle and keeping me from hitting the floor.

His face was close as he bent toward me. The scent of his cologne and leather jacket mingled, creating something intoxicating and unique. Fingertips digging into his sleeve, I clutched a little tighter than needed and drew in a deep breath.

The expression in his eyes left me spellbound. The man I'd filed away into my heart and head as a fantasy was suddenly standing right here… in my reality.

I didn't know how to react or feel.

"You're not supposed to be here," I whispered, still clutching his arms.

"Where else would I be?" he whispered back.

There went my heart again, fluttering wildly and making it impossible to breathe.

The elevator slid to a stop, and the doors prepared to open. Carter righted me swiftly and stepped back.

Shuttering some of the heat in his gaze, he glanced away toward the opening doors. "Why are you wearing heels?"

"Because I'm at work." *Duh*.

"This is a video game company. You can wear sneakers."

"Heels make my legs look better," I grumped, not necessarily speaking to him.

"No one is going to be looking at your legs," he said, harsh.

A woman waiting outside the elevator giggled.

Embarrassed, I rushed past, leaving Carter in my wake. I made it maybe four steps when I realized I wasn't even on the right floor. And I didn't have my coffee.

Turning back, my belly dropped when I saw Carter standing there staring at me like he was just waiting for me to realize I was lost.

I felt my eyes narrow. "How much did you see downstairs?"

His lips pursed. "Don't let him touch you again."

I blinked. I wasn't expecting that. "What?"

"I'll fire him." There wasn't an ounce of humor in his tone.

My mouth dropped open. "Seth? He didn't touch me."

"He had his hand on your back." Then, as if using it as evidence, Carter held up the coffee, which was already dripping with condensation. "He bought you this, didn't he?"

I rushed right up in front of him to hiss, "Oh my God! Did you follow me to work this morning?"

His dark eyes rolled. "I didn't have to follow you to see him drooling all over you."

"How long were you going to let me embarrass myself in front of the guard before stepping in to say you knew me?" I demanded, surly.

He smirked. "Didn't you tell me not to talk to you at work?"

I made a face. "Yet here we are," I said, motioning between us. Straightening, I gazed around. "Where are we anyway?"

Carter tossed my iced coffee in a nearby trashcan.

"Hey!" I gasped. "I was drinking that!"

"C'mon, we're getting your badge." Taking hold of my wrist again, he dragged me forward.

"I didn't even have breakfast! I need that coffee."

His footsteps halted instantly. Turning around completely, his tall frame blocked everything else from sight. "Why didn't you eat breakfast?"

"How can I do anything when you show up here and completely distract me?" The second I blurted out the truth, I realized what I'd done. Embarrassment burned by face, so I dipped my chin.

"That was yesterday morning."

I didn't say anything.

He shifted in front of me, arms wrapping over his chest. "You mean to tell me you haven't eaten since you saw me?"

"Of course I have." I lied. "You aren't *that* distracting."

Saying nothing, Carter unfolded his arms and reached inside his jacket to pull out his cell. My eyes lifted when he held it up to his ear and spoke into the line. "Nora lost her ID at the coffee place down the block. Go get it and bring back an iced coffee with cream and some kind of breakfast sandwich."

I started to protest, but he silenced me with one swift look.

"I'm at HR," he said into the phone, then made a sound. After a moment, he said, "I'll be in my office."

When the phone was put away, he motioned down the hall with his head. "Your ID."

"I can get it myself," I muttered.

"I told you to get it yesterday. You didn't. I had to come all the way downstairs to get you this morning."

How offensive. "I can take care of myself."

His warm chuckle set my heart to bouncing again. *Damn him.*

We rounded the corner into a large office space with a long white counter up front. The second Carter stepped under the archway, everyone in sight stood.

"Mr. Anders," and, "CEO," collectively echoed through the room.

Carter smiled, the curve of his lips transforming his face into something I wanted to stare at.

Fine.

Who was I kidding? I would stare at him even if he had a paper bag over his head.

"Good morning, everyone." He spoke, friendly. "This is our new intern, Nora Williams. She needs her ID badge."

"I have that right here," one of the women said, rushing around her desk toward the long counter.

"Then I will leave her in your care."

Carter started to walk away, but I grabbed his arm. "You're leaving?"

A few whispers floated through the room behind us.

He glanced between where I grabbed him and my face.

Flustered, I pulled back.

A satisfied smile curved the corners of his lips. Leaning down beside my ear, he spoke softly so only I could hear. "Don't worry, good girl. You'll see me again later."

My teeth sank into my lower lip, and I had to force myself not to watch as he slowly walked away.

Sixteen

Carter

"Bro," Bryan announced, striding into my office. "Tongues are wagging."

Glancing up, I noted Aaron appearing out of nowhere to close the office door so whatever was said between my partner and me would be confidential.

"And what is it that has our employees so entranced that they are gossiping instead of working?"

"You."

Looking up from the monitor, I pointed to myself. "Me?"

"In the five years we've owned this company, you've been in the lobby... What? Three times?" He sat down across from my desk. "And two of those times have been in the last two days."

"I wasn't aware I needed permission to walk around my own damn company."

Bryan raised both eyebrows. "You and the intern, huh?"

Picking up the mug of coffee at my elbow, I sipped it while regarding him. "Is that what people are saying?"

"You can't really expect people wouldn't notice when you—the most unsocial CEO in Miami—starts venturing off the top floor and dragging a mere intern around by her arm."

"I don't drag people anywhere."

Bryan's smile was swift. "Pardon me. What I meant was you held on to her while she ran behind you to keep up."

Rolling my eyes, I set down the mug. "Is this what you came in here for?"

"I want details."

"Seems like you already got them in the hallways."

Cursing beneath his breath, Bryan sat forward. "Don't play me like that, Anders. I'm just as shook as everyone else around here. You never show interest in anyone."

Pressing my hand to my chest, I pretended to be affronted. "But, Bry, I thought you knew how I felt about you."

He laughed. "Fess up."

"There's nothing to tell." Well, maybe there was, but he didn't need to know about our night back on the island.

"You're interested in her."

"Yeah." I confirmed.

"Is that why you hired her?"

"Partly," I allowed. "But her work is good. Have you looked at it?"

He made a face. "Of course I did." He sat back in the chair. "She's got talent."

"Then I guess it doesn't matter if I'm interested or not."

"Don't be an ass, Anders." Bryan called me out. "I don't give a rat's testicle if you do her in your office,

107

because I know damn well you can handle the business. But everyone else in this building is a lot less forgiving."

"Meaning?" I pressed, even though I knew what he was implying.

"Meaning that poor girl is going to get the shit end of the stick from everyone, and no one is going to take her seriously."

The way she'd looked when she found out I owned this place flashed through my mind.

Don't talk to me at work. People will think I slept with the boss to get my job.

I teased her when she said it, but deep down, I knew she was right. I put her in a shitty position because I couldn't help myself. Because for the first time, I wanted something in my life besides work.

Pushing out of the chair, I went to the window to gaze out across Miami. "So what do you propose I do?" I asked my friend.

He made a rude sound. "Fuck if I know. I don't mix business with pleasure. But you better figure out something, or the jealous bitches in this company will rip her apart."

My hand clenched into a fist at my side. Bryan's words brought forth a fury inside me that felt volatile and dangerous.

"It's just a summer internship," I muttered.

"So are you just scratching some kind of itch you got? In a few months, she'll be out of your system and back to wherever she came from?"

I spun, pinning him with a look.

Holding up his hands, he shook his head. "I'm just asking. Do you really want to cause an uproar at the company because you got an itch?"

"She's not an itch," I growled.

"All right." Bry relented. "Like I said, I don't care. She's talented. You're the CEO. You can hire who you want. I'm just warning you of what I see and reminding you there's already enough drama brewing."

"Regal Tech still pissed?"

"Of course they are! You blocked their lawsuit, and ever since, they've been sniffing around, just looking for ways to keep this game from hitting the market."

"You gonna tell me what their latest attempt is?"

Bryan pursed his lips and unfolded from the chair. Reaching into the front pocket of his pants, he withdrew a piece of folded paper. "I got a call just a bit ago."

"And you're just mentioning it now?"

"I got distracted by your love life on my way from my office. I can't help it if women are more fun to talk about than business."

Going around the desk, I snatched the paper out of his grasp. Unfolding it, I glanced down at the number written across the top.

It had a lot of zeros.

Flicking my gaze up at my partner, I waited for him to explain.

"That's how much they want to pay us for the rights to *Zero*."

I let that settle in a beat, then glanced back at the number. "No." Crumpling the paper, I tossed it onto my desk.

I felt Bryan's reaction as I returned to my chair. "Just like that?"

"You're actually considering this?"

"Twenty-five million dollars is a lot of money, Anders."

"Twenty-five million is a fraction of what *Zero* is going to make."

"You're that confident?" Bryan pressed.

Annoyance flashed through me. Was he doubting me right now? "I'm offended you aren't."

His voice turned weary. "They've been applying a lot of pressure."

"That's because they know we're going to rake in a hell of a lot more than twenty-five million. They're desperate and pissed because they should have already done what we're about to do."

"I'll tell them no."

"Don't even answer," I refuted. "Let our silence send a clear message."

"Cold as always." Bryan chuckled, exiting the chair.

"It's business." I reminded him.

"I think I might wander on down to the design department and get a look at our new intern," he goaded.

Not taking the bait, I made a sound. "She's taken."

"Does she know that?" he teased.

I glanced up. "No. But you do."

Bryan chuckled. "CEO's got it bad."

I pretended to work until he was completely gone. Only then did I toss down the pen in my hand and move to stare out the window once more.

What he said bothered me. I put Nora in a hard spot, and now it was up to me to protect her.

Seventeen

Nora

Reality vs. Fantasy Observation #1:
In a fantasy, other people don't matter. In fact, they don't seem to exist at all.
In reality, people whisper and stare, and it is really hard to ignore.

What the hell was I doing? I mean, technically, I was supposed to be working. The badge around my neck and the work in front of me was proof. Honestly, though, I sat here feeling like an exhibit at some exotic animal zoo.

People stared. They whispered. They smiled sweetly when they saw me looking.

"Intern Williams," one of the women from the department called as she approached my desk. Behind her trailed three other employees. "We're heading across the street for some lunch. Want to join?"

Suspicion clouded over the invite, making me feel bitter and annoyed. I couldn't help but wonder if they had ulterior motives because I'd been sure I'd seen them whispering about the CEO's interest in me earlier this morning.

"Umm…" I began.

One of the men stepped up beside the woman. "Think of it as a welcoming party."

"Sure, I'd love to," I replied. "Just let me get my bag." I decided in the moment that I was going to give these people a chance. Truth was I wanted to make friends here. I wanted good working relationships, and I wanted to be able to learn everything I could from the people around me.

I had stuff to offer. Stuff that was mine, and not because I knew the CEO.

As I shut off my laptop and picked up my things, I made a choice that I wouldn't let the rumors I knew were already circling affect the way I interacted with my co-workers. I could at least give them a chance before deciding they were all just out to get me.

Alan made you bitter. I reminded myself. *Not everyone is as awful as him.*

When the elevator arrived to take us to the lobby, the doors opened, revealing a man in a dark suit. My heart sped up irrationally, anticipating Carter, then fell when I realized it wasn't him.

Damn him for telling me he'd see me later, because now I looked for him around every corner.

Exactly why you shouldn't be here! I scolded myself.

"President," one of the girls next to me said, drawing my attention.

Glancing back at the man who wasn't Carter, I paid better attention. He was dressed in a dark suit and red tie. His brown hair was tousled, but in a purposeful way.

He was young like Carter, and I had to admit it really awed me that two men as young as them could found and run a successful company.

It made me want to be here, to learn more about the vibe of this place, to see how it ran daily, and to learn more about the two men who built everything on their own.

"Everyone," the man replied, taking in all of us with a sweeping glance.

His eyes came back to me, and the corner of his mouth kicked up. "You must be the new intern."

The people standing in front of me parted, allowing him to step forward.

Nodding, I held out my hand. "I'm Nora. Nice to meet you."

He took my offered hand and shook it. "Bryan Foster, president of Ansoft."

Everyone was watching us with curious, apt expressions. I couldn't help but wonder if this man often came down to the design department.

"Is there something I can get you, Mr. Foster?" I asked when he said nothing.

Grinning, he tucked his hands in his pockets. "Nope. Just wanted to welcome you. I've seen your portfolio. It's promising."

"Thank you," I said, mildly surprised.

Withdrawing a card from his pocket, he held it out. "If you need anything, feel free to contact me."

I glanced between him and the card before taking it. Behind him, my co-workers were practically peeing their pants.

"I'm sure I'll be fine," I was quick to say.

He smiled, and I cleared my throat. "Well... we were just heading out to lunch."

"Go," he urged, waving us toward the elevator.

I was the last one to file inside, so I was at the front near the doors.

Bryan turned to watch us leave and gave me a little wave. "Nice meeting you, Nora."

I waved back and prayed the doors would close faster. The second they did, I let out a breath.

"Mr. Foster never came to welcome me to the company," Darla observed.

"Me either." Tom agreed.

I shut my eyes briefly and slid the card he'd given me into my bag. "So what kind of place are we eating at?"

"Sushi." Darla spoke up.

Raw fish? My stomach revolted.

The elevator pinged open and revealed Seth standing there waiting. "Going down?" he asked. The smile he gave me was genuine, and it eased some of the tension in my stomach.

Nodding, I gestured for him to take the spot beside me.

"Heading out to lunch?" he asked as the elevator began moving again.

Various noises of agreement went around.

"Mind if I tag along?"

I gave him a warning glance. "We're having sushi."

His eyes danced with laughter. "Sounds good."

My stomach grew queasier the closer we got to the restaurant, which was indeed right across the street.

Seth hung back, waiting for me to catch up, then leaned down to whisper, "Sushi isn't raw fish, but get the California roll. It's the beginner's best choice."

"Really?" I asked, relieved. Realizing what I'd done, I grimaced. "Is it that obvious?"

"Nah," he chuckled. "But sushi is an acquired taste."

"Not anything I'll be acquiring," I muttered.

He laughed. A few of our lunch mates turned to glance in our direction.

"Everyone is very curious about you," he confided.

"I noticed."

Leaning back toward me, Seth added, "I admit I am, too."

All the comfort I'd felt when he stepped onto the elevator evaporated. Suddenly, I was a solitary goldfish in a bowl with a group of spectators standing around.

I didn't like it.

Again, I wondered, *What the hell am I doing?*

Eighteen

Carter

JUST MET YOUR GIRL

THE VULTURES ARE ALREADY CIRCLING

Tossing my phone on the desk, I didn't bother to reply. This was why I never bothered with women. Well, no more than a passing fling.

People in general weren't worth the effort. I'd learned the hard way that most weren't genuine. Most only wanted what would benefit them.

Nora was different. She *felt* different. Maybe I didn't have a lot to base those feelings on… but I was a man who operated on instinct. From the moment she spilled that sugary drink down my chest, those instincts had been screaming she was mine.

I worked the rest of the afternoon, ignoring every urge I had to stomp down to the design floor and see what she was doing. Staying in my office, I did what I was here to do. Work.

With Regal Tech practically humping my ass, the pressure was on. It wasn't that I wasn't confident. I was good at my job. This company and our success proved it.

But my instincts were shouting—this time not about Nora.

I couldn't shake the feeling something was going to happen. That Regal Tech was going to try and pull something before all was said and done.

It was almost six o'clock when Aaron rapped on the door, then strolled in. The white dress shirt he wore was unbuttoned at the neck, and the sleeves were rolled up his forearms. "Should I call for the chopper?"

"I'm staying mainland tonight," I informed him.

Even though I wasn't looking in his direction, I felt his surprise. Lounging back in my chair, I regarded him. "You can call for the chopper. Head home."

Aaron was my right-hand man, but he was more than that. I'd hired him when I was nineteen and so green to the gaming world that it almost killed me. Literally.

He'd saved my life one night and sort of took me under his wing. Even though I was the "boss" in our relationship, I looked up to him. I trusted him more than anyone else, and to me, he was family.

"If you're staying in Miami, then I am, too."

"I might be staying mainland more than usual in the upcoming weeks." I warned him. Neither of us particularly liked staying in Miami.

"I figured as much." The smirk on his face was not lost on me.

Sighing, I kicked up my shoes on the edge of my desk, leaning back. "What'd you find out?"

"Lunch was across the street at the sushi place. By the look on her face, she isn't a sushi kind of girl."

I snickered.

"Then again, it could be the interrogation her co-workers put her through while they ate." Aaron considered.

Any enjoyment I felt dried up. Feet hitting the floor, I stood. "Why didn't you call?"

"'Cause she handled it."

I didn't like that answer.

Aaron cleared his throat. "Seth was there as well."

"Did he not get the hint this morning?" I wondered, annoyed.

"She worked at her desk the rest of the afternoon."

What? Yes, I know what you're thinking. I said I'd ignored every urge I had to go down to her floor *myself*. I never said I hadn't sent someone else to check up on her.

Snagging my jacket off the back of my chair, I picked up my phone and hit the button so the automatic blinds on the windows behind me would close. "I'll be at the apartment later."

"I'll come with you."

Stopping, I held up my hand. "I don't butt into your love life. Don't butt into mine."

"I don't have a love life because I'm too busy babysitting you." He glowered at me.

"I just told you to take the chopper and go home." I made a *what can you do* gesture with my hands. Slapping a palm on his shoulder, I said, "You're obsessed with me. It's unhealthy."

Fast as lightning, Aaron had me in a headlock and bent at his side. I smacked the arm wrapped around my neck while he avoided all my attempted kicks.

"Whose obsessed with whom?" he demanded. I made a gagging sound, and he merely laughed. "Please. Don't be such a drama queen."

Since that didn't work, I changed tactics, shoving a hand beneath the waistband of his pants and grabbing his boxers against his lower back.

"Whoa!" He cursed and let go, leaping back to avoid the massive wedgie I was about to deliver.

"You punk," he spat, reaching behind him to fix his shirt.

"Take the night off, A. Go find a nice girl at a club. Jump-start the love life you so clearly long for."

"You're an asshole!" he called after me, but with affection in his tone.

I laughed.

"Call me if you need anything!"

See? Family.

* * *

Nora's apartment was on the eighth floor of an upscale complex a few blocks from Ansoft headquarters. I'd purposely chosen a building with good security and within walking distance to work.

After knocking on the door, I waited impatiently for her to open it. I wanted to see her face. Missing something wasn't like me... yet here I was, tapping my foot, waiting for the barrier between us to give way.

It seemed to take forever, so I knocked again, wondering what the hell she was doing.

Almost immediately after banging a second time, I felt her. A smile curved my lips as I listened for any sounds on the other side. She was there. I could sense her. I anticipated her.

But she wasn't opening the door.

A moment later, a tentative voice came through the wood. "Who is it?"

Smiling wide, I nodded in approval. I liked that she didn't just open the door for anyone.

"It's me," I called.

The sound of a lock disengaging made my heart jump. The second her face appeared in the partly opened door, the anxiety I hadn't even realized I'd been riddled with calmed. The conversation I'd had with Bryan still bothered me, and clearly, it didn't matter that I'd had someone check up on Nora today. I'd needed to see her with my own eyes.

Tilting my head to the side, I gazed at her.

"I guess I don't need to ask how you got my address," she quipped, leaning against the doorjamb, still holding it partially closed.

Motioning to the apartment with my chin, I asked, "You gonna let me in?"

Nora stepped back with the door, admitting me into her space. She was dressed in a pair of cut-off shorts and a T-shirt with Mickey Mouse in the center. Her blond hair was pulled in a ponytail high on her head. Loose strands had already come free to fall around her face.

Her feet were bare against the wood floor, and her toenails were painted pink.

Sliding the jacket off my arms, I wandered past the small kitchen and into the living room, tossing it on the sofa on my way to the sliders on the far wall. There was a view of the ocean from here and a small balcony just outside the doors.

"Is the apartment okay for you?" I asked, gazing out across the ocean. The turquoise waters surrounding my island were better.

A small choked sound erupted behind me. "Are you kidding? This place is too nice for a mere intern."

Spinning away from the view, I frowned. "Of course it isn't."

"Most interns aren't given a condo with an ocean view *and* paid for their work."

"Anything less than this is beneath you."

A look crossed her face. Then her azure eyes snapped up. "Did you do this?"

"Do what?" I feigned innocence.

Twirling a single finger around, she gestured to the condo. "Are you paying for this condo?"

"Room and board is part of your internship."

Nora practically stomped her foot on the floor. Without another word, she rushed out of the room, disappearing into the single bedroom.

I trailed along behind her because watching her was just too entertaining. Everything she did was with some sort of passion.

Entering in the bedroom, she came out of the closet, hauling a suitcase almost as big as her. With both hands, she towed it up on the bed and flipped the top open.

"What do you think you're doing?" I asked, mild, leaning against the doorframe. Her back was to me as she opened up the top drawer of the dresser and scooped up an armful of fabric, carried it over to the suitcase, and dumped it inside.

"I'm not staying."

A flicker of the anxiety I felt before sparked inside me. Forcing myself to remain in the same calm position, my eyes followed as she made a trip to the closet, coming out with more clothes to drop into the suitcase.

"Mind telling me why?"

A piece of clothing tumbled out of the bag onto the bed. Nora snatched it up and slapped it inside before swinging around to glare at me. "Do you think you can buy me? You think I have no pride at all. That I'll come here and just…" She gazed around. "Live off you?"

Straightening out of the doorway, I dropped both arms to my sides. "I'm not trying to buy you."

Laughing, she surged toward the closet again.

Catching her arm as she rushed by, I pulled her around, gazing down into her fiery blue eyes. "I want you here."

I felt the give in her body, though it didn't shine through in her eyes. I knew damn well she was affected by me. The chemistry between us was undeniable.

You already have part of her… Now just convince the rest.

Nora tugged her arm out of my grasp, and I let go. She didn't step back, though. Instead, she spoke softly. "Why didn't you call, then? Ask to see me?"

"I don't have your number," I answered, holding her gaze.

Scoffing, she rolled her eyes. "Like I'm going to believe you don't have my number."

Stepping a fraction closer, I heard the catch in her breath. "I want you to be the one to give it to me."

"Why?"

"Because then I'll have permission to use it."

The echo of similar words I'd spoken to her flashed behind her eyes, momentarily distracting her. The disoriented look reminded me of that night we spent together and how she felt beneath me, making me want to tug her close and not let go.

Forcing both of us back to reality, Nora retorted, "You didn't ask my permission to bring me out here or set me up with this condo and a job."

Unable to keep my fingers from grazing the side of her hip, I asked, "Would you have come if I'd just asked?"

Visibly she swallowed, tipped her chin up, and met my eyes. "Yes."

A gruff sound ripped from my throat. Honestly, I hadn't expected her to say that. Lowering until our lips were aligned mere inches apart and I had to fight my eyes drifting closed, I whispered, "Have dinner with me."

She jolted slightly, surprised. Stares colliding again, desire danced between us, neither of us moving away.

"I'm packing," she finally said, her body still rooted in place. Like I said, I already owned her body. Now I just needed to claim her mind.

"You can pack later." Reaching down, my fingers entangled with hers. Leading us back through the apartment, I paused only long enough for her to grab her bag and slip on a pair of flip-flops.

"Wait!" She gasped when we stepped out into the hallway. "I need to change."

Allowing my eyes to roam her body, lingering on her long, bare legs, I made a negative sound. "I like you the way you are."

When she didn't say or do anything, I gestured toward the door. "Lock up."

I started down the hall without her, a smile tugging at my lips when I heard her jogging to catch up.

"Where are we going anyway?" she asked.

Glancing over at her, I smiled. "Don't worry. It's not sushi."

"How did you—" She halted in the middle of the hall. "You had someone follow me *across the street to lunch?*"

Backtracking, I stopped in front of her. "When there is something I want, I do my homework. I learn the details."

"I'm a person. Not a thing."

Ushering her onto the elevator, I pressed the button, and we headed down. "There's a Cuban place around the corner. You game?"

She didn't answer, but I felt her stare, so I lifted an eyebrow.

"At least you don't deny your stalker ways."

"Denying implies I've done something wrong. Making sure you're okay isn't a crime."

The doors slid open, and we stepped into the lobby.

"Just one meal," Nora said, as if all this time she'd only been considering eating with me. "Then I'm leaving."

She was cute.

Outside, the Miami heat, traffic, and city noise erupted around us.

"Cuban?" I asked again.

She nodded.

Halfway down the block, I felt her eyes. "Aren't you going to say anything?"

"About what?"

"Me leaving."

It took me a minute to suppress the smile desperately trying to grace my face. Tucking my hands into my jeans, I gazed up at the summer sky. "You aren't leaving, Nora."

Her voice turned sassy. "And how do you know that?"

"Because I'm going to change your mind."

Nineteen

Nora

"Have you eaten at all today?"

I glanced up from my plate, pausing around the mouthful of food filling my cheeks. "It's really good," I replied, going back to chewing.

Carter's deep chuckle floated across the table, making my stomach dip a little. He was incredibly easy on the eyes. After our night together—you know, after I left the fantasy, boarded a plane, and flew back to reality—I convinced myself I remembered Carter through a sort of filter.

And not just any filter. Like the *good* one. The one you always went for when you needed to make your selfie look really hot for social media.

I recalled Carter in almost a surreal way, dreamlike. Everything about that night we spent together was almost too good to be true.

Just like this internship…

Maybe I'd only built up that night in my mind because it was so fantasy-like. I was remembering him as better than he actually was.

That was a lie.

Looking at him now, sitting across from him in a wooden booth with a single light hanging over our table, it was all too obvious that Carter was every bit as handsome as I remembered. I didn't have to build him up in my mind because he didn't lack at all.

I couldn't believe I was here with him right now. Giddiness swam around inside me, making me want to giggle at the most inappropriate times. Occasionally, he would look at me, and my pulse would race. I'd honestly never felt like this before. So... bewitched by someone.

"Eat up." He encouraged, spooning some of the shredded beef from his plate onto mine.

Staring down at the meat, I was oddly touched. "But this is yours," I said, not even meaning to speak.

"If my woman is hungry, I'm going to make sure she eats."

There it went again. My heart galloping wildly.

"But I'm not your woman."

In response, he spooned more of his food onto my plate. "Eat. You look skinnier than you were on spring break."

I went back to eating, scooping up the ropa vieja and taking a big bite. Pleased, Carter grabbed up his bottle of beer and lightly clinked it against my mojito before taking a long sip.

"I thought you lived on the island," I said after a few more minutes of just eating.

Setting aside his fork, Carter gazed over the table. "I do. I just work in Miami."

"That seems like an awfully long commute,"

He smiled. "I take a helicopter."

Surprise had me gulping in air, and with it, rice lodged in my throat, making me cough. Fork clattering against the plate, I bent toward the back of the booth, still hacking, desperately trying to stop.

Warmth settled against my back, and I shot up, leaning against something firm. Still coughing, I looked over my shoulder, where Carter sat close. The coughing continued, and frankly, I considered never eating rice again.

One strong arm wrapped around my shoulder from behind, pulling me against his body. Over the other shoulder, a water glass appeared, heading straight for my lips.

"Drink," he commanded softly.

Gripping the glass, I tried to pull it away, but he wouldn't release it, tipping it against my lips. I swallowed the cool liquid, finally feeling some of the tightness in my throat dissipate.

Carter set aside the glass, and I cleared my throat. He didn't pull back, though. He left his arm wrapped around me, dropping his chin on my free shoulder. "Okay now?"

Nodding, I could feel his chest pressed against my back. His heart was pounding nearly as hard as mine. "You can let go now."

His arm tightened, tucking me closer. "No."

The hollow place just under my ribcage filled with a thousand butterflies, leaving me slightly nauseous, but not in a bad way.

Turning my face slightly toward his, I said, "You take a helicopter to work every day?"

I felt him smile. "I don't usually come to the office every day. Just a couple days a week."

"Oh."

Leaning so close his nose brushed against my cheek, he asked, "What's the matter, good girl? Sad you won't be seeing me every day?"

I sniffed. "It doesn't matter because I'm not staying."

Carter pulled back, making me miss the warmth of his body. My plate slid over in front of me. "You aren't done yet."

Dragging his plate from the other side of the table, Carter settled back into the booth right beside me.

As I sipped my mojito, I glanced at him from the corner of my eye.

With a sigh, he put his fork aside, grabbed my glass, and pushed it away. Picking up my fork, he stabbed at some food and held it to my lips.

Once I was chewing, the full weight of his dark eyes settled on me. "I put you in a hard place."

"What?"

"I didn't think about the position you would be in when I brought you on as an intern."

My knees grazed his leg when I turned toward him. "I still don't understand why you did that."

"I told you. I want you here."

"But why?"

He considered the question while taking a pull of his beer. When he was done, he wiped his lips with the back of his hand. "Because one night with you wasn't enough."

I started coughing again.

Making a disgusted sound, Carter picked up a napkin and dabbed at my mouth. "Are you like this every time you eat?"

I tried to push his hand away, but he evaded and continued to clean me up. When he was done, the water was back in front of me.

Obediently, I took a drink, then made a face. "Why do I always do what you tell me to do?" I muttered, disgruntled.

"Because instinctively, you know I'll take care of you."

Why did he keep saying things like this?

"Carter." My voice was firm, and the glass made a thud on the tabletop.

His hand slid over mine. Glancing down, I marveled at how much larger and deeper in skin tone he was.

"Finish eating. Then we'll talk." He cajoled.

"Promise?"

Lifting both our hands, he made an X over his heart. "Cross my heart."

Feeling playful and maybe a little high because he was so close, I lifted his fork, offering him a bite of dinner. Glittering dark eyes held mine when his lips parted and he allowed me to feed him.

We sat there side by side, his leg pressed along mine, finishing our meal in comfortable silence. Every time he glanced at me, I had to remind myself not to get lost in the fantasy again. There was no place for that in reality.

* * *

By the time we stepped out of the little Cuban place, the sun was fast asleep. However, it seemed Miami was just waking up. The Miami nightlife had a pulse of its own, reminding me I wasn't in Georgia anymore.

"Is it like this every night?" I asked.

He nodded, then added, "It's way busier on the weekends."

"Val would love it here," I mused, gazing at all the lit-up places.

Blurred movement came out of nowhere, and a loud whizzing sound filled my ears. Before I could register what was happening, Carter snaked his arms around me, pulling me out of the way while turning at the same time.

Breathless and clinging to him, I glanced around as a man on a bicycle flew by, swerving all over the sidewalk.

"Damn drunks," Carter muttered, disgusted.

Realizing I was still in his arms, my eyes turned up. The nightlife seemed to fade into the distance as Carter became the focus of my entire universe. Living the moment in slow motion, every nuance of every thing he did next seemed drawn out and that much more palpable.

Cupping the back of my head, Carter dragged his hand down the length of my ponytail while sweeping a concerned, focused stare over my face. "You okay?" he asked, settling his palm against the side of my neck.

Glittering eyes pulled away from me, narrowing on something behind me while his full mouth pulled into a taut line.

"Did he hit you?" he demanded, turning all attention back to me.

How could he when you put your body in front of mine?

"I'm fine," I answered, still feeling the weight of his palm against my neck. His thumb stroked the underside of my jaw, turning all the concern in his gaze into something much more intense and enticing.

Slowly, his face lowered toward mine. My heart was out of control, my lungs burned because, apparently, I wasn't breathing, and the palms of my hands were starting to sweat.

When I turned my face to the side, his lips grazed my ear instead of my lips.

"Ooh!" I exclaimed, taking notice of the place nearby. "What's that?"

Dropping his hands and stepping away, Carter rubbed the back of his head while following my pointed finger. "It's a margarita bar."

Loud music spilled out of the open door and windows, mingling with the sound of rowdy customers and clinking glass. Curious, I went to the door, peeking inside.

My mouth dropped open.

Off to the side, Carter reached around and pushed my mouth closed.

"Are those slushy machines?" I was in awe. Behind the bar, there were giant machines with round clear windows showing off the swirling colorful drinks that looked exactly like the ICEE's you could get at a 7-11.

"That's the margaritas," Carter replied, amused. Leaning down beside my ear, he taunted, "Those are slushees with alcohol… nothing for good girls like you."

His grunt was mildly satisfying when I elbowed him in the stomach. Leaving him there to lick his wound, I strode right inside the crowded place, weaving through the people to make my way to the bar.

Slipping into a free space at the counter, I watched the five different machines churn the margaritas, making the wall look like a rainbow. Bartenders were filling up clear plastic cups with the drinks and slinging them to waiting customers. Beer bottles were also being served up from the coolers I assumed were beneath the bar.

A body slid up behind me, and an arm came around my waist. It didn't scare me because I knew who it was. My body recognized him without even trying.

"What color do you want?" he asked over the music and the crowd.

"Blue," I yelled, then changed my mind. "Wait! Purple!"

Carter ordered the drink from one of the female bartenders passing by, then handed over some cash as the cup was slid across the bar.

Excited, I held it out to look at the bright-purple shade before giving it a try.

Laughing, Carter slid a straw into the slush and guided it toward my lips. "You better be careful." He warned me. "These are strong."

The frosty, thick liquid slid up the straw, bursting over my tongue. Sweetness filled my mouth, and a pleased feeling made me dance a little. "It's grape!" I announced, finally releasing the straw.

The second I did, my mouth puckered and the strong flavor of alcohol hit my senses.

"Told you," he whispered close by.

Turning in the circle of his arms, I held it up for him to try.

I thought at first he might turn it down, but then his pouty, perfect lips wrapped around the straw, momentarily making me forget about everything else.

Afterward, he smiled down at me. "It's gross."

Shrugging, I stuck the straw back in my mouth and took another drink.

"C'mon," he called, taking my hand, leading me toward the door. Trailing behind him, drinking my grape margarita, I wasn't paying any attention, so I wasn't prepared when someone knocked into me from behind.

Stumbling sideways, I hit the corner of a nearby table and cried out.

"What happened?" Carter demanded, materializing right in front of me.

"Someone bumped into—" My words trailed away and all the blood drained from my head when I saw who was glaring at me from over Carter's shoulder.

"Well, look who it is," the man boasted.

Memories of being terrified in the endless black ocean and not knowing which way was land crashed over me. The cup slipped out of my grasp and would have spilled if Carter hadn't caught it.

Rotating, he came face to face with the man that still sometimes haunted my nightmares.

It was the bartender from the island. The man who'd tossed me overboard when I refused to sleep with him.

The muscles in Carter's back bunched, and everything about him changed. Gone was the flirting, almost indulgent man I'd just been with, and in his place was the commanding, cold CEO.

"Pretty sure I told you to make sure I never saw you again," he intoned.

People standing within earshot turned, sensing an ominous scene.

Xander held out his arms and smiled arrogantly. "You kicked me out of the Caribbean. I had to go somewhere. Miami seemed like a good enough place."

"You just got evicted."

"You might have some clout back on the islands, but here in Miami, you have no say."

"I wouldn't be so sure about that," Carter quipped, his voice even and calm. Why did even that simple phrase give me goose bumps?

Unexpectedly, Xander threw a punch at Carter, who dodged it with ease. Frustrated, my attacker swung again. Catching his wrist, Carter twisted the bartender's arm around his back, bending it at an awkward angle. Bent at the waist, Xander struggled and fought, but it didn't seem to matter because Carter clearly had the upper hand.

The crowd all around us moved back, giving them room to fight as if they all hoped they would have front row seats to an impromptu brawl.

"Stop!" I shouted, panic tightening my throat.

Carter shoved him away, making him fall into a table. Xander pushed up and spun, anger flushing his face. Locking eyes with me, he took a single step forward. "You should have drowned," he growled.

With a single, rapid blow, the man folded to the ground, completely unconscious.

A waitress cut through the crowd and gazed down at the body sprawled at her feet.

Carter produced some cash, handing it over to her. "Sorry for the trouble," he apologized, took my hand, and didn't stop walking until we were around the corner and my building was in view.

"Let me see," he murmured, tugging me around to stand in front of him. I stood there, partly dazed, while he checked me over for injuries I didn't have. Cupping my face, he stared into my eyes. "He'll be out of Miami tomorrow."

I believed him. Carter emanated power, so much it was terrifying and exciting all at once.

Pulling away, I lifted his hand to inspect his knuckles, which were inflamed. "C'mon." I started toward home. "I'll put some ice on this."

"I think you'd better kiss it, too." He tried.

"Don't push your luck," I scolded, even though secretly, I really wanted to lift his hand and kiss every knuckle.

Carter

"How did you manage to hold on to this while punching out that guy?" Nora asked, holding up her gross purple alcohol slushy. Condensation clung to the cup, a droplet sliding right off the edge and falling onto her bare foot.

"I'm just that amazing," I retorted, sprawling back on the sofa.

Retreating with the cup, she went around the bar separating the kitchen from the living area to reach into the freezer. After another sip, she set the cup on the coffee table and held out her hand.

My fingers hardly hurt, but I wasn't about to tell her that because she seemed concerned and I liked it. Carefully, Nora took my "injured" hand, studying the knuckles. Unable to take my eyes away from her, the shock of the cold pack I hadn't even seen coming made me jerk.

It fell off the top of my hand, hitting my thigh, and landed on the couch.

Making a sound of distress, Nora leaned close, bending to retrieve what fell. Once retrieved, she pulled back, but I couldn't let her get away. Tugging her gently, she fell into my lap.

Eyes going wide, she tried to jolt up, but I locked an arm around her, forcing her to stay where she was. "I need that ice." I reminded her.

Forgetting about my smooth moves, concern darkened her eyes again. "Let me see."

After I offered my hand, she carefully placed the cold pack over my knuckles. "Why'd you have to hit him?"

"Why?" I gestured toward her with my chin. "You worried about me?"

"Of course not," she retorted, holding the pack in place.

"He deserved a lot more than a single knockout."

Her eyes swung to mine. Electricity crackled between us, making her swallow nervously.

"Your tongue is purple," I mused, trying to make her a little more at ease and hoping the way I'd reacted to that douche at the bar didn't scare her.

Sticking it out, she laughed.

"Are you drunk?"

"Of course not!" Nora refuted. "I only had half of that drink."

"You had a mojito at dinner."

"You took it away from me." Her face showed severe disapproval.

"You're cute when you glower."

She started to get up, but I fought her attempt. "I have to pee," she muttered.

Sighing, I let her go, and she rushed off into the bathroom. A few minutes later, she returned, standing near the couch, but not within touching distance.

"You can just take the ice with you." Her eyes slid across the apartment toward the front door.

"I'm not leaving."

"I have to finish packing."

"We need to talk."

"There's nothing to say," she argued. "You can let yourself out." With that, she skittered toward the bedroom.

"You really want me to go?"

Stopping mid-run, her hand fisted at her side. "Yes." The second she spoke the word, she rushed off again, fleeing into the safety of her bedroom.

Sighing, I stood, dropping the cold pack onto the table next to her half-gone drink. I could hear her moving around in the bedroom, and I pictured her making laps between the suitcase and her closet.

"I'm leaving, then," I called.

All sounds stopped for a long minute.

"Bye!" she finally yelled.

Smiling to myself, I strolled to the front door, opened it, then shut it loudly. Leaning against it, I stood and waited, silently counting. *One, two, three...*

Nora's bare feet slapped against the wood floor when she ran out of the room. I had smoothed my face into a bored expression, but it almost slipped when she came rushing around the corner, wearing a stricken expression.

At first, she didn't see me waiting, but the second she did, she nearly tripped. "Carter," she gasped out.

"You panicked for a minute, didn't you?" I mused. "Really thought I'd just leave."

Flustered, she brushed back the loose strands of hair around her face. "Of course not. I was coming to lock the door."

Pushing off the wall, walking slowly toward her, I smiled. "Liar. It's written all your face."

"You're playing games."

"I'm not. I've never been more serious."

"Tricking me into thinking you left—"

"I wanted you to feel it."

Her brows knitted together. "Feel what?"

"The panic I felt when you got off my boat that morning and walked away."

Her lips fell open. Saying nothing, she shifted from one bare foot to the other. "That was…" Her voice trailed away.

"It was supposed to be one night, but I can't forget." I finished for her.

Her eyes looked everywhere but at me. Tension cramped the condo and I knew she was uncomfortable, but I wasn't going to stop.

"Do you ever think about me, Nora?" I whispered. "About that night?"

"I—" She cleared her throat.

Pulling her hand up, I pressed a kiss to the back of it. "I do. All the time. I can barely sleep in my bed without remembering when you were in it."

"Don't do this," she whispered, a plea in her tone.

"Do what?" I questioned, soft. "Tell you the truth?"

Yanking her hand free of mine, she shuffled back a few steps, putting distance between us. "Drag fantasy into reality!" she cried.

My mouth turned down. "What?"

"What we had that night… it was incredible, like a fantasy come alive. When I got on that plane and left, I honestly thought I'd never see you again."

My stomach tightened. "It was enough for you, that one night?"

Nora glanced at me, so much emotion and unspoken words dancing in her eyes. When she looked away, emptiness clawed deep inside me.

Nearly blind with desperation, I grabbed her, pulling her close to my chest. "Say it. Say everything you're trying to keep in."

A shuddering breath escaped raggedly from her lips. "Every time it rains, I think of you. Some nights, I dream about you and walk around the entire next day like a zombie trying to clutch onto the way that dream made me feel."

Heart pounding, I gave her a small shake. "What else?"

My God, if she stopped talking, if she stopped saying everything I wanted to hear, I would go crazy. I knew what an addict felt like in that moment, how crazed and desperate they must be for a fix. But it wasn't drugs I so frantically wanted... It was her.

Her stare reached out to mine, and I let her see how badly I wanted to know what she was thinking.

"I still have your shirts. Both of them. I wear them to bed. I wear them to class. Val makes fun of me because she thinks I traded one obsession for another."

Puzzled, I asked with my eyes what she meant.

Averting her gaze, she answered, "Alan for you."

Grasping her chin, I said, "I wanted to erase him from your mind."

"You did," Nora confessed. "All that's left is you."

"You haven't let anyone else touch you since then?"

She shook her head.

Closing my eyes, I let out a relieved breath. I'd been torturing myself thinking about some other man's hands against her skin.

"I thought that night was it. But now you're here. Now…"

"Now?" I prompted.

"Now I'm confused. I can't tell what's real."

A sound ripped from my throat, and tenderness washed over me. Her ponytail was in my way, so I slid out the hair band to run my fingers through the long, blond strands. "This is real. I'm real."

Moving closer and dropping her forehead in the center of my chest, she wound her arms around my waist. After a few minutes of standing in my embrace, I felt her draw in a deep breath, then slowly step away.

"This isn't real, Carter. It can't be."

Nora

Reality vs. Fantasy Observation #2:
Fantasy is a great escape. But eventually, you have to go back to reality.

Carter was a juxtaposition.

On one hand, he was commanding and resolve nearly gushed from his pores. The power he yielded seemed to be endless, as he could practically snap a finger, raise a fist, or make a call, and whatever he wanted was done.

These things would have made him intimidating. But he wasn't. Not to me.

I didn't think I'd ever met a man who allowed his emotions to play so easily over his face. Sometimes when I was with Carter, it was like his heart beat right there in his eyes. My entire body hummed beneath his touch, and though he was incredibly powerful, I never felt as though he would hurt me. Instead, his strength would shield me.

It was intoxicating. *He* was intoxicating.

This was exactly why this wasn't real. Getting caught up in a fantasy would only cause pain.

"Explain what you mean," he said, watching me intensely, almost as if he were trying to anticipate my every move.

Walking farther into the condo, gazing around at the gray walls, modern furniture, and new flat-screen mounted against the wall, I raised my hands, gesturing to it all. "Look at this," I implored before going over to the large sliders that offered a view of the beach.

"You don't like the condo?"

Spinning, I gave him a look. "Of course I like it! I already said that."

His face twisted in confusion, and I almost laughed. For someone so damn intelligent, he was adorably clueless.

"This is not the kind of apartment an intern is provided for a summer job," I deadpanned.

Carter straightened, displeasure making his onyx eyes narrow.

Holding up my hand, I continued. "You said it yourself. Ansoft doesn't even take on interns, yet here I am."

"You're different," he muttered.

"How do you know that?" I shot back.

He frowned. "Nora."

"I'm serious, Carter. We had one night together. A night that was so amazing that neither of us could move on. It was too good to be true. Do you know what that means?"

He opened his lips, but I barreled on. "It means that it was. It means all of this... That's just you trying to recreate the fantasy we had."

His eyes flashed, and he started toward me. Evading his hands, I backed up against the doors, which felt cold against my T-shirt.

"You don't really know me. I don't really know you. But look at what you've done. You brought me out here and set me up in an apartment with a job. You have people watching me to get details because you don't know any of them yourself."

"That's not why—"

"I know you have like a bazillion dollars. You're used to getting everything and anything you want. I made you think you could have me because I came so willingly to you that night on the island. But you can't buy me, Carter. I'm not for sale."

Blowing out a breath and rubbing the back of his neck, he laughed under his breath. "That's what you think?"

I made a sound of agreement and nodded once.

He stepped forward, near-black eyes glittering and completely focused on me. My heart jumped, a feeling of being preyed upon skittering down my spine. He looked like a tiger on the prowl for something to dominate. "You think I'm a fantasy," he rumbled, still moving forward.

I started backward, only to realize I couldn't escape. My back was already against the glass, and there was nowhere else to go.

In a last attempt for space, I darted left, but he was faster. His large palm slapped against the glass, blocking my retreat. Dodging right, he did the same, effectively caging me in with his body.

"Carter," I whispered, my voice shaky and weak.

With a low sniff, he grabbed my wrist, dragging it up between our bodies. Placing his hand over mine, he pressed my palm flat against his chest. The silk of his shirt was smooth and soft. Beneath the thin material, his body was solid and strong.

"Doesn't this feel real to you?" he whispered, rubbing his hand over mine, creating even more friction between us.

My eyes closed, body sinking against the window.

"My heart doesn't beat this fast for anyone else," he said, his voice right against my ear.

It was beating fast, thumping exactly the way mine did.

"True, I might not know that much about you. But I know more than you think."

"What your spies reported to you doesn't count."

"Yes, it does," he refuted. "But I'm not talking about that stuff."

Leaning my head against the window, I gazed at him. "Then what?"

"I know you aren't the kind of girl to have a one-night stand. You're the kind of girl who wants stability, who wants to give her heart to one man. You're so loyal you put up with more than you should, trying to make it work when clearly it doesn't. You're the kind of friend who thinks of her friends when you visit places you think they might like. You have a lot of pride. You want to take care of yourself even though, in my opinion, you need someone to look after you."

"Hey!" I gasped.

Chuckling, he bounced his finger on the tip of my nose. "You can't walk in heels, confrontation makes your stomach hurt, and you are a talented graphic designer." Another thought brightened his eyes, and his smile was quick. "Oh, and you have a terrible sense of direction."

"I do not," I muttered.

"When you were lost at sea, you swam *away* from land…"

How annoying. "That was *one* time."

Amusement shone in his eyes. "Am I wrong?"

"You don't know that much," I mumbled, trying to slip past.

His arm shot out, blocking me again. "I also know the way your face looks when I make you come, how your lips feel rubbing against mine, and that the sound of my name on your lips is my favorite."

My knees started wobbling. If my heart beat any more irregularly, I was going to pass out. Using both hands, I shoved at his chest, pushing him back enough for me to skirt by. Pressing a hand against my heart, I willed it to calm. Seeing my melty margarita, I veered toward it to take a hearty drink.

"Why didn't you just call? Why did you have to go this far?" I slapped the cup down on the table and flung my arm out toward the condo.

The air around him changed, growing slightly cooler. The heart-on-his-sleeve man I was looking at slowly closed up and become the powerful millionaire. "In my world, people don't just come when you call. In my world, you have to give something to get something."

"That's not real, Carter," I said, feeling my heart break a little.

"Maybe not for you. But for me, it's all too real."

I wanted to go to him, so much so that my body started forward before my head gave the command. The second I realized what I was doing, I stopped and wrung my hands.

He sighed. "Still don't have that yet."

I glanced up. "Huh?"

"You don't trust me yet."

"I do," I countered, suddenly feeling a thousand pounds of guilt.

His half smile was a little sad, but it was also full of hope. "It's okay, good girl. We'll get there."

"Why do you keep calling me that?" I muttered. "I'm not a dog."

His smile was all joy this time around, and my heart whispered that he could call me that forever if it made him look that way. "Because you are everything good in this wicked world."

Oh, it was hard not to fall under his spell. So hard not to succumb. "I need real, Carter. Something I can trust."

He studied me for long minutes, as though he had an exam. "Can you accept that reality for me is a little different than reality for you?"

"How?"

"Stay," he ordered, and I swear he could have been a siren washed in straight from the sea. I was so ready, so... motivated to do anything he asked of me that it scared me.

Clinging to that fear, I used it as a shield. "How can I do that? I feel like you lured me here. I feel like I don't know you as much as you know me."

"Stay," he said again. "I'll let you get to know me, and I'll get to know you."

"People at work are already gossiping. They've seen us together, and then the president came down and gave me his card, told me to call him personally if I needed anything."

"Bryan is a friend of mine."

"They took me to lunch as a welcome party, but really, they just wanted to know about me and you."

His eyes closed briefly, reopened, and focused wholly on me. "That's not going to change. I won't pretend I don't have feelings for you. People will probably try to get through you to me. I'll try and protect you the best I can."

"Is that why you had someone follow me to lunch?"

He inclined his head. "Partly. The other part of me was jealous I couldn't eat with you."

I liked that he didn't try to hide the fact that everyone would be talking about us. I liked that he held my stare when he said people would try to use me. It made me wonder what his life was really like... if everyone treated him this way.

How lonely he must be.

"Did you hire me because you want to sleep with me?"

His teeth flashed. They were white, but not perfectly straight, something I really liked about him. *Mr. Fantasy isn't perfect after all.*

"I think we already proved I don't have to give you a job to sleep with you."

"Maybe in a fantasy world," I rebuked. "We're in the real world now." Gazing around, I took in my fancy surroundings. "Sort of."

"All right." He raised his hands in surrender. My stomach dipped because it seemed he was about to concede he really did just want sex. "Let's take it off the table."

"What?"

"No sex. We won't have sex while you're interning at Ansoft."

My mouth dropped open. Was he for real?

Chuckling, he closed the distance between us. "If you want me to keep to that, stop looking so damn cute all the time." Tenderly, his eyes roamed my face and his thumb brushed over my cheekbone, trailing so his fingers could tug on the ends of my hair.

Stomach fluttering madly, I stepped back. "You just said no sex."

His eyes glistened. "I didn't say I wouldn't touch you."

"You could have just said you didn't hire me to sleep with me," I muttered, suddenly feeling disgruntled.

He laughed. "Would you have believed me?"

"Maybe." My shoulders slumped. "People will still think that, though."

"Does it matter what other people think if you know the truth?"

No. I shook my head.

"I have faith that your ability as a designer will show everyone at Ansoft why I hired you."

I felt those words in my heart. Like it was putty in his hand. "You do?" I whispered, basking quietly beneath his praise.

"I do."

Making the decision, I nodded. "I'll stay on at Ansoft. I really like your company. It's cool."

Another sunny smile lit his face.

"But I'll find my own place," I added and went to the bedroom for my suitcase.

He caught me in the doorway, arms wrapping around me from behind. "I can't let you do that."

I spun out of his arms. "You don't have a choice."

"I'm not paying for this place. Ansoft is. It's a business expense."

I made a face. "You own Ansoft."

Scrubbing a hand over his face, he cursed low. "Do you have to be so damn difficult?"

"Yes!"

"You said you wanted reality," he said, harsh, holding his arms wide, "This *is* reality. My reality."

"Let me make something clear." Straightening my back, I faced him head on. "I'm not here because of your money. I don't want anything from you in that sense. I'm staying here because I want to learn at Ansoft and because…"

"Because," he prompted, longing in his eyes.

Unable to hold back, I went to him, taking his hand. "Because I want to see you. I want to know you. But I don't care about your money or how many things you own."

"I think you are the first person I've met in a very long time who's said that and actually meant it," he whispered.

I squeezed his hand. "I do mean it. That's why I'll find my own place."

"I can't let you do that."

Yanking my hand away, I fumed. "Look, buddy. I might want to do everything you tell me, but I sure as hell won't!"

Wait. I don't think that came out right.

Confused by my own mouth, I didn't see him coming. Before I knew it, Carter was on me, pressing me against the bedroom wall.

"What are you doing?" I asked, pushing at him.

"Didn't you hear anything I said before?" he asked, impervious to my struggle.

151

I went still. "What?"

"When people find out I'm spending time with you, it will put a target on your back. They'll try to use you. Maybe even hurt you…" His eyes shadowed. Pulling away, he moved across the room. "Fuck. Maybe I shouldn't have brought you here."

"I don't understand."

"I know you don't." His voice was gentle. Then, much quieter, speaking to himself, he said, "This is why I live alone on an island."

I took a step toward him. "You think people will hurt me to get to you?"

"I can't be sure. That's why I said I'll protect you."

When I said nothing, he turned back. "That's why you need to stay here, in this building. It's secure. I won't have to worry about you when I'm not around. You might not like my money very much, Nora, but it's part of me. I won't let my girlfriend live somewhere that I don't deem safe."

"There are plenty of safe—"

"I said no." His tone was quiet but final.

"Who said I was your girlfriend?" I shot out because, really, I had nothing else.

His eyebrow lifted. "You're not?"

"No."

"No sex. No relationship status," he listed. "What exactly do I get?"

Pursing my lips, I held out my hand. "Give me your phone."

Clearly curious, he pulled out his phone from his back pocket and handed it over. I took it, swiped the screen, and made a face. "I need your fingerprint."

Holding up his hand, he smiled. "Come get it."

Crossing to him, I went to take his hand. Abruptly, he held it up overhead and out of my reach.

"Hey!" I complained, reaching unsuccessfully for it.

"Ah," he teased. "Is this why you wear heels?"

"Carter!" I bellowed.

Laughing, he pulled his hand down so I could use his thumb to unlock the device. Once it was open, I gave him a squinty-eyed scowl and turned my back.

"What are you doing?" he asked from behind.

"You really should be more careful who you hand your phone over to."

His body wrapped around mine from behind, and momentarily, my eyes drifted closed because the way he felt against me was so right. "I trust you," he whispered.

My heart skipped a beat. I wasn't sure why, but that seemed like something he didn't often say.

Going back to work, I called up his contacts and added my phone number. "What should I label myself as…?" I wondered out loud.

"Not my girlfriend." He complained.

I giggled.

"Are you laughing?" He was incredulous. When I didn't answer, he poked me in the ribs and made me squeal.

"No!" I squirmed. "I'm not."

"Put Good Girl," he ordered.

I stuck out my tongue. "People will think your dog is calling you."

"Hey, no one looks at my phone but me."

"I don't like it."

We argued about it for so long the screen went dark and I needed his thumbprint all over again.

"Ugh!" I said, annoyed.

"Let me see," he said, taking it from my hands and holding it in front of us. Unlocking the screen, he put an emoji where the name was supposed to go.

It was a heart.

"I like it," he declared, putting it back into his pocket.

I couldn't even argue because I liked it, too.

Carter stepped back. "That's all I get, huh? Your phone number?"

"I don't give that out to just anyone."

He didn't seem very impressed.

"I'll stay in the apartment."

His eyes flared. "Really?"

I nodded. "It seems to be really important to you."

One second, I was on my own two feet, and the next, I was in his arms, against his chest. "Thank you," he whispered into my hair.

Smiling against him, I marveled and how good it felt to be in his arms. When at last I pulled back, I shook my finger at him. "But no more stalking."

I could tell he was about to argue, but I had to put my foot down.

"I mean it, Carter. I said I wanted real. In real life, if you want to know something about someone, you ask them."

"Fine." He pouted.

Sticking out my hand between us, I said, "Let's shake on it."

Taking my hand, he used it to pull me forward. I fell into his chest with an, "*Oomph.*"

"I don't shake with you."

Before I could ask what he meant, his lips brushed over mine. Once. Twice. And then a third time for a lingering soft kiss. It wasn't some soul-crushing kiss that was provocative and toe curling... but *damn*.

I guess, with Carter, it didn't have to be.

When he pulled his head back, my eyes fluttered open, meeting his. "You make me so nervous," I confessed.

The corners of his eyes crinkled with his smile. "I have no idea why. I've already seen you naked."

Because he was getting into my heart... a place that was so much more vulnerable than my naked body.

Leaning down, Carter pressed a kiss to the tip of my nose, almost as if he could read my thoughts. "You gonna let me spend the night?" he asked, giving me a roguish grin.

Hands on my hips, I scolded him. "Didn't you say no sex?"

"Who said anything about sex?" he asked innocently. "You have a filthy mind."

I started to kick him, but he swept me off my feet and into his arms. "I told you I'd convince you to stay."

Maybe I shouldn't have been so easy to convince, but truthfully, I wanted to stay and so I would.

Twenty-Two

Carter

The sun was barely rising when consistent knocking echoed through the condo. The intrusive sound startled Nora, making her bolt upright with a forceful gasp.

Her hand fell onto my bare chest, patting rapidly. "Carter," she whispered.

An unintelligible sound forced its way out of my throat. Automatically, I reached for her hand to hold it.

The knocking continued, making Nora's fingers tighten around mine. "What is that?" she asked, freaked out.

Dragging my free hand down the length of her back, I wondered what the fuck I'd been thinking last night when I told her we wouldn't have sex.

"Carter!" She fussed again, clutching the blankets against her chest as though she were caught naked when, really, she was dressed in shorts and a tank top.

"Someone's knocking on the door," I murmured, still half asleep and thinking about sex.

"Its five thirty in the morning!"

156

That woke me up. Pushing into a sitting position, I glanced toward the bedroom door. "Did you give anyone your address?"

Chewing her lower lip, she shook her head.

Using my thumb and forefinger, I pulled her abused lip out of her mouth. "Don't do that."

"Aren't you worried?" she asked, pointing toward the sound.

"It's probably just Aaron," I muttered, tossing the blankets back and getting out of bed.

"Does Aaron usually come looking for you at five thirty in the morning?"

"Aaron is usually with me at this hour."

She made a surprised sound, and I looked over my shoulder. "We share an apartment in Miami."

Her mouth formed a little O as she nodded.

Picking up the white jeans discarded on the floor, I made my way to the door, tugging them on as I went. Nora's feet smacked on the wood as she rushed behind. The knocking ceased, but it was only because the person on the other side of the door realized there was a doorbell.

I really wasn't sure which was worse—the pounding or the chiming.

Instinctively, I put an arm out, blocking her from stepping up beside me. "Stay there while I answer."

"I thought you said this building was safe," Nora retorted.

"Smart men don't take chances."

I went ahead while she muttered about going to live in the ghetto, making me smile. Unlatching the lock and yanking open the door, I scowled, expecting to see Aaron standing there. "This better be good—"

"Ah!" a woman screeched.

157

I drew back, startled. "Do you have to be so noisy at five a.m.?"

"I thought this was Nora's apartment," the woman exclaimed. Suspicion clouded her face, and she held up a giant bag. "Who are you? Nora!"

"Valerie?" Nora queried, hearing her friend waking up half the building. She rushed up behind me, pulling the door wide. "Val!"

"Step aside, Nora. I've got this," her very loud friend declared, swinging all her attention back to me while heaving the bag backward.

"What do you think—" I began, but Nora skirted around, blocking me with her body.

At the same time, the overstuffed bag came barreling at me like a battering ram. Hastily, I spun, blocking Nora from the hit. My body jolted when it struck me in the center of the back.

Nora gasped. "Valerie! Stop!"

With her body still in the shelter of mine, she looked around the curtain of hair over her shoulder, concern in her eyes. "Are you okay?"

"I'll live."

Ripping out of my grasp, Nora spun around, but I grabbed her back just in case her BFF wasn't done.

Valerie froze, the bag falling on the ground between us as a stunned look crossed her face. "Mr. Fantasy?"

"What?" Confusion made me squint.

"Oh crap! I hit Mr. Fantasy!" Valerie's eyes transferred to mine, then back to Nora. "He *slept* over already?" she whispered really loudly, as if I wouldn't be able to hear. "Damn, you said he was good, but seriously, *that* good?"

"Oh my God!" Nora gasped. "Shut up!" Turning to me with bright-pink cheeks and shy eyes, she said, "I never said that."

I smiled.

"I guess we don't call you Mr. Fantasy for nothing, eh?" Val quipped, smacking me in the stomach on her way into the apartment.

"I don't call you that," Nora rushed out.

Bending at the waist, I lowered until we were eye to eye. Bashful, she looked everywhere but at my face. "Is that where you got all this reality vs. fantasy stuff?" I teased.

"Make yourself useful and bring in her bag," Nora ordered, then rushed away after her friend.

Grabbing the bag, I followed at a much slower speed.

"Valerie, what are you doing here?" Nora asked, following her friend into the living room.

Not answering at first, Val went to the sliders, pulling back the curtains to look out over the view. "Um, wow," she commented, staring out.

"Valerie," Nora demanded.

Still gazing out the window, she said, "I missed you. I decided to come for a visit."

Nora glanced around at me, and I shrugged.

"I thought you were in Atlanta. What about your internship?" She pressed.

"Umm," Valerie said, her voice quieter than I'd ever heard. "I don't think it's going to work out."

Distressed, Nora rushed to her side. "Val." She put a hand on her friend's arm.

A sob burst out, and her shoulders began to shake.

Nora seemed stunned, momentarily gaping at Valerie like her crying this way was something she rarely saw. Banking that shock, Nora lunged forward to hug her.

Leaving the bag by the bar, I went into the kitchen to put on some coffee while Nora comforted her distraught friend.

"Here, sit down." Nora cajoled, guiding a sniffling Val to the sofa. "What happened?"

"It's so embarrassing," she replied, voice watery.

"There isn't anything you can't tell me."

My stomach dipped a little with my girl's words, wondering if they extended to all the people in her life or just her best friend.

"I'll, ah, just go grab a shower," I told them, leaving the coffee to brew and heading toward the bedroom.

"My boss hit on me," Valerie announced.

My feet paused on the wood.

"What?" Nora gasped.

"It's not like I'm that uptight, you know?" Val's voice wobbled. "I mean, if it was just innocent flirting or a couple lewd comments, I could ignore…"

"What did he do?" Nora asked quietly.

"That jerk called me into his office and handed me a hotel room key. When I asked him what it was for, he told me it was my job as an intern to make sure all his needs were met."

"Are you serious?" Nora exclaimed, outraged.

"As a heart attack," Val vowed. "I told him he was crazy, and he told me all I had to do was go there when he called." She took a deep breath and continued. "Then he pushed me onto his desk and stuck his tongue in my mouth."

"Oh my God!" Nora leapt up off the couch and paced. One of the thin straps of her tank slipped over her shoulder, but she didn't notice.

Anger ignited within me as I imagined some dick with a superiority complex putting his hands on Nora that way.

"What did you do?" she demanded.

"I bit him," Val retorted. Proudly adding, "Drew blood."

I smirked. "Should have kicked him in the balls, too."

Both women turned to look at me, their eyes widening as if they hadn't realized I was still there.

Valerie pursed her lips. "Isn't it like sacrilege for guys to tell women to attack other guys' junk?"

"Some guys don't deserve the dick between their legs," I deadpanned.

"I like you," Val mused. She looked at Nora. "I like him."

Nora wasn't about to be deterred from the conversation. "What happened next?"

"I quit, and he told me if I told anyone what happened, he would make sure I never got another internship."

"He can't do that!"

"I'm pretty sure Jon Max can do that," Valerie stated.

I knew that name. "Jon Max, the CEO of Intex?"

Valerie stiffened. "You know him?"

I shrugged. "I've met him a couple times."

Surging to her feet, she worried. "Please don't say anything. I graduate next year. I don't want something like this following me to interviews or hurting my chances at a decent job."

"You're majoring in the same thing as Nora?" I asked.

She nodded. "Please?"

"How many other girls has he done this to?" I wondered, gazing toward the windows.

"I know it's so cowardly of me to keep quiet," Valerie wailed, plopping back on the couch.

Good Lord, she was loud.

"I just feel so gross, you know? He said no one would believe me anyway and he'd tell everyone I came on to him and when he fired me, I made up a sexual harassment story to save face."

Nora hugged her friend, which muffled the loudest of her sobs. Still patting her back, Nora lifted her eyes to me.

"I won't say anything." I promised.

Val lifted her head. "Really?"

I nodded.

Blowing out a shaky breath, she said, "Thank you."

I didn't agree with keeping quiet on this, but getting into a lengthy discussion about it would just end badly. Clearly, this girl was traumatized, and forcing the issue would only make it worse.

"I couldn't stay there. I had to get out." Valerie peeked up at me. "I didn't realize you'd have... company."

"Of course you had to come," Nora protested, hugging her again. "What about your internship?" she asked, pulling back.

Valerie shrugged. "It's too late to get one now. I'll just have to get one next year."

"Stay here," I announced.

Both women looked at me.

"What?" Nora asked.

"I'll give you an internship at Ansoft. You can stay here with Nora."

Valerie lurched to her feet. "What?"

Getting up from the couch, Nora came toward me. "Really?"

"Sure. We could use the help, and I'm sure you'd like having a friend here."

It might make all the assholes whispering behind your back easier to bear.

"I can't let you do this," Nora said quietly, a meaningful look in her eyes.

Great. Did this count as some of her fantasy shit? "I didn't ask for permission."

Her blue eyes narrowed, and it made me a little excited.

"Oh, come on, Nor!" Valerie pouted, reminding me we weren't alone. "If I don't do this, I'll never get a job after graduation."

"It's not a paid internship." I cautioned. Just because I was paying Nora didn't mean I had to pay Val, too. Besides, I was letting her stay in the condo.

"I don't care!" Val insisted. Rushing over, she grabbed Nora's hand. "Pleeease, Nor! Then I can stay here with you. Summer in Miami!"

"We're here to work!" Nora exclaimed, sounding like the good girl I knew.

Val divided a look between me and her friend. "You must have *worked* really late last night."

I laughed.

Nora snatched her hand away and glared.

Relenting, Valerie apologized. "I won't say anything else about you two. I swear."

Nora rolled her eyes. "Yeah, right."

Valerie must have heard something I didn't because she squealed and hugged her while bouncing up and down. Nora laughed. Then Valerie rushed over, throwing her arms around me for a hug. "Thank you! Thank you, Mr. Fantasy."

"His name is Carter." Nora scolded.

Valerie pulled back. "Right. Carter."

"Mr. Anders at work." I reminded her.

"Of course." She agreed.

"You can start tomorrow." I wondered what Bryan would say about this. Turning toward the bedroom once more, I declared, "I'm taking a shower."

"Thank you, again!" Valerie yelled after me. "And I forgive you for looking better in white jeans than most women ever will!"

Nora made a choked sound, and I laughed.

I was tugging on my shirt when Nora let herself into the bedroom, pushing the door shut behind her. "Carter?"

"I'm right here." I turned, a smile breaking over my face when I saw she was standing just inside the room with her hand over her eyes.

"You've already seen it." I reminded her.

"That was different," she explained. "That was the fantasy."

Chuckling, I went to her, moving so close I knew she could feel my body heat. Tensing, she moved to take a step back, but I grasped her wrist, holding her in place.

"Are you naked?" she whispered.

"Why don't you look and see?" I whispered back.

"I can't!"

This girl was so amusing. "I can assure you I'm just as good in reality as I was in the fantasy."

Her deeply indrawn breath was very satisfying.

Allowing my hips to guide, I went closer until my body brushed along hers. At first, she stiffened, but realizing I was fully dressed, the hand not covering her eyes shot out and patted my shoulder and chest, confirming I was wearing a shirt.

Two of the fingers covering her eyes shifted, and her blue irises peeked through.

"You have an odd sense of foreplay."

"I thought you were taking a shower," she said, exasperated.

"I'll just shower at home. I have to change for the office anyway."

"You're leaving?"

"My apartment is on the top floor."

Her eyes rounded. "You live in this building?"

"Did you think I would move you anywhere else?"

She blinked. I could see the wheels in her head going full speed. Leaning down, pressing my lips to her forehead, I murmured, "Stop overthinking."

"Carter." Her head fell back, lips drifting closed.

I kissed her briefly before pulling away. A small sound of protest vibrated the back of her throat.

"Wait for me. I'll walk to work with you."

"'Kay."

Right before I left the room, her arms wrapped around my waist from behind. Freezing at the unexpected embrace, I glanced down, watching her hands lock together while feeling her body press against mine.

"Thank you," she said sincerely. "For what you're doing for Val."

"Just for Val?" I asked.

"For me, too."

"You're welcome," I answered, gruff.

Valerie was in the kitchen, pouring a mug of coffee, when I left the bedroom and headed for the door. "Want some?" she offered.

"I'm going home to change for work."

"I really appreciate what you're doing."

"It's just an internship," I replied, feeling awkward about all the thanks I was getting. Girls were emotional. And noisy.

"Not for me."

Halting at her tone, I turned back.

"For Nora. Thank you for coming back for her."

Is that what I'd done, come back for her?

"Alan messed her up for a while. Then she spent that night with you..." She stopped talking for a moment, clearing her throat. "Anyway, she deserves to be happy, and I think you could do that for her."

Seeing her cell lying on the counter close by, I picked it up and handed it to her. She unlocked it and handed it back without another word. Quickly, I typed in my number, saving it to her contacts.

"Call me if you ever need anything. Or if Nora does." Pausing, I added, "Especially Nora."

Val gazed at me as if she were trying to solve an equation. "You like her, right?"

"Would I do all this if I didn't?"

Shrugging a single shoulder, Val replied, "Maybe this is just some kind of game you rich boys like to play."

"The only kind of games I play are the ones I create."

"All right, then." Val conceded, turning back to the coffee.

The front door was almost closed behind me when I felt it tug out of my grasp. Stopping in the hall, I turned back. Valerie was standing there, her eyes still red from crying.

"One more thing." She smiled. "I might have let the man who harassed me off the hook, but don't think I won't come for you if you do her wrong."

"Fair enough." I shrugged.

I waited to smile until she shut the door. Having Valerie here might take some getting used to, but I was grateful Nora had an ally.

Twenty-Three

Nora

I was at my desk when the design team manager poked his head out his office door and yelled my name.

Everyone in the room looked at me with varying degrees of interest. Clearly, it wasn't every day the manager bellowed for someone.

Standing up and smoothing out my skirt, I answered, "Yes?"

"CEO wants you in his office."

The buzz of whispers and gasps of wonder nearly made me dizzy. "I'm sorry, what?" I asked, hoping I'd heard wrong.

"The CEO called down. He wants you to go to his office."

A million responses formed on my tongue:

But why?

What in the world does he want now?

I told him not to talk to me at work!

He's doing this on purpose!

I didn't say any of those things. I was a pillar of respectability and composure, so naturally, all I replied with was, "Yes, sir."

The second our manager disappeared inside his office, I was swarmed.

"Why'd he call for you?"

"I've never been up to the top floor."

"Did you know Mr. Anders before coming to work here?"

"What did you do wrong?"

Tucking my cell into the pocket of my skirt (seriously, pockets in skirts are the best!) and slipping around my curious co-workers, I started for the elevator.

"She's totally sleeping with him," one of the women whispered as I walked away.

My abrupt turn startled the gossipers, and they all glanced up. "My personal life is none of your concern," I stated coolly. "And since this is an office and we are within working hours, I would assume that whatever it is the CEO wants is work related."

Composed and respectable Nora – 1

Nosy, loose-lipped Molly – 0

PS: Her name isn't actually Molly.

"Of course." Jerry quickly agreed, taking in everyone else standing around, including the women wanting to know about the state of my sex life. "I'm sure she will tell us the work-related news when she comes back. Everyone back to work."

Suppressing an eye roll, I went on my way.

Fuming the entire way up to the top floor, I practiced exactly what I was going to say to Carter and how I would march confidently into his office the second I stepped out of this box.

Ding! The doors slid open to reveal a very modern, sparkling executive floor. All my bravado must have stayed with loose-lipped Molly, because the I walked carefully across the lobby while gazing at the giant Ansoft sign behind the large counter.

The assistants looked up. Both had their hair pulled back and both wore a headset.

Seeing me, their eyes widened and they stood.

"Ms. Williams," the one on the right greeted. "Mr. Anders is waiting for you." Using her arm, she directed me as if we were on some tour of the White House instead of heading down the hall where my boyfriend sat.

Wait. He is not my boyfriend.

A man in a black suit with a black dress shirt beneath stood outside Carter's closed office door. I recognized him as one of the men with Carter when he'd met me in the downstairs lobby.

He was just standing there, hands clasped in front of him, staring at the wall. *My God, he must be bored out of his mind! Is that what he does all day long?*

"Hello," I said, giving him a little wave.

Startled, his eyes slid to me, and I smiled bigger.

"I like your suit. Black is a good color on you."

He looked like a deer caught in a pair of headlights, eyes round and expression blank yet slightly panicked. Putting a fist to his lips, he cleared his throat. "Good morning, ma'am."

"Nora." I corrected.

The assistant made a noise, reminding me she was there. Glancing at her, I noted her displeasure that I was talking to this man. What a stodgy tour guide.

"The CEO is waiting," she prompted, as though I were farting around out here and not following along behind her.

"I'll just go in." I started forward, but she clotheslined me.

Okay, maybe that was a little dramatic. It's not like I fell, but I could have!

Gasping a little, I stared at her. "Didn't you just tell me to hurry up?"

"I'll need to make sure he's ready for you," she retorted, prim.

She had to be in her late twenties, but she was acting like a sixty-year-old grump.

Some of my composure was beginning to slip. People were seriously testing me today. "I'm pretty sure he's ready since he's the one who called for me."

The security guard snickered, which made the assistant bristle, shooting him a dirty look. Instantly, the snicker turned into a cough.

She turned away to rap on the door twice. The guard winked at me.

Opening the door so only she could walk through, she made sure I was stuck behind her. "Ms. Williams is here," she announced.

"Carter, why did you call me up here if I was going to have to jump through all these hoops to get in the door?" I yelled around the woman.

Deep laughter rolled through the office. At my side, the security guard snickered some more.

"Let her in, Meghan," Carter's smooth voice directed.

Meghan turned, giving me a full smirk. My eyes narrowed. Marching past her, I gave Carter a look. It was a good intimidating one, because he called the assistant back.

"Yes, Mr. Anders?" she replied sweetly, glancing at me out of the corner of her eye.

Oh, so before, it was CEO, and now it was Mr. Anders, was it? Someone was trying to prove hierarchy with the boss here.

"Whenever Ms. Williams comes up here to see me, there's no need to escort her. She can come and go as she pleases."

Meghan's red-painted lips dropped.

Glee rang through me.

"But, Mr.—"

"That will be all." He dismissed her swiftly.

Meghan turned to leave, shooting daggers at me the second her back was turned to the boss. I smiled sweetly, resisting the urge to stick my tongue out.

The second the door latched behind her, I dropped the smile. "Just what do you think you're doing calling me up here like this?" Planting my fists on my hips, I scowled.

Damn, he looked good sitting behind his desk. The sun was at his back, making him look like some kind of dark angel, and the smirk on his face only made me want to sit in his lap.

A deep laugh rumbled from my left, making me spin.

"Oh! Hi," I said timidly.

The man stood from the leather club chair, and something seemed very familiar about him.

"Have we met?" I asked.

"This is Aaron. He was on the boat the night we fished you out of the ocean."

"Well, this is embarrassing," I muttered, glancing away while trying to will my face not to turn bright red. Remembering what Carter said about Aaron this morning and that they were roommates, I forgot about my previous embarrassment. "Wait, Aaron the butler?"

Aaron seemed to find that pretty funny. "The butler?"

"Well, you brought me tea. And food." I defended. Looking around at Carter, I asked, "Didn't you call him the butler that night?"

Aaron raised his brows. "Did he now?"

Carter quickly said, "You hit your head that night. I think you aren't remembering correctly."

My lips parted so I could tell him he was full of baloney, but Carter spoke first.

"Aaron is my right-hand man and head of security,"

"That's how you explain our relationship?" Aaron put a hand to his chest. "I'm wounded."

"He told me this morning that you live together here in Miami."

"Roommates!" Carter barked. "I said we were roommates!"

Both Aaron and I turned away from Carter completely.

"Who exactly are you, then?" I asked. Then, without thinking, I added, "Why did I think you were much older than you are?"

Aaron threw back his head and laughed. "Like what you see, do you?" His eyes twinkled as he teased me.

"Ah, that is… umm," I stuttered. "That isn't what I meant."

"When I told you to get a love life, I didn't mean to step into mine," Carter intoned, dropping an arm over my shoulders.

"That night on the boat is such a blur. I guess when Carter called you a butler, I just pictured someone…" Not finishing the sentence, I glanced away.

"Old?" he teased.

I looked up at Carter for help. His dark eyes were filled with amusement. "Aaron works for me, but he's family. Get used to his face. If you ever need anything and I'm not around, go to him."

Aaron nodded immediately, all humor leaving his demeanor. "Nice to officially meet you."

I murmured a greeting, then glanced toward the door. "You're head of security? So is that man outside the door one of your guards?"

Carter nodded, then yelled, "Knox, get in here!"

The man dressed all in black slipped into the room. "Yeah, boss?"

"Come meet Nora."

"We met outside."

Knox's lips tugged into a smile. "Much to Meghan's displeasure."

"Was I not supposed to talk to you?" I asked Knox. "Does she think this is the palace in England, where the guards can't even blink?"

All three men laughed.

"I'm being serious," I muttered.

"She runs a tight ship," Carter explained.

If that's what he wanted to call it….

"Nice to meet you, Nora. I hope we get to see more of you around here," Knox told me.

"Why are all of you hitting on my woman?" Carter spat, irritated.

"I'm not your woman." I reminded him.

"Make him work for it," Aaron whispered.

"Get out!" Carter bellowed. "Everyone out!"

Knox and Aaron shuffled out, not affronted in the least by Carter's rude tone. After a moment, I shuffled along behind them, wondering why I had to come here at all.

"Where do you think you're going?" Carter asked.

I pointed at the door. "You just told everyone to get out."

"You aren't everyone."

"Oh."

Carter's long legs closed the distance between us so easily. The closer he got, the more uneven my heart thumped. Sliding his arm around my waist, he continued until my back came against the wall and he was leaning into me, braced on one arm.

"You interested in Aaron?" His voice was throaty and low.

That darkness in his stare was practically bottomless. I felt I could tumble through it forever and never hit bottom. He had this way of looking at me like he somehow swallowed me whole and there was nothing in the entire universe but him and me, together.

"W-what?" I asked, realizing he'd spoken.

Even though his head tilted, his eyes remained focused, hypnotizing me. "Aaron," he drawled slowly.

Blinking, I tried to focus, pulling my eyes away from his. "All I wanted to know was how old he was," I answered, exasperated.

"He's thirty. Too old for you."

"I'm not interested."

His free hand stroked over the side of my head, fingers dragging through the length of my hair. He leaned so close his nose nudged my cheek. "Did I tell you how pretty you look today?"

Chills raced up my spine and my stomach flipped over. "When we walked to work."

"I think you got prettier since then."

Ducking my head, I smiled. Oh, the charm. He oozed it more than an athlete sweated. It would be quite alarming if it wasn't so freaking powerful.

Lips grazed the top of my cheekbone, then my ear.

"Carter," I whispered.

"I love when you say that," he murmured.

Reaching up to grasp his wrist, I pulled it down, willing myself to untangle from his web. "Did you seriously call me up here to introduce me to your security?"

Pressing another light kiss to my cheek, he pulled away, striding across the room to his desk. "Of course not. We have work to do."

It took me a little longer to shake off our closeness before I could trail after him. "My work is in the design department."

"Not anymore."

"What now?" I grumbled.

Chuckling under his breath, he sat down, hit a few keys on his keyboard, and crooked a finger at me. "Come over here,"

"There'd better be actual work on that monitor and not some pretend nonsense." I warned, going around the massive worktop to look at what he gestured to. "Whoa," I crooned. "That's incredible." Stepping closer, I leaned in to take in all the detail and realism in the graphic that honestly was so incredible, in some lights, I might think it was a photograph of a real person.

"You like it?"

Sweeping my eyes over it again and again, I took in the angles and colors, every detail I could. "Of course." Tearing my stare away, I looked at him. "You don't?"

"No, I like it. I just feel like it needs something. I wanted to hear your opinion."

Straightening, I drew back. "Is this for a new game you're creating?"

He nodded.

"Why ask me? I'm just an intern."

Turning in his chair, he snatched my hand and pulled me into his lap.

Squeaking, I pushed at his shoulders to try and get up. "We're at work!"

"No one's in here."

"But—"

"Knox is at the door."

"I—"

Tapping the monitor, he reminded me. "Tell me what you think."

It was a rendering of a character so polished you couldn't even call it a mock-up. He was dressed head to toe in some kind of gear that I knew could likely be upgraded and changed to fit each user. A bow and arrow was strapped to his back, a dagger on his thigh. The combat boots on his feet were incredibly realistic and detailed.

The eyes were so lifelike it was almost creepy, as if I expected them to follow me whenever I moved. With that thought, I did, swaying back and forth in Carter's lap, just trying to catch it watching me.

"It really is incredible," I murmured, still studying it. "The design team did this?"

"Not the one you're with downstairs."

"There are two design teams here?"

"So you don't think it needs anything?" he prompted, drawing my attention back to the rendering.

"I see what you mean," I mused, thoughtful.

"Really?" He seemed surprised. "Everyone else thinks it's perfect."

I bolted upright. "That's it," I said, glancing at him. "What?"

"It's too perfect."

Carter made a sound. "Do you play games on your phone? On a console at home?"

"Does *Candy Smash* count?" I asked weakly.

His eyes rolled. "You should be embarrassed."

I shrugged.

Incredulous, his eyes widened. "You seriously don't play any of my games? Have any of my apps?"

"No." I apologized.

Snatching a tablet off his desk, he pulled me back into his chest, wrapping his arms around me and holding up the screen so we could both see it. With a few taps, the Ansoft logo appeared, along with some music. Seconds later, a game loaded and exploded to life.

"This is currently our most downloaded game," he told me, his voice right against my ear. Gooseflesh rippled across my skin, and the muscles in my lower belly tightened. "It's basically where you try and survive an outbreak of zombies."

At that second, a zombie lurched out of the dark in the corner of the screen. The sick, realistic sound it made as it grabbed for its prey made me jump.

"Holy crap!" I exclaimed, still plastered against Carter. "That scared me."

More zombies materialized, and the avatar he was controlling stepped into the light and began taking them out with very graphic headshots. A moment later, he ran out of bullets, and I watched him throw the gun at an approaching attacker and pull a sword off his back.

The severed head of the zombie rolled across the floor, and blood splattered the screen, making me jerk again, worried it would splash me.

"You came up with this?" I glanced between him and the game.

"It's not a new concept at all," he said, still playing. "I think just about every company has done zombies. Here." He pulled the tablet closer to me. "You give it a try."

"I don't know how to do play."

"Like this," he said patiently, leaning around me a little more. Hands covering mine, he brought them to the screen and showed me the basics of the game, softly guiding me with his voice.

Eventually, he pulled his hands back, letting them drift down into my lap, watching as I attempted to play.

"Ooh!" I squealed when a zombie ran at me. Screeching, I hit about a million things at once, not really knowing what the heck I was doing. "Eeee," I screeched again, partially turning away as I hit the zombie and blood splattered everywhere.

Carter laughed against my ear.

"Help me!" I demanded. "I'm about to die!"

"You got this." He encouraged. "Hit this." He pointed toward the screen.

I did, and the zombie dropped to convulse on the ground. Picking up a gun I'd found, I took the shot and killed him.

"I did it!" I exclaimed, sitting forward. Turning in his lap, beaming, I asked, "Did you see? I killed it."

Smiling, he tugged the ends of my hair. "I saw."

A bunch of horrible sounds and a blood-curdling scream burst from the game, and I looked just in time to see myself getting attacked and eaten alive.

Oh, it was gross. Pulling it away from my eyes, I buried my face in his neck. "This is the most downloaded game you have?" I complained, my voice muffled against his skin. "But it's so graphic."

"That's why it's the most popular. People love it."

I made a sound, and silent laughter shook his shoulders. Taking the tablet from my hands, he slid it on his desk. I started to sit up, but his palm settled between my shoulder blades, pressing me against him.

"Just give me another minute," he requested softly.

He smelled good, like something expensive and fresh. It reminded me of the island where we spent that first night together. My body melted when he started rubbing my back with firm but gentle strokes.

"Don't you have any other games that won't give me nightmares?"

The indulgence in his tone when he replied made me feel spoiled, even though it was such a simple thing. "I'll download some on your phone. You should get familiar with them."

I nodded against him, and he continued to stroke my back. "This is the market, though. The more realistic, the better. *Zero* is going to blow everything else away."

"*Zero?*"

Carter gestured to the monitor. "Our new game. I've been working on it for a long time."

"Ahh," I mused, understanding.

"You said you thought this looked too perfect?" he prompted. "After seeing another one of our games, do you still feel the same?"

Tugging my lower lip into my mouth, I looked over the rendering on the monitor before picking up the tablet and examining the game we'd been playing.

Decisively, I nodded. "Definitely."

"The objective here was to make it the best on the market, so technically, it should be perfect."

"But it has to also be believable. You know what they say about perfection," I goaded.

"What's that?"

"If something seems to good to be true—"

"It probably is." He finished for me.

"Exactly."

"But this is a fantasy game." A smirk transformed his face.

"Fantasy seems to be your specialty," I teased, ruffling his hair.

"And you're stuck in reality."

"I'm not stuck here. I live here. There's a difference."

"Explain," Carter demanded, clearly becoming frustrated.

"People want an escape, right? That's why they play your games, to go places they couldn't go otherwise. To be a hero when they feel powerless in the real world."

"In some sense," he allowed.

"What you need, then, is a little more reality in your fantasy," I explained, tapping on the monitor. "Make it just a little less perfect so it will feel more real... more..."

"Relatable."

Snapping my fingers, I said, "Exactly."

"If we made it more relatable, wouldn't we just end up making it crappier?" Carter mused.

"I'm not talking about changing the quality of the game. Or the upgrades or whatever else you have going on there." Waving a hand at the image, I carried on. "I just mean tweak certain things so it feels more… lived in. More real."

"For example?"

"Like the boots. Make the shoelaces slightly crooked." I pointed. "Add smudges of dirt on the toe and make the soles look slightly worn, like this person has actually been running around in a fight."

Carter nodded, eyes still locked on the artwork.

"And when the character gets hurt, don't just take away a few of their health hearts."

Dark eyes shifted to me. "Health hearts?"

"You know, when you get hit or fall off a cliff or something, it takes away some of the hearts at the top of the screen. When you run out, you die."

He blinked. Blinked again. "Zero doesn't have health hearts."

I brightened. "Maybe you should add some."

"No."

"It's a good idea," I argued.

"When I take you out in public, don't talk gaming with anyone else, okay, baby? It will embarrass me."

My heart tumbled, and I was rendered speechless… *He called me baby.*

"What else you got besides health hearts?" he asked, grimacing.

My insides were still fluttering, and he didn't even seem to notice he'd tilted my world on its side with a single word. "Besides health hearts…" I repeated, trying to jumpstart my brain.

I needed to put some distance between us. Sitting in his lap, having his eyes on me, his hands… hearing his voice so close—it was causing some sort of short circuit in my brain.

I popped up so fast he wasn't able to pull me back, though he tried. Evading his attempt, I backed up, knocking a dish of paperclips off the desk. They spilled everywhere, and the dish broke into several pieces.

"Oh no!" Dropping to my knees, I tried to scoop up as many as I could at once.

"Leave it," Carter commanded, but I kept working.

"*Ow!*" I yanked my hand back the instant I felt the sting of pain in my finger. Staring, I watched blood well beneath the sliced skin, then slowly drip down my finger.

Twenty-Four

Carter

"If you ever do that again, you're going to see a side of me most people don't like." I fumed, slamming open the lid of the first aid kit.

"I'm sorry." Nora sulked. "I'll replace the dish I knocked over."

I threw the Band-aid I was holding down into the kit. "I don't give a damn about that dish!"

Her eyes widened, confusion swimming in her unshed tears.

Cursing low, I laid a hand on her thigh. "I meant hurt yourself."

"I didn't do it on purpose!" she insisted.

Turning back, I grabbed the bandage. "Well, if you would have listened when I told you to leave it, you wouldn't be bleeding!"

"It's just a little cut."

I grunted, lifting the gauze I'd been holding on it to help soak up the blood. The second I pulled it back, the cut started oozing red once more.

"See!" I yelled, pointing at her injury.

Her lower lip wobbled. "It stings."

184

"Fuck." Gently dabbing at the blood, I reached around for some antiseptic spray that claimed it also relieved the burning of cuts and scrapes.

"Hold my arm." I cajoled, putting her free hand on my forearm and giving it a pat. "If it hurts, just squeeze."

Nora turned her face away as I sprayed. "Okay?"

"Mm-hmm," she said, still turned away.

Smiling, I worked quickly, making sure it was clean and slowing the bleeding to barely anything. "Almost done," I whispered while ripping open a large bandage.

Her hand tightened a little on my arm, and a rush of tenderness flowed through me.

Once the cut was covered, I pressed a soft kiss to the injury. Lowering her hand, I saw she was watching me.

"Thank you," she whispered, eyes wide.

"What were you thinking, leaping out of my lap like that?" I asked, still irritated she'd gotten hurt.

Her eyes skirted away.

Grasping her chin and forcing her head back around, I ordered, "Tell me."

"I can't think when I'm that close to you." Her words rushed out, nearly tripping over each other. "You make me all nervous and dizzy. I couldn't concentrate."

Up until this point, I'd managed to hold back. Up until this point, I sort of enjoyed the sweet torture of anticipating her.

That was over.

Unfolding from where I was kneeling, my body covered hers, pushing her back into the leather chair until we both reclined and she was deliciously beneath me.

Stunned by the sudden switch, Nora gasped and gripped my shoulders.

My lips sought hers, knowing exactly where they belonged, exactly where the sweet spot of her surrender was found. The fingers gripping my shoulders, so tight, fell away so her arms could wind around my neck. Sliding an arm between her and the chair, I lifted so our bodies melded together.

Without lifting my lips even once, I kissed until my brain when silent, until the gnawing hunger I felt for her was muted. Rocking closer, my tongue stroked over hers, and my body began to hum. I'd been waiting for this. I'd been waiting for this from the moment she stepped off my boat and walked away dressed in nothing but my shirt.

It was supposed to be one night. She was supposed to be a fantasy.

She was real. Blissfully, maddeningly real.

Nora's hands danced up the back of my neck, fingers delving into my hair, and I felt the fine tremor in her body.

Gentling the kiss, I pulled back slowly, still so enraptured with her I couldn't go far. Resting my forehead against hers, we both panted, her arms at her sides.

"I've been waiting for you to do that," she quipped, voice shaky.

I answered with my lips, kissing her cheek, her nose, then each of her eyelids.

The phone on my desk buzzed, then buzzed again.

Forcing myself up, I strode over to snatch up the line. "What?" I growled.

"Your twelve o'clock is here," Meghan informed.

"Give me a few minutes," I ordered, then hung up.

Nora was packing up the first aid kit, cheeks flushed and lips red from my assault. "I should go back to work."

"I have a meeting now, but come back up here after lunch."

"I have to work," she hissed.

"We aren't finished with the meeting we were having."

"That's because someone can't keep his hands to himself."

"You like it."

"I'm going to get lunch," she declared, instead of agreeing.

"I mean it, good girl. I want you back up here. We have a project to discuss."

I wanted to kiss her again. I wanted to pull that skirt up around her waist—

"Stop looking at me like that," she snapped.

"Like what?"

"Like I'm a snack."

"You said it was lunchtime," I teased.

"Aren't you coming?" She was puzzled.

"Meeting."

Her face fell as though she were disappointed. "But you have to eat."

I very rarely ate lunch. I was usually too busy. I was about to inform her of that fact when she brightened.

"Want me to bring you something back?"

"You'd do that for me?" I asked, my heart fluttering. I wasn't used to someone worrying about whether or not I ate.

"What do you want?"

"Surprise me."

"Okay, but no complaining." She warned, heading for the door.

"Aren't you forgetting something?" I called, starting toward her.

"Oh, no, you don't," she said, holding her hands out as if she were trying to ward off the plague. "Keep those hands and lips away from me."

Her blue skirt billowed out around her when she spun and yanked open the door. "Knox!" she bellowed.

My security rushed forward, eyes wide. "What is it? Boss?" He worried, glancing past her to where I stood.

"You're worrying about *him*? I was calling you to protect me!" Jabbing a finger in my direction, she said, "He's a menace."

Knox didn't know how to react. No one ever accused me of such things, and if they did, it was Knox's job to show *them* the door. He didn't move, though, which told me he had a soft spot for her.

"He's my guard, not yours." My voice was dry.

Nora paused beside him, laying her hand on his shoulder. "I thought we were friends." With a sigh of disappointment, she left us there, staring after her.

"Where'd you meet her again?" Knox asked once he'd recovered.

Chuckling, I went around my desk to clean up the broken glass. "You can send in my appointment."

Twenty-Five

Nora

Going back to my desk after lunch was a no-go. There was no way I wanted to face off with the staff just waiting to ask me a thousand questions about why Carter had called me to his office.

Plus, I'd have to tell them I was going right back up there the second I put my purse down.

Down in the lobby, security waved me through with barely a passing glance at the ID around my neck. It had been that way since Carter showed up my second day and personally escorted me in. And then did so again today.

Now the guards practically tripped over themselves making a path for me to glide through easily, which honestly made me all kinds of uncomfortable.

It wasn't as if I were some VIP. I was an intern, for crying out loud. And it was embarrassing as hell. All the other employees saw the way I walked right into the building with a free pass. Some stared openly, others whispered, and some flushed with anger because a lowly newbie intern was somehow getting better treatment than them.

Carter wasn't kidding when he said this wasn't going to be easy.

Stepping onto the elevator with a drink carrier filled with iced coffees and a white paper bag holding Carter's lunch, I hit the top floor. Turning so I could see the woman who'd stepped in right after me, I smiled. "What floor?"

She started to speak, then saw the illuminated button I'd just pushed on the panel. Her eyes widened a little, then refocused on me. "You're the new intern?"

My stomach dipped, but I forced my smile to remain bright. "It's nice to meet you. Which floor can I press for you?"

"Oh, um, never mind. I'll take the next car," she hurried to say and rushed out of the elevator as if I smelled.

Wrinkling my nose, I called after her, "There's plenty of room in here!"

"You go on ahead," she insisted, waving her hand at me.

Another female employee approached, heading for the elevator. Putting my arm out, I kept the doors open for her.

The woman who'd just run off grabbed her arm and tugged her back. She leaned in and whispered something, making the other lady cut me a glance. I knew just by the look on her face that she wasn't getting into this elevator.

"The ice in my coffee is melting," I said, stepping back so the doors could close. "No one likes watered-down coffee."

Both women stared as the doors closed between us. The second I was alone, I sagged against the back wall and let out a breath. *Good Lord.* What kind of reputation did Carter have?

I couldn't figure out if these people were jealous or scared.

Maybe it was both.

Carter definitely had a cool dominance about him. He was shrewd and clearly had a brilliant mind. If he didn't, he wouldn't be the CEO of a million-dollar company at such a young age. He was also extremely good-looking and mysterious. He took a helicopter to work, for crying out loud. I wondered if people here knew when he flew off, it was to his own private island.

How many women in this company have tried to get close to him? Did any of them succeed?

Jealousy tore into me when I thought of any woman sitting in his lap the way I had this morning. "You better slow your roll, Nor," I muttered to myself. "You're only here for the summer. Carter is not boyfriend material. He's just a fantasy."

The elevator slowed, so I straightened off the wall and adjusted my bag, which I'd slung across my body so I wouldn't have to fuss with it while I carried the coffee and food. Stepping out, I also turned to make sure my skirt was around me properly and not exposing anything it shouldn't.

Steeling myself for another private escort from Carter's guard dog, aka Meghan, I looked toward the counter.

Meghan and her desk mate weren't alone. The steady clapping of my heels against the floor ceased abruptly. Squeezing my eyes closed and drawing in a deep breath, I reopened them, refocusing exactly where they'd been.

Ugh. He was still there.

Meghan's partner noticed me just standing there staring and gave me an odd look. I knew she was going to call me out, and honestly, it made me panic. Turning back toward the elevator, fully intending to rush away, I hit a roadblock. The doors had already closed.

Damn.

Slowly, I pivoted back around. Lifting my chin, I dared the unnamed assistant to say anything and started walking again, confidence in my steps.

Maybe he wouldn't notice.

Maybe he would—

"Ms. Williams, you're back."

I nearly winced when she basically shot an arrow at me with her words.

Have I mentioned how much I disliked Meghan?

Only a hundred times? Make this one hundred and one.

I'd almost made it past him—almost past the entire counter to escape into the hall. It was a good try. A solid effort.

Plastering yet another friendly work smile on my lips, I turned toward them, avoiding looking in his direction. "I'm just heading back for another meeting."

"Nora?" Alan questioned as if it'd been years since he'd seen me last.

I wish.

Sliding a glance at my ex, who was not supposed to be in Miami, I kept my voice cool and uninterested. "Alan. What are you doing here?"

"You know him?" Meghan butted in. She seemed shocked, and that grated on me. Did she think I lived in a box before this?

It's not like I wanted to talk to Alan, but I didn't particularly want to talk to Meghan either. And here I was, looking at them both.

"Yes!" Alan claimed instantaneously.

Put off by his enthusiasm, I drew back slightly.

"Tell her, Nora. Tell her who I am." His eyes were hopeful, and he nodded at me as though I were a toddler that needed encouragement to wash my hands after I peed.

Pursing my lips, I debated. I could handle this in one of two ways:

1.) As composed and respectable Nora.

2.) As a jilted ex-girlfriend.

It had been nice knowing the respectable and composed Nora Williams, but she was just too heavy a burden to bear.

"This is Alan. He's a two-timing cheater who uses force when his shriveling charm doesn't work. Better call security."

I started to walk away.

I could have sworn I heard both assistants gasp.

"Nora!" Alan roared.

For a second, a split second, I was back in my apartment and his hands were on me. The sinister look that sometimes darkened his eyes made my stomach knot.

I turned around bravely. "Oh, and one more thing…"

Alan relaxed, rolling his shoulders back like he knew I had come to my senses.

"That tie doesn't match your suit."

A sound of shock ripped out of him, but I didn't look back. I was afraid I'd see that look. The one that sometimes scared me.

"You can't just go back there!" Meghan demanded.

I rolled my eyes.

She chased after me, frankly sounding like a clown on stilts. "Ms. Williams!" Her hand closed around my upper arm.

Wrenching free, I gave her a look. "Don't touch me."

"You—"

"Didn't you hear the CEO earlier?" I asked. "He said I could come and go as I pleased."

"I still need to notify him that you're here."

"You're going to see the CEO?" Alan erupted, shock lacing his tone.

My God! Why was he still here? "Go home, Alan. I don't want you here."

Sliding a cool glance at Meghan, I practically dared her to challenge me. "Go ahead. Call him."

"Nora!" Alan shouted after me.

My footsteps sped up and I turned the corner, the ice in the coffees banging against the sides of the cups.

Seeing commotion, Knox straightened and turned. "Ma'am—"

"Wait a minute, Nora!" Alan bellowed, his voice much closer than before.

"I told you, you can't go back there!"

"I know her. She'll explain to Mr. Anders."

Wrinkling my nose, I turned to see both Meghan and Alan stumble to a stop close by. "You're here to see Carter?"

Something passed behind his eyes, and suddenly, it felt like I hadn't swallowed the last of my lunch and it was sitting like a bolder in the middle of my throat. Involuntarily, I stepped back.

Clearing his throat, Alan smiled. It was a fake smile, one that relayed that he thought I was stupid enough to think it was genuine.

"I came to see you, of course. Couldn't stand how we left things. When Dad found out where I was going, he asked me to have a meeting with the CEO."

"You didn't make an appointment," Meghan said, surly.

What in the world was Alan trying to have a meeting with Carter for? Why was his father involved? These people were giving me a headache.

"I told you Nora will vouch for me." Alan turned back to me. "I didn't realize you knew the CEO."

"I'm an intern here." I sniffed.

"Shouldn't you be in the mailroom?"

Meghan snickered.

Something inside me slumped. Why did Alan always want to make me feel miniscule? And why did it always work?

It isn't going to work anymore.

"Is there a problem?" Knox asked from his post in front of the door.

"They were all just leaving," I told the guard.

"I need to see Anders," Alan insisted.

"That's *Mr.* Anders to you," Meghan quipped.

"Nor," Alan implored, "ask your boss to talk to me. Please."

"No."

Locking my eyes on Carter's door, I moved ahead. Suddenly, the urge to see him was intensified. I wanted to escape right into his arms.

I was so focused on where I was going that I didn't pay attention to who I'd left behind.

Big. Mistake.

Commotion erupted at my back. The sheer force of it seemed to knock me unsteady. Or maybe I'd already been that way from the moment I stepped off the elevator and saw Alan.

Either way, I wasn't prepared when Alan's palm smacked against my back, his fingers bunching my shirt to pull me back. I cried out and spun away. The bag of food I was carrying slapped against the floor so I could grip the drink carrier with both hands. Alan let me go, but the momentum of my own movements caused me to lurch to the side. Grabbing my arm, he pulled me upright, making me fall into his chest.

One of the coffees in the carrier smashed into his chest, the lid popping off, and iced brew spilled down his white dress shirt.

"Ahh!" he yelled, shoving me and the coffee away.

My ankle turned, the heel under it slipping out from beneath me. The drink carrier went flying one way, and I went the other.

Ice exploded everywhere, and coffee splattered everything it could possibly touch.

My ankle throbbed and so did the heel of my hand, which took the brunt of my fall.

"Nora!" Knox worried, abandoning his post in front of the door and rushing to help me.

"I'm okay," I told him, pushing up with my uninjured hand. There was so much coffee and ice everywhere that I slid, falling back onto the floor with a slap.

"I got you," the guard said, reaching down to help me up.

"You ruined this suit!" Alan fumed, glancing up from the mess on his clothes.

That sinister look I sometimes saw in his eyes? It was there in full force.

"Are you kidding me right now?" Knox demanded. Reaching up, he hit a button on something by his ear. "Send me some backup," he muttered.

The look in Alan's eyes hardened. "Did you just call security on me?" He switched from the guard to me. It was everything I could do not to wilt beneath the hostility. "You're going to let him call security on me? This is *your* fault!"

Alan lunged, and a panicked sound ripped out of me.

Knox stepped in front of me, using his honed body like a shield. "Don't come any closer." He warned, his voice deadly calm.

Peeking around him, I looked to see where Meghan was. She was standing on the outskirts of the mess, staring at all of us in shock.

"You trying to block me from my girlfriend?" Alan questioned.

"I am *not* your girlfriend!" I yelled, cradling my hand against my chest.

Alan tried to rush around Knox, but the guard flipped him onto his back in record time.

Carter's office door ripped open, and footsteps came rushing out.

"What the fuck is going—" Aaron yelled.

Carter's voice cut him off. "Nora!"

The second I saw him, all the bravado I'd been clinging to itched to abandon me.

He was beside me in two seconds, hands hovering around me. "You're covered in coffee..." he said, bewildered. Then he looked down. "Where are your shoes?"

"They fell off." I gestured to my heels, which were scattered apart, one of them lying in a puddle of coffee.

"What's the situation?" Aaron asked Knox.

"I'm suing!" Alan announced, getting up off the floor. "This is assault!"

"Man, sit down." Knox snarled, glancing around at me. "Are you okay?"

I nodded, and Carter's eyes narrowed.

More men in black suits rushed into the hallway, eyes searching for a situation that needed diffused.

Knox gestured to Alan. "This intruder tried to gain unauthorized access to the CEO and manhandled Ms. Williams."

"He did what?" Carter's growl rumbled along the entire hallway, making everyone pause.

"Pushed her right over. Made her spill the coffee she was carrying."

"She spilled it first!" Alan rebuked.

"Because you grabbed me!" I hollered back.

Alan took a menacing step toward me.

Carter stepped in front of me, and Aaron and Knox stepped in front of him.

"Move," Carter told his men.

Without a single moment's hesitation, both guards stepped to the side, offering Carter a clear path to Alan.

"You shove her?"

"Anders," Alan said, "I'm here on behalf—"

"I asked you if you shoved her." Carter's voice didn't rise a single decibel.

All the men in the hallway glanced away as if they were nervous.

"She's just an intern!" Alan burst out. "I've come about busi—"

He didn't get to finish his sentence because Carter plowed a steady fist right into the side of his jaw. A low grunt forced its way out of Alan, and he fell into a heap on the floor, splashing the coffee around some more.

Tucking his hands into his pants pocket, Carter stood over him and said, "Don't ever show your face in this building again."

Bracing myself, I expected to see the same kind of evil look Alan often wore when Carter turned and looked at me.

It wasn't that at all.

That lump in my throat began to dissolve when the tenderness in Carter's eyes caressed me. The tailored, deep-green suit jacket he wore slid off his wide shoulders, and he tucked it around me.

"Meghan," he called without looking away. "Call someone to clean all this up. And get Ms. Williams a new iced coffee."

I gasped. "Your lunch!" His jacket flapped around my back when I rushed forward to where the paper bag lay. It was soaked with spilled coffee.

I frowned. "Oh no," I crooned, holding it up for him to see. "It's ruined."

"You brought him lunch?" Alan asked from the floor.

Everyone ignored him.

"I'll eat later. Come on," he beckoned, crooking a finger at me.

"I can order you lunch," Meghan offered. Just hearing the little bit of glee in her tone made me want to kick Alan in both his knees.

"Just get Nora the coffee," Carter replied.

Yes, it gave me immense satisfaction.

"Wait!" I gasped again. "There were four coffees."

"Four?" Carter asked.

"One for me, you, Knox, and Aaron."

"You got me a coffee?" Knox and Aaron asked simultaneously.

I nodded. Turning toward Knox, I added, "I got you a sandwich, too, but it's ruined."

"Ma'am, you got me lunch?"

"You've been standing there all day." I looked at Carter, disgruntled. "You have to feed him."

Knox laughed.

"He eats," Carter muttered.

I started to cross my arms over my chest, but the action made me wince and I pulled back.

Carter's attention on me intensified. I felt the weight of it from where I stood. Putting his arm around my waist, he guided me toward his office. "Make it four coffees, Meghan!"

"Nora!" Alan wailed.

I leaned into Carter a little farther, and the hand at my waist tightened.

"Let me go!" Alan yelled. Sounds of him struggling gave me no satisfaction whatsoever. Just before we disappeared into the safety of the CEO's office, Alan gave it one final shot. "I'm Lewis Regal's son!"

Stiffening, Carter turned back. "What?"

"I'm here to talk about *Zero*."

Carter paused but quickly covered it with a rude sound. "You expect me to believe that Lewis Regal's son just walked up in my building like this, assaulted my intern, and made a huge commotion?"

"I was provoked," Alan spat.

"Where's your ID?" Aaron questioned, suspicious.

Alan shook off the guards' hands and reached into his suit to pull out an ID. He tried coming forward to show Carter, but the guards all stepped between them.

Aaron checked the ID. "So you have the same last name. That proves nothing."

"Tell them, Nora."

A beat of silence blasted the hall as everyone turned to look at me. I wasn't concerned with anyone but Carter.

Sensing how uncomfortable I was, he moved closer and reached out to tuck his jacket around me a little tighter. "You know him?"

I felt like I was choking again, like there was a rock stuck in my throat.

"Yes," I finally admitted. "I know him. He is Lewis Regal's son."

"How do you know him?" Carter questioned.

"Can we go in your office?" I kept my voice down.

His eyes searched mine, looking for an answer I hadn't yet spoken.

"Please," I whispered. I felt sticky and cold from the coffee, my hand still stung, and worse than anything physical, my emotions felt like they'd been run over by a freight train.

"Yeah," he allowed, resting a hand on my back.

My relief lasted all of one second.

"She's my girlfriend!" Alan announced.

Twenty-Six

Carter

"Watch him," I ordered before escorting Nora into my office and shutting the door. Her shoulders jerked from the abrupt slam of the door, making me angrier than I already was.

This was a side of her I hadn't seen before. Timid. Leary.

Does it mean she's guilty? Does it mean she knows she got caught in a lie?

Gripping the edges of my jacket, she turned. Her face was pale, clothes wet, and her shoes were still lost out in the hall.

"Carter…" She started, a slight tremble in her voice.

I couldn't do it. Despite experience and the lack of trust I had in almost everyone, I couldn't bring myself to think the worst of her.

My voice was harsher when I cut her off. "Don't say anything." Lifting her off the ground and into my arms, I strode across the spacious office toward the back.

I felt her stare, though I didn't look down. Carrying her into the adjoining full bathroom, I carefully sat her on the wide white vanity top beside the sink. Grabbing a small white towel, dousing it in warm water, I knelt level with her bare feet.

"I'll do that." She huffed, pulling up her foot.

Snatching it back, I cleaned off her feet, which were splattered with coffee. The instant my hand closed around her right ankle, she sucked in a breath and jerked back.

"You're hurt?" I demanded.

"I just twisted it."

"Am I going to have to make it company policy that women stop wearing heels to work?" She probably thought it was an idle threat. It wasn't. I'd told the damn woman to stop wearing them, but she refused to listen. "Now just look at yourself," I muttered.

"What?"

"Nothing." My voice was gruff. Gently lifting her foot, I checked the ankle for any signs of swelling or bruising. It was slightly red on the outside, but I didn't see a bruise. "I'll take you to the hospital."

I stood to lift her back into my arms, but she pushed me back.

"I don't need a hospital! I fell over in my stupid shoes. I'm fine."

Lifting an eyebrow, I challenged her. "And what about that wrist you keep cradling?"

Both hands fell into her lap. "I just sprained it when I fell. It's fine, too."

The wet rag hit the inside of the sink with a forceful slap when I threw it down.

Nora jumped, and my blood boiled.

"You scared of me?"

"No!" The denial was swift and sure. Her blue eyes were round and sincere when they met mine. "I'm not. I swear. I know you wouldn't hurt me. I'm just a little jumpy. I'm sorry."

Grasping her chin and holding her stare, I said, "Don't ever apologize for something you didn't do. Not even to me." Releasing her face, I held out my hand. "Let me see your wrist."

Once it was in my hand, I got mad all over again. Nora wasn't the smallest person I'd ever met, but she wasn't big either. And though I admired her tough, independent streak, to me, she was fragile. She was someone I felt compelled to protect. It really pissed me off that someone had done this to her right outside my office while I'd been sitting inside, clueless.

"It's fine." She assured me, rotating it to prove it. "It's just a little sore."

Cupping her hand to still her movements, I stared down at the underside of her wrist, thinking how delicate her skin appeared. Carefully wrapping my free hand around her forearm, I dragged my thumb up and down the inside of her wrist, caressing the injury I couldn't see.

My heart beat irregularly, pounding suddenly, abruptly skipping beats, then slowing to a thud. Breathing seemed to take heavy effort, and honestly, I really just wanted to kiss her.

Instead, I stood there against the vanity, between her legs, focusing all my energy down on where I held her, hoping even half of what I was feeling transferred from my caress to ripple across her skin.

The sound of her swallowing echoed in my ears. Her hand settled over mine. "It's not true."

I looked up. "No?"

"Of course not. There hasn't been anyone. Not a single man since the night I spent with you."

The way those words made me feel almost hurt. The relief, the validation, and the building tension between us all mixed together, making my stomach drop. Pulling my hands away from hers, I cupped her face and laid my lips against her forehead.

"You just taught me something," I whispered.

Abruptly, her head pulled back, so I slipped my hand around to cup it, stopping it from hitting the mirror.

"You really need to be more careful," I scolded.

Unconcerned that she'd nearly brained herself, she asked, "I taught you something?"

I nodded.

"Tell me!"

"I guess I'm the kind of man who would steal someone else's girl."

Her mouth fell open. That stupefied expression of hers hit me every single time. Chuckling, I dipped quickly, pecking a kiss to the corner of her open lips.

Smacking my shoulder, Nora said, "What did you just say?"

My stare lingered on her when I pulled back. "The second that dickbag out there declared you were his, all I could think about was hauling your ass into this office and demanding that you never see him again."

"Dickbag?" she echoed.

"Never before would I ever have messed around with someone else's woman. But you aren't anyone else's good girl. You're mine."

"I am?"

Nodding, I guaranteed her. "You are, and I will steal you away if I have to."

I loved it when she whispered, sort of like her voice was a secret only I knew. "You don't have to steal me away."

Hooking my hands behind her knees, I dragged her over the counter until she nearly fell off the edge. Stopping her with my body and planting both palms on the counter on either side of her hips, I kissed her.

Stroking my tongue into her mouth, seeking hers, and dancing while our lips created the music. Breathing in deeply without lifting my head, both arms closed around her so there wasn't a single millimeter of space between our chests.

The second her legs wound around my hips, the blood in my veins pounded, the tips of my ears grew hot, and we melted even closer.

Out in my office, my cell went off. I ignored it, turning my head so I could kiss her just as deeply from another angle.

Nora's fingers slid up my arm and gripped my shoulder. Pushing back just slightly, I chased her. Making a sound of protest, my body followed hers until we were kissing just as passionately as seconds ago.

"Anders!" someone familiar called from out in the office.

Nora squeaked and pulled back, clutching at me.

Keeping her in the circle of my arms, I yelled over my shoulder. "What?"

"You need to come deal with this."

Settling her farther back on the counter, I went to the bathroom door to look out at Aaron. "He sent his son, huh?"

Aaron shrugged.

"Bring him in." I decided.

Nora gasped.

Going back inside the bathroom, I shut the door this time. Against the wall was a black armoire. I pulled open a few drawers to grab a white T-shirt and some socks. Kneeling back in front of Nora, I put the socks on her bare feet.

"You can wear this shirt," I said, lifting the edge of my jacket to glance at her ruined top. "Use whatever you need in here to clean up."

"Why did you let him in here?"

Folding my arms over my chest, I regarded her. "Because his father has been trying everything he can think of to get his hands on *Zero*."

Her face wrinkled, lips turned down. "Why in the world would Lewis want a video game?"

She was on a first-name basis with Regal Tech's CEO?

"How do you know his son?" I asked. "Why would that douche out there even claim you were his girlfriend?"

"I used to be," she answered, catching me off guard.

"What?"

"That's Alan Regal," she explained.

Alan...

"Awful Alan." She tried again.

My upper lip curled. "That's your ex?" I pointed at the door. "That's the guy you went to the Caribbean to forget about?"

She nodded miserably.

My laugh was humorless. "I mean, I expected him to be a piece of work, but that guy?" Jealousy hammered at me from the inside out. "Lewis Regal's son?"

"When I first saw him today, I thought he was here because of me… but then I heard him trying to get past Meghan to see you."

My eyes narrowed. "You thought he was here for you?"

Her eyes lowered, fingers twisting in her lap. "He wasn't very happy with me when I refused to go to Boston with him."

The way she'd looked when I'd stepped into the hall earlier flashed through my mind. The way Knox was standing between her and her ex and the way he described what happened assaulted me.

I took a menacing step toward her. "He treat you like that all the time?"

"Not all the time," she refuted, but it was weak.

No wonder she'd looked timid and meek. It wasn't because she'd got caught lying. It was because that bastard ex of hers abused her.

"I'm going to kill him." I decided and moved stiffly to the door.

"No!" Nora exclaimed. When she leapt off the counter, her hiss of pain hit me between the shoulder blades.

Forgetting Regal, I turned back to see her massaging her ankle. Cursing low, I slid her back onto the counter.

"Please don't fight," she pleaded, grabbing my arms. "He's not worth it."

"Has he put his hands on you before?" I asked, barely controlling my temper.

"Please."

That was a yes. As if I didn't have enough reason to dislike Lewis Regal, now I had another. His son was a giant wanker.

"It's not as bad as you're thinking." Nora went on.

I laughed. "If it was anything like what I saw in the hallway, it's bad enough."

"He said he was here about business."

I grunted. "So?"

"So this isn't about me. What could Regal Tech possibly want with *Zero*?"

Voices out in my office made me look around. "We'll talk about it later."

"Wait!" Her fingers caught my shirt when I started away.

Glancing down, I lifted a brow.

"Just see what he wants, okay? Keep things about work. Whatever was between me and Alan ended a long time ago. I don't care about him."

It wasn't that simple. Thinking it could be was wishful.

"Clean up. I'll come get you when he's gone," I said, pressing a kiss against her temple.

Any other protest she made fell on deaf ears as I stepped out into the office.

Twenty-Seven

Nora

Reality vs. Fantasy Observation #3:
Fantasy is breaking up with a guy and thinking it's completely over.
Reality is learning you have really shit taste in men and he's a stalker.

First of all, this was a really nice bathroom.

Secondly, was Carter smoking crack?

Dude must be because he actually thought I would hide in the bathroom after he just so nonchalantly declared he was going to kill Alan.

Um, yeah right.

Not that I actually thought Carter would resort to murder, but as he proved earlier, he was not above throwing a punch. It was a damn good punch, too. Knocked Alan right on his ass. I admit it made me a little gleeful to see Alan go down like that.

Okay, a lot gleeful.

What were the odds that Alan would show up here like this? That he would somehow have business with

Ansoft? Alan didn't even work for his dad yet. Why would he be here on Regal Tech business?

The questions and curiosity were relentless.

After hopping down from the counter, I washed my face (bye-bye, makeup) and found a brush to run through my hair, pulling it back into a bun and securing it with a hair tie I found in my bag still slung across my body.

Once that was done, I exchanged my stained white blouse with the white T-shirt Carter gave me. Luckily, the blue skirt I was wearing was high-waisted, so I tucked in the shirt and rolled up the sleeves a bit to make it a little more polished.

Quickly wiping down my legs, I noticed a bit of coffee on my skirt, but there was nothing I could do about that. Wondering what was going on out there, I fished some tinted lip balm out of my bag, applying it to my lips and then the apples of my cheeks. I needed to hit the beach this weekend. I was not tan enough for Miami.

The second I was finished, I pulled open the bathroom door and nearly collided with Knox. "Ahh!" I pressed a hand to my chest.

Knox turned around with a concerned look in his eyes. "You okay, ma'am?"

"I told you to call me Nora," I said. "Why are you in front of the door like this?"

"'Cause you were in there," he said as if it were obvious.

"Oh, hey," I said, dropping my voice so no one else could hear. I felt oddly secure saying this now because the guard blocked everyone else from view. "Thank you. For before."

Holding out his fist between us, he smiled. "You ever need anything, just holler."

I bumped mine against his, and someone behind him cleared his throat. Knox stepped aside for Carter, who gave me an unreadable look.

"I said I'd come get you when we were done."

"I'm not hiding in the bathroom," I rebuked.

Meghan rapped on the door, then strolled right in without waiting for permission. I glared at her because she had so many rules regarding everyone else, but she seemed to think she could roll on in without any care in the world.

"I have the coffee you requested," she said, looking around for Carter. "And the crew is almost done cleaning up the hallway."

"Thank you, Meghan," Carter said, and she acted as though she'd been nominated for an Academy Award.

Beaming as though she'd soaked her face in too much highlighter, she stopped before Carter, retrieving an iced coffee and holding it out. "Just the way you like it."

Her eyes cut to me as if to say, *I know how he takes his coffee.*

I started at her, but Carter smoothly intercepted by angling himself between us. Plucking a coffee out of the holder, he passed it to me. I passed it to Knox.

"Thanks, Nora."

Carter slid his guard a glance, and Knox cleared his throat. "I mean, ma'am."

Carter handed me the next one, along with a couple creamers. "Go mix it at my desk," he said softly.

Meghan's eyes narrowed, and I smiled sweetly as I took the coffee over to Carter's desk.

"Should I send your shoes for cleaning?" Meghan asked. "They're a mess. You'll probably have to go home for the day."

"I can—"

"Throw them out."

A choked sound ripped out of my mouth. "No way! I like them."

"I'll get you some sneakers," he replied, then nodded at Meghan.

"Yes, sir."

"Who are you to be buying shoes for my—" Alan spoke up, the first time he'd said a word since I stepped out of the bathroom. I'd been avoiding looking at him, but now that he had spoken, it was hard to pretend he wasn't there.

"She's my intern." Carter cut in coolly, practically daring my ex to keep talking.

Meghan handed off the last iced coffee to Aaron, who was standing close to Alan (which I know was not a coincidence), then quietly left the office.

My ankle was throbbing, so I sat down in the closest chair and sighed.

"Nora!" Alan scolded. "What the hell are you doing?"

Alarmed, I sat up rigid. "What?"

"Interns don't sit in the CEO's chair."

Wincing, I glanced down. Yep, I was sitting in Carter's chair. Behind his desk.

I started to get up, but Carter subtly shook his head. "She's fine where she is."

"I apologize on her behalf," Alan said. "She needs some more training in—"

"It is not your place to tell me what my interns need and don't need." Carter's voice was cold.

Almost as if cued by his boss, Knox came over to stand beside the desk.

"Can we get back to the meeting, please?" Alan said, shifting into business mode.

"There is nothing more to talk about. I said no. *Zero* will remain with Ansoft."

"Once I walk out of here, so does the thirty million."

I nearly choked on my coffee. "Thirty million *dollars?*"

"Nora, tell your CEO he'd be crazy to turn down that kind of cash. Tell him that Regal Tech is a good company."

I felt my nose wrinkle. "Is Regal Tech getting into video games?"

Alan turned his full attention on me. "You know about *Zero?*"

Carter remained completely unchanged. Knox and Aaron remained completely unchanged. But everything felt different. No one but Alan even looked at me, but they didn't need to.

"Should I?" I asked. "I heard you mention it before, and I just assumed... Ansoft *is* a video game company."

Alan stood. His shirt was stained with coffee, and his tie still looked damp. "They develop apps and other simple technology as well." He goaded me, trying to see what I would say.

"If it's so simple, why can't your father just make whatever it is himself?"

Aaron chuckled beneath his breath, and Carter full on grinned.

Alan flushed, but his lips flattened. "Eh," he grunted. "Why am I even asking you? You're just an intern." Cocking his head to the side, he asked, "How'd you get hired here anyway? Ansoft doesn't take on interns."

"We are this summer." Carter spoke up. "Another one is joining us tomorrow."

No one reacted as if this were any kind of big news. I was impressed by Aaron and Knox and the two guards I didn't know standing just inside the door.

Dismissing me completely, Alan turned to Carter. "I think if we just sit down and go over some figures, maybe draw up—"

"No," Carter insisted. He didn't yell, but the finality of his tone was more effective.

"You're going to regret this, Anders," Alan threatened.

"Give your father my regards."

The guards stationed at the door moved forward, totally in sync, both reaching for one of Alan's arms.

He avoided them, making a rude sound. "I'm going."

"Allow us to see you out, Mr. Regal," Carter offered. "It's something we do for all our VIP guests."

Picking up my coffee, I took a sip, using it to conceal the urge I had to smile.

Just before exiting, Alan turned back, blue eyes finding mine. "I'll call you later."

My stomach twisted. "Please don't."

Carter made a motion with his head, and the men dragged Alan out, closing the door behind him.

Melting back into his chair, I groaned. "Thank goodness he's gone."

"Put a tail on him," Carter instructed Aaron. "I want to know exactly what he does until he's on a plane out of here."

Aaron pulled out his phone, and Carter came around the desk, picked up the landline, and hit a button. "Come to my office," he said, then hung up.

Turning to Knox, he gave out more orders. "Call a car, then escort Nora home. Make sure you take her all the way to the door of the apartment."

"What?" I exclaimed. "It's the middle of the workday!"

"You've done enough for one day."

Pushing up, I rested my hands on my hips. "If you're trying to imply that I was somehow the cause of all of this—"

"You can't work the rest of the afternoon in my socks and shirt." He cut in reasonably. "People's tongues are already wagging enough."

Oh. He had a point.

"I'll be down the hall," Aaron said, then slipped from the office.

Knox headed for the door, too. "Just come out when you're ready, ma'am. I'll get you home safely."

The second everyone was gone, Carter turned to me. "You lied to Alan about *Zero*."

I executed a very unladylike snort. "He lied about being faithful."

The muscle in Carter's jaw flexed. "Is that why, tit for tat? You wanted to get even for the way he treated you?"

"Of course not. I already did that when I donated the designer limited edition leather jacket he left at my apartment to charity."

The corner of Carter's mouth turned up momentarily. His lackluster but obvious enjoyment of my revenge made me wish I'd thought of it. Actually, that had been Val's idea. I'd just gone along with it.

216

"Then why?" he pressed.

Pushing back into his giant chair, I swung my feet back and forth because they didn't touch the floor. "You didn't want me to."

"I never told you it was a secret project."

"But it is, right?"

Slowly, Carter nodded. "We have a special team working on it. No one else knows about it."

"But Alan knows."

"I can't believe you dated that cocksu—"

"My ears will bleed!" I yelled, slapping my palms over them to keep from hearing his filthy language.

Rolling his eyes, Carter got back to business. "Don't tell anyone about *Zero* or about the rendering I showed you. As you heard, it's worth quite a lot of money."

"That much for a silly video game," I mused, frankly shocked.

He smirked. "I take a helicopter to work, and you're surprised?"

"No one likes a braggart." I grabbed my coffee and prepared to leave. "I do miss your island, though."

"Do you now?" The suggestion in his voice made me think back to that night and the way he'd made me feel.

"Knox is waiting," I declared, stomping across the floor in his socks.

I was pretty sure they were cashmere. "I'm keeping these socks," I informed him. "Probably this shirt, too."

"Hey!"

I stopped.

Carter came around to stand in front of me. "I'm sorry I can't take you home. I have to deal with this."

I put a hand on his chest to stop him from speaking. "Don't ever apologize for anything you don't do wrong," I said, then followed up with, "even to me."

He smiled, and it lit up his endlessly onyx eyes.

Unable to resist, I brushed some of the hair falling over his brows off to the side. "You have really beautiful eyes," I whispered.

Surprise flashed in them, but then I was against his chest, wrapped tight in his arms. I hugged him back, laying my cheek against his chest.

"Do everything you need to do. Don't worry about me. I'll hang out with Val. Maybe hit the beach."

"I'd rather be with you."

It kinda made me all mushy inside when a commanding guy like Carter said things like that to me. It made me feel kinda commanding, too.

"You shouldn't say that to a woman who isn't your girlfriend."

Carter pulled away. "Maybe I should go tell Meghan, then."

I took a running leap and jumped on his back. He laughed, catching my legs just before I slid down his body.

"What is this?" he questioned, lifting me higher and glancing over his shoulder.

"I'm trying to stop you from doing something you will most definitely regret."

"Says who?"

"Me."

"Good girl," he mused. "Are you jealous?"

"Of course not."

Carter's office door swung in, and Bryan stepped inside. The second he saw Carter standing there with me on his back, his eyes widened. "I don't even want to know," he muttered and continued by as though he hadn't seen a thing.

Carter carried me over to the door where Knox waited. Offering his back to the guard, he said, "Make sure she gets home safely."

Knox pulled me off Carter and planted me on my feet.

"See you later," he said, keeping a respectable distance between us.

"Bye."

After a moment of us just standing there looking at each other, Knox reached around and pulled the door shut between us.

Twenty-Eight

Carter

Alan Regal.

Nora's ex.

Son of the unscrupulous Lewis Regal.

Awful Alan.

I had a bad feeling about this.

Twenty-Nine

Nora

"Don't forget we both have to work tomorrow!" I called over the blasting music.

"I know. I know!" Val assured as she shook her hips.

Grabbing her, I looked directly in her eyes to make sure she was listening. "It's your first day at Ansoft. No getting drunk."

Holding up her hand in solemn vow, she proclaimed, "No drinking, just dancing."

Satisfied, I let her hips return to the beat. "Good. I'm getting a drink!"

"Hey!" Val protested. "You just said—"

"I said tomorrow is *your* first day. It's not mine!" Cackling at her sour face, I went off to the bar to order a vodka and cranberry juice.

I'd earned this drink. Today was all kinds of messed up. Facing off with Meghan, the secretary from hell. Dealing with nosy and jealous co-workers. Busting my ass in the hallway and ruining my shoes. And let's not forget the cherry on top of this crap sundae... Alan.

I was still confused as to why he showed up here and what he could possibly want with Carter's game.

Seeing him again brought back a bunch of unpleasant memories that I preferred to block out. It wasn't like I was still pining away for him. I was totally over Awful Alan. But judging from the way my stomach collapsed when I saw him, I was willing to admit I might not be over all the shitty things he'd done to me.

Betrayal and broken trust leaves behind wounds that take a long time to heal.

Coming to Miami was a way for me to start over. To get away from all of that.

Then he showed up. The twerp.

The second the drink was in my hand, I took a giant gulp. Then another.

A man standing nearby sidled up to me. "Bad day?"

"I'm a lesbian," I blurted.

Taken aback, the man's eyes widened. "What?"

"I'm not available. I'm a lesbian. That's my girlfriend over there." I pointed to Val on the edge of the dance floor.

She waved.

"Good for you," he said.

I laughed and downed the rest of my drink. Leaving the empty glass on the bar, I went back to Val, allowing her to lead me out onto the crowded dance floor filled with flashing lights.

"I told that guy we're together," I said by her ear as we danced.

Val laughed.

The song switched to an equally upbeat one. The music was so loud it vibrated my skin. The vodka I'd sucked down sloshed around in my empty stomach, making my limbs feel loose and warm. I probably shouldn't have chugged it so fast, especially since I hadn't eaten dinner, but I didn't care.

We continued to dance until a guy with a sleeve of tattoos came up behind Val and pulled her around. She glanced at me, and I waved her off, telling her it was okay.

I was hot from all the dancing I'd done, so I headed back to the bar for a bottled water. I debated ordering another vodka but decided since I was already feeling kinda buzzed from the first one, I'd better stick to the water.

I'd downed about half the bottle when Val appeared to steal the rest.

"This place is great!" she yelled, setting the empty bottle on a nearby table. "Let's dance some more."

I made a face, and she rolled her eyes. A waitress wearing a bright-yellow tube top, carrying a tray of colorful shots, happened by. Val squealed and grabbed two, one red and one green, handing them over so she could dole out some cash.

She turned back and reached for one, but I held it back. "You said…"

"It's just one," she whined. "I'll dance it all off."

Shrugging, I handed it over, and we clinked the tubes together before downing them in one shot. My lips puckered at the strength of the alcohol, but then we were dancing again and I didn't care.

I don't know how long we grinded in the crush of people beneath the flashing multicolored lights. I was good and buzzed, maybe slightly tipsy. The vibration of the music coupled with the strobe lights made me feel even more off-kilter.

Someone slipped up behind me, arms going around my waist to plaster close, matching my movements. For a second, I leaned back, thinking it was Carter, but even tipsy, I knew right away it wasn't him.

Pushing at the man's arms, I jerked around, accusation in my eyes.

"What's the matter, Nor? You used to love to dance with me."

"What the hell, Alan? Are you stalking me now?" I yelled.

Grabbing my hip, he tried pulling me close again. I attempted to shove him away, but all I managed was to bump into someone dancing beside me.

"Val!" I yelled, scanning all the people for my friend.

"C'mon, sweetheart. Don't be like that," Alan insisted, pulling me close again.

"Don't touch me!"

A few people turned to look, and Alan played it off, slinging his arm around my shoulders and forcibly walking me off the dance floor. I struggled to get out from beneath him, but all he did was clutch me tighter.

"How about a drink? Vodka and cranberry, right?"

Was I supposed to be impressed he remembered what I drank?

"I'm going home." Turning back to go look for Valerie, I hoped he would get a clue.

"Just talk to me," he pleaded, making me turn around. "Please."

"We don't have anything left to say."

"I came all this way to see you. The least you could do is give me five minutes."

"You came for work. Not for me."

Adamantly, he shook his head. "That's not true!" he yelled over the music. "I came for you. The business thing is just a favor for my dad."

I glanced around some more, hoping to see Valerie, but there were just too many people.

Alan's hand closed around mine. I glanced down at where he held me and then up at his face.

"Five minutes."

"Four."

His dimple made an appearance, and I wondered to myself why some bad guys had to be so easy on the eyes. I let him lead me farther from the dance floor and the crowded bar, toward the front where there were less people.

Finally, he stopped and turned to face me.

Yanking my hand out of his, I crossed my arms over my chest. "What do you want to say?"

"I miss you."

I laughed. "Are you kidding me? You miss me?"

"It's true."

For a minute, there was a pang of hurt inside me, but then I remembered how easy it was for Alan to look sincere even when he wasn't.

"You don't miss me. You miss having someone you can put down to make yourself feel superior."

"I hurt you, and I'm sorry."

I didn't say anything.

"I took advantage of you, and I want to make it right."

"Then leave me alone. Stop coming around."

He nodded, again doing a good job of looking like he really understood how I felt. "I will. If that's what you truly want, I'll leave you alone."

"Bye, Felicia!" I sang and went off to find Valerie.

Yes, I know. I could have come up with a better retort. Let's just say it was the alcohol talking, shall we?

He grabbed my arm, pulling me back around. "I'll leave you alone. I swear. But first you have to do something for me."

I made a disgusted sound. "You're such a creep!"

"You owe me."

Flabbergasted, I stared. "*I owe you?*"

"I gave up an internship in New York for you. I was willing to go to that shithole Boston just to prove how sorry I was. And you bailed!" he accused, anger making his face a lot less handsome. "I had no choice but to go work for Regal Tech with Dad."

I scoffed. "Poor little Alan had to go work for a huge tech company under the guidance of his mogul father."

That flat look came into his stare. The alcohol swimming around in my system put a damper on my fear response, which actually was kinda nice.

"You know I wanted to get some experience at other places first."

I held up my hand and made a talking gesture. "You talk too much," I said. "Me, me, me. Blah, blah, blah."

Grabbing my wrist, Alan jerked me forward. "What do you know about *Zero?*"

"What?" I struggled against him, but he just squeezed my wrist tighter. It was the wrist I'd fallen on earlier, the one that was still tender.

"How did you get an internship at Ansoft? How did you manage to get so close to Carter Anders?"

"I'm just an intern!" I insisted, my head spinning. The alcohol in my stomach lurched, threatening to make a reappearance.

226

Without another word, Alan tucked me under his arm and ushered me out of the club. The hot Miami night hit me in the face the second we stepped onto the sidewalk.

"It's so hot out here," I murmured. It was a lot darker out here, too, despite the lit-up entrance and neon sign.

The absence of the strobing lights didn't make me feel any better. If anything, the world tilted more.

Leaning against the wall, I dug my cell out of my purse. I would just call Val and tell her to meet me outside.

Alan took the phone the second I held it up, tucking it into the pocket of his shorts.

"Hey!" I grasped for it.

"You want it, go get it," he said, his voice disgustingly suggestive.

"I don't need it that bad."

It started ringing in his pants, and I glanced down, stricken.

Tilting his hip toward me and taunting, he asked, "You sure you don't want to get that?" When I didn't try to retrieve the phone, he sighed. "I need you to get me as much information on *Zero* as you can."

"I already told you I don't even know what that is."

"Don't lie to me."

"The only liar out here is you."

He raised a hand, and I flinched. Chuckling, he gentled his movements to caress my cheek.

"If you want to keep that hand, you better move it right now." The sound of the controlled, deep voice cleared out some of the dizziness I felt.

"Carter!" I gasped, looking in the direction of his voice.

Three men stepped out of the shadows just down the street, all of them strikingly tall and graceful. They walked in a line, taking up the entire girth of the sidewalk, with purposeful strides and serious expressions.

Carter stood in the middle, Aaron and Knox flanking each side. All three wore black, and all three of them drew the stares of everyone in our vicinity.

"What a coincidence," Alan quipped, "that you should just happen to run into your *boss* at a club after hours."

The way he said it made me feel like Alan somehow knew there was more between Carter and me than I'd told him.

Forgetting about Alan, I rushed toward my three dark angels. I heard his feet scuffle behind me, so I quickened my pace.

There was no need, though.

Carter was there, wrapping his arms around me and spinning so he was between me and my ex. Over his shoulder, I watched Aaron and Knox form a wall behind him, totally barricading us.

"You okay?" he asked, grabbing my shoulders and staring into my face.

"I'm okay." I agreed.

"What the hell is this?" Alan fumed. "We were having a conversation. I was trying to talk to her."

"I don't want to talk to you," I called.

"You promised me four minutes."

I made a sound.

Carter glanced at me. "Is that true?"

"I had a few drinks," I murmured. "I want to go home now."

Gasping, I remembered my BFF. "Valerie's still inside!"

Rushing forward, Carter caught me around the waist and lifted my feet off the pavement.

"Carter!" I yelled, feet still running even though they weren't on the ground.

"She'll be right out," he retorted, amusement in his voice.

"Your time's up," Aaron told Alan. "Get lost."

"Why are you even here?" he asked. "What's going on with you and these guys, Nora?"

I giggled. He made it sound like I had a harem of men.

"I called them," Valerie announced, marching up behind us.

"Val!" I was so relieved. "I tried to find you."

"I saw you right as jackass was dragging you off the dance floor."

"You called them?" Alan demanded.

"Just Carter." She confirmed. "I told you to leave her the hell alone."

Alan lunged for Valerie, and I screamed. Carter blocked me, but before I could get mad, Aaron stepped in.

Grabbing Alan by collar of his polo, he yanked him back, slamming him up against the building. He leaned in so close, with such menacing vibes that I stared even though I couldn't hear anything he was saying.

A second later, Alan's shoulders slumped and the top of his head bobbed. Aaron stood there a second longer before stepping back so Alan could walk away. Which he did. Without looking back.

"He has my phone!" I called, pointing at his retreating figure.

"I got this." Knox jogged after him.

Practically collapsing against Carter, I breathed a huge sigh of relief.

"Who are you?" Val asked, staring wide-eyed at Aaron.

"What the hell are you doing here?" Carter scolded.

Shushing him, I turned back to watch Aaron introduce himself to Valerie. Val giggled—she actually giggled—when he held his hand out for her to shake.

Elbowing Carter, I pointed at them. He rolled his eyes, then turned all his focus back on me.

Rotating, he crossed his arms over his chest to glare. Almost at the same moment, Knox moved beside him, mirroring his position, my phone in one of his hands.

"Well?" they both demanded.

"I don't have to explain myself to you!" I huffed.

"You do when I get frantic texts from Valerie saying your ex is dragging you out of a club and onto the street!"

"Valerie," I groaned.

"Well, he was! And after what happened at the apartment…"

"He was at the condo?" Carter's deadly quiet voice made me shiver.

"I mean at our apartment in Georgia." Val corrected

"What happened in Georgia?" Aaron asked.

"Nothing," I said, giving Val an *I will kill you* look.

"Let's go," Carter said, taking my hand and drawing me toward the curb where he whistled for a cab.

One pulled over almost instantly, making me scowl. "Do you know how long it took to get one earlier?"

Not saying anything and yanking open the back door, he looked at the other three on the street. "I'm taking Nora to our place. You stay at hers in case he shows up there."

Aaron nodded.

"Wait, what?" Valerie and I both exclaimed.

"What about me?" Knox asked, handing over my phone.

"You're off the clock 'til morning."

"Amen," he muttered.

"Traitor!" I called.

"See you tomorrow, ma'am." He winked.

"I'll bring you a coffee." I promised.

"Get in the cab. You're drunk."

"I am not," I argued, ducking into the car. I would have hit my head on the roof if Carter hadn't smoothly injected his hand between my forehead and doorframe.

"Drunk," he repeated.

After giving directions to the driver, he sat back against the seat. When I rested my head against his shoulder, he glanced down. "Why do you keep doing things that make me worry about you?"

"I'm sorry," I mumbled, rubbing my cheek against his T-shirt.

Sighing, he lifted an arm, draping it around me and pulling me close.

"Alan followed me to that club," I told him.

"Yeah."

"I'm glad you're here."

"Don't go out like this again without me or some of my security."

I didn't say anything because I didn't want to argue. I just wanted to sit in the back of this stinky, strange cab against a man who was anything but.

"I like you so much I don't even care this cab is stinky and weird."

My body bounced against his quiet laughter, and I liked that, too.

Thirty

Carter

The second Nora stepped into the lobby of Ansoft, she searched for me. I liked watching the way she evaluated every person in her line of sight, quickly disregarding them when she knew it wasn't me.

She wasn't wearing a dress or skirt today, which frankly made me happy. Instead, she wore solid lemon-yellow pants that only came down to her calves and a button-up white top that kind of flared out around her hips and got longer at the back. As she walked, the fabric billowed behind her, making her look like a summer angel.

The second she saw me leaning against the wall behind security, her eyes narrowed and her footsteps increased.

"What'd you do?" Aaron asked, noting her aggressive reaction.

"Beats the hell outta me."

Paul moved out of her way as she approached, calling out a good morning.

"Can't talk now, Paul," she told the security guard. "I have a fish to fry."

"Hey, wait!" Valerie called when she was intercepted by security.

"ID please," Paul said dutifully.

Nora stopped right in front of me, tapping her foot on the floor like I was in for a good scolding.

Amused, I half smiled. "About time you wore some sneakers," I drawled, glancing down at the white shoes.

Now that she was up close, I could see the tiny yellow polka dots on her top.

What the fuck was wrong with me? When did I ever notice or care about what a woman wore? Except, you know, when they were strutting across the beach in a bikini. Even then, it wasn't the bathing suit I noticed, but the skin it displayed.

Azure eyes narrowed, and her finger poked me in the chest. "What did I tell you?"

Aaron snickered.

"You told me a lot of things last night. You were drunk."

Gasping, she looked at Aaron, her cheeks turning pink. "I was *not!*"

"You were totally drunk." Aaron assured her.

"Did you enjoy sleeping over in my apartment last night?" She goaded him, lifting an eyebrow.

Aaron didn't take the bait. "Your couch is uncomfortable."

"That's because Carter picked it out."

Aaron threw back his head and laughed. Straightening off the wall, I shoved him away. "Go get Valerie from the security line. She's holding everyone up."

When we were alone, all my attention focused back on Nora. "You were saying?"

"I told you I wanted real."

"Gonna have to give me more than that, good girl."

"You sent Knox to walk us to work." Flinging her arm out, she pointed toward the lobby doors where Knox was standing as though he were in a time out.

"I couldn't be there. I had a meeting."

"I can walk myself to work." Her patience seemed to be at its limit. It made me want to grab her and kiss her. "Only in fantasies do girls get followed by their boyfriend's security team to make sure they're safe."

"Boyfriend?" I acted surprised. "I thought you said you weren't my girlfriend."

"I'm not!" she declared. Then, flustered, she added, "Don't you try and turn this around on me."

I laughed.

"Carter!"

I sighed. "I haven't even had any coffee yet. Could you keep the noise to a minimum?"

Apology filled her eyes, and my heart squeezed. "Here." She held out her cup. "I'll share."

"Yeah?"

She nodded.

Taking the cup, I lifted it to my mouth, putting my lips where hers had been.

Aaron and Valerie approached, and behind them lurked Knox. "Is it safe?" he asked.

Aaron hit a button for the elevator, and it dinged open almost immediately.

"Come on." I put a hand at Nora's back, guiding her forward. "We're drawing too many stares."

All five of us loaded into the elevator, and I hit the button for Nora and Val's floor.

"No more babysitters," Nora declared.

"Yesterday we were friends," Knox muttered.

"This isn't personal." She assured him.

"If I can't be there, then Knox will be," I told her, finality in the decision.

She gasped, completely offended.

The elevator stopped and the doors slid open.

"Let's go." I gestured.

"You're getting off, too?" she asked, wide-eyed.

"I have an announcement."

Aaron and Knox stepped out but stayed near the elevators while I went with the ladies into the design team offices.

As expected, everyone stopped what they were doing when the three of us walked in. Curious glances were thrown at Valerie, who honestly didn't seem the least bit bothered.

"Morning, everyone," I called out.

The few remaining people in the break room came out, including the design team lead.

"Mr. Anders," he said, rushing forward. "I didn't realize you were stopping by."

"I wanted to introduce you to Ansoft's newest intern, Valerie Harper."

Looks of shock went around the room.

"Another intern?" someone whispered.

"Ms. Harper will be replacing Nora on the design team."

Nora made an abrupt sound. I felt her eyes penetrate me with questions.

"She's fired?" one of the team members asked. She did a bad job of hiding her glee about it.

"I knew they wouldn't last long," someone else whispered.

I shot them a look, and they shut up.

"Of course not," I replied. "Nora is being moved to the special projects team, as I have added more work to their plate and they need some extra help."

I knew Nora was caught off guard and she probably had a million questions, but damn, if she didn't do a good job of standing there acting like she'd already been informed of this. That kind of loyalty and the kind she'd shown yesterday when she acted dumb about *Zero* to Alan was something I valued.

"Since I felt it was unfair to give this department an intern then take her away, we hired a replacement." Glancing at Valerie, I motioned for her to greet her co-workers.

"Hi, everyone." She waved. "Looking forward to learning a lot from you all."

"I trust you will all spend some time today helping her get familiar with our company and all the tasks that were previously assigned to Ms. Williams."

"Of course." The team leader assured me.

"If you have anything in your desk, get it now," I told Nora.

"I don't." Just after the words left her mouth, she made a sound and rushed over to her desk. Reaching in the top drawer, she pulled out a pen. "I'll take this."

"The special projects team has pens." I assured her.

Someone snickered.

She shrugged, looking at the black ballpoint pen as though it weren't plain and boring. "I like this one."

"Good luck on your first day, Ms. Harper," I told Valerie.

"Thank you, sir."

Motioning for Nora to go ahead of me, she took a few steps, then leaned in next to Val and spoke quietly. Val nodded once. Then she continued on.

The four of us got in the elevator, and the second the doors closed, she spun on me. "Why didn't you tell me I was being transferred?"

"If I told you last night, you would have forgotten."

"I was *not* drunk," she declared, looking at all three of us individually, practically daring someone to contradict her.

Knox and Aaron melded toward the back of the car, probably hoping she would forget they were there.

"What's the special project team?" she asked, curiosity winning out over frustration.

"It's the team working on *Zero*."

Excitement sparked in her expressive eyes. Her hand gripped my wrist and squeezed. "You want me to work on *Zero*?"

"We moved up the launch date, so the team is scrambling to get everything done. I thought you could be of some help to them."

"Whatever I can do," she said, instantly ready for the task. "Even if it's getting coffee while they work."

"You'll probably be doing some of that."

"Of course, that's what interns are for." There wasn't a hint of irritation in her voice.

We reached our floor, the doors opening to reveal the large counter and Meghan standing behind it. Aaron and Knox went ahead, stepping onto the floor first.

"Where is the special project team located?" Nora asked, hesitation in her tone.

Gesturing out, I replied, "On the top floor, where I am."

Suspicion clouded her face. "Carter Anders, you didn't move me up here because you wanted to spy on me, did you?"

Aaron snickered. "She's almost as suspicious as you are, Anders."

I was not amused. She wasn't supposed to be suspicious of me.

"I told you. I moved up the launch date. The team needs extra help, and since you already know about the project, I figured you'd be a good fit."

Aaron and Knox led the way toward the special team's office. Instead of going left at the counter, we went right.

Aaron rapped once on the door, then opened it.

A team of four people sat in the large square room. A table filled the center, covered in monitors and laptops. Around the edge of the room were more computer stations and various equipment the team needed.

Everyone looked up from what they were doing, eyes going to Nora.

I could feel her sudden nervousness. Glancing down, I watched her take a steadying breath, almost as if she were fortifying herself for whatever this team would think of her.

"This is Nora." I began. "Bring her up to speed and hand down anything you need done. Even if it's just coffee runs and delivering materials to my office for approval."

"Anything you need," Nora echoed.

"Hey, Nora." Sean lifted a hand to wave.

The other two guys on the team did the same.

The only woman on the team, Anna, pushed her glasses up on her head and waved Nora into the room.

"Thank God you're here. I've been outnumbered for too long. These guys think proper communication is burping and code talk."

Nora giggled.

Tension I didn't even know gripped me dissolved, making me feel a hundred times lighter on my feet.

"Burping is not a form of communication." Nora agreed, moving forward.

"Tech geeks." Anna shook her head sadly. "I'm Anna, by the way." She pushed out a chair beside her. "Come sit here."

"I'll leave you all to it," I said. Everyone waved eyes still on their computers.

Frankly, I was hurt Nora didn't even look up to see me go. I cleared my throat, but that didn't get her attention either.

Anna pointed to something on her monitor, and Nora leaned in to look.

Stalking over, I towered behind her shoulder until she turned. Without a word, I reached over her, plucking the coffee out of her hand. "I'm taking this."

Nora blushed, her eyes slipping to Anna and then back to me.

"I already told them we're involved. No one in here is going to bother you about it."

Her eyes almost popped right out of her head. "You told them *what*?" she hissed.

"Don't worry." Anna consoled her. "None of us are going to be jealous hags like I'm sure you encountered downstairs."

She made a choked sound.

Cutting a look at her, Anna asked, "I'm right, though, right?"

I felt Nora's attention even though she didn't look at me. "It wasn't anything terrible."

"Terrible or not, you don't need to worry about it here. We're glad to have you." Anna patted a surprised Nora on the back.

Suppressing a smile, I headed for the door. "Oh," I said, turning back. "Nora has some ideas I liked for minor modifications to some of the art. Make the changes as you see fit."

Nora's eyes bugged out again. "They're really not that good."

"Let's hear what you got." Devin challenged.

Sipping her coffee that was now mine, we left the team to work. I liked having Nora upstairs with the rest of us. Finally, everything seemed complete.

Nora

The arm wrapped around my body glided upward until his palm cupped my face to gently pull it around. A sleepy sound rumbled out of me, cut off by the velvety sensation of his generous lips covering mine completely. Though I was still caught between sleep and awareness, Carter kissed me slowly and provocatively, eliciting my body to respond in kind.

When I turned toward his warm chest, his hand settled against my hip, rubbing suggestively while he deepened the kiss. As he pulled back to nibble on my lips, arousing even more desire, the lower half of my body turned liquid, making my hands reach around to pull his head fully back into mine.

Tongue delving deep, he rolled so I was pinned beneath him. The weight of his body was so incredibly delicious. The hold I had on his face tightened, and the kiss continued until I was lightheaded.

The second I turned to gulp in some air, his lips took advantage of my exposed neck, sucking on the sensitive flesh and making me tremble.

His hips thrust against me, and raw need rippled through me. I grasped his ass and pushed him closer against my core. Groaning into the pillow beside my head, Carter quivered, and though he didn't thrust again, I felt the evidence of his want between my legs.

Holding himself prone, he moved just so he could gaze down into my face. The intensity of his obsidian stare left me feeling swallowed whole, as if the only thing those endless eyes could see or want to see was me.

No one had ever looked at me like this before, as if he could confess the secrets of the universe without even saying a word. As if the greatest secret of all was being allowed into his heart, and the invitation was right there in his eyes.

Three words were right there on the tip of my tongue. They felt so natural it was hard to keep them in. But I was afraid. Afraid of putting them out there. Afraid of getting hurt.

Most of all, I was afraid the second I said I love you, moments like these would come less and less, which would be far more painful than keeping the words inside.

My head left the pillow as I leaned up, initiating another kiss. Everything about Carter quieted, so I glanced up. Lips still touching, our gazes connected. My heart beat wildly beneath my ribs, and a case of the flutters filled my stomach. Confessing wordlessly what I was way too scared to speak, I didn't even have to wonder if he heard because it all reflected right back in the depths of his eyes.

He began kissing me again, making my body melt back into the bed, surrendering completely.

Abruptly, he rolled away onto his back, flinging an arm over his face.

"Carter?" I asked, completely breathless.

"What the fuck was I thinking?" he muttered. "I never should have taken sex off the table."

I giggled.

The arm covering his eyes flung away so he could glare. "You think this is funny?"

"Maybe a little…"

"I'll just fire you." He reasoned. "I'll fire you, and then it won't matter how much sex we have."

"You wouldn't!" I gasped, propping up on one elbow to give him an incredulous look.

"You like the special projects team, huh?"

Oh, the way he looked at me. It was something that could never ever be duplicated.

Reaching out, I brushed the hair from his eyes, letting my fingers play in the softness before pulling away. "I do like it."

"I like it when you touch me," he whispered, and something about the way he said it made my heart squeeze. Almost as if he treasured it as something he'd always wanted but never really had.

Leaning down, I brushed a kiss against his cheek.

"You're fired," he deadpanned.

"I am not!" I argued.

"Fine. But I can't stay down here with you anymore. I won't be able to hold myself back."

"I never asked you to."

He groaned. "I'm trying to prove a point. This isn't helping."

"What point was that again?" I teased.

He glowered up at the ceiling, and I hid my smile. "That I didn't hire you so I could sleep with you."

"You're sleeping with me right now," I whispered, dragging a finger down the center of his bare chest.

Shuddering, he caught my hand and nearly jumped out of bed.

"Carter," I whined, patting the empty space beside me.

"Wicked woman," he chanted and went into the bathroom.

Burying my face into the pillow, I smiled wildly while wondering if my heart would ever return to normal. I'd never felt like this before. Equal parts giddy and electrified.

A few minutes later, Carter's voice drifted from above. "Are you planning to stay in bed all day?"

"Since I got fired, I have nothing else to do," I called from beneath the covers.

All my blankets were ripped away, and cool morning air assaulted my bare legs, making me squeal.

"If you're late, I'm docking your pay."

"Maybe I'll just quit!" I threatened.

I didn't really mean it.

Grabbing hold of my ankle, Carter dragged me halfway out of the bed until my feet were on the floor. Slapping both hands on either side of me, he leaned down, almost touching his nose with mine. "You're not going to quit." His words were confident. "Because if you did, you wouldn't have a reason to see me every day."

Before I could retort, he kissed the tip of my nose and spun away, leaving me half hanging off the bed and reeling from his closeness.

"I'm going to my apartment to shower and change. I'll see you at the office later." Before disappearing completely, he knocked on the bedroom doorframe, making me lift my head. "Knox will be here to escort you, so wait for him."

Launching up, I threw a pillow at him. I had bad aim, and it hit the door instead.

"You're a violent woman," he admonished, then left me and Val to get ready for work.

We managed in record time, already used to sharing a bathroom. I felt bad she was sleeping on the pullout couch, but she insisted it was fine because the apartment was so nice and she had a view of the ocean.

Just as Carter said, Knox was waiting outside the apartment door when we opened it to leave for work.

"Ma'am." He greeted each of us with a nod.

"Good morning!" I chirped happily even though I was annoyed Carter forced him to take us to work. I liked Knox, and it wasn't his fault Carter was a giant control freak.

The three of us walked to the coffee shop just down the block from Ansoft, something that had become part of our normal morning routine. We did the same even when Carter was with us.

I'd been at Ansoft for a little over a week now, and ever since being moved to the special team to work on *Zero,* things had been crazy hectic. The launch date was fast approaching, and everyone was scrambling to make last-minute adjustments and preparations. Along with the rest of the team, I'd been working long hours and a few late nights, trying to get it all done. I mentioned once it would be easier if we had more people, but everyone shook their heads adamantly, saying Carter preferred less people in the know.

I couldn't help but wonder if the high level of secrecy had to do with Alan and his father. I also wondered if Ansoft planned to market this game before dropping it. For something that had been developed for so long and cost so much, I would think getting a buzz going about it would be essential.

I didn't mention either of those things to Carter for two reasons:

1.) I was an intern, and it wasn't my place.

2.) I trusted that Carter knew what he was doing.

When we arrived, Miami Java was busy as usual, but since the line always seemed to move quickly, we headed in without any hesitation.

"Nora!" Seth waved from farther up in the line.

"Hey, Seth!" I waved back.

After he'd gotten his coffee, he came over. "You look pretty today," he said, gesturing toward my floral baby doll dress and the white tee I was wearing beneath it. It was loose and breezy, something I appreciated in the Miami heat. Plus, it looked cute with the sneakers Carter constantly insisted I wear.

"Thank you," I said, noting the way Knox moved closer to my side to glower at Seth. I elbowed him lightly in the waist, and he gave me a knowing glance.

"Have you met Valerie?" I asked, then introduced them.

The line moved up. Knox nudged me and practically told Seth to get lost.

When he was gone, I swung around. "Seriously? He was just saying hi. We're co-workers."

"That man does not think of you as a co-worker," Knox remarked.

I glanced at Val for help. She shrugged. "He was giving out interested vibes."

Thankfully, I was saved from this stupid conversation when the barista called for us to order. Since I ordered extra coffee and bagels to take to the team—and one for Carter—we had to step off to the side to wait.

A prickly, uncomfortable sensation of being watched crawled over the back of my neck. Turning around to glance around the shop, I found the source of my discomfort fairly quick. At a table by the window, Alan sat with a coffee parked in front of him.

I couldn't even pretend not to notice him because he was already staring.

The sound I made drew Val around. "Are you kidding me?" She groaned.

Alan got up from his seat, leaving his coffee where it sat, and came forward.

The barista yelled that my order was complete, but I didn't look away from my ex.

Knox stepped in front of me, slowly shaking his head. "Turn around and walk away."

"Nora, I just want to talk to you," Alan said as if Knox weren't there.

"She's not interested," Valerie insisted.

The barista called for me again, so I went to grab the bag of bagels and drink carriers. Turning back, I saw Alan was still standing there, facing off with Knox.

"It's just a conversation," Alan implored. "We're in a public place."

"Did you follow me here?" I asked.

"I wouldn't have had to if you would answer my calls."

"I don't have anything to say to you."

"Just listen, then."

I wavered. I'd dated this man for a year. Yes, he hurt me, but we had some good times, too. All he was asking for was a few minutes.

"Fine."

"No!" Valerie insisted. "Knox!"

Knox gave me a disapproving glance. "It's not a good idea."

"If I don't hear him out, he'll just keep coming back."

"It's true." Alan agreed.

"Carter isn't going to like this." Knox warned me.

The last time I spoke with Alan, he asked me to get information on *Zero*. True, Carter wasn't going to like hearing I'd talked to him, but Carter wasn't the boss of me. *And* maybe I could learn what Alan and his father wanted with *Zero*. That would help Ansoft.

"Here," I said, handing over a drink carrier to Val. Then I handed the other one to Knox, along with the bag of bagels. "That one is Carter's," I said, pointing to one Knox had.

"I'm not leaving," he intoned.

"Me either," Val echoed.

"Fine. Then go sit over there like good little shadows."

Knox turned back to Alan. "I'll be right over there."

Alan rolled his eyes.

"There's a bagel in that bag for you, Knox," I called as he walked off. "You should eat it."

Motioning with his head, Alan led me to his table. Sitting down across from him and wrapping my hands around my hot latte, I waited for him to speak.

"Things have gotten pretty messed up between us, huh?" he said. He sounded a lot like the guy he was when I'd first met him. The laidback, charming, boy-next-door kind of guy I'd been so drawn to.

Funny, that didn't appeal to me at all anymore. In fact, I sat there looking at his blond hair, blue eyes, and dimples, wondering what I'd seen in him at all.

"I guess that's what happens when you cheat, manhandle, and basically scare the shit out of me."

Alan leaned over the table, and I sat back, keeping the distance between us. "It wasn't all bad, though. Was it, Nor?"

"No." I admitted. "It wasn't. But the good stuff was a really long time ago."

"I'm sorry about the other night. I was pissed off and jealous."

"Jealous of what?"

"Come on, Nora. I'm not stupid, and anyone with eyes can see you and Anders have something going on."

"My personal life is none of your business."

"I just wish it was me." Regret was thick in his tone as he lounged back in the chair. I ~~might have~~ *would have* fallen for that once.

Not today.

"I have to go to work."

When I stood, his hand shot out over the table to grab mine.

On the other side of the shop, a chair scraped across the floor, making everyone turn. Knox was up, his heated expression aimed at Alan.

I waved him back down, pulled my arm free, and sat. "What?"

"You won't give me another chance? A chance to prove it could be like it was?"

I laughed.

"Then can I at least make it up to you?"

"I don't want anything from you."

"How about from my father?"

"Your father." I scoffed.

"He's offering you a job at Regal Tech. As soon as you graduate, there will be a spot for you at the company. And not just an entry-level position, a good one. One that can grow as you do."

Regal Tech was arguably the largest technology company in the country. They had their hands in just about everything computer related…

"Is that why he wants *Zero*?" I asked.

Alan's interest sharpened. "What do you know about *Zero*?"

"Nothing." I lied. "But I know you're interested."

Alan took a drink of his coffee and glanced out the window.

Leaning in, I pressed for more. "Is Regal Tech trying to get into the gaming industry? Are they wanting to expand, and they were hoping to do it with…?"

His eyes narrowed. "With?" he probed.

With the hottest, most advanced game to hit the market. I couldn't say that, though. That would be way too much info. Instead, I replied, "With something Carter has."

"I know you know more than you're saying."

Shaking my head slowly, I clutched my cup. "No. I don't."

The muscle in his jaw jumped, and an uncomfortable feeling settled in my chest. Alan made me nervous. As much as I hated to acknowledge it, it was impossible to ignore.

"Is that it, then?" I went on. "You're here because you want something Carter has."

"It's not his!" Alan erupted, his hand slapping the table.

People all around stared.

Without turning around, I lifted a hand, silently telling my friends I was fine. "You're saying it's yours?"

With flashing eyes, Alan leaned over the table. "Yes. That game is rightfully ours. It belongs to Regal Tech. Anders has no rights to it at all, and when it launches, he's going to make a laughing stock of us."

I wrinkled my nose. "If he doesn't have any rights to it, then how did he get it?"

"Look, Nora, I know you hate me right now. I was a shitty boyfriend, and I've apologized for it. But you know me," he entreated. "Deep down, you know I'm not a terrible guy. You know how important my future is to me and that I'll one day take over my dad's company."

"What does any of that have to do with me?"

"I need your help. I have no right to ask for it, but it's true. I still love you, and I think you still love me."

"No." I cut in firmly. "No, I don't."

The conviction in my voice surprised him. Momentarily, he sat back, cleared his throat, and averted his gaze. After another minute, he spoke quietly. "I need all the information you've got on that game."

"I don't have any—"

"Then get it," he growled. "I know you have access. The way that Carter guy looks at you, he'd probably hand it over if you asked."

"I don't take advantage of people's trust," I spat, disgusted.

I stood, and so did he.

Quickly coming around the table, he grasped my arm and stepped close. "Get me the information. My father is offering you a job most college students would kill for. It has a generous salary, benefits, and room to grow."

Is this really what he thought of me? After all this time, Alan didn't know me at all.

"And me… I'll spend the rest of my life making up for the way I hurt you. You'll never want for anything."

"Let go of me," I said softly, a clear warning in my tone.

"Think about it."

"I don't have to. The answer is no."

His fingers tightened on my arm, and I stiffened. "Let go, or you'll be wearing this coffee."

He released me, his face a mask of frustration, and even though it was early morning, I was suddenly exhausted.

"If you change your mind, call me."

I left the shop, not even pausing for my friends. A few moments later, they caught up.

"What'd he want?" Val asked, curious.

"Nothing important," I answered. "We'd better go. Carter said if I'm late, he'll dock my pay."

I started off without them, my mind crowded with too many unpleasant thoughts.

Thirty-Two

Carter

"Boss?" Poking his head inside the office, Knox called for me.

Not glancing up from the game I was playing on the tablet, I called, "Yeah?"

"I got a coffee for you," he said, coming farther into the room.

"Since when do you bring me coffee?" I asked, still battling it out on the screen.

"It's from Nora."

Forgetting the game, I looked up at the large iced coffee he held out for me.

"Nora got me this?"

He nodded.

"Why didn't she bring it, then?"

Noise from the game reminded me I'd been playing. Turning back, I saw the red flashing in the center of the screen. Game over.

"Aish," I swore, tossing the tablet on my desk.

"She said she had work to get to," Knox answered.

"What's more important than coming to see me?" I muttered but picked up the drink and took a sip. It was good. She knew exactly how I liked my coffee. And I liked that she thought about me enough to bring it.

Knox didn't say anything, but he shifted uncomfortably.

"What happened?"

"Her ex was waiting at the coffee place."

Pushing out of my desk chair, I paced to the window to gaze out. "He just can't stay away from her, can he?" I intoned. Spinning around, I asked, "You got rid of him, right?"

Knox averted his eyes.

"Knox!"

"She said she wanted to talk to him."

"I told you to keep him away from her."

"She kept it short, and they stayed where I could see them."

"She okay?" I asked. It irritated me that she even entertained the douche, but I still worried about her.

"She was a little quiet afterward. Asked me to bring you that." He gestured to the coffee I was still holding. "But I think she's fine. That girl is tough."

I appreciated her resilience. I just wished she didn't have to utilize it so much lately.

"I'll drop in on the team, check on her." I decided. "Thanks for the coffee."

"She got me a bagel," Knox announced, clearly thrilled.

"If I didn't know any better, I'd think your loyalty was shifting to my girlfriend."

"You never give me snacks."

"Get out of my office," I snapped.

Knox laughed the whole way out. I waited until he was gone to smile.

The phone buzzed, so I picked it up. "Yeah?"

"Sir, there's someone here to see you." Meghan spoke quietly.

Usually, Meghan sent anyone without an appointment packing. The fact she was calling to tell me this piqued my interest.

"Who is it?"

"It's Lewis Regal, sir."

I felt my eyebrows lift. "Lewis Regal is here right now?"

She made a sound of agreement. "He said he flew in this morning to talk to you."

Running my tongue over my teeth, I made a decision. "All right. Send him in."

"Right away, sir."

A few moments later, Knox opened the door, allowing Regal inside. Nodding once to my guard, I silently let him know it was fine to wait outside.

"Mr. Regal," I said, not bothering to come around my desk for a handshake. It would be a false politeness anyway. "I'm surprised to see you."

"You've been so tough on the negotiations. I had no choice but to fly here myself."

"I didn't realize we were negotiating anything. I said no. I meant it."

He chuckled good-naturedly, as if this was going to be a conversation between friends. I guessed he had more tolerance for fake politeness than I did. "I like to say everything in business is a negotiation until the ink on the contract is dry."

"I feel that you've wasted your time coming here today. I won't change my mind. *Zero* is a personal project of mine, one that I'm very proud of, and I could no more sell it to you than sell one of my own children."

"You don't have children, do you, Mr. Anders?"

"No. Maybe that's why I feel so paternal toward this project."

"My son told me his meeting with you didn't go well."

"With all due respect, Mr. Regal, your son needs some more lessons in business negotiation."

The older man sat in one of the leather chairs, indicating I should join him. He was tall with slightly stooped shoulders and dark hair that I'd bet my helicopter was dyed. He wore a traditional navy-blue suit with a matching tie and black dress shoes he probably paid someone to shine and polish for him.

Lewis Regal was a shrewd businessman. Formidable. And he wasn't used to hearing the word no. I admit I'd never said it to him until recently.

He chuckled fondly when I basically dissed his only son. "Alan is young and passionate. I was the same at his age."

That really wasn't something he should be proud of.

Sitting down across from him and crossing one leg over the other, I resigned myself to this waste of time. "Should I call for some coffee?"

"No need. Let's get down to business."

I gestured for him to say whatever it was he'd flown all the way here to say.

"You're well aware that *Zero* is a knockoff of *Primal Fear,* Regal Tech's most profitable game."

I made a face, considering his claim. "Knockoff? No. A far superior game with upgraded technology and capabilities with some similarities would be my take on things."

"Thirty million dollars is a very generous offer. Far above market price for something like this."

"The reason you're offering such a generous amount is because you know as well as I do you would recoup that cost and make a heavy profit on top."

"If that game launches under Ansoft's label, Regal Tech will become a laughingstock in the gaming world."

Shrugging one shoulder, I said, "Regal Tech is the biggest technology company in this country. You don't even need a gaming division. Just leave this sector to the people who know how to play."

His hand gripped the arm of the chair, and he pulled himself forward. "Name your price."

Leaning forward, I mirrored his stance. "This game—and any of Ansoft's future work—is not for sale. No matter the price."

"You're messing with the wrong company." He warned me.

Sitting back, I mused, "I think you've got it all wrong here, Mr. Regal. I'm not the one messing with anyone. You keep coming at me."

"You little shit. You think you've finally managed to get one up on me. You're still bitter about what happened all those years ago."

Both feet hit the floor, and all traces of my amusement were gone. "Now why on earth would I need to be bitter about something when I've risen above it?"

His eyes narrowed, and the wrinkles around his mouth seemed to deepen.

"You did me a favor all those years ago. I might not have recognized it then, but once I pulled the knife out of my back, I realized I didn't need you." Gazing around my office, I added, "The fact that you're sitting there with your checkbook open proves I was right.

"I'll tell you what..." I continued. Getting out of my seat, I paced across to my desk. "How about I offer you a price for *Primal Fear*? You can close down your gaming division that never quite took off and use the money to put it toward your more profitable ventures."

Lewis chuckled, coming to stand in front of my desk. Facing off, my workspace between us, he reached into the inside pocket of his jacket and tossed a white envelope onto the tabletop.

Clearing my throat, I opened it up, unfolding the letter-size papers inside.

"I'm prepared to go public with everything," Lewis informed me quietly.

As I read over the words, my fingers tightened, making the pages crumple. "Where did you get this?" I asked, hoarse.

"Did you think I wouldn't do my homework? That I wouldn't want to know how a nineteen-year-old kid ended up in my office with a game to sell?"

"I was trying to survive." My words were angry. "And I trusted you to help me!"

He laughed. The sound made me sick. "I did help you." Lifting his arms, he gestured around. "Look at where you are now. You wouldn't be here if it weren't for that check I wrote you."

The papers in my fist balled up. "Get out."

"Did I finally shake that cool façade of yours?" he mused. "I see the boy from back then"—he pointed to the wad of papers—"is still in there somewhere."

"Get out of my building and don't ever come back."

"Sell me all the rights to *Zero*, including the team who built it. Name your price, and I will be sure that information never sees the light of day."

"Now I see it," I said, controlling my anger. Keeping my face expressionless, I jammed my hands into my pockets, not wanting him to see the way I shook with anger. "I see that your son is just like you."

Regal's eyes narrowed. "If that gets out, it won't matter how many state-of-the-art games you create. No one will buy from a killer."

"Get out!" I roared.

The frame on the double doors leading into the room shook as Knox barged in. Looking up from beneath my brows, I saw it wasn't just Knox, but Aaron, too.

"Boss?" Knox asked.

Aaron and I locked eyes. He didn't say anything, just stalked forward to take Regal's arm. "Let's go."

"Think about it." Regal coaxed. "If you want to keep everything you have, including that new girlfriend you seem to be so attached to—"

My eyes and nostrils flared before he even finished threatening me. The wadded-up paper hit the floor, and both my hands slammed onto my desktop, knocking several things over.

Aaron and Knox dragged him from the room. Halfway to the door, he started to protest, realizing he was going to be seen in the lobby, looking way less composed than his image would allow.

"Get your hands off of me!" he declared.

My guards ignored him. A few more of my security team met them at the doorway, and a small group formed around the man, escorting him out.

Stepping out into the hall, I watched as he was led away. The second he turned the corner, out of sight, Meghan appeared, hurrying toward me.

My eyes snapped up, and her steps faltered.

"Hold my calls," I ordered, then went back inside, slamming the door behind me.

Hand closing over the first thing it found, I launched it across the room. The heavy award crashed into a piece of art on the wall, shattering the glass and making the entire thing clatter loudly to the floor.

Thirty-Three

Nora

Anna slipped into the room, wariness written all over her face. "Guys," she whispered.

All of us looked up from what we were doing.

"Apparently, the CEO is on the warpath. It's probably best to hide out here for a while."

When I stood, the chair slid out from under me, rolling away. "Carter? What's wrong with him?"

"A few people in the hall said they saw some man in a suit being dragged out by security. Whatever happened has even Meghan cowering at her desk."

"I'll be back," I said, rushing to the door.

"Whoa," Anna said, blocking my path. "Maybe you should give him some time to breathe."

Devin made a sound of agreement. "I know you and our CEO've got something going on, but we've been here longer. He can be scary when he wants... Best to give him some space."

Well, that was advice I wasn't going to take.

When I continued forward regardless of the warning, Anna blocked me again.

Frustrated, I glared. "I'll be fine. Move."

Forcibly, the door pushed open, and all of us looked up.

Carter's dark head appeared, his eyes blacker than usual. The very air around him shimmered with danger.

"I was just coming to find you."

Not glancing at anyone else, he grasped my wrist, towing me to the door. Before leaving, he paused and looked back. "How's progress?"

"A little ahead of schedule," Devin answered.

His voice was swift, no-nonsense, and in no way invited any reply. "Good. Keep working. If you have any updates, call my personal cell."

I had to jog to keep up with his long strides as he pulled me down the hallway. I thought we were going to his office. Instead, he pulled me into an empty conference room at the end of the hall.

Pressing my body against the closed door, he rested one hand on the wood beside my head. His eyes glittered like a vast galaxy, so intense it was almost unfathomable. Anger simmered beneath the surface, reminding me of a caged animal who was pacing to be set free.

"What happened?" I asked, reaching up to touch his face.

He jerked back, and I froze. Dropping my hand, I refused to look away from his eyes. If I couldn't physically touch him, then my stare would have to be enough.

"Come with me." He said it almost like a challenge, like this was somehow a test.

The wildness in his eyes didn't scare me. I didn't care where he wanted to go. Moving slow, I reached out again, this time my fingers slipping into his.

"Let's go," I whispered, conviction in my words.

Surprise flickered in his eyes. Then his fingers tightened around mine. The door banged against the wall when he yanked it open, and once again, I was jogging to keep up.

Aaron waited at the end of the hallway. The second he saw us, he spoke into the phone at his ear. Knox and another guard were at the elevator, standing in the door to keep it open.

Carter walked right in without stopping. The guards smoothly stepped in, backs turned, and the doors slid closed. There was a black car with heavily tinted windows waiting at the curb just outside the lobby. A man in a black suit and black cap opened the door the moment we stepped from the building. Carter stopped long enough to usher me into the back seat, joining me immediately.

The car door shut.

A thick glass divider slid up, blocking the back seat from the front.

Gliding away from the curb, the car sped up, the city of Miami passing by.

"Don't you want to know where we're going?" Carter questioned.

"No."

The way his Adam's apple moved against his throat when his head turned to look at me made my fingers clench in my lap. "Why not?"

"Because I don't care."

Neither of us said a word as the car drove to our unknown destination. When we stopped, Carter didn't wait for the driver to open his door. Pushing out, he unfolded from the back seat, reaching a hand inside for me.

The sun was so bright it was nearly blinding. My eyes watered and blinked, trying to adjust. A heavy breeze ripped the strands of my hair away from my cheeks, and the scent of salt was thick in the air.

As Carter led me around the front of the car, I spied his glistening white yacht, the one he'd rescued me in the night I'd gone overboard. It was even bigger in the daylight, much more luxurious than I had realized.

Ocean waves did their best to rock the large boat anchored at the end of the long dock, but in no way did they succeed. A man stood on the dock beside the craft. He was dressed in a suit, and I assumed it was the captain.

Halfway down the pier, Carter stopped abruptly. Pushing the hair out of my face, I gazed up, questions in my eyes.

"If you step on that boat with me, our no-sex deal is over." His voice was sandpapery, making my stomach quiver.

Never had a warning made me so feverishly excited. Never had I wanted anything or anyone as much as I wanted this ebony-eyed man's body covering mine.

That's how it happened.

Reality stayed where we left it on the dock, and we sailed off into fantasy.

Thirty-Four

Carter

Irony - a sometimes humorous state of affairs or events that is the reverse of what was or of what was to be expected.

It was truly ironic that Nora thought of me as Mr. Fantasy. Me. The man who preferred to be alone because reality was just too harsh.

I understood where the moniker came from. I supposed, from the outside, it was the way I appeared. Rich, young, with various successful businesses to my name. I lived on a private island and used my resorts and the city of Miami as my playground.

Money and success didn't make me Mr. Fantasy, though. It just gave me the means to make me appear that way.

What made me Mr. Fantasy was Nora.

From the very moment I heard her fantasizing about the man who supposedly lived on the island— *about me*—I began fantasizing about her. That night with her was a chance to be something more than I was. A chance to be someone's fantasy. A chance to be better than my reality.

She didn't know it, but I needed her. More than she could ever need me. On the outside, some people looked as though they didn't need anything at all. Usually, those were the people who needed the most.

Nora might want reality, but what I needed right now was a fantasy. *Our* fantasy.

The dress she wore billowed behind her, giving glimpses of the backs of her bare thighs as it waved in the ocean breeze. Her arms leaned on the railing, face upturned toward the shining sun as she gazed out across the endless turquoise sea.

Coming up behind to spoon my body against hers, I wrapped my arms around her, careful not to spill the champagne I held.

"What's this?" she asked, taking one of the glasses.

Using my teeth to drag back the cap sleeve of her T-shirt, I kissed the top of her bare shoulder. "Your skin is warm," I murmured.

"I am standing in the sun."

We sipped at the champagne while the yacht glided through the waves, carrying us farther away from Miami.

Rotating in my arms, Nora's back rested against the rail, her blue eyes beguiling. "What happened today?" she asked.

Catching a strand of hair before it blew into her eye and tucking it behind her ear, I shook my head. "I don't want to talk about it right now."

"Then what is it you want to do?"

I couldn't look away from her. I didn't want to. "So many things. I want to do so many things with you."

Wearing a soft smile, she brushed the hair off my forehead, dragging her fingers through it more than once. My eyes drifted shut, and a feeling of peace washed over me.

When I looked at her again, she was watching me, and the tender expression in her gaze made my heart somersault.

"Will you stay with me, good girl? Will you do all the things I want to do?"

"Where'm I going to go?" she answered, a teasing smile lifting the edges of her lips. Turning back to the railing, her hand swept out, gesturing to the view. "I'm in the middle of the ocean with no land in sight."

Draining the rest of the alcohol in my glass, I stated, "Guess that means you're mine."

I could feel the tension coiled within me easing with every passing moment she was in my arms. No amount of money or success or luxury had ever been able to do that.

Leaning back into me, she said, "You ever wonder what's down there under the surface of the water? There could be a shark or a whale right beside us and we don't even know it!"

"Let's go see." Linking our hands, I led her to the stairs so we could descend to the lower level. It was cooler here because the sun was mostly blocked.

"It's just how I remember it," she mused, gazing around as we stepped into the master bedroom.

"You didn't see everything," I confessed, flipping a small switch nearby.

The quiet sound of a motor running startled her. Her eyes rounded and turned to the floor. "What's that?" she asked, wary.

"You said you wanted to see what was below us."

A section of the bedroom floor rolled away, slowly revealing a solid sheet of thick glass.

Gasping, Nora jumped back onto an unmoving section of floor. Looking at me, then quickly back down, she pointed. "Is that the ocean?"

I nodded.

"For real?"

Laughing, I stepped onto the glass, which gave a clear picture of the turquoise waters below. Several fish swam by, one of the them a bright yellow.

"Look!" she gasped, pointing again. Instead of taking my offered hand, she smacked me repeatedly on the shoulder. "Look, Carter!"

"Come closer," I proposed, completely amused by her awe.

When I tugged her forward, her feet dug into the floor. "I can't step on that! What if it breaks?"

"Then I guess we'll get an even closer look."

Squealing, she jumped back.

Ah, so incredibly cute.

Laughing, I picked her up, stepping back onto the glass with her cradled in my arms.

"I weigh a lot, Carter! This isn't funny! It's going to break!"

"It's not going to break." I assured her. "Don't you trust me?"

She stopped squirming and bit her lip nervously. "Yes, I do."

Leaning in, I kissed her.

"Have you ever seen a shark?" she asked when I pulled back. Her eyes lit up. "A dolphin?"

"A dolphin way under the boat?" I asked, completely skeptical.

Her shoulders slumped. "Right. Too bad. I've always wanted to see one up close."

Sitting down in the center of the window, I kept Nora in my lap. The bedroom glowed from the little bit of light filtering up through the water, and the waves seemed to ripple right along the walls.

"I feel like I'm inside a fish tank," Nora observed, still staring down at the moving water beneath us. "It's so beautiful."

I didn't bother to look at what she was referring to because, honestly, there was nothing down there that could even compare to her.

"Oh! Look!" she exclaimed, nearly falling out of my lap onto her hands and knees. Blond hair fell around her shoulders, creating a curtain that hid her face. "Look!" She tapped on the glass.

A school of orange fish swam by, their small fins working overtime.

She gasped again when a small coral reef came into view. "It's different colors!"

I smiled.

Finally peeling her eyes from the ocean floor, she scowled at me. "You aren't looking."

"I've seen it all before, but watching you… It's like seeing it for the first time all over again."

She didn't look back down. Suddenly, there was an invisible tether tightening between us. The atmosphere shifted, dissolving all the comfort and fun in the space and replacing it with tension and thick desire.

My stomach clenched and my pulse quickened, making me forcibly swallow. Her eyes drifted down to my throat, and when they came back up, the blue was darker than before.

Spider-crawling my fingers over the glass, I caressed hers, rubbing my thumb over the back of her hand. Her breathing hitched, and I knew she felt the same tug.

Moving so she was between my legs, I cupped her cheek, caressing it the same way I had her hand. "You really are so beautiful," I whispered. I knew I didn't have to say it, but truthfully, I wanted her to know that's how she looked to me. "I thought about you almost every day since that night we spent together. It drove me crazy. So crazy I had to find you again."

She whispered my name, but it was more than that.

I grazed her lips at first, teasing us both. Opening my eyes again to hold her stare, I said nothing, waiting until her eyes went unfocused before putting my lips on hers again.

I kissed her deeply, the way I'd longed to do from the moment I'd snatched her from the office. Palming her head, I had my way, kissing until she began to melt and I wasn't just supporting her head, but all of her weight.

Easing us back, I laid her across the window, kissing her still. Settling between her legs, I felt them trembling, so I glided my fingers over her bare thigh and all the way to her calf.

Her hands went to my shirt, fumbling with the buttons but unable to get even one undone. A sound of frustration rumbled in her throat. Pulling away from my lips, she stared accusingly at the shirt still covering my chest.

Rising above her, I ripped it off. The sound of buttons scattering and rolling across the floor was like music to my ears.

After pushing herself up off the glass, her hands went everywhere, sliding over my chest, across my abs, and dragging up my arms. Leaning forward, she flicked her tongue over my nipple, making me shudder. My fingers tangled in her hair as she sucked and taunted my flesh with her hot little mouth.

Ripping the dress over her head, I threw it aside with my shirt, then tugged off the rest of her clothes until all she wore was a pair of lacey pink briefs.

Catching her arms and forcing her back down, I pinned her wrists above her head. With her body stretched out, I took my time kissing and sucking every inch I could reach.

She was panting when I finally released her arms, and immediately they went to the waistband of my pants, her quivering fingers trying to undo the button. After the third try, she glanced up, her eyes unfocused and so incredibly blue. "You make me too nervous."

Gently pushing her hand away, I undid them while claiming her mouth.

"You weren't this nervous the night we met," I murmured between kisses.

"It's because now I lo—"

I jerked back only far enough that I could see the look in her eyes.

Nora bit down on her lip, averting her gaze.

My heart fell a little because I'd been sure she was about to say the words I really longed to hear. "You know this makes me angry," I whispered, tugging her lip from beneath her teeth.

"Why?" she whispered, eyes searching mine.

"I don't like anything that hurts you," I explained, cupping her face in my hands. Her cheeks were flushed, and her lips were plump. "Because I love you."

Her breath caught, and surprise filled her expression. "Y-you do?"

Smiling gently, I took her hand and pressed it against my chest. "You're the first person I've let in here in a really long time... Take care of it, okay?"

Her chin wobbled slightly, but then she smiled. "I promise."

"Good girl," I praised, then kissed her again.

Cupping the back of her head, I pushed her down so we were skin to skin.

Below us, something swam into view, and I grinned. Moving fast, I flipped her over, pressing her naked torso along the glass.

"It's cold." She gasped, squirming.

"Look."

A large stingray glided gracefully through the water, its body deep brown and spotted with white. It looked almost like it was flying, fluttering its fins, which really looked more like wings.

Nora made a small sound of awe.

Moving her hair to the side, I kissed her neck, over her shoulder, and then started moving across her back. A low moan filled the room when I reached under her to palm her breast.

Slowly, her legs parted, and I fit myself between them. Grinding against her warm, round ass was sweet torture, and so were the sounds she made every time I moved. Pushed to my limit, I ripped the panties off her body and tossed aside my boxers. Slipping an arm under her hips, I pulled her ass into the air, sliding my rigid erection along her slick core.

Burying her face in her arm, she thrust against me with a deep moan. The sweet warmth of her core enticed me, but I held back from plunging deep in favor of rubbing along her slit to tease the sensitive nub above it.

Reaching around behind her, she grabbed at my bare hip, trying to pull me in. Giving in, I pushed the swollen tip into her entrance. Her upper body melted against the glass, and a shudder moved through her.

Every part of me tightened. The need for her was so intense. Desperately, I wanted to pound into her, to lose myself.

Rocking just a little, I let my eyes slip closed for a moment of bliss before pulling away.

A sound of protest filled the room, and she looked over her shoulder. "Carter?"

I stood, staring down at her naked form on display, lit from behind by the ocean. "I can't."

Flipping around, her bare ass hit the glass. "W-what?"

Sliding my hands under her arms, I lifted her off the floor. She seemed wobbly on her feet, and her face was still a mask of confusion.

She whispered my name again.

I picked her up, cupping her bare cheeks as her legs wound around my waist. Under her, my cock jerked, desperate to be inside her again.

As I carried her to the bed, the slick desire of her core coated my lower belly, making me even more impatient.

The second her back hit the bed, I bent over, locking eyes with her. "I can't take you on the floor from behind. Not right now. I want to see you. I want to look into the face that I love when I claim you."

"Carter," she whispered, letting her fingers drag down my chest.

"After this, you're mine, Nora. Completely. No more denying. No more saying you aren't. Got it?"

Her throat worked, and the nerves she spoke of before befell me in a vicious way. I'd just filleted my heart for her. I let her into a place no one else was allowed. What if she rejected it? Rejected me?

"I love you."

A deep roar filled my head, echoing through the rest of my body. Possession, hard and forceful, slammed into me, knocking out everything else.

When I plunged into her, we both cried out. I wanted to take her slowly and sensually, but there was no way. Her confession drove me to the brink of madness, making me operate on pure instinct.

Nora was warm and wet, sheathing me with far more than just her body. Groaning, I fell forward, burying my face in the side of her neck, thrusting deep.

Her fingertips dug into my back, anchoring me to this moment, anchoring me to her.

Too soon, the bliss between us erupted, and I was free-falling through satisfaction. Entire body quivering with ecstasy, I milked every last ounce of pleasure I could from the both of us. I collapsed over her and our slick bodies stuck together, but I didn't care. It could be glue fusing us together, but I wouldn't ever complain.

Nora

Reality vs. Fantasy Observation #4:
Fantasy is having a sexy one-night stand and thinking you're his
only one.
Reality is knowing he has a name for all the women he's dragged
home.

The opening and closing of the bedroom door aroused me from the satiated state my body had succumbed to. Glancing beside me, I realized Carter was no longer acting as my personal heater.

"Hey," I called, lifting my head. "Where'd you go?"

"I don't know if I should be offended or proud that you just noticed I was gone," he quipped, walking toward the bed.

Proud. He should definitely be proud.

Pushing up into a sitting position, I spied what he carried. "Ooh, what's that?" I said, wiggling my fingers in a gimme gesture.

The sound of his warm chuckle made my belly tighten, and everything we'd been doing in this bed for the last few hours whispered through the rest of me.

Oh, if Val only knew how right she was when she called him Mr. Fantasy.

"You want one of these?" he teased, holding out a drink inside a real pineapple, complete with umbrella and straw.

I went to take it, but he pulled it back, just out of reach.

"Hey!" The sheet around me fell to my waist, exposing my naked chest.

"I was hoping you'd do that," he mused, fixing his stare on my breasts.

I scoffed, and he winked.

I grumbled, and he held out the pineapple, offering it like a truce.

"Is it alcohol?" I asked, wrapping my lips around the hot-pink straw.

"You're supposed to ask that *before* you drink it." He scowled.

Batting my eyelashes, I said, "Even when you give it to me?"

"Except me." He relented, slipping into bed with his identical drink.

"It's juice," I said, taking another sip. The pineapple was a little prickly against my palms, but I didn't care. How often did a girl get to drink out of an actual hollowed-out pineapple?

"You haven't eaten enough for me to ply you with alcohol."

I glared. "I'm a big girl."

"I want you sober," he whispered, leaning in to kiss my shoulder. "I don't want you forgetting any of this."

"As if I could."

"Sometimes good memories get overshadowed by bad ones," he said, a more serious note creeping into his tone.

Lowering the pineapple and turning to him, I asked, "Hey, what's wrong?"

He shook his head and smiled. "I have a surprise for you."

"What could be better than turning the bedroom into an aquarium?" I asked, gazing over at the glass floor.

"C'mon." He motioned, getting out of bed again. It was the first time I noticed what he was wearing.

"Is that a swimsuit?"

He lifted an eyebrow. "Should I go get drinks from the staff naked?" His hair was mussed, dark eyes playful, and his all-black swim trunks accentuated his long torso.

"I need my dress," I asserted, covering my bare chest with my arm.

Pulling my arm down, he said, "There's a suit here for you."

An icky feeling came over me, and I held the pineapple out for him to take.

"What's wrong?" he asked. "Is it bad?" Immediately taking a sip of my drink, his face filled with concentration as though he was studying the juice to make sure it wasn't sour. "It tastes fine," he concluded.

Standing, I dragged the sheet with me, covering myself. "I'm not wearing any of the clothes you keep on this boat for all your conquests."

"Nor—"

"I know you're rich and sexy and single... but could you maybe at least act like you don't parade women on and off this boat and your island?"

As I lectured, Carter lowered his chin to stare up at me from beneath his strong brows. I swear, the more I talked, the more amusement lit his eyes.

Squinting, I pursed my lips. "You think this is funny? Should I tell you about Alan—"

The drinks were put aside, and he tackled me before I could even finish my threat.

"Hey!" I gasped, falling against the tangled sheets while being jailed in by his body.

"Let's get a few things straight." He half growled, eyes roaming my face like a predator checking for weaknesses in his prey.

You know, if this had been Alan on top of me, I'd probably be queasy and timid. I'd probably be worried I'd said something wrong and his anger was all my fault.

This wasn't Alan.

(Thank God.)

Leaning over to where he held my wrists, I sank my teeth into his hand.

"Ow!" he hollered but remarkably didn't let go. "What the hell are you biting me for?"

"You tackled me!"

"Because you were about to put images in my head I don't even want to imagine."

"What the hell do you think you just did to me?"

His lips actually tugged up into the beginnings of a smile.

My eyes narrowed.

"It's brand new."

The expression dropped from my face. "What?"

"The bathing suit, the clothes…" He began, eyes bouncing between mine. "I had them brought onboard for you."

"Oh." I pressed my lips together. That was a relief.

Above me, his body shifted so he was no longer holding me down, instead cradling me in his arms.

"Yes, there have been other women on this boat," he admitted, his voice matter-of-fact. Feeling me bristle against him, he kissed my nose, then hurried to say, "But I've never kept clothes for them. I've never even considered it."

"Really?"

He nodded. "I've never taken a woman back to my island."

"Liar." I accused.

He laughed under his breath. "It's true. Ask Aaron. I never let anyone see that much of me, of my personal space."

"But that night…" I refuted. Memories of his beautiful island, the views from the terrace, and the pure white sand on his beach assailed me. "You brought me there." Considering something else, I said, "Was that not your island? Do you have *two*?"

His teeth flashed when he laughed. "I'm not that rich. Not yet anyway."

I rolled my eyes.

When he pressed against my back to draw my attention, I noted the seriousness in his eyes. "You're the only woman I've brought there. The only woman to ever be in my bed."

"But why? We didn't even know each other."

He shrugged. "I felt it. My heart just recognized you. It was fate."

"You believe in fate?"

He smiled fondly, as if we were talking about an old friend. "I have a healthy respect for fate. And yeah, I think it exists, as long as you're paying attention."

"You're like really for real right now?"

"Really for real." He confirmed, eyes shining like polished gems. "You're more to me than just a sand dollar, and I'll never treat you like one."

My nose wrinkled. "A sand dollar?"

"Beach girls, random hookups. You step onto the resort and they're a dime a dozen, just like dollar bills. Not worth much but maybe enough for a good time."

I punched him in the side.

"Ow!" he wailed, rolling off me. "Since when did you become so violent?"

"That's a horrible way to talk about women."

"I said that's *not* how I think about you!"

"That still doesn't make it right," I declared, leaning over to pinch his nipple.

"Okay! Okay!" He surrendered, holding out his hands. The surrender was completely nullified by his laugh. "I won't say it again."

"Unbelievable," I muttered. Still, I was secretly delighted he thought of me in a better light.

"Don't be mad, good girl," he crooned, sitting up and pulling me against him. "I love you."

What a dirty trick. Pulling out those three words in a voice more charming than coffee at a five a.m. wake-up call. How was I supposed to be mad when he tucked me against that long, sinewy body of his and made my heart flutter?

Winding my arms around his waist, I sighed.

"If you don't get dressed, you're going to miss your surprise."

I pulled back. "Huh?"

"Probably swimming away right now." He sighed regrettably.

Bounding out of bed, completely naked, I rushed toward... Well, wait... Where was I rushing?

"Top drawer," he instructed.

Pulling it open I saw three bathing suits in a neat row, all of them still tagged. There were two bikinis and a hot-pink one-piece with a zipper up the front.

"A one-piece?" I feigned surprise, lifting it with my finger.

"It's got a zipper. Easy access." He winked, and I nearly swooned.

Naturally, I put that one on. It fit like a glove, and I kinda marveled at how he knew my size.

Handing me the pineapple, he grasped my free hand and led me onto the deck of the yacht.

"We aren't moving." I noticed when the ocean came into view before us.

"We dropped anchor for a bit."

"Why?"

Smiling, he tugged me toward the back of the boat where a section of the side was lowered, sort of like a tailgate on a truck.

Beyond that, waves bobbed, but something else moved with them.

"What is that?" I asked, feet stalling.

Carter swung back, scooping me off my feet, and carried me the rest of the way. "You said you wanted to see dolphins."

I gasped. "Dolphins!" Nearly falling out of his arms, I craned my neck so I could look. "Oh my gosh! Dolphins!"

An entire pod was right beside the boat, swimming and playing. They cut through the water so gracefully like the waves were no resistance at all. I clearly recalled when I'd been tossed overboard and just how much resistance the ocean could put forth and how quickly I'd grown tired.

Standing on a little platform attached to the boat, Carter helped me down, cool ocean water rushing up over my bare toes.

"How did you do this?" I asked, gazing around in awe.

The water here was bright turquoise, and the surface glittered like a handful of diamonds under a bright light. There were no other people to be seen. Miami was long gone, and the sun was lowering in the sky, creating streaks of color overhead.

Warm, balmy air blew around us, caressing my skin just like the water flowing over my toes.

"This is a well-known spot where dolphins like to play. Must be good eating or waves or something, because usually, they gather here quite a bit. When you said you wanted to see them, I had the captain point the boat in this direction."

"You really are Mr. Fantasy," I murmured, watching a dolphin crest before diving back down.

His arms wound around me from behind, and he rocked our bodies together rhythmically.

Nearby, a dolphin jumped, its whole body leaving the water in a beautiful arch, then plunged below.

"Oh!" I gasped, gripping his forearms. "Did you see?"

"Want to pet one?"

"Can I?" I asked.

"They're pretty used to boats and people," Carter explained, going to the edge of the platform and slipping his hand into the water. "Tour guides bring people out here."

A grey body swam close, passed by, then turned back.

"You just have to hold still," he said, watching the mammal.

Sure enough, it came back, swimming close enough that Carter was able to reach out his hand and stroke it.

"They're a lot bigger than I imagined," I said, suddenly apprehensive. "Do they bite?"

Holding out his dripping-wet hand, he coaxed me forward. "Come here."

Cautiously, I moved closer, surrendering my hand to his. Crouching beside him, I gazed out warily.

Wrapping his fingers around mine, Carter put our hands down into the water. I waited, barely breathing, heart pounding, for a dolphin to approach.

After a few moments when none came, I took a deep breath. "I don't think they want to."

"Hold still," Carter said, patient.

The sea breeze was blowing the hair away from his face, and the sinking sun kissed his cheekbones, making him glow. I forgot about the dolphins and the magic of being out here. All I saw and felt was him.

"Here he is," Carter whispered, and something smooth and slick grazed against my fingers. Startled, I jolted, but he held my hand still, pressing my palm on the side of the dolphin. My hand dragged the length of its body, then it flicked its tail and coasted away.

"Oh my gosh!" I exclaimed in a hushed tone. "I just petted it!"

Carter sat down with a chuckle, letting his feet plunge into the water and tucking my hand in his lap. "Sit with me."

Following his lead, I hung my feet over the platform, water coming up to almost my knees.

"Next time, we'll bring some fish and feed them."

"We can do that?"

"We can do anything."

"This is some world you live in, Carter Anders," I mused, gazing out over the horizon.

Lifting my hand from his lap, he kissed the back. "It's our world now, remember?"

How could I forget? The way he rose above me, declaring I was his, would be embedded in my brain forever.

A dolphin whizzed by, splashing us and making me laugh.

"I think this is the perfect spot to watch the sunset," he told me.

He was right. It was perfect.

Thirty-Six

Carter

Reality vs. Fantasy Observation #5:
Sometimes there is a thing as too much fantasy… like when it has birds.

Have you ever woken up with a woman's lips wrapping around your morning wood and her warm, wet mouth sliding down until there was nothing left to take?

No?

Dude. You don't even know what you're missing.

Men everywhere have wet dreams about this… but this morning, I wasn't dreaming.

Not a single thought drifted through my mind. Everything remained peacefully quiet as she slid up and down my rod, chasing away literally everything but the feel of her mouth and hands. As her head bobbed, the ends of her hair tickled my abs, creating another layer of pleasure I didn't even know I could experience.

Tilting my hips up, I thrusted into her mouth. Nora dragged back until just the tip was caught between her lips. One palm wrapped confidently around the base and began pumping while her tongue swirled around the head.

Small grunts of pleasure burst from my throat as she assaulted me with sensation after sensation. My entire body melded boneless against the mattress, and I tossed an arm over my eyes. The second she moaned, my body shuddered because the vibration quivered my already sensitive dick.

Pulling back, her mouth left me, and she sat back. Cracking my eyes open, I gazed unfocused at her rumpled blond head perched right beside my stretched-out body. A little smirk pulled at her shiny lips, both hands still wrapped around my shaft.

My eyes drifted closed again, and her mouth slipped down over me. The slow, seductive way she milked my erection changed, becoming more fevered and faster. Unable to even drag in a full breath, I moved restlessly under her. Pumping my hips to try and match her pace, feeling myself rise and rise and rise…

And fall.

I tumbled into an endless wave of ecstasy. I don't know if I shouted or called out her name. Pleasure had its iron grip on me, paralyzing me.

When I finally came out of it, I was still in her mouth and the warmth of her still tenderly around me made a rush of emotion roll over my chest.

She made me feel vulnerable in a way I had never been before. I'd worked hard for a lot of years to build up a world for myself in which I was king.

Even Lewis Regal's threat didn't shake me as much as Nora did right now. I was letting her inside places I'd purposefully sealed off.

Purring like a cat, she eased away from my cock, straying upward to kiss across my stomach and chest, and nestled against my shoulder.

I palmed her head, holding her against me. "I think that just earned you the title of Mrs. Fantasy."

The throaty sound of her laugh made me smile.

"Don't even think about it."

"So you can call me Mr. Fantasy, but I can't turn it around on you?"

"*I* don't call you that. Val does."

"But you secretly agree," I teased.

She poked me in the stomach. After a few moments, she said, "I should probably call Val. She's probably worried because I didn't come home last night."

"Aaron told her."

"Aaron?"

I made a sound of agreement.

"You're really close to him, huh?"

"He's my family," I said, trailing my fingers along her shoulder. "The only family I have."

Lifting her head, she whispered, "You have me now, too."

I pressed a long kiss to her forehead and prayed I'd never lose her, knowing I might. "You ready for breakfast?"

"I'm starving," she admitted.

We dressed in our suits, and she pulled her hair back into a messy-looking knot. Before leaving the bedroom, I grabbed a black silk shirt and held it out for her arms.

Once it was on, she turned, smiling. "If you keep putting your clothes on me, you won't have any left."

"You look better in my shirts than I do," I teased, reaching between the unbuttoned sections to play with the zipper at her breasts.

Her stomach made an angry grumbling sound, and I laughed. "I guess I've held you captive for too long."

"I'm pretty sure I'm here willingly."

Emotion clogged my throat. It was a sensation I didn't like. As if I were choking on emotions I'd managed to avoid for so long. "Thank you for this," I said, releasing some of the pressure inside me.

Pausing at the bottom of the stairs leading up top, she tugged my hand. "For what?"

"Being here with me like this." *For not asking questions I'm not ready to answer.*

"There is nowhere else I'd rather be."

When we walked on deck, home was a welcome sight. I liked Miami, but I'd spent far too much time there recently.

"We're here." Nora's deep-blue eyes gazed toward the island. "I think these are the biggest palm trees I've ever seen."

"Watch your step." I cautioned as we disembarked, walking across the long dock to shore. Instead of going toward the house, I tugged her toward the beach.

"Where are we going?"

"Didn't you say you're starving?"

"Isn't food usually kept *inside* the house?" she muttered, scurrying along behind me.

Sand kicked up around our feet and squished between my toes.

Amused with her continued muttering, I made a mental note that Nora might not be the perkiest morning person, and if she went too long without eating, she got crabby.

"Will this do?" I asked, putting my back to the beach to meet her gaze.

Curious, she peeked around me, but every move she made, I made, too, effectively blocking her from seeing.

"Stop that!" she scolded, smacking me in the stomach.

Snickering, I stepped back to let her see. She did that thing I liked. You know, when her mouth dropped open into that adorable little O.

"You did this?"

"Technically, no, but I did ask someone to do it."

A gleeful little sound erupted from her, and she rushed off, the silk shirt billowing out behind her as she ran.

The table for two was draped in a long white cloth, two white folding chairs pushed up to the sides. Bright-pink tropical flowers graced the center, along with covered platters of food, white porcelain plates, and silverware that gleamed beneath the morning sun.

"Come here!" She waved an arm to me, then turned back to the table. Blond hair blew around her face like a tornado while she lifted one of the lids to peek inside. "Bacon!" she exclaimed, snatching a piece and taking a bite.

With her other free hand, she seized a flute of juice.

Tucking my hands into the pockets of my swim trunks, I made my way toward her, pace unhurried. I'd been rich a while now, but honestly, I'd never really enjoyed it that much, other than the solitude it could buy.

Seeing Nora experience so much joy in just the little things I was able to do for her gave me a whole new appreciation.

"Who said you could eat that?" I teased, delivering a stern look.

Her chewing paused for a brief second, and she smacked me with the remaining hunk of her bacon. "I'm starving!" she announced.

Some of the bacon I was being abused with snapped off and fell into the sand.

She made a sad face. "Look what you made me do."

With an incredulous expression, I pointed to myself. At the same moment, a seagull swooped out of the sky, diving for the morsel.

"Agh!" Nora cried, launching herself at me. The flute in her hand went flying, juice splattering across the sand. Both her arms wrapped tight around my neck, and we tumbled to onto the beach.

Instinctively, I rolled so I was over her like a shield. Ducking into my chest, she cowered while her fingers dug into the back of my neck.

"It's a bird," I mused, lifting so I could gaze down at the top of her head.

"What?" Her voice was muffled against me.

"It was just a bird after the food you dropped."

Slowly, her head lifted. Wary eyes glanced around to where the bird was perched in the sand a safe distance away, staring at the table like it was anticipating more.

"It's vicious!" she declared, pushing at me so she could sit up.

Laughter I'd been trying to suppress bubbled up and spilled over.

She looked charmingly affronted as she stared daggers at the bird. "Don't laugh!" She complained.

I kept laughing. "You're scared of birds?"

"Only the ones who try and pluck out my eyeballs," she stipulated.

If her goal was to make me stop chuckling, she failed.

Nora crossed her arms over her chest and made a disgruntled sound. Her cheeks were flushed, but her eyes kept going back to the seagull.

Jumping up from the sand, I ran at the bird, making it fly off over the water. Offering a hand to her, I said, "He's gone now."

Nervously, she looked up at the sky.

"If he comes back, I'll scare him away again, okay?"

Note to self: It is too much fantasy for Nora to eat on the beach.

I pulled her up and helped her into the chair. Dragging my chair closer to hers, I sat down beside her and lifted the lids on all the plates.

Fruit, pastries, egg frittata, and, of course, bacon was spread out before us.

Nora poured coffee into two mugs, handing one over to me. "Do you do this often?"

"Never."

She gave me a side eye filled with doubt.

Popping a slice of pineapple into my mouth, I rested a palm against her thigh. "I know it's probably hard to believe, but there are a lot of things I haven't done. I've always kind of used this island as an escape, nothing more.

"Sounds kinda lonely."

I never realized how much until I met you.

"I have Aaron," I said. "And Bryan comes out a lot on the weekends."

"I thought you said you lived here alone?"

"Aaron has a place on the other side of this island."

She gasped. "Do you think he saw us that morning?"

Ah, yes, sex on the balcony. "No." I promised. "The balcony faces the opposite direction."

"Eat this," she said, shoving a bite of frittata against my lips. I obliged, then fed her the same.

The breeze off the ocean was refreshing and kept the sun from feeling too hot. As we chowed down, Nora would occasionally glance at the sky as if anticipating another attack from a hungry seagull.

"I got you." I promised after about the fifth time she looked up. Putting an arm around her shoulder, I pulled her close. "Just eat."

"I hope you don't think I'm ungrateful." She grimaced.

"Everyone has things they're scared of."

"What about you?" she asked, curious. "What are you scared of?"

I answered without considering my words. "Trusting people."

Nora turned in her seat, tucking her legs beneath her, sitting so close her knees brushed my leg. "Something had to have happened to make you that way."

My heart squeezed, but I worked not to show it. Lifting an eyebrow, I smirked. "Does that mean you've been attacked by angry birds?"

"That's different," she declared.

Grabbing her chin, I smiled. "How?"

"Birds are vicious creatures! Just look at their beady eyes and creepy feet. You don't have to experience anything evil to know they are capable."

This girl was a riot.

After my laughter died down, seriousness settled over me once more. "I think sometimes people can be that way, too. Although, what makes them scary is they don't always look like they aren't worthy of trust."

Her voice was soft and all her attention was focused solely on me. "What happened at the office yesterday?"

I knew I was going to have to tell her. But maybe not today. Shaking my head once, I cupped the back of her neck. "I just want some time with you. Can you give me that?"

Her eyes searched mine for the span of a few heartbeats. Just when my lungs burned with nerves, she nodded. "Of course I can."

Leaning in fast, I kissed her swiftly, relief making my limbs like Jell-O. "That's my good girl."

She barked at me.

She was a brat, and this required payback.

"Watch out!" I gasped, putting an arm over her head like the bird was swooping in.

She screamed and curled into me.

"You are so mean!" she yelled, shoving away from me. "I'm leaving!"

I knocked her chair over when I burst out of mine to pull her back. Shrieking, she landed in my lap but still tried to get away.

"You're going to make me angry." I cautioned, grabbing some fruit and chewing.

A few seconds later, she halted mid-struggle, collapsing against my chest. "Don't do that again."

"I won't." I promised, kissing her cheek, then offering her a bite of food.

She ate a muffin while sitting in my lap, watching the waves crash against the beach. I wished we could stay like this indefinitely, but tomorrow would come too fast.

Thirty-Seven

Nora

Carter was good. *Sooo* incredibly good at turning my world into a fantasy.

He was right.

Secretly, I did think of him as Mr. Fantasy. I wouldn't tell him that, but it was true.

I had exactly one hour. One hour to get myself ready for work and reality. It didn't seem like near enough time, considering just a few minutes ago, I'd been flown here via my boyfriend's helicopter.

Boyfriend. Helicopter. Private Island… Fantasy.

We stayed on the island last night, sleeping with the giant sliders in his room wide open so the sounds, scents, and feel of the tropics surrounded us.

I honestly couldn't tell you which was better—his arms or everything else.

Actually, I could tell you. It was him.

After letting myself into my apartment, the scent of coffee wafted from the kitchen.

"You're up," I said, coming around the corner, expecting to see Valerie leaning against the counter like a zombie.

"Agh!" I screeched, realizing too late it was *not* Val.

Aaron froze for a few seconds, then calmly went back to what he was doing.

Do you want to know what he was doing?

Standing in front of our open fridge, in his boxers, drinking out of the milk carton!

So many things. There were so many things I could start with. "You slept here last night?" I asked, averting my gaze.

My heavens, he wasn't even embarrassed to be practically naked in front of me.

"Yep," he said, pushing the fridge door closed but keeping the milk. "Coffee?"

"After I just caught you slurping out of the milk? I'll pass."

"I was totally waterfalling it." He scoffed.

"Water-whating it?" I repeated.

Instead of explaining, he gave me a demonstration. How considerate of him.

Waterfalling = pouring the milk into your mouth without wrapping your lips around the container.

Apparently, in Aaron's eyes, this made this behavior acceptable.

"Carter upstairs?" he asked, setting aside the carton and grabbing a mug for coffee.

"Make yourself at home," I muttered.

Aaron turned, his blue eyes ornery and amused. "I have."

"Clearly." After giving him a dry look, I answered his question. "Yes, he's changing, then heading to the office."

He put down the mug, forgetting the coffee. "Gotta go, then."

He started past, and yeah, maybe I checked him out a little. You know, because it was my duty as a Val's BFF to see what kind of man she was involving herself with.

Plus, I mean, dude was standing around in his underpants. If he didn't want me to look, he should have worn clothes.

Aaron wasn't thin like Carter. His body was thicker, more muscular. His chest and shoulders had clear definition, and so did his taut waist. There was a tattoo on one of his biceps and a smattering of dark hair in the center of his chest. His hair was buzzed short, which seemed to make his jaw appear wider.

Basically, he didn't look anything like the butler I originally thought he was. But he did look like a bodyguard, and considering he was head of Carter's security, that was a good thing.

Backtracking a little from the living room, he leaned in to say, "You checking me out?" He tsked. "What will Carter say?"

I smacked him in the center of the chest.

"Ow!" he wailed, rubbing the spot.

Rolling my eyes, I told him, "Don't be such a baby."

Grumbling under his breath, he went back into the living room, grabbing up his clothes from the coffee table to pull them on.

"You slept on the couch?" I asked, seeing the rumpled blanket and pillow.

"Where else was I supposed to sleep?"

"I thought maybe you and Val..." I actually blushed a little, averting my gaze.

He grunted. "I'm working on it."

I forgot I was embarrassed, my eyes lifting again. "You are?"

"Why else would I park my ass on that uncomfortable couch?"

"Because Carter asked you to."

He barked a laugh. "Carter and I are close, but my love life is mine."

"You're interested in Val?"

"Didn't I just say that?"

Well, not really. But I guess he thought so. Of course, he also thought waterfalling was an acceptable thing.

Completely dressed, he looked toward the bedroom. "Tell Val I'll see her later."

I nodded, and he brushed by.

"Hey." he called.

I turned, curiosity in my eyes.

"Don't hurt him, okay?" The sincerity with which he said that clutched my heart. I couldn't even be offended that he might even think I would do such a thing because it was so clear he was coming from a completely caring place.

Shaking my head, I promised. "I won't."

When he turned away, I pressed a hand to my heart, suddenly missing Carter like crazy.

"Hey!" I yelled, remembering.

Aaron came back.

I pointed to the milk on the counter. "Take that with you."

Cackling, he snatched the milk, letting himself out of the apartment.

Val was buried under her blankets, the top of her head just barely visible. Snatching the covers back savagely, I stared down at her.

"Val!" I demanded. "Why didn't you tell me about you and Aaron?"

Groaning, she reached around for the covers, but I wouldn't let her have them.

"We have to be at work in less than an hour."

Her eyes popped open. "Crap! Why didn't you wake me up sooner?"

"Because I was busy watching your boyfriend waterfall milk out of our fridge."

"He's not my boyfriend," she grumped, her still-sleepy face scrunched up. "What's waterfall?"

"Val!" I hollered. "Why didn't you tell me about you and Aaron?"

"There's nothing to tell," she said, climbing out of bed.

"Really? 'Cause just a few minutes ago, out there"—I pointed toward the living room—"he said he was totally interested in you."

She gasped. I'd never seen anyone wake up so fast in all their life. "He did?"

I made a sound.

She clutched my arm. "Did he really say that?"

"He really did."

A gleeful little shout peeled from her, and she fell back onto the bed as if she were fifteen and just got a new poster of her favorite celebrity crush.

"He's so hot," she proclaimed. "He insisted on staying here while you were gone because he didn't want me to be alone." Her heavy sigh filled the room.

Clearly, I didn't need to ask her how she felt. "So what was he doing out on the couch?"

Val sat up, acting offended. "Just what kind of girl do you think I am?"

I raised my eyebrows. "You've slept with guys you've liked a lot less than Aaron."

Her mouth dropped open.

Holding my hands up in surrender, I shrugged. "I'm not judging. I'm just pointing out the obvious."

"That *is* the obvious," she said, completely unoffended by my frank observation. Really, what was there to be offended by anyway? Val could do what she wanted as long as she was safe. "I like him. Like *a lot*."

"Okay…" I said, inviting her to elaborate.

"I can't just give it up like that. He needs to work for it."

I laughed.

"I'm serious!" She smacked me. "He's more to me than some fling. I want… more."

"Aww!" I crooned, rushing in to hug her.

"We have to get ready," she grumped but totally hugged me back.

"You picked a good one," I told her, going to the closet to choose an outfit. "I can tell he really likes you, too."

"So, hey, what's going on with you and Carter?" she yelled from the bathroom.

"What do you mean?"

Her head appeared around the doorframe, toothbrush hanging out of her mouth. "I mean there's all these rumors that he flipped his lid at the company the other day, smashed a bunch of stuff in his office,"

I frowned. Carter did that?

"Then you up and disappeared with him." Val went on. "I was worried until Aaron told me you were on the island and swore Carter would never hurt you."

301

"He wouldn't." I firmly agreed.

"Are you sure?"

"Valerie!" I gasped. Dropping my clothes on the bed, I turned on her totally. "How could you even imply that about Carter?"

Plucking the toothbrush out of her mouth, she brandished it like a weapon. "You don't have the best track record with men, Nor. Look at Alan—"

"Carter is not Alan!" I yelled. Protective instinct roared inside me. I wouldn't listen to anyone—not even Val—disparage him.

Slinking off into the bathroom, Val said nothing else. A few minutes later, she came out carrying a white hand towel. "I didn't mean anything bad against Carter. I like him. I really do. I was just worried."

The anger inside me evaporated. "I know. I'm sorry."

"Everything is really okay?"

Honestly, I didn't know. We hadn't talked about whatever it was that was bothering Carter. He'd just swept me away and asked for some time. I didn't tell her any of that, though. Instead, I nodded.

Satisfied, Val chattered the rest of the morning about Aaron, describing their first kiss in great detail.

I was partly finished curling my hair when someone rang the bell.

"It's probably Knox," I called, grabbing another strand to loosely wrap around the wand. Carter had to head into the office right away, and that meant my escort would be arriving.

A few moments later, Val rushed into the bathroom, her cheeks flushed. "It's Aaron!"

"Is Carter with him?"

She spoke in a hurried, hushed whisper. "No. He said Carter is already at the office, so he came back to walk with me."

I'd never seen Val so frazzled over any guy before. It was amusing and endearing at the same time. "Well, what are you standing in here for?"

"What about you?"

"I'm not ready yet." I motioned toward the wand. "Besides, he came for you, not me."

Her teeth sank into her lip. "We can't let you walk to work alone."

I rolled my eyes. "You sound just like Carter. I'm a grown woman. It's broad daylight."

"But—"

"But Knox will be here any minute."

Her eyes brightened. "Oh! Right."

Shooing her away, I said, "Go."

"Let's have lunch?" she said excitedly.

I nodded.

"Do I look okay?" she asked, twirling.

She was wearing a floral romper that looked like a dress but was really shorts, and she'd added a sheer white kimono and a pair of brown leather sandals.

"Ten out of ten." I promised.

She rushed off, and I laughed beneath my breath, turning back to my hair.

Seconds later, a large figure loomed in the mirror behind me, making me jump.

"Ow!" I wailed, the curling wand falling out of my grip and into the sink.

Aaron swore and rushed closer. "Did you burn yourself? Let me see."

Tilting my head to the side, I showed him my neck, which was stinging with pain.

His blue eyes darkened. "You should be more careful."

"You scared me!" I countered.

"Shit. Carter's gonna be pissed."

"I'm fine." I sighed. Gazing into the mirror, I winced. There was definitely going to be a blister. "What are you doing in here anyway?"

"To remind you not to go anywhere without Knox."

"Why does everyone around here think I'm five?" I grumbled, fingering the area around the burn.

"Carter's lost a lot in his life. The fact that he put a bodyguard on you shows how important you are to him. Just let him have this, okay? It doesn't hurt you, and it makes him more at ease."

Forgetting about the stinging, I met Aaron's eyes. "Why does it feel like there's a lot about Carter I don't know?"

"He'll tell you when he's ready."

"You know everything?" I pressed.

He nodded.

"And what do you think?"

"I think you should you should wait for Knox before heading into the office."

Nodding, I turned back to the sink.

I guess it wasn't as hard as I thought to step back into reality, because here I was, already waist deep. I wanted to give Carter all the time he needed, but I also thought it was time for us to talk.

I was finger-combing through the curls to create loose waves when the bell rang again. Finishing up, I grabbed my bag and slipped into my heels.

"I need coffee!" I declared, pulling open the door. "I'll get you a bagel—" The words died on my lips. It wasn't Knox. "Alan?"

"Expecting someone else?"

"How did you get my address?"

"We need to talk."

I swung the door closed, but he slammed his hand against it and pushed.

"Leave, now!" I demanded, then threw all my weight into the door. We struggled against each other, the door pushing open, then closed... like a tug-of-war I was destined to lose.

"Just go!" I cried, stumbling back when he shoved hard.

The door banged against the wall, and he stepped in.

"I'll call the police," I threatened, fumbling for my phone.

"I wouldn't do that if I were you."

The cool, calm tone he used made me pause. "Why?"

"Because you're going to want to hear what I have to tell you about Carter."

Thirty-Eight

Carter

"Where the hell have you been?" Bryan demanded, barging into my office not even five minutes after I arrived.

"Home."

"You haven't answered any of my texts or calls." Bryan fumed. "Have you even checked your messages."

"Why bother? You're here now."

"Dammit, Carter!" He slapped the file he was carrying onto the coffee table. "This isn't the time to be all nonchalant about things."

"I'm always like this, and it isn't like I haven't gone off the grid before," I rebutted, much calmer than he was.

"Well, it's the first time Lewis Regal strolled into the building and pissed you off so badly you had security cart him away."

"I needed some time."

"What the hell happened?" he asked, standing on the other side of my desk with a pleading look in his eyes. "What did he say that could make you disappear like that?"

"You act like me disappearing is something strange. Up until recently, I never worked more than a few days a week."

"Until Nora got here."

Maybe it was his tone. Maybe it was the irritation I felt at having to come here and deal with this. Or perhaps I felt more bonded to Nora than ever. But the fact he brought up my girlfriend really pissed me off.

"Nora isn't part of this conversation." The command in my tone was clear and final.

Holding up his hands in surrender, he backed away from the desk to drop into a chair. "Are you going to make me ask again?"

"He threatened to leak the sealed documents," I answered.

Sitting forward, his face paled. "He did what?"

"He knew about the case, of course." I continued. "Said if I don't sell him *Zero*, he will bring me and Ansoft down."

Shooting up out of his seat, Bryan stacked his hands at the back of his neck and paced. "This is bad. This is really bad. The whole company could go up in flames."

"I'm not going to let that happen," I said, watching him. In between the sexy times, playing around on the beach, and skinny dipping in my pool, I'd had some time to think. To plan.

"You're going to sell him the game?" He surmised, relief in his words. "I think it's a smart move. We can—"

"I'm not selling him the game!" I snapped. How many times did I have to tell him?

"There's only one other option, then."

I lifted an eyebrow. "Which is?"

"Step down as CEO. I'll take over control of Ansoft, and then Regal won't be able to do anything to us."

Lifting the coffee Meghan had supplied, I regarded my business partner as I sipped. My silence must have rattled him because he stopped moving and stared.

After a long, charged silence, during which I didn't blink or look away from him, I set down the mug and folded my hands over my chest. "You think I should step away from the company that I built? The company I own?"

"We built it together," he rebuked, his tone much less confident.

I lifted an eyebrow.

He cleared his throat. "It's not like I meant permanently. I just mean until after we released *Zero* and it's dominating the market. Regal wouldn't have any reason to leak what happened all those years ago because the game would already be out there." Scratching behind his ear, he went on. "You can come back, and it will be like nothing ever happened."

"Pretending nothing happened when something did is the way cowards live. Do I look like a coward to you?"

"Of course not." Straightening his tie, he went to the water cart to pour himself a glass. "If you aren't selling or giving up the CEO title, then what are you going to do?"

I smiled. "I'm going to call his bluff."

He spun to face me, the water in his glass sloshing onto his hand. "What?"

"Meghan is scheduling a press conference as we speak. I'm going to disclose it all myself."

"Anders, that's career suicide!" Bryan exclaimed. "We need to be doing damage control right now, not creating more fallout."

"I don't think that's what I'll be doing."

"This isn't just about you and the warped relationship you have going on with Regal! We have an entire company to protect. Our employees depend on us for their livelihoods."

"That's exactly why I'm doing this." Standing up, I adjusted my jacket and the T-shirt beneath it. "Regal thinks he can threaten me by exposing my past. By making me look like some... killer." I nearly choked on the word. Memories from years ago assaulted me, bringing back panic and pain. "He seems to be forgetting one thing, though."

"What?"

"I'm innocent."

A strangled noise came out of my partner's throat. "No one cares!" he yelled. "It's all about public opinion, about the way you look. You know damn well this will hurt Ansoft's image. There is no parent out there who will let their kid download a game from a company whose CEO is a rumored murderer."

It was hard for me to say, but it was ten times harder for me to hear it come out of Bryan's mouth. It was almost as if he didn't think I was innocent. Or he didn't care.

Regarding him for a long moment, I picked up the phone and called Meghan. The second she picked up, I said, "Get Carl Frost down here. I have some urgent documents that need drawn up."

"What the hell are you calling your lawyer for?" Bryan asked when I hung up.

"I'll buy you out."

309

"Wh-what?"

"I'll buy your portion of the company. I'll give you double its market worth, and then I'll give you a cut of *Zero's* first two quarterly profits. You'll never have to work another day in your life."

"Are you fucking crazy?"

"I was just sitting here wondering the same thing about you."

His expression transformed into a mask of confusion.

"It's obvious you think of me as a murderer, and so I sit here and wonder how you've managed to work with me for so long."

His expression turned more incredulous by the second, and a lot of the color seeped out of his skin. "Carter, you know me. We're bros. I don't think you're a murderer. I said that's what *other* people will think."

"And since we're friends, I'm cutting you a check and sending you on your way so you won't need to worry about what other people think."

"When people called you cool and emotionless, when people whispered you were antisocial and didn't have a heart, I thought they were being stupid. I thought they just didn't see what I see." Bryan sounded shell-shocked.

"And now?" I inquired.

"And now I realize it was me who couldn't see what they did."

It felt like the barbed wire I had guarding my heart suddenly betrayed me and attacked. "All the more reason to get paid and get out." I was good at hiding my emotion, good at keeping my voice casual and strong.

Forging to his feet like a battle star in one of our action games, he declared, "No. I won't let you buy me out. I'm not giving up all the hard work we've done together."

"But just a few moments ago, you wanted *me* to go."

"Temporarily!" he insisted. "Just until things calm down."

"I can't say things will be calm after the press conference, but business won't suffer."

"How can you be so confident?"

"Because while I'm *spilling all the tea,* as all of those online bloggers like to say, I'll also announce *Zero* and that it will be dropping next week."

"Next week?"

"Of course. If I'm going to whip up this kind of media frenzy, I might as well use it as free publicity for our new launch." Pursing my lips, I considered. "I think you'd be surprised at how many people will want to download a game that inspired so much corporate scandal."

Bryan's wide-eyed stare followed me as I walked to the door. "Where are you going?"

"I need to talk to Nora."

"She knows about all this?"

The first inkling of fear introduced itself. It was cold and sharp and made me feel I was doing the wrong thing.

"Not yet." I admitted. "I'm telling her now before the press conference. I won't go on record about any of this until she knows about it first."

I left Bryan standing in my office, things between us not really settled but my position made clear. I didn't have time to hash this out with him right now, not when there was Nora. I'd put this off until I literally couldn't anymore.

What if I told her everything and she left me? What if she looked at me the way everyone else did back then?

I'd let her in. All the way in.

I really hoped I wasn't about to regret it.

Thirty-Nine

Nora

"What could you possibly have to say to me about Carter?" I demanded.

"Obviously, you think I know something, because here I am." He gestured around the condo. His face turned thoughtful. "I'm impressed. This place is pretty nice. I assume you aren't the one paying for it."

"Say whatever it is, and then get out." Did he think insulting me was going to buy him any bonus points? The *only* reason he was standing in my living room was because he claimed this involved Carter.

It wasn't as if I would blindly believe anything Alan told me, but I wanted to at least hear what it was. Knowing Alan and his father had some kind of business rivalry going on with Carter was reason enough to get any details I could that might help Ansoft.

"Have you thought any more about my offer?" Alan asked, placing the file folder of papers he was carrying on the coffee table. The blanket Aaron used last night was still in a heap, and I admit I thought about throwing it over Alan's stupid head and bolting.

"I'm not interested." I kept my reply clipped.

"I think you should reconsider."

God, he was so freaking smug. Arrogance clung to him like the worst kind of aftershave, nearly making me gag.

Folding my arms over my chest, I sighed. Loud.

Using one finger, he pushed the documents toward me. "Go on. Have a look."

My feet stayed where they were, my stare bouncing between my ex and whatever was in that folder.

"Carter Anders is not who you think he is." Alan gestured again toward the file.

Stomping forward, I snatched up the file, flipping it open. A photograph fell toward me, almost sliding to the floor. The second I lifted it, my stomach lurched. Dropping it onto the stack of papers, I turned my face away. "What is this?"

"That's who your boyfriend really is."

The photo was of a dead body. No more than a teenager, the boy lay limp and lifeless against a pale tile floor. His skin had a bluish-purple cast, and his lifeless eyes were open, staring at something no one else could see. He wasn't wearing a shirt, and there were red scratch marks all over his chest as if he'd been scratching at himself excessively.

Though he looked cold, the hair on his forehead was matted with sweat, and all the muscles in his entire body seemed wilted. A single rivulet of deep-red blood dripped from his nose, proof that his body had given up.

There wasn't anything especially gory about this photo, but it didn't matter. I would have nightmares about this image for many nights to come, and the endless thoughts of how, why, and who would plague me maybe forever.

Glancing up through teary eyes, I pinned Alan with a hard stare. "Why?" I rasped. "Why would you show me something like this? No warning, no consideration."

That was Alan, though. He never had considered me at all.

"Sometimes the best way to get through to someone is with shock."

"This isn't shocking." I disagreed. "This is cruel." Punctuating my words, I took the photo and flicked it to the floor, where it fell face down near my feet.

"That boy right there." Alan pointed at the photo. "That's the boy Carter killed."

I sucked in a breath. For long moments, the world around me tilted. "What did you just say?"

"It's all right there, Nor. In black and white. I knew you'd never believe me if I just told you. I had to bring proof. I needed you to see who you've allowed into your life."

Shocked, I glanced down at all the papers. My vision was blurred and my brain sluggish, so I couldn't even see what I was looking at.

An impatient sound ripped out of Alan's throat as he bolted aggressively toward me. I cringed away, the reaction purely instinctual.

"You're scared of me?" He fumed, eyes incredulous. "Me? I just handed you proof that your boyfriend is a murderer, and it's me you flinch away from!"

"We both know I have reason to be wary of you."

Rage lit his face, the heat in his eyes scaring me. "This!" He slapped his hand on the papers in my hands. "This is what you should be scared of."

315

The second slap flipped the entire folder out of my hands. Papers scattered over the coffee table.

I took a step away from Alan.

Closing his eyes, he dragged in a long, ragged breath, blowing it out slowly. Seconds later, when his eyes reopened, they were kinder, but I was still afraid.

"My father met Carter Anders when he was seventeen years old," he said, bending to scoop up all the papers. "That game, *Primal Fear,* the one that used to be really popular?" he asked, glancing up at me.

I nodded. I knew the game.

"Regal Tech owns that game."

"They do?" I answered, surprised. "I didn't know your father's company was in video games."

"Regal Tech is involved in everything technology has to offer. Gaming is one of those things. However, it is not our strongest department. We're working on building it up."

"What does this have to do with Carter?" *And that body I just saw?*

"Carter is the one who created *Primal Fear.* He sold it to my father."

Carter created a video game when he was seventeen? Not just any video game, but one that was purchased by one of the biggest tech companies in the country.

"Why would he sell it?" I wondered, not really asking Alan, more like just thinking out loud.

"Guilty conscience maybe?" Alan quipped.

Remembering he was there, I looked up. "What?"

"That dead kid? That was his best friend. The friend who helped him create that game. Just as they were about to sell it to my father for a huge payday, his friend"—Alan pointed to the floor where the photo still lay—"died."

The first thing I felt was sympathy. It hit me hard and swift, punching a hole right in my stomach, making it hard to breathe deep.

"How did he die?" I asked, wrapping an arm over my waist.

"Overdose. From pills your boyfriend fed him."

"No," I whispered, shaking my head.

"Yes. Carter Anders didn't want to share any of the millions my father was paying for that game, so he got his friend and partner drunk and then convinced him to take a handful of pills."

"You're lying!" I yelled, tears streaking down my cheeks.

"It's all here!" Alan roared, brandishing the papers like a well-sharpened sword. "Because they were minors at the time, the case was sealed, unavailable to public record."

I dashed away the tears on my face, only to have them replaced with more.

Alan rushed forward, grabbing me by the shoulders and forcing me to look into his face. "When I found out you were involved with him, I did everything in my power, me and my father, to get these records to prove to you that you can't trust him."

I struggled to get away, but he only gripped harder. The papers crinkled and pressed against me beneath his fingers, and I looked at them, horrified, not wanting any of their ink to touch me.

"Get off of me!" I finally yelled, stomping down on his foot with my heel.

He wailed in pain and fell back on the couch. I rushed around the coffee table, putting it between us.

"You bitch!" He snarled. "I do all this for you, and this is the way you repay me?"

Anger rose to meet the hurt and confusion I felt. "Oh, so you didn't do this for me, then. You did this so I would owe you a debt. Isn't that right, Alan? What is it that you want? Huh? Inside information on *Zero*? Why is that? Because Regal Tech's gaming division is so bad you have to steal from Carter?"

Alan rushed me, but I held my ground. I was done cowering to him. I was done being afraid.

"That game is rightfully Regal's! Everything Carter has, his entire company, he wouldn't have any of it if it weren't for my father."

Grabbing his arm, I dragged him forward. "Get out! You disgust me. I can't believe I ever loved you."

An inhuman sound drowned out everything else. One minute, I was pulling him, trying to force him to the door, and the next, it felt I was flying, free-falling backward with no sign of a net.

Crack!

The base of my skull hit against the edge of the coffee table, and sharp pain burst through my entire neck and head. My body slumped, and unable to hold myself up, I dropped over onto the floor.

"You still choose him? Even after hearing he's a fucking killer, you dare try to kick me out of this place!" Alan roared over me, but I only heard half of what he was saying. Things were fuzzy.

I tried to look up at him, but my eyes only got as far as the photo lying halfway under the couch.

A sharp splintering sound cut through the heaviness dropping over me. Then a loud yell and grunts of pain followed.

Reaching for the table, I tried to pull myself up. My grip wasn't strong enough. My fingers didn't seem to want to work. Every time I'd grab the edge, my arm would fall right back to my side.

"Ma'am!" a familiar voice called out.

I felt myself smile. "Knox… I was hoping you'd come."

My bodyguard's worried face came into view.

"There's two of you," I murmured. "Two is better than one."

"Hang on, ma'am. I've got help coming."

"Alan," I said, trying to lift my hand. Knox grabbed it and held it in his. "He was here."

"I got him." He assured me. The tone of his voice changing dramatically.

"I want Carter," I whispered, suddenly feeling the weight of unconsciousness pulling me under.

"Stay with me!" he yelled, lifting me against his body. "Stay with me, Nora!"

"Carter…" I gasped, a thought suddenly coming to me. "The file," I told Knox. "You have to get the file. Don't let anyone else see." I struggled to get up, to get out of his hold so I could find those papers.

"Sit still," he insisted, but I struggled still.

"You have to hide those papers!"

"Okay, okay." Knox eased me back, a string of curses cutting through the room.

"You have a foul mouth," I mumbled.

Through blurry, darkened vision, I watched him strip off the black jacket he always wore so well. He leaned down, pressing it at the back of my head, making me whimper in pain.

"We gotta stop the bleeding," he said.

"The papers…"

319

"I got them." He assured me.

"You did?"

"Yes." Then to someone I couldn't see, he yelled, "I don't care. Get him on the goddamn phone! *Now!*"

Somewhere else in the room, a phone went off, the ringing extremely loud. I moaned.

"Ma'am." Knox worried, applying more pressure to the back of my head.

"That hurts!" I complained.

Abruptly, the ringing was cut off by Alan's voice. "Yeah?"

"I thought I fucking knocked you out." Knox jolted forward, but I cried out, making him come right back. "What is it?"

"Stay with me," I pleaded.

"Okay, shh." He agreed. "Where the fuck are the paramedics?"

"It didn't work," Alan said, his voice sounding thick with pain. "Go to plan B."

"Plan B?" I echoed. "What's plan B?"

"Fuck this," Knox announced, and suddenly, I was no longer on the floor but in his arms as he ran way too fast.

"I think I'm going to be sick." I gagged.

"It's okay. Go ahead." If anything, his steps increased.

My body tensed, and vomit burned the back of my throat. My stomach heaved, making the pain in my head so severe I was finally granted with unconsciousness.

Forty

Carter

I left my phone on my desk.

I realized when I stepped into the elevator, but going back to get it involved seeing Bryan again, and I was done with him today.

He was a traitor. I knew it with every fiber of my being.

I started suspecting back when he tried to convince me to take the twenty-five million, but I'd given him the benefit of the doubt, realizing that kind of money was enough to make anyone go a little crazy.

But just now? Offering to take over my company "temporarily" for the good of everyone?

Bullshit.

I didn't know just how deeply he'd deceived me yet, but I would find out. Oddly, the betrayal didn't hurt as much as I expected. Maybe because I'd already suspected, or maybe because I had never let Bryan all the way in.

Still, I'd trusted him. Something I did with very few people. I thought this kind of betrayal from him would be enough to send me scurrying back to my island to protect myself.

But I wasn't thinking of me right now. I was thinking of Nora. Of finally opening up and giving her what she'd been asking for all along: reality.

I would be okay. I'd be okay if she could understand, if she didn't look at me the way everyone else had back then. Everything would be fine when she knew I was doing exactly what I said I would: outing myself.

With Regal involved, being outed was inevitable. If I was going to be thrust into the spotlight this way, I would do it on my own terms.

I wasn't a scared seventeen-year-old anymore. I was beyond manipulation, and even if all this blew up in my face, I would be okay.

I would.

As long as Nora understands.

Our building came into view, and I boarded the elevator. Every floor that I went up, my nerves frayed just a little bit more. My past was not something I was proud of. My past was something I had to live with every single day. It was the kind of past that would forever be part of the present because living with it was part of my penance.

The second the doors opened onto her floor, I was distracted by commotion in the hallway. Uneasiness propelled me forward toward several paramedics wearing full gear and carrying equipment as they stepped out of Nora's apartment.

Every drop of blood in my body went cold. Frantically, I looked around for Knox, hoping he could offer some sort of explanation. He was nowhere to be seen.

"Excuse me!" Jogging the rest of the way to the apartment, I stopped, craning my neck to see inside the open door. "What's going on here?"

"This your apartment?" one of the EMTs asked.

"I own it." I confirmed.

"We received a 9-1-1 call about an injured female—"

"Nora!" I yelled, shoving past them into the apartment. "Nora!" I yelled again, rushing back into the bedroom, banging open the bathroom door.

She wasn't there.

"Sir!" one of the men yelled.

I ran back out, skidding to a stop in the living room. There was blood on the floor and smeared on the coffee table.

"What the hell happened?" I demanded, pointing violently toward the mess.

"We don't know. When we got here, the door was open, but the place was empty."

"Empty?" I echoed. Reaching into my pocket for my phone, I cursed. I didn't have it.

Grabbing one of the EMTs by his jacket, I dragged him close. "Who called you? What did they say? Was it Nora?" My heart was racing, and there was a low ringing sound in my ears.

"We don't know. We—"

I shoved him away.

"Hey!" one of the other men yelled, but I ignored them all.

Going over to the blood on the floor, I knelt beside it, as if being close would tell me whose it was. The corner of a white piece of paper sticking out from beneath the couch caught my attention. It was near the blood… so much blood.

My fingers quaked as I lifted the paper—a photo—and turned it over. I was assaulted by images, memories of that horrible night, of the weeks that passed after it. The betrayal, the pain…

"Carter!" Aaron yelled, running into the apartment.

"Get Knox on the line!" I bellowed, not even thinking to ask how he knew to come.

Cutting through the paramedics still standing around, he held out his cell. "He's here."

"Knox!" I bellowed. "Where's Nora?"

"Boss." Knox's voice didn't sound right. It was low and flat.

"Nora!" I yelled.

"We're at the hospital right now. I had to bring her into the ER."

Standing straight become too great a burden, and I sagged forward. Aaron was there, shoving his shoulder underneath me to offer support.

"Put her on the phone," I insisted.

There was a pause.

"The phone, Knox!" I yelled. "Put Nora on the fucking phone!"

"I can't."

If I thought I was cold before, now I was experiencing frostbite. Every part of me was numb, and if I allowed it, my teeth would chatter. "Why?"

"She's unconscious," Knox said but then quickly added, "She's going to be okay."

"Who did this?" I asked, the temperature in my voice matching that of my body.

Everyone in the room stilled and looked at me.

Good. Let them stare. Let them learn that I was not a man to be crossed.

"It was Alan."

I sucked in a breath. Against me, Aaron tensed.

"You take care of it?"

"I tried—" He began, anxiety in his voice.

"Don't you leave her side," I demanded. "Not for one fucking second!"

"I swear."

"I'm on my way," I growled, shoving the phone back at Aaron. "We have to go."

"She's already at the hospital, guys," Aaron explained to the confused paramedics. "Thanks for coming."

My legs felt like rubber, but I ran out into the hall anyway. Too impatient for the elevator, I shoved into the stairwell and ran down every flight.

Aaron kept pace with me as we erupted out of the building and onto the sidewalk.

"Taxi!" I yelled, running to the curb.

Occupied taxis passed by, not a single empty one in sight.

"Knox said she was gonna be fine," Aaron told me, trying to get me to bring it down a notch.

"I'm gonna kill him." I fumed.

Grabbing a handful of my shirt, he yanked me back, nearly wiping my feet out from under me. "You know you can't talk like that. Don't let me hear you say anything like that again."

"She's unconscious," I whispered, feeling something inside me crack. "She's fucking unconscious, and I'm not there."

Swearing, Aaron released me and waved toward the street. "Taxi!"

After a few endless moments of both of us screaming at every car that passed, I caught sight of one bright-yellow cab turning onto our street. Stepping off the curb, I waved both arms, signaling for it to stop. The unoccupied sign on the roof flipped to occupied, and the cab slid into a lane closer to us.

Anxiously, I waited, stepping a little farther out onto the pavement.

"Aaron!" I called, glancing back over my shoulder. "I got one!"

Aaron turned, and his face transformed almost instantly. Panic made him age about five years right before my eyes, and he started to run.

"No!" he yelled. "Carter, no!"

Confused, I turned to look, and realization slammed into me.

The cab coming to pick us up wasn't slowing down. Instead, it was heading right toward me, and I swear the sound of it accelerating filled the street.

Something slammed into me. The wind whooshed right out of me, and everything around me turned white. The sounds of tires squealing and people screaming filled my ears.

Hitting the ground with blunt force, I felt the skin on my elbows and forearms rip open with painful clarity. I rolled, falling onto my back and staring up at the Miami blue sky... thinking that the color reminded me of Nora's eyes.

Nora!

Forgetting I was just hit by a car, I lurched up, swaying on my feet.

Someone nearby caught my arm. "Are you okay?"

It took a moment to register it wasn't Aaron beside me.

"What?" I said, more confused than I realized.

"You almost got hit! Do you know the man who pushed you out of the way?"

Awareness came flooding back, overwhelming me with its sudden force. Whipping around, I looked out onto the street where there was a crowd of people gathered around something on the road.

Not something… someone.

"Aaron!" I bellowed, staggering forward. "Aaron!"

The crowd parted to reveal my brother, my best friend, lying in a bloody heap. Moaning, I dropped to my knees beside him, grabbing his face and screaming his name again.

"Carter," he answered, shocking me silent for long seconds.

Leaning down until we were almost nose to nose, I stared at him. "Don't you dare die," I threatened. "Don't you dare fucking leave me alone."

He tried to laugh, but it turned into a cough, and blood splattered my shirt.

"Help!" I roared. "Someone get some fucking help!"

I glanced around as the paramedics I'd just seen upstairs came out of the building.

"Get them!" I yelled, pointing. "Help! Over here!"

Seeing an emergency, the EMTs rushed over.

I turned back to Aaron, my heart nearly stopping with relief when he was still looking back at me. "How bad is it?" I asked.

"Bad enough I need a raise." His voice was weak, and the joke wasn't funny.

"Don't ever fucking do that again." I raged. "Don't you ever!"

"B-be c-careful," he rasped, pain twisting his face. Blood dripped from his cut lip and the gash in his forehead.

"Shh!" I shushed. "Don't worry about me. Take care of you."

The paramedics arrived, and I was forced to let them work.

When the ambulance pulled up and someone tried to look at the cuts on my arms, I rebuffed their attempts. "I don't care about me!" I seethed. "Take care of him!"

When they loaded him onto a stretcher and into the back of the ambulance, I climbed in beside him, taking his hand.

"Nora," he mouthed under the oxygen mask.

"I'll see her when we get there." I promised, totally not missing the fact that the two people who meant the most to me were currently in crisis.

Forty-One

Nora

"Nora?"

The voice calling out to me sounded a light-year away.

"Nora, can you hear me?"

His familiar voice beckoned like a single star in an otherwise black night. Just knowing he was nearby alleviated much of the loneliness I felt trapped in the dark like this.

"How much longer will she be out like this?" The anguish he clearly felt motivated me to battle back to him.

Slowly, I was able to open my eyes, the overhead light making me recoil.

"Nora?" I felt him lean over me. His frame offered a barrier against the light, making it so I could blink up at him.

I smiled. He was so beautiful... even if he looked like he'd been dragged into hell.

The thought was jarring and immediately made me afraid. "What's wrong?" I asked, trying to sit up. "What happened?"

"Shh, shh," he insisted, gently pushing me back onto the mattress. When he moved, the light blinded me again.

"It's so bright."

"Turn off the lights," Carter demanded to someone close by. "Get the doctor!"

The light switched off, making me sigh gratefully. Carter still floated over me, his hands hovering close, clearly wanting to touch me but also clearly unsure.

I looked around, trying to recognize where we were.

"Look at me." He cajoled. "Just look at me."

I did, searching his face for answers.

"We're at the hospital. There was an accident, and you passed out."

The explanation unlocked all the memories of earlier today as feelings and images replayed inside me. Pain radiated in my head, and I reached up.

"Don't touch it," he commanded gently, taking my hand and linking it with his. Kissing the back, he said, "You hit your head and have seven stitches."

"I just wanted him to leave," I said, a catch in my voice.

Carter stilled, but his eyes and touch remained gentle. "Who?"

"Alan." His name brought on a whole other host of thoughts, and I gasped. Springing up, wooziness overcame me, and I put a hand to my forehead.

Carter sat down on the side of the bed, wrapping an arm around my waist. "You need to rest right now."

"Knox." I worried. "Where's Knox?"

"He's getting the doctor."

Grabbing a fistful of Carter's shirt, I said, "Knox has some papers… papers we can't let anyone else see."

Something passed behind his expression, but my brain was too befuddled to make sense of what I saw. "Don't worry about that right now."

"I have to!" I pushed at his chest, thinking I could just get out of bed. The IV that was stuck into the back of my hand tugged, and I glared at it accusingly.

The door opened, and Knox rushed in, followed by a doctor in a white coat.

"Ms. Williams, you're awake," the doctor announced as if it weren't already obvious. "How are you feeling?"

"I'm not sure," I replied, still trying to get a handle on everything.

Even though I was awake and it seemed there was nothing seriously wrong with me, Carter appeared really stressed.

"I'll just do an examination, ask a few questions, and maybe make things a little clearer."

I nodded. Carter nudged me back against the pillows, staying very close.

The doctor cleared his throat. "I take it you also will refuse to leave the room?"

"Also?" I repeated.

"It's not happening," Carter replied, crossing his arms over his chest.

"Miss, are you okay with these gentlemen staying in the room for your exam?"

Carter made a rude sound, unfolding his arms.

Catching his hand, I pulled it into my lap, giving it a squeeze. "It's fine with me."

"I'll be over here." Knox assured me. "I won't look, ma'am. But if you need me, just yell."

Looking past the doctor, I watched Knox turn toward the corner. Something seemed strange about him, and then I realized. "Where's your suit? Why are you wearing scrubs?"

I didn't think I'd ever seen him in anything other than black before.

"Uhh…" Knox hesitated.

"Knox…" I warned.

"It's not important." Carter chimed in.

Knox looked between me and Carter as if he didn't know who to listen to. But then he sighed and glanced toward the floor. "You got sick all over my suit. The staff offered me these."

"Whose bodyguard are you?" Carter accused, betrayed.

"Mine," I announced. Glancing at the doctor, I said, "That's my bodyguard."

He nodded cordially. "He hasn't left your side since he brought you in."

"I'm sorry I threw up all over you," I told him.

"I needed a new suit anyway."

"Oh," I said, an idea coming to me. "We should get you something that isn't black."

"You're a patient." Carter reminded me, his voice strained. "This is not the time to talk about shopping."

Knox turned back to the corner, and the doctor came closer. Carter stood over us the entire time, watching his every move.

"Well then," the doc said, stepping back to make some notes in my chart. "It appears the blow to your head didn't do any serious damage. You do have a concussion, the stitches, and you'll probably have quite the headache for a day or two, but otherwise, I would say you were rather lucky."

"Why was there so much blood?" Carter asked, suspicious.

"How do you know how much blood there was?" I asked.

"Head wounds always bleed quite a lot," the doctor replied. "We'd like to keep you overnight for observation, and the nurse will be in later to tell you about wound care."

Carter thanked the doctor rigidly while Knox held the door open for him to leave.

My heavens, these guys were rude.

"Thank you," I called out, hoping to soften the way these boneheads acted.

When he was gone, I glared at both of them. "Why are you being so rude?"

Carter grunted. "If I act too nice, then he won't do his job right."

Knox made a sound of agreement.

"He's a doctor!" I exclaimed, then put a hand to my forehead.

Carter rushed close, putting his arm around me and easing me back. "Watch your head." He worried.

"Ma'am." Knox stepped toward the bed, concern in his tone as well.

Carter flicked a glance upward. "Go see if you can find any info on Aaron."

"Aaron? What's wrong with Aaron?" I stressed, sitting up again.

Knox hesitated nearby, but Carter gestured for him to get out.

The second we were alone, I turned questioning eyes on him.

"You need to rest."

"Where is Aaron?"

Sighing, Carter kicked off his shoes and climbed into the bed. Noticing the cuts and scrapes all over his forearms and the blood all over his shirt, I put a hand to his chest, stopping him.

"You're hurt!" Grabbing his wrist, I tried to look at his injuries.

"I'm fine," he insisted, shrugging off my hands.

"Knox!" I called.

"He already left—"

Knox burst into the room, cutting off Carter's words.

"Ma'am?"

"I told you to check on Aaron," Carter muttered.

"I need something to clean this," I told him, pointing at the injuries on Carter's arms.

"Right away." Knox agreed, disappearing.

Glowering, Carter asked, "How did you manage to get the loyalty of my men?"

"You're the one that said I had to have a bodyguard," I countered.

"Probably the same way you got mine," he murmured, petting my head.

My stomach dipped, and all I could think about was all the things Alan just told me about Carter. I couldn't believe him. I couldn't believe all the accusations he so callously offered up. How could I? How could I believe the man sitting here so obviously worried about me was a killer?

"What happened?" he asked quietly, realizing my thoughts were troubled.

Taking a breath, I shook my head. "I want to know about Aaron first."

Visibly, he debated. I could practically hear the turmoil going on inside him. Grasping his hand, I said, "Please tell me."

As he wrapped an arm around me, I leaned into him more than the bed.

"On our way here, he was hit by a car."

I gasped. "Where?"

"Outside our building. I'd gone home to see you, but then we got the call from Knox."

"He's here at the hospital?"

Carter nodded, his face slightly ashen. "He's in surgery."

"Surgery!"

"You need to stay calm."

"How bad is he?" I pressed, ignoring him.

"He was conscious the whole time. He has some stitches, broken ribs... a collapsed lung."

Groaning, I leaned into him. The back of my head felt tight and oddly numb. There was pain, but it was muted somehow.

"Did they give me pain medication?"

"Is it not working?" he demanded. "Are you in a lot of pain?"

"No." Tugging him back down, I tried to assure him. "It's not as bad as I thought it would be."

"I wasn't here when they gave it to you. I was with Aaron."

"You should go be with him now."

"He's in surgery. There's nothing I can do right now."

Our eyes met. His were bleak and tired.

With a sigh, he pressed his lips against my forehead, holding them there. "Thank God you're awake. Thank God you're okay."

A nurse entered, Knox trailing behind. "There's need for first aid in here?" she asked, carrying a small kit.

"Here." I pointed to Carter. "He's all scraped up."

"I told you I'm fine." Carter complained.

Looking over his injuries, the nurse made her own conclusion. "It will get infected if you leave it like this."

"See!" I insisted. Reaching for the kit, I said, "I'll do it."

"No." Carter shook his head. "You need to lie down."

"Over here," the nurse directed, pointing to a chair near the bed.

Carter slipped away and sat down. "Any news on Aaron?" he asked Knox.

Knox's face was somber. "Not yet. He's still in surgery."

The nurse worked quickly and efficiently, cleaning up Carter's arms and covering them with large bandages.

When she was gone, Carter looked at Knox. "Why don't you take a breather? Get some coffee and food."

When he looked to me for confirmation, I smiled. "Maybe bring a coffee back for Carter?"

He started to go, but I called him back.

"What about those papers? The ones I asked you to take from the apartment?"

Reaching behind him into the waistband of the scrubs, he pulled out a folded stack of papers. Laying them on the bed beside me, he said, "I'm sorry I didn't get Alan. At the time, I had to choose between him and you."

"You made the right choice," Carter said.

"Thank you for being there." I agreed, my eyes suddenly welling with tears. "If you hadn't come…"

"Ma'am." Knox leaned over the bed to hug me.

"Watch her head!" Carter barked.

I hugged the bodyguard, sniffling into the scrubs. He patted my shoulder.

"All right, enough," Carter said after a short period of time. "Out."

When we were alone, Carter's eyes drifted to the papers lying beside me. "What happened between you and Regal?"

Laying my hand protectively on the stack, my stomach twisted and the back of my head throbbed a little more than before. Still, I didn't shy away. I couldn't. "I was on my way to work when he showed up. I told him to leave, but he said he had information about you, information I needed to know."

"You let him in," Carter quietly surmised.

I couldn't read his voice. I couldn't tell what he was thinking, and that scared me.

"I only did it because I wanted to know what he was planning. I wanted to know so I could protect you."

"And look where that got you."

"You're mad."

"You're damn right I'm mad!" He exploded. The Adam's apple in his throat bobbed furiously, and his black eyes glittered. "He could have killed you."

"He didn't."

"You think that makes it okay?" He scoffed, planting his hand on his waist, dropping his chin toward the floor. "Death isn't a game. It's final. Once you lose, there's no turning back. And the people you leave behind..."

Whispering his name, I slid across the bed, throwing my feet over the side.

"What would I have done if you'd died?" he whispered, his voice tortured and filled with so much pain.

But more than just pain. *Experience.*

It was the voice of a man who'd lost to death. A man who deeply feared death would steal from him again.

"You have to think about that now," he implored, eyes seeking out mine.

My legs were wobbly, the floor icy against the balls of my feet. I felt like I'd been in a car accident. Every muscle in my body ached, and my scalp prickled with pain.

I moved forward anyway. There was literally nothing that would keep me from following the broken voice of the man I loved.

"You have to think about what will happen to me if you die. Our lives might not be tied together, but you're my heart." His voice caught, and the palm of his hand rubbed against his chest. "A man can't live without his heart."

The IV stand rolled past me when I wrapped my arms around his neck, plastering against him as tight as I could, hugging him fiercely. The tears dripping from my eyes soaked into his shirt, the fabric already stained with his best friend's blood and now his lover's tears.

"Sorry," I whispered. "I'm sorry." It didn't seem to matter how close I got. It just wasn't close enough. I needed more... He needed more.

Pulling back abruptly, I reached for the buttons on his shirt.

"Nora."

"Closer," I told him as I undid one after the other. When finally the shirt was open, I put my arms against his waist, stepping nearer to lay my cheek against his bare skin.

A shuddering breath vibrated his body, and he clutched me close.

It didn't matter. Those papers laying over there on the bed, the unsealed court documents revealing such a dark secret, might as well be blank.

I loved Carter.

I loved him in a way I thought only existed in fantasy.

Except this was reality. Scary, ugly, dangerous… but I loved him still.

Pulling back only enough to look up, I said, "We should   talk."

Forty-Two

Carter

She said she wanted reality.

But how much was too much?

I think perhaps I'd just found out. The papers lying on the hospital bed were sort of like a premonition of bad things to come.

"I don't regret it," I told her, pulling back completely.

"Regret what?"

Glancing at the papers, then back at her, I said, "Not telling you everything right away. I wanted you just for me. You wanted the reality, and I wanted a fantasy."

Tugging on one open side of my shirt, she stepped closer. "I want you just for me, too. But how can I have that when you hide part of who you are?"

Is this where it was? The point where reality and fantasy crossed? The point where they met and existed together?

A sharp knock on the door made us both look around. A uniformed police officer pushed open the door and walked in, followed by a man dressed just like him.

I knew they would come, but their presence felt like an intrusion. Did I mention my distrust for people in general started with police officers?

Sworn to protect and serve, they said.

My experience said otherwise.

Moving around Nora, I gazed at them directly. "Officers."

"Ms. Williams? We have some questions about what happened today."

"She's not up for twenty questions."

"The sooner we can get a statement, the better," the officer rebuked, coming farther into the room.

"Carter." Nora's voice was soft, and so was her hand when it clutched the back of my shirt. I turned, noting her anxiousness. Easing an arm around her waist, I guided her and the IV pole back to the bed.

Not allowing her to climb in, I lifted her to place her in the center. Her hand clutched at my shirt again, firmly holding me in place. The question in my eyes was answered as she smoothly reached over to grab the papers Knox left and tucked them beneath her pillow.

Surprise caught me off guard. Was she protecting me right now?

Why?

"I'll tell you whatever it is you want to know," Nora said, releasing my shirt.

I stayed at her side but shifted so the police officers could see her.

"You were assaulted in your home earlier today. The paramedics were called, but you didn't wait for them to arrive at the scene. Is that correct?"

Nora nodded. "My bodyguard thought they were taking too long, so he rushed me here himself."

"Your bodyguard…" He glanced down at the notepad in his hand. "Knox Wilson?"

She nodded.

"And you employ this bodyguard yourself?" the officer asked, but both of the men looked at me.

"I think we all know that Knox Wilson is employed by me."

"And you are?"

I decided to play their silly little game. "Carter Anders, CEO of Ansoft."

"How are you doing today, Mr. Anders?" the second officer asked.

"I've had better days."

"Ms. Williams, what is your relationship with Mr. Anders?"

My breath caught with the simple question. Perhaps if she'd been asked before this happened, I wouldn't have even thought of it. Though, now that she was hiding a stack of my secrets under her pillow and she'd been attacked because of me, the question was like a stick of dynamite just needing a match.

"He's my boyfriend."

My lungs deflated like a balloon that had just been stabbed with something sharp. I turned to look at her, seeking out answers for questions I hadn't been able to ask.

When she'd said we needed to talk, I figured it was the end for us. But she just called me hers.

Feeling my gaze, she looked up at me, offering the faintest of smiles.

"How long have you been dating?"

"A few months," I said, but at the same time, she answered, "A few weeks."

"Which is it?" he asked.

Nora cleared her throat. "We met a few months ago, but we just made it official a few weeks ago."

"You met before you started interning at Ansoft?"

Their knowledge didn't surprise me. In fact, I would have been shocked if they didn't know the answers to ninety percent of the questions they were about to ask.

"Yes. I met him at one of the resorts he owns."

"Why is it you have a bodyguard assigned to your girlfriend, Mr. Anders?"

"Because I value her safety."

"Did you have reason to believe her safety was at risk?"

I shrugged.

"Is it true that you've been having some intense business negotiations recently and that could be the reason?"

"They weren't negotiations. Lewis Regal of Regal Tech offered, on numerous occasions, to buy a new game I've developed, and I told him no. When money didn't work, he resorted to threats," I deadpanned.

"What kind of threats?" He quirked an eyebrow.

"Personal ones."

"You're going to need to be more specific," the officer pressed.

A pained sound came from the bed, making me forget about the two men.

"Nora?" I questioned, gently holding her face. "What is it? Should I get the doctor?"

"Can I have some water?" she asked, her voice weak.

Quickly grabbing the pitcher nearby, I dumped some water into a cup and held it to her lips. As she sucked through the straw, she gazed into my eyes.

Was she trying to distract everyone? To move the subject away from me?

"Thank you," she whispered, releasing the straw.

"If you need some time," the officer offered, and I started to take him up on it.

Nora spoke first. "Alan Regal, Lewis Regal's son, was trying to get me to betray Carter and hand over inside information on the game they wanted."

"Alan Regal is the man who was at your apartment this morning?"

Nora nodded. "He said he wanted to talk. When I asked him to leave, he got upset and shoved me."

My teeth snapped together. When I got my hands on that guy...

"And you hit your head?"

"On the coffee table." Nora leaned forward to point to the large bandage on the back of her skull. "I have seven stitches." Her eyes lowered. "They had to shave part of my head."

Pulling her hand away from the injury, I leaned down. "Good thing I don't love you because of your looks."

She giggled.

"Then what happened?" The officer continued.

"It's all a little fuzzy after that. I was bleeding a lot, lying on the floor. Knox must have heard Alan yelling at me and came inside..." Confused, she glanced at me. "Does Knox have a key?"

"He kicked the door down." I clarified.

Nora nodded. Then alarm flashed in her eyes. "It's okay. I told him he could!" she told the officers.

Pressing my lips together, I tried to hide the amusement I felt at her trying to protect Knox.

"Your bodyguard isn't in trouble," he informed her. "At least not for that."

Nora gasped. "He's in trouble for something else?"

This was the first I'd heard of this.

"Alan Regal is pressing assault charges against him."

"No!" she yelled. "He can't." Her hand went up to her head, and she made a small sound of pain.

"That's enough," I told the officers. "You're upsetting her."

"No!" Nora protested. "Let's finish." Peeking around me at the men, she said, "Knox only did what he had to do in self-defense. Alan attacked me. I was lying on the floor, bleeding, and he was ranting like a madman, blaming me for everything. He would have hurt me more if Knox hadn't showed up." Her breath caught, and pink bloomed in her cheeks.

"Okay." I soothed, sitting down beside her and slipping an arm behind her back. "Calm down."

"How can I?" she wailed. "Knox can't get in trouble for protecting me. He can't!" She started crying.

I got pissed.

Turning hard eyes to the officers, I stared at them.

"No charges have been filed." One of them spoke up. "He's just threatening at this point. We have to investigate to ascertain if he even has a case."

"Does he?" she whimpered.

"Your story and your bodyguard's match. Since he was asked to leave and then attacked you, I'm very confident in saying that any charges Alan Regal might bring will likely be thrown out."

Nora wrapped her arms around mine, leaning into my body. Feeling her rub her damp cheek on my sleeve made me look down. Tenderness swelled my heart. She was the injured one, but I hadn't seen her cry until Knox was threatened.

"I'll take care of Knox, good girl," I said quietly. "He'll be fine."

The officer's attention turned to me. "We understand you were involved in an incident today as well, Mr. Anders?"

"A hit-and-run," the other officer added.

I nodded.

Nora griped my arm tightly. "The person who hit Aaron just drove off?"

"Yes," I replied to everyone.

"What kind of car was it?"

"It was a taxi. The same kind that are all over Miami."

"Was there anything unusual about this cab?" The officer scribbled something on his notepad.

"Besides the fact that it tried to run me down?"

Nora jolted upright. "It tried to hit you?"

The officer's attention sharpened.

"Maybe we should take this outside," I suggested, starting to stand.

"Don't you even think about it, Carter Anders!" Nora scolded. "Sit down."

I sat. "I stepped off the curb to hail a cab. We were having trouble getting one and were in a hurry because I'd just gotten the call about Nora." As I spoke, I linked our hands. "The cab turned onto our street and changed lanes to come pick us up. I turned back to call out to Aaron. He noticed the cab was heading right for me and pushed me out of the way." Pausing a moment, I remembered thinking that I had been the one struck.

I wished I had.

"So the driver was trying to hit you, but your friend got in the way."

"That's right." I nodded once.

"Can you think of anyone who might want to hurt you?"

I scoffed. "Lewis Regal and his son."

"Because you refused to sell them a game."

I didn't like their tone or what it implied. As if a businessman as prestigious as Lewis Regal would do something so shady for a silly "game."

I made eye contact with each officer before answering. "He offered me thirty million dollars."

Both men visibly choked on the air.

"Excuse me?"

"It's not just some game. It's going to be the biggest game to hit the market since *Primal Fear.*"

"Are you saying you think Lewis Regal is behind the hit-and-run?"

I shrugged. "I wouldn't be surprised."

"Do you have any proof?"

I guess a thirty-million-dollar business deal wasn't proof enough.

Did I mentioned I didn't like cops?

"He just told you the proof!" Nora exclaimed.

I had to suppress a smile.

The man cleared his throat. "We need something a little more concrete."

"Of course you do. You want someone else to do your job for you."

"Carter!" Nora gasped.

Both men bristled.

"I'm sorry," she told the cops. "This has been a hard day for him. First me, then Aaron…"

I started to say something, but Nora squeezed my arm.

"Would you like to press charges against Alan Regal, ma'am?" the officer asked.

"Can I?"

The second officer nodded. "You would also be within your rights to get a restraining order."

"She'll do both," I declared.

"That's not your decision," the officer said coolly.

I stiffened, and Nora patted my arm. "I'd like to go ahead with both." Then in a quieter voice, she added, "Alan scares me."

They'd better lock him up, because if they didn't, I might get to him first.

"Is there anything else we need to know? Perhaps about the personal threats Lewis Regal made."

Nora tugged my sleeve. "I'm really tired."

"All right, baby, come on and lie down," I said, concerned she'd overdone it.

She turned on her side, resting on a pillow and closing her eyes.

"That's enough for today," the officer said. "If we have any further questions, we'll contact you. And if you remember any other details about the hit-and-run, please give me a call." One of the men stepped forward to hand me his card.

I took it and watched them leave.

"Are they gone?" Nora asked, cracking open an eye when the door clicked shut.

Lifting my eyebrows, I asked, "Did you do that to get them to leave?"

"Of course."

"It's almost like you were trying to protect me from their questions," I mused, thinking of how she interrupted them the first time they'd asked about the personal threats.

"I was."

I blinked and blinked again. Pointing a finger at her, I said, "You were trying to protect me?"

"Duh. That's what you do when you love someone."

"Love," I echoed, pressure crushing my chest.

Could it be? Could what Alan have told her not mattered?

Cautious, afraid to hope but already doing it, I asked, "What exactly did Alan tell you?"

Just then, Knox burst into the room. "Aaron's out of surgery."

Nora

Reality vs. Fantasy Observation #5:
Fantasy is having more than enough time.
Reality is never having enough.

Do you know how hard it was to have a private conversation with the man I loved in a hospital?

It was impossible.

Literally impossible.

I woke up confused. First, because when I reached for Carter he wasn't there. Second, because it took me a minute to remember where I was. The hospital. Overnight observation.

If the stark-white walls and antiseptic odor of the place hadn't been enough of a reminder, the pain in my head would have been. Whatever feel-good juice they gave me yesterday had officially worn off.

Gently probing the back of my head, I could tell the area was most definitely still swollen. The feeling of the buzzed area around it was jarring against my fingertips, but at least the length of my hair covered up the shorn section.

When I went to bed, Carter had been beside me. After the full day of events, we'd both been too exhausted to have the conversation waiting for us.

Worrying something happened while I'd been asleep, I slipped out of the bed. I had on Carter's socks again. He literally took off the ones he'd been wearing and put them on my feet last night.

I liked his clothes. I think I probably liked them better than my own.

Rolling the IV pole with me, I headed toward Aaron's room. His surgery had gone well, and the doctor said he would make a full recovery. He was heavily sedated the entire day, which made Carter doubt the good prognosis. I supposed it went back to his lack of trust. He needed to hear it from Aaron himself and not the doctors he didn't know.

The door to his room was open when I approached. Inside, I could hear both Carter's and Aaron's voices. Relief I didn't know I'd been seeking relaxed my body, making it easier to breathe.

"Did you get a good look at the driver?" Carter asked.

"Man, midthirties, baseball hat," Aaron replied. "Which could describe half the men in Miami."

Carter cursed low. "You shouldn't have done that. You should have let him hit me."

I pressed a hand to my mouth. The thought of it was just too horrible.

"I'm head of your security. This is my job."

"You're more than an employee to me, and you know that."

Aaron grunted. "Even more reason for me to protect you."

"You could have died. How would you have protected me from that?" The low anguish in his voice tightened my stomach. Carter was gruff and cold on the outside, many people probably thought he didn't have a heart. In actuality, though, his heart was tenderer than anyone else's.

Alan painted him out to be a villain, some kind of ruthless killer. I knew better. I knew the events that happened all those years ago were probably what shaped Carter into who he was today.

"I'm not going anywhere, punk. Someone's gotta stick around to keep you straight."

Peeking around the door, I watched Carter lean forward in the chair beside Aaron's bed. "Regal is going to pay for what he did to you."

"A man like that, you know he's going to be hard to take down."

"He's getting desperate, though, and desperate men always make mistakes."

Feeling a little guilty for eavesdropping, I stepped farther into the doorway. "Can I come in?"

Carter jumped up, put down the coffee in his hand, and rushed over. "What are you doing out of bed?" he asked, slipping an arm around my waist.

I missed you. "I wanted to check on Aaron."

"How's the hospital treating you, Nora?" Aaron asked.

"Probably about the same as it's treating you." I grinned. "Don't these make great accessories?" I motioned to the IV in my hand and his.

"The best." He agreed, chuckling.

He looked pale and tired, but the life in his eyes was all there. He also had stitches, his in his forehead.

His lip was busted, and I could see a few other cuts and scrapes on his arms.

"How's the ribs and the lung?" I asked, sitting in the chair Carter had just vacated.

"I'll be good as new faster than you can blink."

Leaning forward, I put my hand over his. Mildly surprised, he glanced down, then back at me. "Thank you for what you did," I told him, sincere. "I'm so glad you're going to be okay."

Emotion moved behind his eyes. Then he looked away. "What's with you two this morning?" His voice was gruff. "Getting all sappy and shit."

"You just wait 'til Valerie gets here," I teased.

He groaned. "Think the nurse will give me something to knock me out?"

Carter laughed.

"Be nice!" I scolded. "You should be thankful a woman like Val cares so much."

Aaron smiled. "I do."

"How much longer are you going to have to be here?" I asked.

"Not long," Aaron answered.

At the same time, Carter replied, "A few days at least."

Aaron made a rude sound. "I got shit to do."

"The only thing you got to do is get better."

"Don't make me get outta this bed," Aaron threatened, sitting forward.

Carter wasn't intimidated at all. "I'm your boss. I'll pull rank."

"Shit, kid. You're only my boss in name."

Carter took a step toward the bed, but I put my hand against his stomach. He was still dressed in the same bloodstained clothes from yesterday.

"What do you mean in name only?"

Aaron laughed.

"It's not in name only," Carter muttered. "I sign his paychecks."

"I work for your boy here because it's the only way he can keep me close enough."

I looked up at Carter for confirmation.

"You know it's hard to find people you can trust."

"So you aren't actually his butler, bodyguard, and head of security?" I asked, confused.

"He's all of those things."

"Butler, my ass," Aaron grumped.

"Carter said you were family."

Aaron's face cleared, and he nodded. "We are."

"I think I might still be confused," I mumbled, rubbing my forehead.

Carter leaned over me, concern in his face. "Should I get the doctor?" Brushing a strand of hair away from my face, he added, "You okay?"

"I'm fine." I promised. "I think the pain meds wore off is all."

"I'll get you some more." He started away.

I grabbed the tail of his shirt, tugging him back. "No, I'm fine. I need as clear of a head as I can get right now."

"Why's that?" Aaron asked.

"Because we need some kind of evidence proving Lewis Regal is behind this hit-and-run."

"That's not your job," both men said at once.

I rolled my eyes. "But I can help."

"No," Carter insisted, but Aaron seemed intrigued. "How?"

"I heard you talking before. You said everyone makes mistakes."

Carter's brows wrinkled. "So?"

"So…" I pursed my lips, thoughtful. "Lewis Regal and I share a common mistake."

Forty-Four

Carter

I pitied Aaron. And I'm not talking about his punctured lung, broken ribs, and host of other injuries.

I'm talking about the noisy woman currently making a fuss at his bedside.

Valerie was a serious piece of work.

But she was loyal, a good friend to Nora, and clearly into Aaron. That meant she was sticking like glue.

Maybe I'd get used to her volume.

Maybe—hopefully—Aaron could get her to tone it down.

With Aaron out of the woods and currently being worried over by his soon-to-be girlfriend, all my attention was back on Nora.

Not that it really ever left her.

Maybe now that she was sprung from the hospital, we'd actually get a chance to talk. I was more curious than ever about what happened between her and Alan. First, she protected me from the police and said she loved me. Then she tried to involve herself in catching Regal.

"Hey," she called softly, tugging on my hand.

My footsteps paused in the hall when our eyes collided. Forgetting the bustle of the hospital around us, the bright lights overhead, and the constant noise from the intercom, Nora was all I saw.

"Did you forget something?" I asked, gesturing back toward the room.

She shook her head.

Shifting closer, I tightened my hand around hers. "What is it?"

"I want to tell you something."

"We can talk when we get home." A private conversation in this hospital was clearly not going to happen.

"I can't wait," she said, glancing up and down the hall. Smiling secretly, she tugged my hand. "C'mon."

Nearby was a storage closet, no more than a box packed with medical equipment and who knew what else. The second the door closed behind us, the room was plunged into almost absolute darkness. The only light was from a small rectangular window in the door.

There was only enough room in here to stand, close enough that her chest brushed against me every time she took a deep breath.

It really wasn't the time, I know, but desire uncurled inside me.

"What is it you had to say that couldn't wait?" I asked, amused.

Her blue eyes found mine, even in the dim light. "I love you."

My heart skipped. "I already knew that."

"You *knew* it," she emphasized. "But do you *know* it?"

I swallowed thickly. Suddenly, the closet seemed much smaller than before. I wanted to touch her, but I was afraid to. "I know Alan probably told you some really bad stuff about me. I know he showed you this." Fishing out the now bent photo I'd found under her couch, I held it up.

Nora averted her eyes and pushed the photo down. "You were at my place?"

"Ironically, I was on my way to tell you everything. When I got there, I found this and your blood everywhere."

Grabbing the front of my shirt, she leaned in, resting her forehead against my chest. "I want you to tell me everything. I need to know."

"Right here in this tiny closet?" It didn't seem like the best place for something like this, but okay, if that's what she really wanted.

Her low giggle filled the darkness, making my heart skip again. "No. Not right here." Looking up, she smiled. Lifting onto tiptoes, she pressed her lips to mine.

It was a brief kiss, but I felt it all the way to my toes.

"You're nervous," she whispered.

"Yes." I agreed.

"You don't need to be."

My eyes searched hers for any indication of doubt.

Nora didn't back down from the interrogation my stare inflicted upon her. Instead, she merely smiled, confident in what I would find.

"I love you, Carter. Nothing is going to change that. I just wanted you to know that. I don't want you to be afraid."

"I'm not afraid," I refuted, even though her words were making it hard to talk.

"Yes. You are."

I picked her up, legs automatically winding around my waist. Turning so her back was pressed against the wall, I cupped the back of her head to protect it. "Say it again."

"You're afraid."

"Not that."

"I love you."

"Again."

"I love you."

I stole her lips and considered never giving them back. Her words replayed over and over inside me until they replaced the beat of my heart. That beat became the rhythm in which I kissed her, soft and gentle but without even once lifting my head.

I forgot we were in the hospital, forgot about all the words left unsaid. I wanted closer to her. I wanted to feel her around me. The small closet grew warm. My tongue stroked deep into her mouth.

Sliding my free hand beneath the hospital gown she was still wearing, I caressed the inside of her thigh and stroked over her core.

Nora shuddered against me, her kiss deepening.

"Nora," I whispered, breaking the kiss.

"I love you."

Reaching between us, I freed my throbbing cock, then pulled aside her damp panties.

Her arms tightened around my neck. Our eyes met.

In one push, I was inside her, her slick, tight core gripping me. Burying my face in the side of her neck, I thrusted upward, taking it slow as if we weren't in danger of being caught.

The muscles in my back rippled from pleasure, my balls drew up against my body, and inside her, I throbbed for release.

Tugging on my hair, she dragged my head back, meeting her unfocused gaze with mine. I watched her while her low moans filled the small closet.

Ready to burst, I buried myself deeper. Nora rocked slowly, her forehead falling to my shoulder. Both my arms wrapped around her, and we fell together, quivering and shaking as one body.

Her body went limp in my hold, so I leaned her against the wall while straightening her clothes and mine.

"Damn," I whispered, feeling satiated on a soul-deep level. "I feel like we just had some epic make-up sex before we had the fight."

Grabbing a fistful of my shirt, she pulled me down. "There won't be a fight, okay? Just be honest with me."

That I could do.

Forty-Five

Nora

"When I was a teenager, I ate, slept, and breathed video games," Carter said, his voice fond as he recalled. "It drove my parents crazy because I never wanted to do anything else. I woke up thinking about the game, and I fell asleep with some kind of device in my hands."

He'd never mentioned his parents before. He said the only family he had was Aaron, so it surprised me to hear him talk about them now.

"It was the same for my best friend, Chris. We were so into it, you know?"

I nodded, afraid if I said anything more, he might stop talking.

"We started messing around, building a game we wanted to play. The deeper we got into it, the more we wanted to do. Eventually, we created a whole world we knew other people like us would love, too."

"*Primal Fear?*"

He nodded. "We posted a few demos online and a few videos of us playing it in some forums. It took off. People wanted more. They wanted to know where to get it, how to play… It went viral."

"And that's why Lewis Regal wanted to buy it."

He nodded. "If I had known what a serious douchebag he was, I never would have agreed."

"What happened?"

"He approached us. Offered us the kind of money we'd never even dreamed of. I mean, here we were, these seventeen-year-old kids who hated school, had no promise for the future, and this man was offering us enough money that neither of us would ever have to work."

"You agreed to sell it."

Carter shrugged. "Sure, why not? Not only were we getting paid, but we could see our creation in the hands of millions of people. It was surreal."

"I would have done the same thing," I said, knowing in my heart it was the truth.

"Chris had always been a bit of a partier..." He began, his voice changing. "We both liked to drink and get high. For a while, it was becoming a little bit of a problem, but when we started building *Primal Fear*, he got better, like he had something to focus on."

I nodded. "Makes sense."

"Right before we signed the final contracts, he wanted to celebrate. We were about to be millionaires." Carter got up from his chair and went to the window, gazing out over the ocean view from my apartment. "Who wouldn't want to celebrate that?"

I hated the self-blame I heard in his voice, the regret.

"I drank until I passed out." His voice was bleak. "When I woke up, I found him..."

The picture of the dead body Alan showed me flashed into my mind. It was a horrible sight, even in a photo. I couldn't fathom what it must have been like to see it up close and personal. To know the person who died.

"Alan said there were pills involved."

His dark head nodded, but he didn't turn around. "Yeah, I guess after we'd gotten drunk, he'd taken some pills. I never saw him do it. Maybe I was already passed out or he did it in the bathroom." His voice trailed off as though he were reliving it all over again. "It was probably in the bathroom, since that's where I had the pills."

My throat tightened as if someone were squeezing it. "They were your pills?"

"They were in my bathroom. Someone gave them to me at a party I'd gone to. I never took them. I should have just thrown them away."

His palm flattened against the glass. The bright sunlight made him look like a shadow standing there instead of a flesh-and-blood man.

"They interacted with all the alcohol in his system. The cops said it was an overdose." His head bowed as if the weight of the past were too heavy to hold.

Going to him and wrapping my arms around his waist, I pressed against his back. At first, he stiffened, and I thought he might try and push me away. But then his body relented, and he allowed me to hold him.

"I sat with him until the police showed up. I never saw his body again. I never even got to go to his funeral."

One of my hands flattened against his chest as I pushed a little closer against him. "Why didn't you go to his funeral?"

"Because I was in jail."

"Jail!" I exclaimed, jolting back.

Carter turned, leaning against the window. Hair fell into his eyes, but he didn't bother to push it away. His jawline was shadowed with stubble, and it made me realize I'd only ever seen him with a clean shave.

"Alan told you I killed him, didn't he?"

"I didn't believe him," I swore passionately.

"It's true."

I gasped. "You just said it was an overdose."

"If I hadn't had those pills, he wouldn't have taken them. If I had stayed sober enough not to pass out, I could have called the paramedics and had his stomach pumped. There are a million things I could have done differently that might have kept Chris alive."

"What happened to Chris was an accident. A horrible, sad accident. I don't believe, not even for a second, that you are responsible for his death."

Carter's lips lifted in a half smile. "Then you're one of the only ones who believe that."

"Impossible!"

"Did you look at the papers Alan brought here?" Carter's eyes went beyond my shoulder, gazing into the apartment like he was imaging where Alan and I had been standing before.

I shook my head. "Very briefly. I saw the picture and got upset. Alan knocked the folder out of my hands before I could read them."

"You didn't look at the hospital?"

"Why would I? I wanted to hear it from you."

Pushing off the wall, he cupped my face, holding it tight. "Sometimes I think you're too good to be real."

"I'm all about the reality of things. You should know that."

A low laugh rumbled his chest. Taking my hand, he led me to the couch. "You should sit down. You have a concussion."

"I'm fine," I insisted, but I sat anyway.

Carter grabbed a bottle of cold pressed juice out of the fridge, along with a bottle of water, and brought them both over to me. Before sitting down, he draped the blanket still laying out over my lap.

"No one really believed you?" I asked.

Slowly, he shook his head. "Not even my parents."

My heart collapsed. How was that even possible? How could his own parents turn their backs on him?

"The police treated me like some kind of drug addict, like a dealer who got caught. Because of the money we were set to be paid, they acted like I just wanted Chris out of the way so I could keep all the cash for myself."

"That's crazy."

He laughed humorlessly. "That's what I said. Why would I kill him when my share alone was more than enough to live off of forever?" He turned thoughtful. "Now that I'm older and have more money than I will ever need, I understand why they thought that way. I understand that money changes people. It makes them greedy, and it makes them do things they wouldn't normally do."

"How long were you in jail?"

"A month."

"You finally convinced them it was all an accident?"

"Aaron did."

Surprised, I leaned forward. "Aaron?"

A little bit of light came back into his eyes. A little bit of life replaced the bleakness deep within. "If it weren't for Aaron, I might still be in jail."

"Tell me," I insisted, grabbing his hand and squeezing.

"Aaron was one of the responding officers the day I called 9-1-1."

"No." I gasped as though suddenly I was watching a Lifetime movie and we'd gotten to the plot twist.

"Yes." Carter's eyes widened. "He was a rookie back then, had only been on the force for a year or so."

"I really can't imagine him as a cop."

He smiled swiftly. "Probably why he isn't one today."

"Aaron believed you, then?"

Carter nodded. "Said he knew right from the minute he stepped onto the scene that the kid sitting next to his dead friend, crying, wasn't putting on a show."

Oh, the picture those words created. My heart ached just imagining it. "I wish I'd been there," I whispered. "I wish I could have been there for you."

"You're here now," he rasped, lifting my hand to kiss the back.

"He wouldn't let the case go. Even when all the other cops told him to. He pushed and prodded and built enough evidence to create enough doubt that I had actually killed Chris for money." Grabbing the juice, he uncapped it and held it out. "You're going to get dehydrated."

"I had an IV the entire night. I'll be peeing for the next century," I muttered.

"Drink," he insisted.

I did as he asked, then forced him to drink some, too.

"Aaron took a lot of crap for what he did for me. Everyone wanted me to go down. They wanted me to be some kind of poster boy for overdose and drug dealing. When he took all the info he had to the chief of police and they had to let me go, he was ridiculed."

"Is that why he quit?"

He shook his head. "Nah. Aaron's too stubborn to quit because of something like that."

"What happened once you were released?"

Hurt passed behind his eyes. Then he answered, "My parents kicked me out. They turned their backs on me completely."

"What kind of parents would do that?" I yelled. "If I ever meet them, I'm going to give them a piece of my mind." Shaking my fist in the air, I said, "And my fist, too!"

Carter laughed. "All right, Rocky, simmer down."

"I will not," I replied, indignant.

I was about to go on even more of a rant when Carter cut me off. "They aren't worth it, good girl."

I slumped, suddenly weighed down by sadness.

What are you afraid of?

Trusting people.

The conversation we'd had replayed in my mind, and so much of it began to make perfect sense.

"Almost right after I got cleared, Lewis Regal paid me a visit."

My eyes flew to his face.

"He still wanted the game. He offered me both shares of the money."

"You agreed?" I surmised, knowing the game belonged to Regal Tech.

"I told him I only wanted my share of the money, not my best friend's. I also asked for a job."

"You asked Lewis Regal for a job?"

He nodded. "I wanted to stay close to the game I'd created with Chris. I wanted to be able to update it, keep it evolving, and make sure it stayed true to what Chris always envisioned it to be."

"Why not just keep it?"

"What was I, an underage guy with a bad reputation, going to do with it? I had no job, no money, and I was crashing on Aaron's couch. I thought if I took just my share of the money, it would be okay because I'd earned it. Because that was the amount I was supposed to get before Chris died. I could get my own place, and I could continue to work with the game we both loved."

"Lewis wouldn't give you the job?"

"He agreed to give me the job. Said I would be an invaluable part to their gaming division. I signed the contract, and he deposited the money. When I showed up to work the first day, security wouldn't even let me in the building."

"What?" I squinted in confusion.

"It was my first lesson in reading between the lines," Carter replied, no trace of contempt in his voice. "He used a well-worded loophole to renege on the job offer. He laughed in my face and told me he would never hire a criminal like me into his empire. So I took the money and ran off to the Caribbean. I bought my first resort not long after and then bought the island where I live."

No wonder he didn't trust people. The ones he should have been able to trust the most had betrayed him. No wonder he lived on an island alone. It was better than being surrounded by people who would only try and take advantage.

How many times could a man be burned before he stopped getting close to a flame?

"About a year later..." Carter continued, and I admit I was shocked there was more to this story. "Lewis contacted me. Asked me to update the game. I guess the people on his team were doing a shit job and didn't quite grasp all the original coding Chris and I had done."

"Karma."

Carter smiled like a cat. "Technology is ever-evolving. It's a constant process to stay current. That's true even with something like video games. You have to keep players coming back. You have to introduce more and better. You have to evolve with them or the game will go stale and become nothing but a relic."

"That's what happened with *Primal Fear*."

Carter nodded. "Lewis Regal might be a technology giant, but his gaming division is only as good as the people he hires."

"You refused to help him with the game," I concluded.

"I wasn't quite as polite about it," Carter remarked, a glint in his eye. "Even though I was living in the Caribbean, doing well with the resort, my heart was still with gaming. Regal's call reignited the passion, so I took some of that money he'd paid me and started up Ansoft."

"That's why Alan said everything you have rightfully belongs to his father."

Carter raised a brow. "Is that what he said?" He scoffed. "I guess in their twisted minds, they would think that."

"How close is *Zero* to *Primal Fear*?"

"Not very. It has some of the same aspects and features, but it's updated and current and filled with all the things *Primal Fear* could have had if Regal had the right team."

"He's jealous."

Carter nodded. "I hurt his pride when I created *Zero*. When I started up a company that can outperform any gaming division he creates."

"And he threatened to leak the sealed police records about what happened to you and Chris."

A strange expression crossed Carter's face.

"What?" I asked, sitting forward. The stitches in the back of my head tugged, but I ignored them. "Did I say something wrong."

"No one's ever referred to it as something that happened to me *and* Chris. It was always just what happened to Chris."

A sound ripped from my lips. Scooting forward until I was perched between Carter's legs, I said, "You are just as much a victim as Chris. Your entire life was torn apart."

"Most people would say I turned out okay."

"Because you have money? Because you take a helicopter to work and own your own company?"

The intensity of his onyx eyes captivated me. "Because I have the most beautiful girlfriend in the world."

"You don't have to sweet talk me." I scoffed. "Clearly, I'm already on your side."

"Which is exactly why you can believe what I said."

Oh.

"You know what I think?" I asked, tilting my head. He gestured for me to tell him.

"I think money has allowed you to protect yourself. It's given you the opportunity to appear to live a fantasy when you're just hiding from reality."

"Then you came along, squawking about how you wanted real." As he lowered his hands into his lap, the smile on Carter's face disappeared. "What do you think of me now, good girl? Now that you know I'm not Mr. Fantasy, but just a guy with a fucked-up life and a big bank account."

"You know the difference between fantasy and reality?" I mused.

A smile curved his lips. I knew he was remembering when he'd asked me something very similar. "What's the difference?"

You figure out the difference between a dream and reality yet?

You!

"Me."

He laughed.

Easing into his lap, I wound my arms around his waist, gently resting my cheek on his chest. "Thank you for telling me." Lifting my face, I scowled. "Although, you should have told me sooner."

"I should have." He agreed.

"If you can't trust me, then what we have will never work."

Staring intently into my eyes, he whispered, "I do trust you, Nora. As scary as it is, I do."

"I won't break that trust, Carter. I promise."

We lay together for a long time, not saying anything at all.

After a while, my voice broke the silence. "So when did Aaron quit the police force?"

"When I asked him to head up security for the first resort I bought. He's done all the security on all my resorts, and now he does it for Ansoft."

"So he was never your butler?"

Carter laughed. "Not really. We just let people think that sometimes. Or my personal assistant or my bodyguard… Whatever suits the situation. He's sort of like a shield for me. Before you, he was the only person I trusted in this world."

"I guess he'll be suitable for Val," I mused.

Carter groaned. "I should probably head back to the hospital," he added. "I want to make sure he's still doing okay."

"Will you be back later?"

He gave me a dubious look. "You think I'm going to leave you here alone?"

"Yes?"

"Try again."

I whined.

"Alan is still lurking around Miami," Carter growled. "He's probably waiting for the chance to pounce."

I knew that. I was counting on it.

"This isn't over yet, good girl. The reason Alan attacked you, the reason his father tried to run me over with a car… You can't be alone until I settle this. I'm not letting you out of my sight."

"Okay then." I relented. "Let's go."

If I couldn't go to Alan, then Alan would have to come to me.

Carter

Did she think I wouldn't notice how easily she gave in?

How she didn't so much as grumble when I insisted she come with?

First, her veiled comment about her and Regal sharing a mistake, and now her following along behind me to the hospital like a good little duck?

Nora was up to something, and you bet your ass I was going to find out what it was.

So here I was, trailing her as she so innocently went to the hospital cafeteria for some coffee. No one drank that shit. It was nasty.

I stayed back just far enough that she wouldn't suspect. Although, for all the attention she gave her surroundings, I could have practically breathed down her neck and she wouldn't have noticed. Clearly, I was going to have to give her some lessons in awareness.

When she turned in the opposite direction of the cafeteria, I knew I'd been right to stalk her.

Heh. Look at me. Guess I was the stalker she claimed me to be after all.

Don't wait for an apology. I'll never give one.

I watched her pull out her phone, her fingers flying over the screen. Seconds later, the same phone dinged, and she glanced back down.

At the end of the hall, she made another right, heading in the direction of the gift shop.

Using a giant potted palm as camouflage, I watched between the leaves as she ducked into the shop, waiting for a few passing people to move on, then quickly rushed back out, slipping into some room beside it.

Is this what the rest of my life was going to be? Following along behind her while she did shit that gave me gray hair?

That's it. I was getting her a tracker. I'd put it in a nice piece of jewelry. And Knox wasn't getting another day off until never.

After another moment, I hustled to the room she went into and pushed open the door, silently praying it didn't squeak and give me away. Maintenance was clearly up to par because the door was soundless.

The low murmur of voices floated to my ears.

"I'm surprised you asked to meet me."

Alan's voice was unmistakable, and it took everything in me not to barge into the room swinging and kicking like a karate star gone rabid.

"Or maybe that blow to the head knocked some sense into you."

Forget rabid karate star, I was going to Mike Tyson his ass and start biting.

"If anything, it knocked the sense I did have out," Nora replied.

"What the hell is that supposed to mean?"

"I changed my mind."

"About...?" Alan cajoled.

"About giving you the information on *Zero*."

Even though I was already standing there motionless, I froze, paralyzed by the words she'd just said.

"You expect me to believe you changed your mind just like that?" Alan punctuated his words with the sharp snap of his fingers.

"I talked to Carter," Nora said, her voice hollow. "I can't get that photo you shoved in my face out of my mind."

My eyes slid closed. Had our talk not gone the way I thought? Was she just playing me when she said her love hadn't changed?

"So he admitted it, then?" Alan mused. The know-it-all tone of his voice really grated on my nerves. This guy needed a fresh punch in the face.

"He said he was guilty." She agreed.

Alan laughed. "If only you had listened to begin with, things wouldn't have had to go this far."

"I'm ready now," she replied. "Is that job your father offered me still on the table?"

"Of course."

"There's something else I want."

"Bold, aren't you?" he said. "All right then, what is it?"

"The truth."

"The truth about what?"

"About everything you and your father have done lately."

I perked up on the other side of the door. Was she doing what I thought she was doing?

"I don't know what you're talking about."

"Then I guess we have nothing left to discuss." She must have started to walk away, because Alan called out for her to stop.

"If you're done with Carter like you say, then what do you even care?" he asked.

My stomach twisted, and my upper lip curled. Just the thought of Nora betraying me this way made me utterly sick.

"It's not about that. It's about honesty. I'm risking a lot by giving you Ansoft secrets. It's only fair if you risk something by giving me yours."

The room was thick with silence for long minutes. Nora didn't even so much as breathe heavily or relent. I felt her standing there, boldly waiting for Alan's reply.

Finally, he gave in. "Ask."

"Your father was behind the hit-and-run, wasn't he?"

"How could—" Alan started.

"Spare me your phony outrage and answer the question." Nora cut in calmly.

"Yes."

My hands balled into fists at my sides. That son of a bitch put Aaron in the hospital. He could have killed him.

"What the hell were you thinking?" Nora exclaimed, her voice shaking with emotion for the first time since entering the room.

"That bastard was on his way to holding a press conference." Alan raged. "You wouldn't give us the information, and he was about to take away our only advantage. Something had to be done!"

He knew about the press conference?

Only one other person knew about that.

And now I knew just how deep Bryan's betrayal went. All. The. Way.

"So hitting him with a cab was your plan B?"

"You knew?" Alan intoned, his voice dropping a few decibels.

Nora laughed, disgust clear in its tone. "While I was lying there bleeding on the floor, I heard your phone ring. I heard you say it was time for plan B. Right after that, Aaron was hit by a car aiming for Carter. I'm not stupid, Alan, despite what you think."

"You little…" He began, and I heard some commotion.

"You stay right where you are." Nora cautioned, her voice a little less confident than before.

I shifted all the weight onto the balls of my feet, ready to launch into the room.

"Is this a setup?" he demanded. "Are you really here alone?"

Nora ignored his question and asked her own. "How did you get those sealed police records? Who did your father pay?"

"I've answered enough of your questions. It's time for you to keep up your end of the deal."

"And if I don't? Are you going to hit me with a car, too?"

An angry sound ripped out of him, and the noise of chairs scattering clanged loudly. Nora shrieked, and everything inside me went on full alert.

The door hit the wall when I shoved it open, but no one noticed. Alan was leaning over Nora, who had fallen back in a chair.

"I recorded everything!" she blurted, holding a phone between them. "If you do anything to me, I will send your confession straight to the police."

Alan smacked the phone out of her hand, and it went flying. "You stupid bitch." He snarled. "My lawyer will have that pathetic confession thrown out in seconds. You can't record someone without their consent."

Bringing her knee into her chest, Nora propelled her foot forward to kick Alan right in the chest. He stumbled back, and she bolted from the chair. Alan roared, tackling her from behind.

"Get off!" Nora demanded.

I leapt over the first two rows of chairs, then swept the rest out of my way as I charged forward. Surprised, Alan looked up, but there was no time for any other reaction.

Launching myself right at him, I bulldozed into his side, knocking him off Nora. Both of us fell to the floor, him beneath me. We struggled, but I had the advantage, straddling his waist.

Without hesitation, my fist plowed into his face, rocking his head to the side. I hit him again and then again.

"Carter!" Nora called close by. "Carter, stop!"

"You and your father are scum," I growled, hitting him again.

Nora grabbed my arm when I pulled it back again. "Carter," she pleaded. "That's enough."

Breathing hard, feeling my pulse hammering in my veins, I looked at her.

Her eyes were wide and beseeching. "Stop."

Shoving off the nutsack on the floor, I stood, looking her over. "Did he hurt you?" I asked. "Are your stitches okay?"

"I'm fine." She assured me.

Alan stood, spitting blood onto the floor. "You're going to pay for this."

"Don't you ever get tired of saying cliché shit?" I quipped.

Roaring, he came at me. I stepped out of the way, and he crashed into a few overturned chairs.

What a moron.

"Guess Daddy's money didn't buy you any coordination. Probably why you only ever try and beat on women, 'cause they're the only ones physically weaker than you."

Alan flipped over, sitting up amongst the disarray. "The next time we send someone to kill you, I'll make sure they finish the job."

Nora gasped and rushed forward as though she was going to throw some punches of her own. Catching her around the waist, I towed her back. Her feet kept on running like they were still on the ground.

I loved when she did that. Like a little Energizer bunny.

"Stay away from him," I said quietly. "Unless you want me to start punching again."

Slumping against me, she nodded.

"Go get your phone," I urged, gently guiding her to it, making sure my body stayed between her and Alan.

"It's broken." She stressed. "You broke it!"

Alan laughed. "So much for my confession."

"Now there's nothing to prove I wasn't lured here and beaten by the CEO of Ansoft."

Reaching into my back pocket, I pulled out my cell and hit a button. A few seconds later, Alan's voice filled the room.

"The next time we send someone to kill you, I'll make sure they finish the job."

Underneath the blood smearing his face, his skin went white.

"Big deal." He fronted. "So I mouthed off after you beat me up."

Tsking, I rewound the recording a bit further.

"Your father was behind the hit and run, wasn't he?"

"How could—"

"Spare me your phony outrage and answer the question."

"Yes."

"I heard all of it," I said, tapping the screen a few times. "And I just sent this recording to a few of my closest friends, so now they've heard it, too."

Alan scoffed. "Like I said, my lawyer—"

"Yes, your lawyer can have this thrown out in court. But what about public opinion? You were going to release those sealed records—the ones you probably bribed someone to get—into the media because of public opinion, right? Because you and your father both know a businessman's reputation is more important than what any judge says in court. What do you think the public opinion will be of Regal Tech's CEO and his successor when they find out you aren't above bribery, murder, and assault?"

Launching off the floor, he charged.

Nora shrieked, and I put my arm out, blocking her while kicking him away. "I wouldn't make things worse for yourself if I were you."

"You bastard."

"What we have here is a stalemate. You have info on me, and now I have info on you. We could both release everything we have and see which of us comes out on top, or we can stop this now and walk away."

Alan snarled. I held up a hand. "Should I call your father and see what he has to say?"

"What's going on in here?" a man yelled from the doorway.

Alan turned toward the hospital security that had finally decided to show up. I didn't take my eyes off Alan, though. Only a stupid man looked away from his enemy.

"Arrest them!" he screamed. "Look what they did to me!"

The men moved farther into the room, coming around to see my face.

"Carter Anders?" one of the guards asked.

I nodded. "Sorry for the trouble." I began. "This guy here has assault charges and a restraining order pending against him. He's the reason my girlfriend has those stitches in the back of her head."

Dutifully, Nora turned around and lifted her hair, showing the large bandage.

"Did this man come after you again, ma'am?" the officer asked.

She nodded. "I was really scared."

"You lying bitch!" Alan roared, taking a threatening step forward.

"Whoa!" The guards cautioned as I stepped in front of her.

"Call the PD," one of them requested.

"I just came down to get a gift for our friend who was hit by a car yesterday." Nora sniffled while gesturing to the gift shop outside. "I don't know how he knew I was here." As she held up her phone, her lower lip wobbled. "He broke my phone when I tried to call for help."

I put my arm around her for comfort and hid my smile. Damn. My girl deserved an Academy Award.

"All right now, ma'am," the guard said, trying to soothe her. "Security is here now."

"You mind if I take her out of here?" I asked. "Seeing him is very upsetting."

"Sure, sure." The guard allowed.

I told them the room number we'd be in and left my phone number so they could contact us if the police had any questions.

"PD is on their way." One guard confirmed, hanging up his phone. "There is a restraining order and arrest warrant issued for this one."

"I never got a restraining order," Alan protested.

"It will be served as soon as they get here."

"You two go on ahead."

"Thank you," I said, offering my hand to the guard.

"Anytime, Mr. Anders. My kids sure do love your games."

I grinned. "Glad to hear it."

Alan was making noise about his lawyer and making a phone call when we stepped out of the room.

"What the hell did you think you were doing?" I scowled the second we were alone.

She seemed incredibly naïve and innocent when she replied, "Getting evidence."

"You can't just meet up alone with the man who put stitches in your head."

"I wasn't alone. You were with me."

"Because I became that stalker you always accused me of being."

Nora rolled her eyes. "You always were that stalker. That's how I knew you would follow and I wouldn't be alone."

This girl was unbelievable.

Her eyes twinkled when she leaned close. "I did a good job pretending I didn't know you were there, didn't I?"

I'd never tell her she had me fooled.

I was still putting a tracker on her sneaky butt.

Glowering, I said, "That was dangerous."

She took my hand as we turned the corner into a surprisingly empty hall. Directing me against the wall, Nora lifted her chin. "You didn't believe it when I said I would betray you and hand over all my info on *Zero*, did you?"

The idea of it definitely punched me in the heart. But did I actually believe it?

I shook my head. "No. I trust you."

"Do you really?" she pressed.

Spreading my feet so my back could slide down the wall and I was closer to her level, I wrapped my hands around her waist and pulled her close. "I trust you."

"I think those words might mean more to me than *I love you*."

Smiling, I said, "I love you, too."

"I just wanted to help. I knew I could make him confess." Dipping her head against my chest, she said, "I didn't know we couldn't use it in court."

Tipping up her chin, I stared into her eyes. They were so blue it was like having a piece of the Caribbean with me even when I wasn't there. "That confession was everything we needed. Lewis Regal will back off now. He doesn't have a choice."

"You really think so?"

"I know so." Without a doubt.

Regal Tech wasn't the leading tech company in this country because Lewis Regal was stupid. He would know it was time to back off, because if he didn't, I'd bring him down. Even if it meant going down with him.

I'd do it because I wasn't afraid. I could leave Miami in shambles and go back to our island with my girl and my best friend and never look back.

"It's really over?" she whispered, looking for more reassurance.

Slipping my hands under her arms, I lifted, standing to my full height. Her feet dangled over the floor when I held her at eye level and pecked a quick kiss against her lips. "The drama with Regal and Ansoft? For sure." Putting her back on the ground, I smiled. "But everything between you and me? That's never going to end."

"Good thing I like you, then."

I laughed.

"I'm tired of walking. Give me a piggyback ride back to the room?"

As I dropped to offer my back, my heart did a little tumble when she wrapped her arms around my neck.

So which was better? Fantasy or reality?

With Nora in my life, I had the perfect combination of both.

Epilogue

Nora

Reality vs. Fantasy Observation #6:
Sometimes reality is even better than fantasy.

Sun-kissed arms wound around me from behind, pulling me away from the railing and against a familiar chest.

Waves crashing against the private, white-sand beach carried through the balmy breeze, creating music I would now always associate with home.

"How did I get so lucky?" I asked, cuddling into the arms holding me tight.

"It wasn't luck. It was fate." His voice brushed against my ear, making gooseflesh rise along my arms and legs.

Rotating, I kissed him, licking the salty ocean waves right off his lips. No matter how many times I kissed Carter, I always wanted to kiss him again.

"Eventually, I'm going to have to go to work," I said, my lips still against his.

Swatting my bottom, he scolded me. "I just got you back, and already you want to leave?"

Laughing, I hopped onto the railing to sit. The sea breeze blew my salty hair around my cheeks. "You've always had me."

"But I had to share you with college. Now that you've finally graduated, I get you all to myself."

Finishing my degree in graphic design was important to me, even though Carter tried to sweet talk me into staying at Ansoft and just accepting a permanent position.

I couldn't do that, though. I wanted to earn a place at his company. I wanted to feel like I deserved the job. So for the last year, I divided my time between here and Georgia. It made Carter grouchy, but it wasn't anything a few strategic kisses couldn't fix.

The day I graduated, Carter showed up with a moving crew and packed our entire apartment (yep, Val's stuff, too), and two weeks later, I was still here on the island and still partially dressed.

Despite my insistence for reality, I'd come to realize that, to me, Carter would always be Mr. Fantasy.

Not because of his island, his helicopter, or his money.

Because of the way he made my heart flutter. The way he turned my insides to mush, and most importantly, because of the two people he trusted on this planet... one of them was me.

"Tongues already wag enough because you gave your former summer intern and current girlfriend a permanent position on the special project team. Don't you think people will really cry unfairness if I only go to work when you let me off this island?"

"I could give you Bryan's unfilled position and really stir things up," he teased, wagging his brows.

I laughed. "You still haven't filled his position?"

He shrugged. "I'm in no hurry."

"His betrayal really hurt you." I empathized, wrapping my arms around his neck. I think out of all the chaos over *Zero*, Bryan's betrayal cut him the deepest.

(By the way, *Zero* was an even bigger success than Carter had guessed. It launched Ansoft into a whole new playing field.)

"Bryan is the past," Carter said. "I don't want to talk about him. Besides, I'm sure he's living it up somewhere with the pile of cash I paid him for his shares of my company."

"What do you want to talk about, then?" I asked, nuzzling the side of his sun-warmed face.

"There's something in my pocket for you," he whispered.

Chuckling, I pulled back. "I'm pretty sure that present in your pants was already given to me this morning." I held up two fingers. "Twice."

"Well…" He sighed regretfully. "If you don't want the present I got you—"

"Wait!" I laughed, pulling him back. "There's really something in there for me?"

His smile was wicked. "One way to find out."

Plunging my hand into the pocket of his swim trunks, I let my fingers caress his cock. "This it?" I teased, eyes dancing with laughter.

"You're in the wrong pocket." His voice was dry.

Pulling back, I swatted at him. "You could have told me."

"Now why would I want to do that?" He winked.

Delving into the other pocket, I fished around until my fingers brushed over something cool and small. My eyes shot to his.

He chuckled. "I told you."

"What is it?" I whispered.

"Pull it out and see," he whispered back.

Drawing my hand out of his pocket, I looked down at the object resting against my palm. The dainty gold band glinted under the rays of the sun.

My breath faltered. "What is this?"

Lifting the ring out of my palm, he held it up. The large round diamond sparkled beneath my gaze. "This is a promise," he said. "to keep you and love you forever."

It was a beautiful ring, a perfectly cut round solitaire centered in a thin gold band. But more beautiful than any ring could ever be were his words.

"Carter," I whispered.

"Will you marry me?" he asked, a sincere, tender expression filling his eyes.

My heart was hammering. Tears shimmered in my eyes, and everything around us had a dreamy quality. "Is this real?"

"Very." He assured me. "Mr. Fantasy needs his missus."

I laughed, and a tear dripped down my cheek.

"An answer would be nice," he quipped, waving the ring.

"Yes," I burst out. "Yes!"

I nearly fell off the railing into him, but his arms were strong, holding me up so I could wrap my legs around his waist. Carrying me through the long, billowing white curtains, he laid me across the bed, his onyx eyes smiling into mine.

Straddling my hips, he gestured for my hand. The ring slipped effortlessly over my knuckle, proving something I otherwise might never have believed.

Sometimes reality really was better than fantasy.

Author's Note

This book started out with an invitation. An invitation to a secluded island by a super handsome fella that slid into my DMs.

It was accompanied by an unsolicited pic of his genitalia.

I'm just kidding.

Got your attention, though, didn't I? Ha!

This book DID start with an invite, though. An invitation to join an anthology called *Spring Fling*. It asked for a short story about a fling or a one-night stand. So I wrote "Overboard." And "Overboard" turned into *Mr. Fantasy*. The problem with me is that I have a hard time writing just a short story. The beginning of this book, "The Fantasy," originally titled "Overboard," ended with Nora going back home after spring break.

I was supposed to move on to another full-length novel. You know, something I actually had plans to write.

Nope. My brain doesn't work that way.

I'd really been struggling with writing, coming up with inspiration, and generally liking anything I actually typed out. Once I wrote the short story, I kept coming back to Nora and Carter and what happened after she went home. I just felt like their story wasn't over yet.

So "The Reality" was born. And both of them together (the fantasy and the reality) created this book.

I had fun writing this one because I felt like there weren't many rules. Maybe because of the "fantasy" aspect, I felt I could get away with more. Or maybe my mutinous brain just overruled everything else. Either way, it was fun and a good escape from reality and from all the other words I was supposed to be writing.

I won't say this book is "different" from what I normally write, because I feel like I say that all the time. And really, I just write what I feel like writing, so is there really a normal? LOL.

I hope you enjoyed Carter and Nora, and I also hope this book was a great distraction from your everyday reality and it brought you a little fun fantasy.

I want to give a shout-out to my editor, Cassie McCown (Gathering Leaves Editing), for putting up with my ADD and just going with the flow for what I write. Also, for not killing me when I emailed to say, "Hey, you know that short you edited for me for that anthology? Well, I'm using it for a full-length, and now I have to write a new short that needs edited... and I need it like ASAP." So thank you for being a super editor!

Oh, PS: the short story I wrote to replace "Overboard" is titled "Cake by the Ocean," and you can find it in the *Spring Fling Anthology* online.

As usual, thanks to all the readers (you!) for all your support! If you enjoyed Mr. Fantasy, please consider leaving a review, telling a friend, and posting about it online. Word of mouth helps authors!

See you next book!

XOXO,
Cambria

About Cambria

Cambria Hebert is an award-winning, bestselling novelist of more than forty books. She went to college for a bachelor's degree, couldn't pick a major, and ended up with a degree in cosmetology. So rest assured her characters will always have good hair.

Besides writing, Cambria loves a caramel latte, staying up late, sleeping in, and watching movies. She considers math human torture and has an irrational fear of birds (including chickens). You can often find her painting her toenails (because she bites her fingernails) or walking her Chihuahuas (the real rulers of the house).

Cambria has written within the young adult and new adult genres, penning many paranormal and contemporary titles. She has also written romantic suspense, science fiction, and male/male romance. Her favorite genre to read and write is contemporary romance. A few of her most recognized titles are: *The*

Hashtag Series, GearShark Series, Text, Amnesia, and *Butterfly.*

Recent awards include: Author of the Year, Best Contemporary Series (*The Hashtag Series*), Best Contemporary Book of the Year, Best Book Trailer of the Year, Best Contemporary Lead, Best Contemporary Book Cover of the Year. In addition, her most recognized title, *#Nerd,* was listed at Buzzfeed.com as a top fifty summer romance read.

Cambria Hebert owns and operates Cambria Hebert Books, LLC.

You can find out more about Cambria and her titles by visiting her website: http://www.cambriahebert.com.

Please sign up for her newsletter to stay in the know about all her cover reveals, releases, and more: http://eepurl.com/bUL5_5.

Text "Cambria" to 7606703130 to sign up for new release alerts.

CPSIA information can be obtained
at www.ICGtesting.com
Printed in the USA
FSHW020449230319

9 781946 836267